A
Curse Of Silver
And Blood

K. A. Banks

For wayward souls, old souls, and the
souls who are still learning who they are.
Lastly, for those we love that have passed on.

Symbols found at Seven Sisters Road

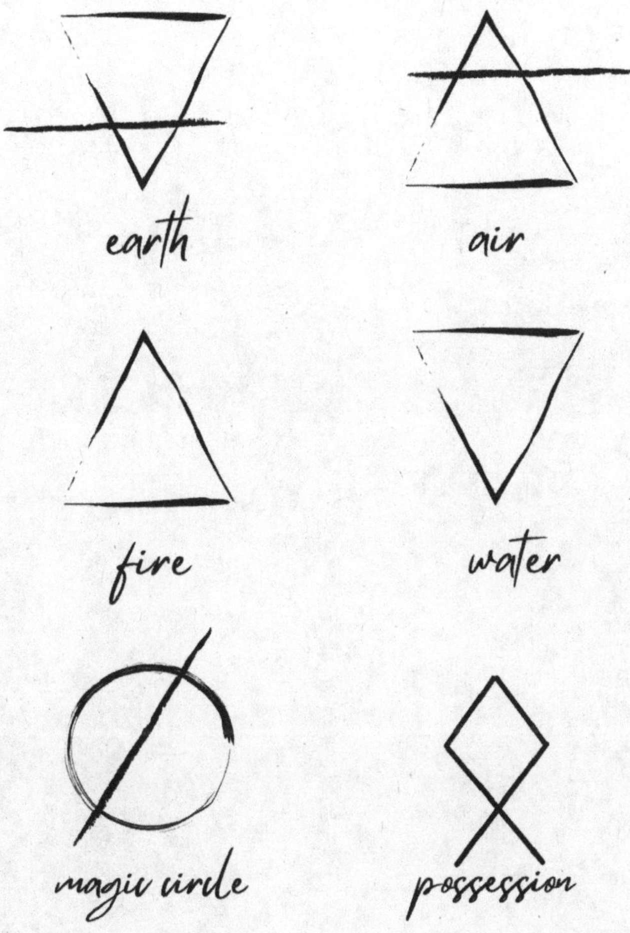
earth
air
fire
water
magic circle
possession

The boundaries which divide life from death are at best shadowy and vague.
Who shall say where the one ends, and the other begins?

Edgar Allen Poe

1

THE STIFLING HEAT INSIDE the shoreline baptist church stuck to Elijah's skin, and the bottle of whiskey from the night before churned in his stomach. Acid rose in the back of his throat, and he clenched his jaw. The massive staples that held the lining of the casket in place dug into Elijah's hands, drawing blood. Owen's wax-like face etched itself into Elijah's mind. His charcoal-gray suit—the one Owen wore to homecoming senior year—was wrinkled. Pale-blue bruising left behind on his neck by the ligature peeked through the makeup the mortician had used. The woodsy scent of Owen's aftershave wafted into Elijah's nose, and he gripped the edge tighter.

"Elijah, honey, you have to keep moving," Owen's mom and Elijah's adoptive mother, Shelly, whispered in his ear, interrupting his grief-riddled thoughts. Tears streamed down Shelly's cheeks, and she wiped them away with an old-fashioned monogrammed handkerchief. Shelly's hair was tied back in a modest bun, and golden flyaways framed her gracefully aging face. Shelly slid a tender hand over his and gave him a half-hearted smile. The same smile she gave him when things were unhinged and beyond terrible. It let him know, in some sort of secret code, that she knew everything was crap, but he had to keep pushing through.

Staying quiet, Elijah cast a glare behind him at the line of mourners who were sobbing and sniffling, waiting to get their last peek at Owen. Their judgment of Elijah's battered face was transparent as they glared at him, whispering gossip amongst themselves. He deserved time with Owen. As long as he wanted.

I'm saying goodbye.

Elijah's throat bobbed, and he struggled against the tears he wanted to let spill out onto his friend's body. The whole scenario didn't sit right with him; something was off. Owen had no reason to kill himself.

"One more minute; then I'll go." Elijah squinted at them, speaking louder so they could hear. "They can wait," he said matter-of-factly.

Elijah knew the three sorority girls criticizing him. He'd met them once at one of Owen's film school functions. They were acquaintances who wanted to attend only so that they could go back to school and *speak out* about how Owen's death affected their emotional state. Making Owen's death all about them. As Elijah stared at the girls, there was a brush against his fingertips. He snapped his attention back to the casket. Crazy as it may seem, Elijah could swear Owen touched his hand.

Binx, the Golden Retriever Shelly bought for Elijah and Owen after Elijah's father died, was curled faithfully at the head of his master's coffin. In the last twenty minutes, Binx had raised his head and glanced at Owen's coffin half a dozen times, whimpering in grief.

Elijah felt overwhelmingly lucky to have Shelly in his life. If it weren't for her, he would have been an orphan after his father's car wreck. Elijah never knew his mother; the only thing he did know is that she abandoned them both after he was born.

Being an only child, Owen was the closest thing Elijah had to a sibling. His dear friend that he made forts with as a child, went trick-or-treating with, rode bikes with, grew up with, wasn't a friend at all—he was a brother. Elijah's ears burned, and his hands trembled. He was lost in a hurricane of confusion.

Understanding how someone so kind and amazing could take his own life at the age of 25 was an impossible task. The long-term, life-altering implications of the vacant and soulless body before him hadn't fully taken shape into reality.

This can't be happening. This is a nightmare, and I'm gonna wake up.

A menacing crow screeched behind Elijah as it soared into the church from one of the open windows, separating him from the casket. Half of the mourners scurried, while others attempted to guide out the black, little devil. Defiant, it perched itself onto a structural beam above the sanctuary and bore its eyes into Elijah. Binx growled with fury at the bird, barking ferociously; he guarded the front of Owen's casket.

The church walls closed in on Elijah, and he adjusted the collar of his black T-shirt. His ribs throbbed where he'd been beaten the night before. Vertigo rushed over him like a tidal wave, and he clumsily darted for the door.

Escaping the heavy atmosphere of the funeral, Elijah stumbled out the front. His legs were heavy, and as a result, his Justin work boots thumped against the aged wood of the porch. The muggy air of the South Carolina July evening was still and silent. Leaning on the dilapidated railing of the country church, he watched a breeze roll over the marsh of the coast. Salty sea air gusted into his face, sending his chestnut-colored, shaggy hair into a frenzy. For a moment, he thought he could hear Owen's voice carried on the breeze, calling for him.

The churning in his stomach settled, and he unclenched his jaw. The sun dipped down past the horizon, and the reflection colored the scattered clouds different blended shades of coral and violet. The deep-green water of the inlet was still, and cicadas sang. It was serene, but the emotional storm that raged inside of him was stark in contrast. Elijah plucked a piece of overgrown wheatgrass from beside him.

"God damn it, Owen." Elijah gave a sharp sigh.

The tension that plagued him all day melted away as he picked off each bud, flicking them to the ground.

"Am I late?" Camilla's velvet, Puerto Rican accent jolted him out of his thoughts of Owen. Elijah's lip twitched at her sing-song tone. It was the trained vocals of a woman practicing to become a leading television anchor. He gave an internal sigh, and heat spread through his face.

"Like always." Elijah shoved himself off the railing and dropped what was left of the grass to the porch. He spun on his heels and narrowed his eyes at her. "You haven't been on time for anything in your life. Except shopping."

"Please." She rolled her cinnamon-colored eyes in annoyance. "*Don't act* like people want me here. I came to say goodbye to Owen." Camilla reached down and plucked a blade of dead grass from her black stiletto and flicked it to the ground.

"The guy did everything for you, and you couldn't even show up to his funeral on time." Elijah's hands were shaking. It took every ounce of strength he had left to maintain control. Camilla was beautiful, show-stoppingly beautiful, but a certain amount of high-maintenance came with her beauty.

She slipped a Kleenex from her cheetah print leather clutch and dabbed the sweat from her flawless bronze skin. If you didn't *know* Camilla, you might think she was elegant—until she opened her mouth. She never had anything to say that wasn't loaded with emotional daggers meant to hurt everyone she knew. Unimpressed, she scanned Elijah up and down. "I see you dressed down. Per usual." Camilla flipped her sleek, ebony hair and flashed an arrogant smile with her full, cherry-colored lips. Elijah expected that reaction from her. He was convinced her heart was made of stone.

"We're at the funeral of your ex, and you're worried about what I'm wearing?" Elijah clenched his fists and reminded himself that it was against his morals to punch a woman.

"Nice shiner. You get into a fight again at the Thirsty Parrot? You're so predictable." Camilla said, rolling her eyes.

Elijah's left eye socket throbbed at the memory, and the scab on his bottom lip pinched. He pointed a furious finger at Camilla. "That's none of your damn business."

She chuckled, enjoying that it was so easy to piss him off. "Relax, Jess told me you were there, and you got into a fight."

"Why don't you do everyone a favor, save the drama, and get the hell out of here?"

"Elijah, honey, are you alright? You're shouting." Shelly eased out the front door. Concern clouded her weary eyes. Elijah noted the horrified expression on Shelly's face when she saw Camilla; it lasted for a fraction of a second. It would have been unrecognizable by anyone who didn't know her. In an instant, she smiled with grace and then gave a trained "Southern hospitality" extend of her hand, welcoming Camilla up the stairs.

"Camilla, my dear ... I thought you weren't going to make it." Shelly cleared her throat, brushing her golden bangs from her tired eyes.

Camilla flicked a fake smile toward Elijah. "Well, here I am." She turned her attention to Shelly, ascending the stairs. "Traffic coming from Savannah was hellish."

"Before I forget, I found this in Owen's things in his dorm room." Shelly gave Elijah a weak smile that barely hid her sorrow.

Shelly held out a manila envelope, and Elijah rubbed the back of his neck, hesitating. Camilla passed Elijah with her shoulders squared, holding her head elegantly. The way she studied the envelope, Elijah could tell she wanted to know whether Owen left her something, too. A waft of her designer perfume burnt Elijah's nose, and he rubbed his temples. His mouth was dry and he needed a Bloody Mary.

"How 'bout you keep it for now." His voice was thin, his heart skipped a beat, and his chest throbbed like he'd been stung by a hundred bees. Aching shot through the muscles of his ribs, and he winced. He already knew that the soldier he picked a fight with probably broke two of them, and he deserved it.

Shelly placed a tender hand on his shoulder and brushed back Elijah's hair from his forehead. "When you're ready, darlin', it'll be here for you." Shelly squeezed Elijah's shoulder lovingly and wrapped her arms around him, hugging him the way she did when his father died twelve years prior.

"Do you know what happened to Owen's leather bracelet with the lion's head on it? I wanted it if that's alright."

"I don't know where it is. I haven't seen it in his belongings, and it's not on him. If I find it, I'll give it to you." Shelly placed a soft hand on his chest, kissing his cheek.

Elijah glanced down at his matching bracelet. Shelly bought them both the exact same one at a renaissance festival their junior year of high school.

They snuck away from Shelly and stole a stein of mead off an abandoned table while she bought the bracelets. It was the first time they drank alcohol. That day was one of the best days of his life.

Elijah's momentary happiness dissipated when the soul-crushing notes of a Sarah McLachlan song floated through the open stained-glass windows. Twelve years ago, at his father's funeral, Elijah would have never guessed he would be standing on the same porch mourning for the loss of Owen. Shelly still had the habit of rocking Elijah the way she did when he was a child, scaring away the monsters for him. The truth was that there was no way Shelly could battle his demons. This time Elijah was a man and not a twelve-year-old, mourning, little boy. This time he would have to wage war alone against the demons nipping at his sanity.

Shelly's chest shuddered, and Elijah heard her sniffle. Elijah squeezed Shelly tighter and knew that neither of them would get to hug Owen again. They were all each other had left. Shelly released Elijah from their embrace, kissed his forehead, and disappeared inside the church.

Muffled arguing came from the other side of the doors, and they burst open. Someone collided with the back of Elijah, sending stabbing pain through his bruised hip and leg. He turned, expecting to unleash a flurry of curse words. Instead, he was met with the cat-shaped, piercing emerald eyes of a young woman. Her curly, coppery-colored hair clung to her alabaster skin. The fresh scent of lavender and vanilla calmed him. A warm gust glided around him, wrapping him in serenity.

The young woman's hair swayed in the wind, and her bloodshot eyes let him know she'd been crying too. "Hey, it's Elijah, right?" He stayed silent.

"Right ... good talk. Have a good night."

"Wait, sorry ... your names Quinn?"

Elijah knew precisely who she was. Except, it felt like centuries since he set eyes on her delicate features. Quinn was his first kiss at the tender age of eight. Shelly, Quinn's aunt, never spoke of her. The last thing Elijah heard from Owen was that she was dating a rich guy named Terry, who left for Florida to play baseball for the Marlins. He promised her everything under the moon, except a monogamous relationship.

"Yeah, the prodigal cousin has returned. To apparently crash my cousin's funeral." She smiled warmly and adjusted her black dress strap, then straightened the collar of her jean jacket. Elijah noted the freckles that covered her chest and nose. "You got a few tattoos since the last time I saw you." Quinn tapped his colorful sleeve tattoo—her touch electrified him. Elijah glanced at his right arm. He made a mental note that he had to find a spot for artwork memorializing Owen.

"A little." Elijah smiled, recalling his last memory of her fishing off the pier without a license and getting yelled at by Mr. Wallace, the fishing and game warden. "The last time I saw you was when we were twelve." Elijah cleared his throat. "How you been?"

"Well, my cousin just died." Quinn crossed her arms.

"Right." Elijah pinched the bridge of his nose.

Her smile faded and was replaced with a mixture of expressions that shifted through grief, confusion, and anger.

"I was doing my best to not make this whole night awkward but did anyway." Quinn turned her tissue over in her hands. Her transfixing eyes studied his face. "Sorry. Didn't mean to bother you. Have a good night."

"No, it's okay. Really." Elijah grabbed her hand, stopping her. "I wasn't ... sorry. You grew up pretty good." As soon as the words left his mouth, Elijah wondered why God ever gave him one.

Shelly stormed out of the church, her eyes furiously landing on Quinn. "You have two seconds to get off this property before I have you removed."

"I'm sure that won't be necessary," Elijah interjected, gently touching Shelly's forearm.

"She shouldn't even be here." Shelly jabbed a finger at Quinn.

"Yeah, yeah, I'm going." Quinn wiped her nose and forced a smile as she shoved the tissue into the pocket of her jacket. "It was good to see you, Elijah."

As Quinn vanished into the steamy Beaufort evening, Elijah's intuition told him he would see her again—very soon.

2

THE VOICES SPEAKING TO Elijah from the unfurling electric mist above him set his veins on fire. The malevolent spirit penetrated his defenses, prodding around his consciousness. He could *sense* it. Sweat trickled down Elijah's forehead and rolled from his bare chest, down his sides to his bed. He was paralyzed. The energy unfolding above him was evil, and it wanted to take his soul.

It had been a year since Elijah saw a ghostly shadow or experienced anything close to a psychic episode. The visions of the dead and tormented were horrors he kept to himself. The intuitive impressions were sporadic and unpredictable. Like every misfortune in Elijah's life, there was no way to control them. He'd wished the universe would have been merciful and given him the visions he needed to prevent Owen's death.

Elijah had finished his self-prescribed medication—a half-bottle of Jack. As of late, the alcohol had lost its effectiveness, and he was overcome with insomnia. The flickering translucent images of the dead started after his father's death, haunting him from a dimension beyond his comprehension. When Elijah was twelve, he vowed to stay silent about the macabre messages. The last thing he wanted was for Shelly to have Child Protective Services take him away after she fought so hard to keep him in her home.

Wind gusted through an open window above his bed, ruffling the mist, and the ghost wailed in pain as if it was being torn apart. The sleep paralysis wore off, and his limbs tingled as they regained movement. Elijah's whole body trembled violently as he gazed into the paranormal abyss. His chest muscles tightened, shooting pain wrapped around Elijah's stomach to his back like he was tangled in a jellyfish. Elijah grunted, and his breath was forced from his lungs. The nightmare that destroyed his sleep only moments before reeled in his mind's eye, and his calf muscles spasmed from exhaustion. For a moment, he thought he was in a forest chasing Owen in an alternate universe. The experience was so real, he could still feel the thick, clay mud between his toes.

The quick visions of: *A rope. Blood. A letter falling to the ground. Screams. An archaic symbol etched into the trunk of a tree. A man agonizingly transforming into a dog.*

The high-pitched sound of his phone ringing jolted him out of his grim standoff with the ghost, and the mist evaporated into the atmosphere, releasing its grip on his mind. Elijah jolted up, grasping at his throat, gasping for air. An uncontrollable pain shot through his chest. It felt like his lungs were going to explode.

Elijah's body stiffened as a vision of Owen's corpse materialized, standing across the room. His face pale, and the line across his neck that marked his death more defined. Pure terror was woven into every molecule of the room. The apparition of his best friend reached out a shaky hand. The hair on Elijah's arms stood, and electricity surged through him.

"Mary," Owen hissed, evaporating into the fringe of the universe where the souls of the tormented resided.

"Jesus Christ," Elijah mumbled, rubbing the back of his sweaty neck. He had no idea how he was going to survive Owen's death. Being psychic wasn't the easiest of gifts. Actually, *only* being psychic (intuitive) would have been easier. After years of research, Elijah discovered he was Clairvoyant, Clairaudient, and suffered from unwanted Astral Projections.

Angry, swollen clouds raged, pouring rain into his open window. It was then that he noticed his soaked bed. He picked up an empty bottle of Jack, sighing. The soothing sounds of crickets and toads in the willow tree outside the window filled his room. Shadows of the old tree danced across his bedroom floor. It always reminded him of the creepy tree from the movie Poltergeist.

Once again, ringing savagely tore through his room. Elijah rubbed the back of his neck, deciding whether or not he wanted to speak to anyone. The blazing red numbers of his bedside clock told him it was 1:30 in the morning. He knew exactly who it was. Sweeping up his phone, Elijah winced as his body protested the movement. Throbbing rippled through the tender muscles in his ribs.

"What do you want, Jess?" Elijah's voice was gravelly.

The sound of a crowd and the booty-shaking beats of Little John boomed through the phone. "Hey, sweetie. What you up to? I was jus' seeing if you wanted to come out. There's a gnarly after-hours ..." She paused and took a drink, then started talking to someone else. He guessed she was probably drinking something fruity like a Fuzzy Navel. He could tell she was bored with her current company. Elijah had no desire to be her *filler* date. Any other night, he might be alright with being a distraction. *Just not tonight*. It had only been twelve hours since Owen's funeral. It seemed like a dick move to be out partying.

Elijah clenched his eyes shut and slouched on the edge of his rain-soaked bed. The scent of hot cement drifted through his room, and he concentrated on the splashing of cars driving past. Judging by the smell of the dampened earth, he could tell the rainfall had started recently. He tried to focus on what Jess was saying, but all he could hear was the hissing of the entity. The apparition beckoned him to Seven Sisters Road. The location where Owen's body was found by the police department, hanging from a tree. Elijah stood and paced the modest room, tripping over a pile of dirty work clothes.

The historic turn-of-the-century mansion was converted into an apartment building in the early seventies after the original family sold it to a real-estate company. The cherry-wood floors were authentic to the house, and on certain nights Elijah could hear them creak as the wood swelled from the humidity. Elijah paused and tacked back down the curling corner of his Walking Dead poster.

Jess continued chatting to a partygoer in the background, and Elijah heard a random person yell, "Hi!"

"I'll have to pass tonight," he said with finality.

A compulsion to record the recent dream overtook Elijah, though he was mystified as to why. He stumbled to his desk, searching through the clutter for a notebook. Elijah froze. He raked a hand through his messy hair, shifting from one foot to the other. He studied the envelope he left with Shelly in disbelief. The envelope with the message from Owen.

How the hell did that get here?

"*Please*, I want to see you tonight," Jess pouted pathetically, and Elijah's patience grew thin.

"No, you just want to get laid." Elijah slid out the envelope and flipped it back and forth, setting it on a stack of books.

Trivialities he once found exciting (like booty calls) were no longer appealing. His mind was processing enough, and he didn't have time to deal with needy women at the moment. Elijah opened his desk drawer and rifled through the organized chaos for a pen. He could never find one when he needed one. *Just his luck*.

"That's not true. I'm worried about you."

"I'm fine. Raincheck?"

"Riley's there, isn't she?" Jess's drunk voice shifted, grating against his ear with jealousy.

"No. I broke up with Riley. Remember? Because I have self-respect."

Elijah spotted a pink pen on the floor, which was Riley's, and snatched it up. "Speak of the devil," he mumbled.

"What is that supposed to mean?"

"Goodnight, Jess. Make sure someone *sober* drives you home."

"You're an assho—"

Elijah clicked end, slapping his cell down. He watched the envelope intently and then pushed it away, not ready for the hell it could unleash on his life. Elijah rolled out the leather desk chair and plopped into it. Flipping through his economics class notes, he searched for an empty page. He cursed under his breath at his need to ensure that *all* information, even the unneeded, was written down.

The forest Elijah chased Owen through in his nightmare was Owen's crime scene, the place rumored to be haunted by seven sisters. They were murdered by their brother, who lured them out and hanged them one by one from seven different trees. Elijah's pulse quickened, and his heart thumped in his throat as he recalled more of the hellish visions:

He ran in mud uphill next to a darkened forest line. A malicious entity chased him. A blip in time. He stood in a room filled with people and screamed. Wind from the energy of his screams gusted against the walls, blowing papers around the room. No one could see or hear him. Terror and panic waved through his body. He looked down, and his hands were translucent. He was dead. The last horrifying image was Owen dangling from a tree, and Elijah was helpless to get him down. Owen was isolated and alone.

The scream embedded itself in his subconscious. The entity that woke him up moments before was the same one that had screamed in his dream. The animalistic shriek overlapped from his nightmare into reality and forced him awake. Elijah was unsure if it had crawled its way out of his grim dreamscape and into his room. A disturbing realization rolled over Elijah: He had heard the voice before. He had heard *that* scream before.

A cumbersome breeze flowed through his room as if Mother Earth was responding to his dismal thoughts. The recollection of the scream chilled him to the bone, and Elijah pulled a sweatshirt over his head. He dug his hand into his thick, chestnut hair, resting his forehead in his palm. He slid the envelope closer. The edges were worn, and the ink that spelled his name was blotched with water (or coffee, knowing Owen). Elijah shoved it in a drawer, then snatched it back out and cut it open.

Owen had always wanted to do a documentary about the murders of the Shaw sisters. He was fascinated by Southern ghost stories and *storytelling* in general. He was incredibly close to making documentaries with Turner Television in Atlanta, except for one hitch—his untimely death.

A small envelope was inside, and Elijah opened it with the tip of the pen. He held it in front of him, and his fingertips tingled. An external hard drive the size of a cell phone slipped out. The taste of iron brought Elijah back from his thoughts, and his tongue ached where he was clenching his teeth.

Uneasy energy rippled through Elijah's shoulders, and goosebumps formed on the nape of his neck. Elijah glanced around the room. *Something* was watching him. Holding up the hard drive, he squinted, wondering what answers it might hold. The energy from the hard drive caused an upheaval in his untamed intuitive abilities. The energy was splintered and hard to interpret, and in Elijah's experience, that meant things were terribly wrong.

A tap at his door startled him, and Hudson peeked through a crack. His rich, reddish-brown skin glowed in the dim apartment lights.

"Hey man, was that Jess?" Hudson raised a thick, dark eyebrow, smiling with amusement.

"She call you too?" Elijah cleared his throat and did his best to fake like he wasn't about to lose his shit. He opened a desk drawer and dropped in the silver external drive.

"She might have daddy issues, but at least she's consistent." Hudson opened the door the rest of the way, holding onto a camo Play Station game controller, and leaned against the door frame.

Hudson was a night owl and spent most of his time online talking shit with fifteen-year-olds playing video games. Neither of those things was of interest to Elijah. He preferred to read and spend his time doing activities that weren't attached to a screen. For some reason, girls found that intriguing, like there was something exotic and dangerous about him.

"How you doin', man? You're pale."

"I'm fine." Elijah leveled his shaky voice, and his eyes shifted from the door to the window, anticipating the return of the entity he'd witnessed moments before. Hudson squinted; Elijah knew he was weighing his current emotional state.

"I know you're not the emotional kind ..."

"Thanks." Elijah forced a fake smile. He knew exactly where this was going, and he was too sober to have the "You'll be alright" conversation.

"Night," Hudson said, his eyes worriedly lingering on Elijah.

"Night. Could you turn off the light and flip on the fan?"

Hudson turned to go and stopped, spinning back around. "Oh yeah, try to get out of bed and clean your room tomorrow. It smells like sweaty balls and sex in here. The open window and car air freshener aren't going to cover the smell forever." He glanced at a small pine tree hanging from Elijah's ceiling fan.

"Thanks, asshole." Elijah reached over his bed and closed his window.

He caught sight of a wolf, its hateful energy reaching him from across the street. The wolf's fur was matted and wet from the rain. The beast stared at him, its eyes blazing like two fury-filled embers.

3

THE STREETS OF HISTORIC Savannah were wet and muggy. Gnats were eating Elijah alive as he strode down an alley toward River Street. The refraction of sunlight through the overcast sky burnt Elijah's tired eyes. He adjusted his black wayfarers, wishing he'd bought the darker UV coverage. Live Oak trees intermingled with palm trees rustled in the streets of the old colonial city. Spanish moss flapped like ribbons from the branches in the moist, gentle breeze, and the sun warmed his shoulders. The delicious aroma of seafood and fried foods drifted from restaurants' open windows and back doors, and his stomach growled.

Elijah was unsure how many days had passed since Owen's funeral; time ground to a halt when he received the call from Shelly, and he saw Owen at the morgue. Every hour melded into the next. His best guess was four days, or maybe five, he'd spent in his cocoon of depression, blocking out the world. Since he started walking, the comfort of his bed beckoned him, but his aching back and legs told him to get moving before he gained bed sores.

Chattering tourists and busy locals honking while driving to work played like a comforting symphony. Elijah had missed being outside and walking through the streets, soaking in the beautiful and historical energy of Savannah. Elijah watched two lovers walking down the street together, intertwined, and a pang surfaced, dulling his hunger. His heart ached for Riley.

The stale smell of Old Spice and sweat from his dirty shirt reminded him that he needed to clean. Hudson was cranky when there was no order to things and relentless until the task was finished. The Pink Floyd T-shirt he found on the top of a mountainous pile of clothes was the freshest he could find. Honestly, his room was a shit show—even by his standards. Sweat dampened his forehead and caused his cheek to stick to his cell phone. He held it away from his face and wiped it quickly with his dirty T-shirt.

"Honey, I'm telling you, I have no idea how that envelope got into your room." Shelly's voice was coated with worry. "I thought I put it back in my car …" Shelly paused, and her voice shuddered as she continued, "But that was a long day for all of us. Maybe it was brought to you by someone at the funeral. I could have set it on a table or left it somewhere in the church. Did you ask your roommate if he found it?"

Elijah sighed at the mundane explanation. In the confusion that followed the vision of Owen's tormented apparition, he hadn't thought of that, even though it should have been the first thing he considered.

"No, I suppose I could ask Hudson. You're probably right." Elijah rubbed his temple as he adjusted the volume on his cell phone, struggling to focus.

"Did you sleep last night?" Shelly's Southern voice dipped. Elijah could tell she already knew the answer.

Stopping next to the Thirsty Parrot, Elijah leaned against the cool brick exterior. A man with long, blond hair sipping a Coke and a woman with blue hair eating ice cream strolled past. The woman was complaining about her professor's standards on artistic expression in a scratchy, stressed tone.

"Yeah, like a baby. So, Quinn. I haven't seen her in a while." Elijah adjusted his stance to accommodate his sore body and his throbbing ribs. His side where he was kicked a week ago had turned from crimson to a bluish-plum color.

Elijah didn't want to admit it, but Quinn was on his mind more than he was comfortable with since the funeral. It was only a fraction of a conversation they shared. There was something mysterious about Quinn that fascinated him.

"She wasn't supposed to be there, the audacity she had crashing her cousin's funeral. It's sickening. That side of my family wasn't invited." Her voice was thick with disdain and judgment.

"Shelly, it was her *cousin's* funeral. Not a damn debutante ball." Shelly quieted at his response. Elijah checked his cell phone for the time, not entirely ready to discuss superficial drama from one of the worst days of his life. "I've got to get going. I have an appointment."

The weight of Owen's death was heavy on Elijah's shoulders, and he wanted nothing more than to hide. The voices and the spirits that plagued him had been making the grieving process unbearable.

"Alright, I have to meet a friend for lunch anyway. Speak to you soon, dear. Much love, and Elijah?"

"Yeah?" Elijah's voice was broken, and for some reason saying goodbye to Shelly felt like saying goodbye to Owen all over again.

"Take care of yourself." There was a sentiment behind her gentle tone that told him he was the only son she had left.

Even if he wasn't biologically hers.

"I will." Elijah waited till Shelly clicked end, noting the numerous missed calls.

None from Riley.

The ethereal core of who Elijah was that connected him to the spirit world kept reminding him he'd lost a piece of himself. Owen was that piece that anchored him in normalcy. Letting go would be impossible, especially since the last time he spoke to Owen, he'd punched him in the face. There was never going to be a chance to tell Owen how sorry he was. The time to apologize had vanished into a black hole of sorrow and melancholy his life had become.

Elijah took off his sunglasses and slipped them over the collar of his T-shirt as he entered the Thirsty Parrot. He judged on a scale of one to ten how pissed off Riley was at him because of the fight he started a few nights ago. Her missing Owen's funeral was bittersweet. Although, Elijah understood why she didn't show up. The number of white daisies she sent in her place was extravagant. They were laid on top of Owen's casket when they lowered him into his grave. Elijah was convinced it was a metaphorical symbol of the two things that would probably kill him.

After Elijah and Riley broke up, he continued to frequent the bar that they both drank at while together. All of Elijah's friends were Riley's friends.

Their break-up was akin to a dysfunctional divorced couple fighting for custody of their children. Even though six excruciating months had passed, the group acted like speaking Riley's name would destroy his fragile world.

The humidity of the Southern afternoon made the bar smell like mold and damp wood. Dust drifted through the room, and daylight cut through the massive, dirty skylight. Two rough-looking men in the back corner burst into laughter while playing pool. The taller of the two sized Elijah up with his beady eyes, taking a drink of his Bud Light. Elijah raised an eyebrow at the man's unspeakably ugly Hawaiian shirt. "Jessie's Girl" by Rick Springfield played softly from the jukebox in the back corner by the dartboards.

"Hey, Ri, you here?" Elijah banged his ribs on the brass bar that stretched the length of the countertop and winced. His bruised eye spasmed.

"No, she's got the day off." Hudson came around the corner carrying a case of Pabst beer. "Went to Tybee with Dylan for the day." Hudson set down the case and stocked the bottles into a mini-fridge under the counter.

"Well, can I get a shot?" Elijah watched the men out of his peripherals; the other man was short and stocky.

"Did you clean your room?"

"What are you, my maw?" Elijah's twang seeped through.

"No, I'm worse. I'm your roommate." Hudson grinned at him, flashing his pearly whites. "And just 'cause I'm a dude doesn't mean I don't like cleanliness." Hudson grabbed a shot glass with gentle precision and poured a double of house whiskey, sliding it a short distance to Elijah.

The shorter man handed the taller one his phone and pointed to the screen. The taller, beady-eyed man was doing his best to try and be inconspicuous. And he failed miserably. Elijah pulled a five from his back pocket and slapped it down on the shellacked bar.

"Keep the rest."

"Wow. Thanks for the twenty-five-cent tip." Hudson raised a dark eyebrow and stroked his manicured beard.

"I do what I can." Elijah took the shot like a pro, and tingling spread across his chest.

"When you finally get your own bar, you better give me drinks on the house, regularly."

"Absolutely." Elijah slid the sticky shot glass back to Hudson, and he dropped it into a plastic tub. "Hey, I have a question. Did anyone drop off an envelope for me the night of Owen's funeral after you got home?"

"No. Why?"

"It's no big deal, just a question Shelly wanted me to ask."

Elijah noticed a new vinyl sticker that had been added to the side of the bar. It was a gold compass rose with the words "True North Trading Company" scrolled across the center. Elijah grazed his fingertips over the top of the sticker, and the bar around him faded away.

"Found this stuck in the crack of our front door this morning," Hudson interjected, slapping a business card down in front of Elijah, tearing his attention away from the sticker.

Elijah picked up the card, inspecting it, then quickly set it back down on the bar; his dark eyebrows pinched together in thought. He leaned in closer to Hudson so that the strange men in the back couldn't hear. "What the hell does Homicide Detective Jensen want with us?"

"Not with us. With *you*."

Hudson flipped the card over and pointed to the note on the back. Elijah stiffened, paused, and hesitantly picked up the card.

Elijah, please call. Inquiring about Owen Percy.

"But Owen committed suicide." Elijah shoved it in his back pocket.

"Apparently, that might not be the case."

Hot sea air drifted from the Savannah inlet and dampened Elijah's messy hair. He couldn't decipher whether it was his lack of sleep or the shot he downed at the bar that was knocking him on his ass. His head ached, and his eyes throbbed. He adjusted his sunglasses, hoping they would do their job. He desperately wanted to go home, eat some Ramen noodles, and climb back into bed.

Elijah rounded the corner of a building into an alley, entering Factor's Walk, making his way to the liquor store. His ribs exploded. An unseen impact sent his fight or flight into overdrive, and his breath shot out of his lungs. Blindsided, Elijah gasped. A blunt, heavy object collided with the base of his skull. Stars shot across his vision.

Swinging blindly, Elijah's fist connected with someone's face. A man's raspy voice cursed in a language he didn't understand. Another blow landed on his lower back, striking his kidneys. Elijah stumbled into a stone wall. His right shoulder rammed into the jagged rocks. A shot of stabbing pain radiated through the joint. He grunted, grabbing his shoulder.

Pain flew from every part of his body and wiped his mind of function. His vision blackened. His head whirled. Before he regained footing, Elijah felt two strong arms dragging him. Elijah fought against the aching in his head, attempting to force open his eyes.

He lost one of his flip-flops as he was dragged behind a dumpster. His bare heels scraped against the cobblestone street. As his senses returned, adrenaline rushed through Elijah. He continued to fight against his attackers. A firm but strong forearm pressed on his chest, pinning him to an ivy-covered wall. Elijah made a pitiful attempt to flee, and another attacker gripped his shoulder, slamming him against the building. His eyes watered at the putrid aroma of rotting food intermingled with sweat and cheap dime-store cologne.

"I don't have any money." Elijah struggled to put together words as he took stock of what was happening to him.

"You hear that, Allison? The kid thinks we're robbing him."

After his blurry eyes regained focus, Elijah saw the two men from the Thirsty Parrot. The short, stocky redhead embodied a ruggedness that reminded him of Murphy from The Boondock Saints. Considering his situation, Elijah wondered how many men were attacked or murdered in the burning streets of Savannah since the late 1730s. Sad, angry, and lonely spirits brimmed the city, perpetually searching for a way to escape their current hell. Silently, Elijah hoped he wasn't about to become one of them.

Allison, the tall, lanky man from the bar, chuckled and grinned, revealing a mouth full of crooked, grayish, corn-colored teeth. "This job is da best. So, you're Elijah?" The man's voice was thick with what Elijah assumed was a Russian accent.

Raising his throbbing head, Elijah met the emotionally vacant eyes of Allison. Instantly, Elijah knew there was a violent history behind that look, backed by a silent rage. He got a sense that those eyes and the hand that pinned him had witnessed and committed many illegal and dirty deeds.

"I asked you a question, kid," said Allison.

"Depends on who's asking? Who the hell are you two?"

Allison's eyes narrowed like a predator's does when they are about to devour their prey. His short, clay-colored hair had frosted ends that made him look like he'd strolled straight out of a ninety's crime drama.

"I'm Allison." He jabbed a thumb toward the other man. "And this is Landon. We're here for Josiah." The pungent scent of cigarettes wafted from his shirt.

"Look, there's better ways to ask a guy out these days. Maybe tell him to swipe right next time?" Elijah was scared shitless, but his voice was steady and condescending.

His left cheek throbbed—the impact rippled down his neck. A trickle of blood rolled down his face.

"You're a smartass … and I don't like smartasses." Allison wiped Elijah's blood from his tanned, calloused knuckles. "It's disrespectful." Allison jabbed a crooked finger in Elijah's face, and his scar-littered upper lip raised with disgust. "What the hell is the problem with today's youth? Speaking before they think."

Elijah's need to poke the angry and hungry lion subsided. "Who the fuck's Josiah? Am I supposed to know who that is?" Elijah dabbed the broken, tender skin of his right cheek with his fingertips. Blood was flowing.

Great, I'm gonna need butterfly stitches.

"Your friend, Owen ... was an employee. He owes Josiah *and* us." Landon nodded toward Allison. Elijah studied Landon, noting he had softer eyes. Whatever they were shaking him down for, Landon hadn't been in the shaking down profession for long.

"Merchandise or money," Allison added.

"Owen dealt drugs?"

A trolley full of out-of-towners stopped at the end of an alley, and the tour guide told them the history of the many historic buildings on River Street. Allison chuckled and backed away, staying cautious of the passersby, watching them out of the corner of his eye. "Hey, Landon, this kid catches on fast."

"There's no way that's true." Elijah clenched his jaw. "Why does he owe Josiah and you too?" Elijah waved his hand furiously at Allison.

Landon rocked forward, pressing his forearm against Elijah's chest. He glared at Elijah, giving him an unspoken warning not to make one move. Landon was short, but he had muscle mass like a Pitbull.

Allison rested his hands on his hips. "I call it a transaction fee. And since I had to drag my ass out here and miss my daughter's tenth fucking princess birthday party to deal with this shit, I'm tacking on a late fee. You have any idea what it's like getting the silent treatment from a kid?"

Elijah stifled a smile, imagining Allison in a silver, plastic tiara, sitting at a pink table drinking tea with stuffed animals. Poetic justice.

"How much does he owe you?" Elijah rubbed the back of his neck, and the distant sound of a train filled the alley as the voice of the tour guide faded.

"Forty thousand in either cocaine or cash. He took three bricks at fourteen grand each."

Elijah wanted nothing more than to punch Owen in his stupid face. How could he leave this for his mother? He rested his weary head on the brick behind him, wincing. Elijah could barely afford to pay his water bill, let alone find forty-grand. He had to figure out if there was any stash left or if Owen had hidden the money somewhere.

"I don't have that kind of money."

"Not my fuckin' problem. His debts are yours now."

Elijah's face flushed red, and he balled his hands into fists. "I'm not paying drug dealers. That's what happens when you make unsecured investments. You lose money."

"No. That's what happens when people commit suicide. Their debts go to the next person in line. Law of the jungle," Landon shot back.

"There's nothing worse than dumbasses avoiding debts," Allison added and laughed.

"What's stopping me from going to the cops?" Elijah shook with an aching need to beat Allison. The hard barrel of a gun dug into his sore side. Allison came dangerously close to Elijah's face.

"You can either pay, or we can go after his sweet mom Shelly for the money." Allison's tone dipped to a sinister level, drawing out the word "sweet." His hot breath brushed against Elijah's cheeks and smelled like taco meat and beer. Elijah stared him directly in the eyes, not wavering once. "If you call the cops, she'll end up like her son."

"No. I'll get it." Elijah's voice was firm. "If you touch Shelly or even go in her vicinity, I'll beat the living shit out of you." Elijah was convinced he either needed to be bitten by a radioactive spider or become a vampire if anyone else kicked his ass. He might even settle for a werewolf.

The annoyance in Allison's eyes faded. He stuck his gun back into his hip holster, impressed by Elijah's morality. Allison placed a hand on Landon's shoulder, and he released Elijah.

"Look, kid, for some ungodly reason, I kinda like you ..." Allison took a pack of Marlboros from his pocket and slid one out. "So, here's the deal." He placed the cigarette in his mouth and lit it. "Josiah wanted you to get the goods or cash to us by next Thursday."

"That's seven days from now."

Allison took a puff, and his body relaxed. "I'll talk to him about giving you two weeks. Business has been pretty good."

"Thanks. Ironically enough, that's the nicest thing anyone has done for me all week." Elijah picked his sunglasses up from the ground—thankful they weren't broken. He glanced at the building and noticed he stood underneath a sign that said: "24-hour tarot readings available." A woman with long, blonde hair and round eyes stood, shuffling cards, staring down at the three men from the third floor, watching their movements with prying eyes. Bored, she turned back into her apartment and shut the curtains.

"Words of wisdom." Landon backed away, regaining Elijah's attention, standing next to Allison. "At some time, we all have to pay for our sins. You might want to figure out what brought you to this crossroad."

"Very true." Elijah sighed at the thought that such insightful advice came from the strong arm of a drug dealer. "You should probably go before you miss the rest of your daughter's tenth birthday."

4

BY THE TIME ELIJAH made it out to Shelly's, he wanted a nap. The exhaustion he'd been pushing back all day had finally sunk into every part of his body mentally, physically, and spiritually. The safe haven where he spent his life after his father died had turned unbearable and distressing. The whole place was a painful reminder of what he'd lost—and all the emotional shit he now waded through.

Exasperated was the word Elijah searched for when he paused, rifling through Owen's belongings. He was on the third box that Shelly packed and brought over from Owen's dorm room. There wasn't a shred of evidence that pointed to drugs. He needed to find out what was on the hard drive as soon as possible. He knew he couldn't let his avoidance win for too long. The answer he needed *might* be there.

After his encounter with the cocaine dealers, he'd halfway patched up the cut on his cheek with a liquid band-aid and coagulant. His cheek stung where Allison had punched him, a painful reminder that Owen had been dealing drugs. That image didn't fit and was the opposite of the person he knew. Elijah's mind played a strange dance between anger and grief as he thought about the vulnerable position Owen had placed him and Shelly in.

The crow at Owen's funeral was a harbinger. The intuitive thought had been nipping at his mind since Owen's funeral—something far worse was on the horizon. Elijah always believed terrible things came in threes. He had an inkling that there were more secrets and lies to come. Ones that would destroy his delusions of reality. Elijah hoped that after it hit three, there wouldn't be any bonus rounds.

A faint scent of saltwater and algae floated in on hot violent gusts through a half-open window above Owen's bed from offshore. Torrential rain poured in sheets, and charcoal-colored clouds blanketed the sky. Thunder shook the walls of the small three-bedroom coastal home where Elijah had spent his childhood. Binx anxiously spun around in doggy circles. His beautiful, golden coat shimmered in the gloomy afternoon, and Binx clumsily jumped onto Owen's bed, curling into a ball, cocooning himself under the down blanket. Binx huffed, snorting through his snout. Elijah scratched behind Binx's ears.

"Gotta love hurricane season." Shelly smiled, taking a sip of her merlot. "What was it the friend said they needed?"

"I'm not entirely sure, to be honest. They were pretty vague." A pang of guilt surged through Elijah with the bald-faced lie. He'd been biding his time, waiting for her to leave so he could do a *genuine* search for the drugs, and it was taking longer than he expected.

"Who was this friend? It better not be Quinn." Shelly dropped a trinket back into the box and gave Elijah a motherly glare.

"It's not." Elijah raised his eyebrows, holding out his hands in surrender.

"You promise?"

"Yes. I promise." He sighed, disquieted. "You know I am an adu—"

"You stay away from her. She's bad news."

Shelly's voice shook, and her eyes were bloodshot. The last two weeks, she had been through hell, and her defense lawyer ex-husband, William, had made it even more unbearable for her, blaming her for not raising Owen the right way. His way was always the only way, and that was one of the reasons they divorced. It didn't shock Elijah that he wouldn't shoulder any of the responsibility.

Elijah placed a tender palm on her cheek. "You don't need to do this with me right now."

Shelly hesitated before setting down a film textbook. "Are you sure?"

"Yes. Go take a nap. I'll clean up before I leave, feed Binx, and come and say goodbye." Elijah wrapped his arms around Shelly, resting his chin on her head. "It'll be alright. I'll always be here."

"You know you have a room across the hall. It'll always be here for you if you need it." Shelly hugged him tightly, and her chest shuddered against his stomach. "I'll always consider you my son too."

"I know." Elijah smiled.

"I have no idea how I'm going to make the payments to the funeral home. I have three months to pay off fifteen grand," Shelly murmured.

He squeezed her tighter, and she rubbed his back. "Thank you for volunteering to pack up the rest of his dorm. I know this is hard for you too." Shelly removed keys from her pocket and handed them to Elijah.

Elijah wiped the tears from her face, and he could see the heartbreak in her eyes. At that moment, he made a silent vow to never tell her about the drugs.

"Anything I can do to help. We'll get the money situation figured out. I'll talk to Hudson about doing a fundraiser at the bar."

"I don't know what I'd do without you." She turned away, then turned back. Taking a sip of her wine, she picked dog hair from her oversized black sweater, the sleeves covering her hands. "I need to tell you something. It's still early, but ... " Shelly wiped her nose with a tissue and shoved it in the pocket of her pink sweat pants. "They think there might be more to Owen's death."

Elijah's heart shuddered, and his shoulders tightened. He played with the edge of the box and stayed silent, not sure how to continue. There were countless ways this could go wrong, and he didn't want to make things worse.

"A Detective Bohannon from Beaufort came by and said there were some inconsistencies in Owen's autopsy. They think he was murdered."

Elijah bit his bottom lip; the intuitive nudge he'd received was correct in the worst way. His intestines twisted into knots, and his head whirled.

Shelly pinched her earlobe, played with her earring, then took another sip of wine. Loose, blonde tendrils from her untamed ponytail framed her delicate jawline. It hit Elijah that the oversized, black sweater she wore was Owen's.

"Elijah, did you hear me?"

"Yeah, it's ... unexpected, that's all," Elijah stuttered as his mind tried to produce cohesive words.

"You need to take the envelope he left you to the police. Did you open it?"

"No, not yet." Elijah swallowed heavily and rubbed the back of his neck.

When Elijah had a psychic episode or connection with a spirit, it had usually been manageable. The nightmare and apparition of Owen, the night of the funeral, flickered, burning in the back of his mind. Every ounce of fear and terror Owen felt during his death hijacked Elijah. Every ounce of pain Owen had experienced when he left the Earthly plane soaked into Elijah's soul with that ghostly visit. It was the most emotionally cataclysmic thing Elijah had experienced; helplessness consumed him.

"He said he would be contacting you to talk about Owen. He's trying to establish if he was suicidal or not, which he wasn't," Shelly said with conviction.

"I'll talk to him, don't worry," Elijah assured her.

She patted his face. "You need to stop getting into fights. You're gonna go to jail if you keep doing things like that." Her gentle raspy voice turned rigid.

Shelly meandered out Owen's bedroom door and paused in the hallway, her weary eyes on Elijah. She flashed him a hopeful smile. "Let's go, Binxy." The dog scurried off the bed, and they both disappeared down the hall.

Elijah could hear Shelly shove her bedroom door closed twice, then rattle the knob. Shelly's door used to give a soft *click*. But now, it took force every time. Owen and Elijah jimmied the lock one Christmas and snuck into her room to find their Christmas presents when they were thirteen. It was always a thing of Owen's to shake the box and guess. Elijah preferred the thrill of the unknown, being patient and waiting to unfold the mystery. Finding exciting surprises under the wrapping on Christmas was half the fun. The anticipation had always given Elijah a rush.

Owen's room hadn't revealed anything worth a second glance. Most of the boxes were filled with pictures of his film friends and him on set. There were a couple of Owen and Camilla. Movie project binders, editing software boxes, and crappy film theory textbooks Elijah didn't care about filled the rest.

"Where the fuck did you hide it?" Elijah mumbled as if he thought Owen could hear him. He had no way to tell if Owen would show himself again or if his spirit had moved on. Elijah stared out the window in thought at the fishing boats rocking in the marina. Palm trees were now whipping around in the violent winds.

The humidity drifting through the window faded. The air conditioning clicked on, and Elijah felt an icy blast. No one could understand why he always had the window open, but he loved the fresh air for some reason, whether it was hot or cold. Elijah found pure pleasure in being connected to the Earth around him. Being grateful for the little things. On some subconscious level, the open window reminded Elijah he always had a way out, that nothing lasted forever, and everything eventually came full circle.

Elijah closed the bedroom door, walked to Owen's closet, and squatted, thumping the floorboards with his sore knuckles. He found the spot he was looking for and pulled up the small, wooden puzzle piece. The only things Elijah found in the hidey-hole were a Sublime cassette tape and a Playboy featuring Sandra Nilsson, Miss January 2008. They stole it from the corner store when they were twelve. She was a favorite of both Owen's and Elijah's.

No bricks of illicit drugs there. A grainy substance brushed his fingers. He bent over, reaching further into the hidey-hole. Still, no drugs. Elijah pinched out the pinkish substance and sniffed. A sweet, floral, chemical odor hit the back of his throat, burning.

Elijah stood, wiped his hand off on his jeans, and ran his fingers through his thick hair in thought. His heart raced. Elijah had researched the drug online before going to Shelly's. He knew that the granules had to be traces of cocaine. The smell and color were exactly as described. Owen had sold the illicit stimulant and hid it at his mother's house. Elijah grunted, annoyed, then decided he needed to clean the evidence out of the hole before leaving.

It was impossible to know the number of people Owen had sold to, and as a result, overdosed or became addicts. Not to mention the friends he'd exposed to it in college.

Sinking with disappointment, he dropped onto the edge of Owen's bed.

Elijah ran his fingertips over the soft, flannel sheets. For a split second, he could hear Owen's footsteps down the hall. He expected him to walk through his bedroom door and say, "Hey, asshole, quit bein' a creeper." Elijah swiped a textbook, and it crashed against the floor, sliding.

It knocked over a desk lamp and cup full of pens. Elijah wanted to tear down every single movie poster and rip them to shreds. The walls closed in, and his breaths shallowed. A sheen of sweat formed on his face, stinging his busted lip. He needed to get out of the room before he suffocated. The air around him crystalized, and Elijah felt like he was sitting in a walk-in freezer.

Steam billowed from his mouth, and he waved his fingers through it in amazement. The digital thermometer on the wall flipped through numbers, rapidly falling from ninety degrees. It reminded Elijah of a falling elevator that had lost its cables. Whispering blasted his ears. It sounded like a chorus of a thousand voices, and it pierced his eardrums. The unsettling desperate sound of their calls vibrated through him, shaking him to his core.

Elijah jumped up in time to witness a wolf trotting down the street. It stopped in front of the docks and fixated on Elijah. The canine's cold gaze unsettled him, and his stomach lurched.

One tortured, disembodied voice rose above the rest, hissing, "Mary." The same name Owen had communicated to Elijah a week before. Frigid breath brushed Elijah's ear. He instinctively spun away from the spot and toward the empty room. An unseen force grabbed his forearm, and searing pain penetrated through layers of his skin and muscle. Elijah clenched a weak fist, grunting. A mild electric shock immobilized him, and before his eyes, a welted imprint of a hand appeared. The pressure released after what felt like hours.

He regained control of his body, and Elijah returned his attention to the malicious canine. The canine's shaggy, blended gray and white fur rustled in the summer coastal wind. Furious clouds and lightning framed the creature. Its primal black eyes bore into him. A ravenous desire to devour him sparked behind those hollow, black windows of rage, and Elijah's heart felt like it seized. The world faded around Elijah, and it silenced; he was standing in the eye of a spiritual storm. All Elijah could hear was the hell-beast's primal grunting. Its lips curled back, exposing its razor-sharp teeth, giving a hungry grin. Adrenaline surged through Elijah as the rumbling engine of a beat-up Chevy truck raced past, breaking the bizarre standoff, jolting Elijah out of his supernatural black hole.

5

THE STUPID DOOR WOULDN'T open. Elijah tried what seemed like a hundred times to swipe the key card through. Every time, a high-pitched "denied" sound beeped, and a tiny red dot flashed at him. He had no idea how many SCAD students passed him staring, like he'd lost all his senses and belonged in a padded room. He wasn't entirely sure he shouldn't be committed to one after hearing the disembodied voices in Owen's bedroom. The mystery of who *Mary* was, ravaged his thoughts, making it difficult for him to focus. His arm throbbed where the entity seared its handprint into his skin, marking him.

Over the past few days, he had a growing list of both supernatural and real-world complications that needed to be shoved away into the back of his mind. His psychic senses were in overdrive and weren't going to allow him peace. He knew his ordinary life and supernatural life were bound to collide, creating further devastation, making a mockery out of what he'd worked so hard to achieve. *Being normal.*

Spinning away from the door, Elijah threw his hand in the air. Sitting on a bench, he rubbed the back of his neck, turning his leather bracelet around his wrist, playing with the metal lion head bead. He thought of Owen's and how soon, hopefully, he would recover his matching bracelet and wear them both. Elijah knew they both would be a daily reminder not to squander his relationships and be *present* every second of his life.

Making sure he was in the right place (for the hundredth time), he double-checked the name of the building. *Yep. Victory Village. Right place. This is a sign from the universe. I'm not supposed to go in there.*

Elijah stood and tugged at the bottom of his sweaty, black T-shirt and strode toward his car. His sanctuary. It was the place he could recall the good memories of his father and Owen at the same time. It was a security blanket after his father died. Restoring the 68 Nova SS was the best thing he and Owen had done with their summers. The cassette tape player would, from now on, always play Owen's favorite music along with his father's. Except, now, Elijah would be sitting on the hood of the beautiful silver-bullet-colored piece of machinery at Tybee Beach drinking beer by himself.

"Can I help you, son?" the trained, military tone of a no-bullshit man boomed behind him.

Damn.

Elijah pivoted in mid-stride, turning around. A middle-aged, slightly bald security guard poked his head out of the glass door.

"Yeah." Elijah cleared his throat. "I'm ... my friend. I'm here to pack some things for my friend's mother." Elijah's cheek twitched, still raw from the abuse earlier that morning.

"I'm sorry, son, but you're gonna need the tenant to do that." He watched the security guard's eyes skim over his battered face, then over his sleeve tattoo. His shoulders squared, and he turned his body, blocking the entrance. Elijah strolled to the door.

"Well. See ..." Elijah adjusted his sunglasses, pointing at his name tag. "Henry." Attempting to be as charming as possible, he gave a crooked smile. "The thing is—"

"You've been drinking, kid. I can smell it on ya. Sorry, you're gonna have to come back with the student that's renting the room." The security guard shut the door. Elijah knocked on the glass with desperation harder than he intended. Henry threw his head back and turned around, then cracked it open.

"Go. Don't make me detain—"

"Look, I'm here to pack stuff up—"

Out of patience, he closed the door. "Go sober up. Take a shower, for Chri —"

"Will you please let me finish?" Elijah's voice was a mixture of firm and pleading. "I have a good reason."

Henry raised his eyebrows, sighing, leaning against the door frame. He cracked it open. "Sure. Go ahead." He crossed his arms, narrowing his eyes in skepticism.

"My best friend died recently." There was a hitch in his voice. "His mother, Shelly, sent me to pack his things," Elijah said the last part slowly as if every word was a hit from a baseball bat beating the shit out of his fragile heart.

Henry's face turned from stern to sullen. "Oh, Owen."

"Yes. Owen." Elijah sighed. He stuck his hands into the pockets of his jeans.

Being emotionally exposed to a stranger made his chest tighten. Dealing with vulnerability was a skill he'd let weaken and fade away after his father's death. Being vulnerable led to more pain.

"He was a good kid …" Henry looked past Elijah in thought. "One of my favorite students." He gave a quick corner-mouth smile. "Always treated me with respect." Henry gave a shallow sigh, turning his attention back to Elijah. "Remembered all my kids' birthdays and mine and my wife's anniversary. Brought me apple pie on occasion. I sure am gonna miss him." He tucked his thumb under his belt, tapping his behemoth flashlight.

The two men sat in silence as if they were under an unspoken understanding to give Owen's memory respect.

"Come on in, kid." Henry opened the door wide for Elijah. "I get why you're drinking. I would be too. He was on the third floor. Sorry about giving you a hard time. We've had some strange guys loitering around here lately. Trying to sneak into the building." Henry pointed Elijah down the hall. "Elevators are on the right-hand side past the commons area."

"Out of curiosity, what do they look like?" Elijah took off his sunglasses, sliding them on the collar of his shirt. "The loiterers."

"Tall, lanky guy with an ugly Hawaiian T-shirt. He wears a different colored one every day; I know 'cause I have to put it in the log. He's usually in the company of a short, red-haired kid. I called the cops on 'em, and they haven't been back since."

The truth hit Elijah, his throat tightened, and his head throbbed. Owen had changed tremendously in six months. Elijah had been far too stubborn and prideful, and he shouldn't have let anyone come between them. He should have been there for Owen.

Owen's dorm room was messy as all get out. It didn't surprise Elijah one bit. They both had that in common. Elijah stood, taking in the studio apartment. It was the first time he'd seen it since Owen moved dorms. Six months in the span of eternity was a flash in the existence of time, but it felt like millennia to Elijah. A pungent, earthly scent filled his nose—disarrayed, chaotic energy pulsed against Elijah. There were small areas through the apartment where Shelly had cleaned. Elijah slid his keys into his pocket and studied the open living space. There were numerous movie posters, artwork, and photography covering every square inch of the studio. Among them, *The Godfather*, *The Sandlot*, Tim Burton's *Alice in Wonderland*? Elijah chuckled.

A fan on Owen's bedside table was still turned on, facing his pillow. Old pizza boxes and crumpled up empty bags of spicy pork rinds were strewn through the kitchen. Heat radiated from the window over his desk, and the sunlight set afire every white surface in the room. Elijah closed the curtains and turned on the air conditioning.

There was a soft knock at the door. Elijah opened it, and a timid, short girl with a pale face and long, black hair smiled sweetly. She held a blue laundry basket filled with folded clothes. Pink rose in her cheeks, and she chewed on her bottom lip.

"Hi. Umm. I'm Harper." She gave a short wave, keeping her hands on the basket. "I live two doors down." She nodded down the hallway.

"I'm Elijah."

"You're Owen's friend, right?" Her beautiful hazel eyes widened.

"Yeah, how'd you—"

"He has a picture of the two of you on his desk standing in front of a sweet silver Nova. I'm a huge fan of classic cars."

"He does?" Elijah raised a dark eyebrow.

"Or he did." The girl bit her bottom lip, and she slouched with sadness.

"Right." Elijah rubbed the back of his neck and leaned against the door frame.

"Sorry, I didn't mean to bother you. I noticed you coming in the door. So, I thought I'd bring these over. They were left in the laundry room by Owen. I folded them for his mother."

Elijah took the basket, setting it inside the door. "Thanks. I'll make sure she gets them. I didn't notice you at the funeral."

"Oh, yeah. I wanted to be respectful and let the family have their time. I remembered Owen in my own way. I watched a bunch of crappy horror films." She smiled, and her eyes sparkled. Her black summer dress ruffled from the ceiling fan.

"He did love those," Elijah said.

"Yeah." She paused, rubbing her nose. It seemed like she had something else to add. "Well, have a good day."

Elijah let the door close. Kneeling next to the basket, he sifted through the clothes. The fresh scent of the laundry reminded him of the simple pleasures of life. Since he was a child, he'd always loved the smell of clean laundry. He had no idea why.

After a short search, Elijah found what he was looking for. Owen's favorite band shirt, Florence And The Machine. It was the one Elijah bought him for his sixteenth birthday at a summer concert in Charleston, South Carolina.

A mountain of packed boxes sat next to the front door where Shelly had already started packing. He grabbed a stack of medium-sized boxes from the corner, leaning against Owen's TV, and set them on the coffee table.

Another knock at the door interrupted Elijah. He cracked it open cautiously, hoping it wasn't Allison. Elijah released a sigh of relief. It was

Harper.

"There's something I need to tell you."

"Sure, what's up?"

"Do you mind?" Harper motioned toward the inside of Owen's room.

Elijah opened the door for her to come in.

"I'm not sure how to say this, so I'm gonna spit it out. I study Wicca. Owen came to me a few months ago, scared. Said there were animals following him."

Elijah draped the shirt around his neck and moseyed over to Owen's desk. He leaned against it. "What kind of animals?"

"A gray wolf and a crow. Both harbingers of death. It seemed uncanny that they were following him, and now, well, you know."

Elijah crossed his arms. He had seen the crow at Owen's funeral and the wolf this afternoon. "What did you help him with?"

"Basic protection spells against curses. I bought him Sage and Palo Santo wood. Both clear out negative energies." Harper drew her hair back into a ponytail. "Sometimes, if you wait it out, the spell's power will lessen and pass over time. If this is a result of black magic, the witch is strong."

"Were there a lot of people that came in and out of his room?"

"Well, yeah. Owen was freakin' awesome at what he did. A natural. Which meant there wasn't a short supply of students that wanted to work with him. Owen had numerous collaborations and projects going. He worked all day and night. It got weird for some of our friends, though, working with him. Owen was extremely secretive about his current project, *Seven Sisters Road*. Made some of the crew sign privacy waivers. It got to the point where he left campus to do all of his editing." Harper paused, squinting in thought. "There was a curly red-headed girl I'd seen him leave with a few times. I don't think she's a student here."

It hadn't occurred to Elijah that Owen might have bought the drugs for himself and his friends. Owen told him about the crazy deadlines. The overwhelming stress of being in a top-notch school of the arts wore on him and his health. Owen notoriously bit off more than he could chew. The success came with its downfalls. Elijah was never immersed in the creative process, but it sounded like hell.

"Okay, thanks." Elijah smiled and ran a hand through his dark hair.

Harper turned hesitantly. "What happened to your arm?"

"That's none of your business," Elijah snapped.

A flush crept across Harper's face, and she grimaced. "Sorry, I wasn't …"

"No. I'm sorry," he said softly.

Harper cautiously padded to the door, then stopped and turned before walking out.

"Be careful," her beautiful eyes dropped to the floor in deep thought, then she spun, swung open the door, walked out apprehensively, and closed it behind her.

Elijah removed everything from the cupboards in the kitchen, emptied the refrigerator, and checked under the sink. No sign of drugs. He uncovered the picture of Owen and him hidden in the corner of his desk. It was buried under piles of manuscript drafts of *Seven Sisters Road*. It was taken six years prior, right before he drove Owen to SCAD and dropped him off. Owen was so close to gaining his master's in filmmaking. Elijah wrapped the band T-shirt around the picture and set it on the corner so he wouldn't forget it when he was done packing.

Judging from the sophisticated equipment he saw open and laid out along the wall in Owen's living area, Elijah knew that's where he must have spent his drug money. There were many nights where they stayed up late in the fort in the backyard, talking about their dreams. Owen was constantly flipping through American Cinematographer, gawking at cameras and lenses.

Elijah was sure that some of the money went to Camilla, his gold-digging ex-girlfriend. He searched through Owen's closet and clothes, took the hangers out and laid them in a chair. A picture poking out from a shelf caught his attention. It was a picture of Quinn, Owen, and himself when they were thirteen. They were all sitting on the dock across from Shelly's house, fishing.

He smiled at the memory; it was a good day. It made him wish he'd gotten Quinn's phone number.

Darting to Owen's dresser, Elijah pulled out the drawers, setting them on the ground. He searched the inside for any sign of drugs. He opened the bedside table drawer, hoping to find Owen's bracelet. It wasn't there. Elijah's phone rang; Camilla was calling him. He clicked it onto the speaker, setting it down.

"Hey," she drawled it out like she wanted something from him.

"Why you callin' me?" Elijah asked flatly.

"Why is it the first thing you assume is that I want something?"

"We haven't spoken in six months, and when I saw you at the funeral, we didn't exactly play nice."

"I spoke to Shelly today. She mentioned needing money for the funeral. I wanted to tell you Turner still wants to go forward with the documentary." Her voice dipped and turned to velvet.

Elijah sifted through the contents of Owen's dresser drawers, nothing of use there. Elijah dashed to the half-empty bookshelves, pulling the rest of the books off and flipping through each of them.

"Are you serious? You're not considering finishing that damn thing, are you?"

"Maybe." Her voice perked, and she took a drink. Elijah was sure it was white wine. That's what she preferred. Plus, it was a Thursday evening; just about every woman he knew (for some reason) drank on Thursdays. "I assumed after Owen's ... they ..." She went silent. Elijah could tell he wasn't the only one having trouble saying Owen was dead out loud. "Anyhow, I can act as an ambassador on Shelly's behalf." Her voice was professional. Firm. "Get her the funds she needs."

Grabbing a roll of tape, Elijah put a box together and dropped the books into it. This would be Camilla's big break. Going straight from journalism school to a contract with a major broadcasting company would be like winning the lottery. Owen worked a pretty sweet deal with Turner, making it a contingency during the optioning of the series that Camilla got a contract.

Elijah plopped onto Owen's bed out of habit, and a waft of Owen's cologne whooshed around him. The cedar scent comforted him. He laid back on the bed, tucking one hand behind his head. The jostling of the plop made all of his wounds throb. And the softness of the mattress made his eyes heavy. He turned the phone off the speaker.

"Elijah, are you there?"

"Yeah, I'm here." His voice cracked, and he cleared his throat. Elijah stared blankly at the ceiling. It wasn't an ideal way to get money, but he did have angry, homicidal drug dealers following him, waiting to dismember him.

He had no idea where Owen hid the drugs. There was clearly no place for him to hide them in his tiny apartment. The bathroom sink didn't even have a cabinet door. The AC unit vibrated the wall as it turned on, and cold air gusted from the vent.

"Look, I know you hate me, but I promise I'll do what I can to help Owen and Shelly." Camilla's voice lowered. "Owen deserved this. Despite what happened. It was his passion. I'm not gonna let it fade away. I have to do this last thing for him. I have to finish it."

Unbelievably, Elijah understood how she felt. For the first time, they were on the same page. "I believe you. And you're right. He did."

Elijah needed to ask her about the drugs. It wasn't a conversation he could have over the phone. Elijah rolled off the bed and onto his feet, darting to a vent next to Owen's closet.

"Meet me at Monroe's at 9:30 tonight. There's something I want to talk to you about. In the meantime, get ahold of Turner and figure out what we need to do." Elijah clicked end and slid his phone into his back pocket.

He grabbed a chair and drug it to a high vent on the wall. He jumped up on the chair and peeked through the slits. There was a book in there. He could see the corner of it flapping. Elijah took a pocket knife out and unscrewed the vent cover. A leather-bound journal packed to the gills with loose pieces of paper shoved between the pages waved in the wind as it gusted past and into

Elijah's face. It was the sweet, earthly aroma he had noted when he walked into the room. Elijah pulled out the journal, studying the pentagram branded into the leather cover, and flipped to the first page. There was a post-it attached.

Elijah,

I hope this journal makes it to your hands and finds you in good health. This is the beginning of the story of how you, I, Camilla, Quinn, Riley, Hudson, and Parker all lived and died. If you're reading this then I'm no longer alive, and you need to leave town before you're murdered.

6

THE CLOUDS WHIRLED THROUGH the skies as if they were racing to escape the depraved world they surrounded. The hissing of the name "Mary" was still echoing in Elijah's ears. He flipped to a page in Owen's journal, quickly reading an entry.

> *Its voice called to me from the darkness of the forest. I couldn't move at first. The fear it unraveled in me debilitated my mobility. It sounded exactly like my mother, shrieking in pain, calling for my help. An urge to run and save her took me over, even though I knew the voice beckoning me into the woods wasn't hers—because she was across town eating dinner with Elijah.*

Elijah skimmed over notes Owen wrote on past life hypnosis therapies, marking them to read later. Specific tidbits of the writings were in sync with visions that Elijah experienced in his nightmares. Some others spoke about Benjamin and Samuel Shaw and how Owen believed that he and Elijah were once each one of the brothers. He thought that Samuel might have been innocent of the so-called conspiracy to murder his sisters out at Seven Sisters Road.

Wind gusted, shaking Elijah's Nova; he slapped shut Owen's journal and shoved it under his seat. Elijah gripped the steering wheel, and his body shuddered. Everything he'd felt about the supernatural his whole life was being validated. The scary part was that Riley's spirit had been connected to Elijah for many lifetimes if Owen was right. And from what Owen wrote, Camilla was Owen's twin flame. The other half of his soul. Elijah rubbed the back of his neck, locked his door, and jogged into the diner. The vintage jukebox in the corner softly played a love song Elijah recognized from a chick flick Riley made him watch once.

Camilla was already sitting inside the diner when Elijah arrived. She sipped on coffee in a booth across from where the group congregated before they were torn apart. Monroe's Diner was the place they all caught up with each other. In a matter of six months, all their lives had shattered like glass, and the shards were cutting through Elijah's existence like a razor blade.

Camilla's red designer purse rested perfectly next to her as she fiddled with the silverware. Her bronze skin glowed under the diner's fluorescent lights, and her ebony hair was tied back in a stylish bun. Her white, collared dress shirt was pressed, and her black, high-waisted pencil skirt showed no signs of wear. She had pristine makeup on and was TV presentable.

"Hey." Elijah slid into the booth. The comforting scent of freshly made waffles, hash browns, and coffee wrapped around him, hugging him like an old friend.

"Finally, you took long enough." Her voice was rigid. "Five minutes early is ten minutes late." Camilla took a sip of her coffee.

Elijah smiled, "I had some things to take care of."

"What happened? You look worse than you did when I saw you last time." For a moment, there was a flicker of concern on her face. Camilla smoothed her sleek hair, checking her flawless bun in the reflection of the window. Aware she had been empathetic, Camilla's face tightened, and she adjusted the collar of her shirt. Elijah stifled a smile at her transparency and how physically uncomfortable her concern for him made her feel.

"I've had a rough few days. So, did you talk to Turner?"

"I left a message with the intern that works for the producer interested. They should get back to us by tomorrow afternoon."

A petite, pink-haired waitress strolled to the table with an iPad. "What can I get ya, dear?"

"Coffee, black. And some hash browns with scrambled eggs and cheese. A side of bacon."

"Commin' right up." She paused after tapping in the order and smiled at him. "My name's Sage. If you need anything, please don't hesitate to ask."

"Don't worry, I'll be fine with the coffee. Thanks for asking." Camilla's catty tone caught Sage off guard and her shoulders slumped.

"Are you a new waitress? I've never seen you here before." Elijah raised an eyebrow, attempting to diffuse the awkwardness. He could tell Sage was the type to dig bad boys. And well, at that point and time, he definitely fit the bill of a bad boy. He figured he might as well use it to his advantage.

"I am, started a month ago. I love your sleeve." She drug a finger over Elijah's tattoos and then gave a sexy smile.

"Thanks. It took about two years to finish." Elijah leaned toward her, rubbing his arm in pride.

"The coloring is gorgeous." Her cat-shaped, sapphire eyes admired his arm. "Where'd you get your work done?"

"As cute as this display is ..." Camilla's Puerto Rican accent thickened, and she flicked her finger back and forth between the waitress and Elijah. "We have business to attend to. So, if you don't mind?"

"Sorry." The waitress's cheeks blotched with crimson; "I'll be back with your order." She rubbed one of her eyebrows, tucking the iPad under her right arm, and swayed behind the fifties-style bar.

Elijah kept his eyes on her plump booty as she strolled away, swinging her hips. He raised an eyebrow to piss off Camilla. There was something about the jukebox that drew his attention, but it wasn't the song anymore because it was an awful tune he didn't recognize.

"Ugh. God. Can you please keep your sex drive in check for one second?"

"There's no need to be rude, and I'm a single man."

"Don't get me started—"

"So, how much still needs to be done?"

Elijah hadn't meant to open Pandora's Box with that statement, so he steered the conversation back to Camilla's favorite subject. Herself.

"There're specific shots they're requesting. Ones that can't be worked around. Each ghost hunting docuseries has a formula ..." Camilla paused and adjusted herself in the seat. Elijah already knew what her unspoken words were.

"We have to go out there, don't we?" Elijah leaned forward onto his elbows and started picking apart a napkin.

"Yes." Camilla's tone was low and slow. She brushed back her bangs, sighing. "But I can do it by myself with some newbies that don't know Owen." She straightened her shoulders as if she was shrugging off the dark thoughts of working in the same place her ex-boyfriend had died. It didn't do any good because Elijah could sense the heaviness radiating off of her. It was apparent that Owen's death affected her more than she let anyone know.

"Cam. I know we haven't always gotten along, but I'm not going to let you go out there with a couple of kids you don't know."

Camilla raised her eyebrows and took another sip of her coffee. Pausing, she wrapped her hands around the mug. She kept her eyes locked on the dark liquid, staying silent.

"I know this is going to be difficult ..." Elijah said.

Camilla smiled. "No one's called me Cam since ..." Her smile disappeared. "This was the last place he called me that." Her saddened cinnamon-colored eyes whirled around. "Besides you, he's the only person that called me that."

"If it bothers you, I'll stop."

"No, it's comforting ... in some way." Camilla's remaining iciness melted. Her grief surfaced, and Elijah witnessed a vulnerable side of her she'd always kept hidden. "I wish I would have talked to him ... maybe I could have stopped him."

"You and me both." Elijah's throat tightened. "So, how much money are we talking about?"

"One-hundred and fifty grand. Seventy-five for me and the rest for Shelly."

Elijah sighed. He was gonna regret giving in and helping, but he didn't want to get murdered either. "What do you know about *Seven Sisters Road*? What was Owen like when you guys were working on the project?"

"At first, he was normal, but then things changed. He became obsessed. Spending all of his time in the archives, doing research on the metaphysical. Started discussing past lives and the possibility that he and I lived on Seven Sisters Road. He compiled so much information that he bought an office space."

Heat rippled through Elijah's back and neck. "Why didn't you tell me about any of this?"

Camilla slapped the table. Her cheeks burning crimson. "What the hell was I supposed to say? We've never truly talked. I figured that as long as I was around him, working with him on the project, I could watch him. And he would be alright. It was all going fine until Riley started working on the project too. She believed every word he said and indulged his paranormal fantasies. He started shutting people out of the production, not telling anyone about the shooting dates. Completely cutting everyone out."

"Riley fucking knew about this too? Are you kidding me?" Elijah's voice was thick with anger.

Camilla's eyes filled with tears. "I blame myself for this." Her fist pounded the table with every word.

A pang of guilt surged through him. He felt the exact same way. The truth was they all failed Owen when he needed them the most.

"The cops dropped by today." Camilla wiped her eyes. "They say that he might have been murdered."

He had been murdered. Elijah could sense it on such a deep level that it made his whole body ache. Someone hated his best friend enough to string him up and leave him like trash. Elijah swallowed hard and rubbed the back of his neck.

"There's something I have to ask you about. It kinda relates to why my face is even more fucked." Elijah went silent, contemplating the perfect words. He wasn't excellent at communication and wanted nothing more than to let the whole thing fade. But he knew Josiah would send his henchmen back eventually.

"What is it?"

"When you and Owen were together ..." Elijah paused, sat up straight, then tapped his finger on the table. "Did he ... was he ..."

"Any time now," Camilla said impatiently.

Elijah leaned over the table closer to her. "Was Owen selling drugs?" His voice was a whisper.

Camilla's face flushed white. She sat back and crossed her arms, staring down at the table. "I confronted him about rumors that I'd heard. That kids were getting uppers from him to finish projects. He denied it completely."

"Well, this here ..." Elijah pointed at the wound on his cheek and lowered his voice even more. He glanced around the diner and decided to slide in next to Camilla. She slid quickly out of the way. "Is the handiwork of a cocaine dealer named Allison. He came looking for the payment. And apparently, they're tagging me with his bill. So, I have to do one of two things in seven days. Find the drugs, or come up with forty grand."

"Jesus. Are you serious?"

"I'm pretty sure that if we don't find that shit soon, then you'll be attending my funeral."

"We have to go to the cops."

Elijah shook his head. "We can't."

"Bullshit. They could have been the ones that murdered Owen."

"It makes no sense to kill him if he owed them money."

"I'm going to call the detectives."

"They threatened Shelly," Elijah said slowly, monitoring his surroundings. The warm and welcoming energy shifted, turning stale. "They insinuated that they would ..." Elijah's throat tightened. "We can't tell the cops right now. I'm not saying we won't, but not right now. You can't tell anyone about this. I don't want Owen remembered like that."

The lights pulsed and clicked through the diner, then blacked out. Camilla's eyes widened. "Crap."

Elijah felt the temperature drop, and Sage dropped a glass behind the bar;

the shatter reverberated through the empty diner.

"Mr. Monroe, is that you?" Sage said quickly. Elijah deciphered the tone in her voice. She was frightened.

The sound of heavy footsteps walking through the kitchen caught Elijah's attention. A door creaked in the dark as it swung open. "I'll go check the fuse box." Mr. Monroe's voice was deep. And after pretty much living in the diner for five years, it was unmistakable for Elijah.

Static whispering came from the jukebox on the wall, and the neon lights from inside flickered on, turning itself into a beacon.

Camilla's eyes widened and she pointed out the window. "What the hell is that?"

A shadow slowly glided across the parking lot, and the lights outside pulsed.

A scent filled the area, and Camilla stiffened. "That smell, it smells like—"

"Owen." Elijah stood, and Camilla stood with him, grabbing his arm. They both moved together toward the window, staring out into the dark, empty, gravel parking lot. Silence resonated through the restaurant. The air thickened, and Elijah could hear Camilla huffing, terrified.

"Elijah, someone is squeezing my arm." Camilla attempted to gain her faculties, her eyes skipping across the room. Elijah could feel her searching for a way to rationalize the ghostly visitation. "There's no one standing next to me." She stammered.

A handicap parking sign burst into flames and Elijah bolted out the door to the front of the building, followed by Camilla. They stared at the burning sign and charred metal in shock, as Sage came from behind them, throwing water over the flames. With the fire out, Elijah and Camilla saw the letters "OMR."

The thickness in the air dissipated, and as if a storm had passed a dense energy cleared.

The lights inside blinked back on, and Elijah heard Mr. Monroe's low baritone voice from inside. "Fixed it!"

They sat in silence. The cute waitress swayed her way to the table and set Elijah's food down. "Don't worry about paying for anything tonight. It's on the house." Her voice dipped to a honey-coated Southern accent. "Anything else?"

"No, this is good, thanks." He gave her a smile, winked, and she quickly walked away, biting her bottom lip.

Elijah turned his attention back to Camilla, unfolding his silverware. "So, how much research does he have?"

"At least an office full." Camilla sipped her coffee, shifting her eyes from the window back to Elijah's face. She was still trying to process what she'd witnessed, and at this point, he wasn't entirely sure Camilla was ready to accept what she'd just gone through.

Elijah had never experienced anything paranormal in a public place before, and the whole scene played back in his mind. What did OMR mean?

"There're a few boxes that Shelly has at the house. It was all stuff from the studio at SCAD."

"Well, Shelly has the keys to his dorm. His key for his office is on there," Camilla said, drumming her fingers on the coffee cup.

"Do you have any idea where it is?" Elijah said, shoving his mouth full of hash browns.

"Yeah, well, kinda. I've only been there once. Owen was tired of people bothering him at school after a while." Camilla adjusted herself in her seat. A door slammed in the back as four loud drunks stumbled into the diner. Camilla's eyes shot toward the noise in paranoia, breathing heavily.

Elijah poured ketchup onto his hash browns and eggs. "I might go out there tonight. Maybe the drugs are there."

Doing her best to get back to some normalcy, Camilla plucked lipstick from her purse and started reapplying. "Dear God, you're gonna die of a heart attack. I'm so glad I don't eat meat."

"Not eating meat is un-American. I almost forgot. I brought this external hard drive Owen left me; it's what was in the envelope."

"Why are you giving it to me?"

"Crazily enough, you're the only one I trust to keep it safe for me till I can look at it."

Digging into his pocket, Elijah produced the external hard drive in a sandwich bag. Camilla curiously looked it over, then grabbed it from him.

"What's on it?"

"Hopefully, the location of the drugs?" Elijah shoved his mouth full of hash browns, enjoying the salty goodness. "Don't know. I haven't ..." Elijah stopped chewing. A heartbreaking silence grew between them.

Camilla put up her hand. "It's okay, I get it."

Elijah gave a hopeful smile and took a sip of his coffee. "Meet me at the office in the morning. We'll open it together, and not a minute before then. I'll stop by Parker's tonight and talk to him about helping with the rest of the documentary."

Camilla tapped the drive in thought, then shoved it into her purse. "You do realize by us not taking this to the cops, we could be charged with obstruction of justice?"

Allison was sitting on Elijah's trunk when he walked around the front of the restaurant. Elijah had escorted Camilla to her car and waited until she safely drove off before walking over to the Nova. Allison flipped the top of an old Bic lighter back and forth. The metal scraped and clinked. An angry coastal breeze whipped through the parking lot, and Allison's Hawaiian t-shirt flapped against his stomach. The humidity of the day made the stiffness of Allison's clay-colored hair disappear, and it was now a fuzzy mess. From the angle he sat, Elijah wasn't sure whether or not Allison had seen him.

Elijah's eyes darted to the front door of Monroe's; he backed away slowly.

"I already saw you, kid. They have cameras, so I'm not gonna kick your ass. Don't worry." Allison turned his head toward Elijah and flickered a devious smile. His pupils were dilated and echoed a demon's eyes. "Where're the drugs?" Allison hopped off Elijah's car, facing him.

"I haven't found 'em yet."

"You didn't find anything at the dorms? How long till you get me that money from the Turner deal?"

"I just learned about that ..." Elijah hesitated and studied the drug dealer.

Allison was stalking him. Waiting to make his move—itching to tear him limb from limb.

"I have ears everywhere." Allison waved to the pink-haired waitress in the diner, and she blew him a kiss.

"Fuck," Elijah mumbled.

"You touch my side piece; I'll tear your dick off." Allison's Russian accent thickened, and he moved in closer. "Time is tickin'," Allison tapped his watch. "Pretty soon, you'll be joinin' Owen if you don't get me that money. Or I could take it out on that hot ass you put into the Camry. Isn't that Owen's girl? You fuckin' her?"

"No, I'm not." Elijah's hand trembled, and he balled it into a fist.

"Hell, I would be." He reminded Elijah of the devil at the crossroads. Elijah was waiting for him to offer a deal that he knew would fuck him over. Allison's crooked teeth and menacing grin disappeared. "If I don't get that money, you die." Allison was inches away from him now. "'Cause, my boss gets real pissed off when he doesn't get what he wants. If he takes it out on me, I take it out on you." Allison's pupils were dilated and primal as he poked Elijah in the chest. "'Cause it's either people in my family die, or people in yours do. And it ain't gonna be anyone in mine."

"We don't get the money for the Turner deal until we're done with the documentary."

"You have seven days. Make shit happen, or I'm gonna cut you into pieces and bury you where your best friend hanged himself," Allison growled.

7

THE MUFFLED SOUNDS OF an obscure rap song drifted through the muggy summer night. Moths buzzed around the front porch light, where Elijah saw Hudson talking to Jess. She put her hand on his forearm and flipped her shoulder-length, brown hair flirtatiously. Hudson held what Elijah presumed was a rum and Coke. Smiling, Elijah shook his head; he was incorrigible when it came to a pretty face. Jess was so flakey. Elijah believed she came by it honestly, though. Jess liked to have a good time and loathed any dull moments. In some minuscule way, he admired that about her; Jess lived in the moment. With Owen's untimely death, it seemed like Jess's thinking was spot on; life was fragile. Why waste any time?

Parker's little one-bedroom historic house was on the edge of town outside of Savannah. The aged home featured wood siding and a massive wraparound porch twice its size. Parker's grandmother and grandfather built it shortly after purchasing the land in the late 1940s. His whole family, except for Hudson, still lived on the property, scattered through the expansive acreage. The isolation of the home offered a comforting privacy that Elijah wished he had in his life.

Elijah had no idea why he was so hesitant to go inside, sitting in his car like a stalker watching his friends from the outside like a stranger. Parker was most likely sitting on his usual crappy, black, torn leather couch in the exact same spot he was in every day. The right-hand corner next to the end table.

There were people in there Elijah had no desire to be around. At least not since Owen had died. He also knew Riley was in there with Dylan; her beat-up, two-toned, red and black Honda was parked adjacent to the tree line.

I'd rather have dinner with Hannibal Lecter.

Elijah rubbed his forehead. He didn't know the first thing about making movies, and besides Riley, Parker was the only one he knew who could do it competently. Even if he spent most of his time stoned, the kid had a natural talent.

Flipping through the pages of the journal, ice shot up Elijah's spine, and he paused. His eyes instinctively scanned over the pitch-black forest line next to the Nova. After he'd satisfied his paranoia, he turned his attention back to the journal. There were necromantic spells with notes in the margins. Articles about Seven Sisters Road and the hauntings. Protection spells and a list of stones and herbs used in witchcraft. One section of his journal was dedicated to a strange creature that he studied in Navajo traditions.

> *Skinwalkers never die. To kill them without the original spell that changed them, you have to find out their birth name first, remove their heart, and burn it. From what I've been able to find, the most dangerous ones are on the fringes of both the magical and Navajo societies, mixing magical beliefs that even the most skilled witches have a hard time deciphering. Commonalities show they have a tendency to practice some form of Necromancy and hang out in graveyards. During the rites, they are required to eat the flesh of the ones they love to complete the change. Once changed, they are skinwalkers and shapeshifters combined. Giving them the ability to transform into a wolf or crow and any human.*

Closing the journal, Elijah placed it under his seat. Furious vibrations from the land around him rippled through the air. The energies of the dead were intense, and his sensitivity to them had grown since Owen's death. His abilities were expanding at an accelerated pace, and he had no clue how to keep his sanity.

Elijah watched partygoers sprinkled around the property joking and drinking, the light of their phones flickering like fireflies in the night. Some were dancing around a bonfire singing to a poorly played acoustic guitar. *They were all superficial*. In a matter of six days, the same things that once brought him pleasure fell to the wayside and seemed pretentious. If Elijah was honest with himself, he knew that none of those things ever brought him joy—they were only a distraction from his pain.

He was different from the rest. An old soul. He'd known it his whole life. All he'd done was wear a mask that allowed him to blend in for a while. The act allowed him to forget he spent his time with the dead. With the tortured. Elijah thought he knew himself and Owen so well. Now he wouldn't be able to recognize his own face in a crowd.

Jumping out and slamming the door, Elijah made his way through the sea of cars to the back porch. There were no lights in the backyard, so it wasn't hard to hide out when a party raged. A memory flickered in the back of his mind; he and Riley sneaking away to a massive live oak tree about twenty yards from the house to make out. She had a way of shutting down every ounce of his self-control. It frightened him. He could still smell the sweet, floral perfume she wore.

"Holy crap, look who decided to show up!"

"Hey, what's up, man?" Elijah hugged Hudson, slapped him on the back, then turned to Jess, wrapped his arms around her, lifted her off the ground, and set her back down. "Your brother here?"

"Same spot as always." Hudson's caramel eyes glistened in the porch light. He was stoned.

Elijah cast a cautious glimpse out toward the darkened yard. Crickets were singing, and the bonfire smoke drifted over the porch where they were standing. There was something out in the woods stalking him. Preying on him. And it wasn't human; it wasn't *Allison*. All the unknowns of the past few days were racing through his distressed mind, prompting him to decide whether or not he should relocate entirely away from the East Coast.

"I do need to tell you, though, Riley and Dylan are inside," Jess said. "I'm pretty sure he wants to kick your ass for getting Riley in trouble at work."

"What're you talking about?"

Dumbfounded, Elijah opened the door, and voices echoed into the night. Weed smoke billowed out into the evening, and it was so strong Elijah thought he was going to get a contact high. Heat rushed over his skin from inside, and the faint smell of sweat drifted out. The hum of fans buzzed in the background. He guessed that the air-conditioning unit must have gone out again.

"When you got into a fight with that military guy, Matt wanted to have you blacklisted from the bar." Jess paused and took a sip of her beer. "Riley stuck up for you. Said it was because you were grieving over Owen. Matt didn't care, and they kinda got into it. She almost got fired."

"You couldn't have mentioned this sooner?" Elijah closed the door slightly, giving Hudson an annoyed glare.

"Yeah ..." Hudson paused, taking a sip of his rum and coke, "I didn't want you to get arrested. I also didn't want to get fired because you kicked my boss's ass."

Jess twisted her long, fine hair into a bun. "If you ask me, she's still not over you."

"Well, he *didn't* ask you." Hudson raised an eyebrow.

Satisfied with Hudson's answer, Elijah sighed. "I suppose those are valid points."

He slipped through the door, closing it behind him, leaving the two of them to banter about his crap love life. Elijah weaved through the packed bodies. The mixed emotions of everyone in the house swirled around, creating a thick energetic atmosphere. Doing his best to focus, Elijah concentrated on a protective shield around himself. Being in large groups made him vulnerable to others' emotions. He had learned that in the most inconvenient way.

There were tremendous trial and error phases before Elijah had the spiritual epiphany that he could absorb what others were experiencing. The only thing he hadn't discovered was how to effectively keep others' emotions from seeping into him. Most of the time, it was only after he'd taken on others' rage, anger, and frustration that he'd figured out what had happened. By that time, the damage was already done to the people around him, and it was too late. He was still trying to find a way to separate himself from others.

Getting in and out without being noticed by Dylan would be difficult; it was a small house, but Elijah was pitted against worse things at the moment. Making a mental note that becoming invisible should be added to his supernatural powers, he headed toward Parker. He received some hellos from his so-called friends as he covertly ducked his head, working his way through the packed living room, using the many partygoers to block him from view.

A platinum blonde with a pixie cut, watermelon-sized breasts, and a lime-green tube top handed him a jello shot. Elijah walked down a hallway, through the doorway to the family room, and set down the shot on a seventies-style side table. He knew someone would be trashed, out of alcohol, scavenging. It would be picked up eventually. A couple of stoned kids in the corner played Mario Cart and cursed at each other as they animatedly turned around corners in the game.

Riley's silky laugh surfaced over the sea of noise coming from the kitchen, and Elijah scoured the crowd. Finally, he caught sight of her reflection in the window over the kitchen sink that looked out into the backyard. Dylan was faithfully at her side with his arm around her waist, which was nothing surprising. That guy was like a damn lap dog and never gave her space. Everywhere Riley went, he was there by her side. A sting of longing formed in Elijah's chest as his eyes lingered on her reflection. Riley's wavy, brown hair flowed over her shoulders, and she wore a tight-fitted, hot-pink shirt. Her cheeks were rosy with sunburn. Wearing form-fitting clothing was never something he could get her to do.

Riley's waist was slimmer. She complained about being overweight when they were together, but she was perfect and had curves that rivaled Marylin Monroe. Riley was a natural beauty, the kind of woman that was gorgeous in a ball cap and no makeup. She glowed and was happier without Elijah. He hadn't noticed before because he was usually five drinks in by the time he saw her—the only way to make their separation bearable.

Elijah never told her how much she meant to him, but he assumed she already knew. *They were together*. But apparently, *choosing* her wasn't enough. Elijah was sure his emotional constipation and lack of communication were two (of the many) reasons she lost interest. He pulled the bill of his camo hat down over his eyes, directing his mind back to his mission of the evening.

"Holy shit! Elvis has arrived! 'Bout time you got here! Where the hell you been?" Parker shouted, and everyone in the kitchen shot a glance his way, curious what the excitement was about.

So much for getting out unnoticed.

"It's only been like five days since I've last seen you." Elijah walked to Parker's seat on the couch and bent over, giving him an overcomplicated handshake that Elijah was never a fan of but did anyway because it was Parker's thing. "I need to talk to you."

"Fo sho." Parker turned to a seafoam-color-haired woman with bloodshot eyes next to him and shooed her down the couch. "Make way for my man, move yo' ass."

The woman raised her eyebrows, pursing out her lips. She stuck her shoulders back, pushing out her breasts, then adjusted the strap of her skintight pink dress. "What eva."

Elijah dropped down into the seat next to him, and Riley walked out of the kitchen. He looked up, catching eyes with her. Elijah turned away from her, angling his back. Seeing her with another man was far more hurtful when he was sober.

Parker adjusted his worn and sun-bleached Atlanta ball cap, grabbing a roach clip from the bill. His blond shaggy hair was curled up over the edges. He had a likeness that reminded Elijah of a southern Shaggy from Scooby-Doo. Except Parker was tremendously shorter than Shaggy, and *Shaggy* was probably less stoned all the time.

"So, what's up, dude?"

"You know my friend, Owen, right?"

"The asshole that hung himself," Parker said, taking a shot of vodka.

Elijah clenched his eyes shut and pinched the bridge of his nose. If he hadn't been Hudson's brother and needed his help, he'd probably given him a right hook.

The beautiful blue-haired woman stopped her conversation with the girl next to her, reached over Elijah, and smacked Parker in the back of the head. "Don't be a dick." She smiled apologetically, touching Elijah's knee. "Sorry, sometimes he doesn't have any tact. I'm Chelsea, by the way."

"Yeah, he's kinda blunt sometimes, and it's nice to meet you." Elijah smiled at the girl.

Dylan's voice pierced through the blaring music and chatting of the drunks. "What the fuck's he doin' here?" His voice was sharp and annoyed.

Even though Elijah couldn't see him, he knew Dylan glared at him with a jealous intensity.

"I didn't mean it the way it sounded." Parker rubbed the back of his head. "She keeps me in line."

"It's fine …" Elijah could hear Dylan in the background getting louder in the kitchen.

"No. I'm gonna go say something to him."

Elijah turned his attention back to Parker and grabbed a shot of what he thought was vodka off the coffee table. The tone in Dylan's voice was familiar, one he himself had used on plenty of occasions. It was the voice of determination and rage. After the ass kicking's he'd received the past few days, a spark of insight told Elijah he would be getting *another* tonight. And he needed the shot.

"So, anyway, my friend had a deal with Turner Television. This was supposed to be his big break." Elijah twisted the bill of his camo hat to the back.

"Yeah, I heard, man. That sucks." Parker took a joint and lit it, trying to hand it to Elijah, letting him know he was genuinely sorry.

"No thanks." Elijah waved off the joint. "Anyway, Camilla says that the deal is still on the table. She needs help finishing the project. I'm not sure what's going to happen as far as compensation yet."

Parker's eyes lit up, and Elijah knew at that instant he was interested. He opened his mouth to answer but was interrupted by Riley's asshole boyfriend.

"Why the fuck did you have to come here? When are you gonna *get it* that she doesn't want you anymore?" Dylan stood in front of the coffee table now, and his beady, fury-filled eyes were staring down at Elijah.

Elijah raised an eyebrow at Dylan, his expression condescending. Uninterested in Dylan's drama, he turned back to Parker. Everybody in the party stopped, and all eyes were on Elijah.

Waiting.

Adrenaline surged through Elijah; his nostrils flared. His feet bounced uncontrollably. Heat rose across his shoulders, and he dipped his head. Elijah rested his elbows on his knees, considering punching Dylan in the face just because the guy was a dick. Elijah took two calming breaths, steadying his legs, twisting his bracelet around his wrist. It was customary for Elijah to fly off the handle, but not tonight. He had life-altering crap that demanded his full attention. Elijah wasn't going to be submissive to others' emotions tonight.

"I asked you a question." Dylan scooted forward, bumping the coffee table, his movements sluggish.

"I came to talk to Parker, then I'm leaving." Elijah's voice shook with annoyance. "Not to burst your bubble, but I'm not here for your girlfriend. I have other shit to worry about."

Elijah saw Hudson and Jess slip in the back door and move to the side of the room.

Dylan's stubby nose wrinkled, and his fists trembled. "You can't keep showing up and causing problems in her life."

"The way I see it, she only has one problem right now, and he's standing across from me."

"That's it." Dylan pointed a calloused finger at Elijah. "I'm gonna beat your ass. Someone needs to."

"Trust me, you wouldn't be the first jackass to believe that." Elijah rubbed the back of his neck, becoming increasingly uncomfortable in the packed house.

"Call me, Parker," Elijah said quickly. The walls were closing in, and his patience was diminishing. Elijah stood and strode toward the door, dismissing Dylan's invitation for an ass-whoopin', no matter how tempting.

Elijah's eyes gravitated toward Riley, and she watched him with a softness he hadn't seen since they first started dating. It was the look she gave him when she thought she could fix what was broken inside him.

Back then, he didn't *want* to be fixed.

Dylan's face was filled with rage, and before he knew it, Elijah was tackled to the floor, receiving blow after blow. Each strike of Dylan's fist landed on his cracked ribs. The nerve endings on Elijah's sweaty abdomen erupted in agony.

"Isn't that where you got kicked the shit out of the other night, asshole?" Dylan's hot breath brushed against his cheek.

There was a circle around them both, and the spectators made flurried comments, adding to the riotous emotions filling Elijah.

Riley's pleading screams for Dylan to stop penetrated Elijah's ears through the turbulent mass of bodies. White-hot fury erupted through Elijah, and every instance that someone had stepped on his pride ripped him apart like an alligator.

Elijah grunted, his ribs popping, as he flipped Dylan onto his back, and the wood floor rumbled underneath them. The crowd's mixed reactions of shock and excitement caught on like a violent fever and rolled through the house. Elijah landed a blow to Dylan's cheekbone that made a *crack*. Dylan's warm blood flowed over Elijah's fist.

Before he knew it, Elijah was being pinned against the wall by Hudson. Elijah put his hands up in surrender and saw that Riley's beautiful hazel eyes had turned disappointed. Shaking her head, she made her way to Dylan on the floor, who held his face, bitching.

Elijah chuckled as Riley coddled Dylan like a spoiled child. Hudson rolled Elijah down the wall, out the door, and onto the back porch. The heat from the night suffocated him, and his chest heaved. Sweat trickled down his face and burned his eyes. Satisfaction filled Elijah as he wiped Dylan's blood from his hand, shaking out his throbbing knuckles.

"We don't do that here." Hudson's voice was firm, and he jabbed a finger in the direction of Elijah's car. He was only three years older than Elijah but was skilled at giving him a guilt trip.

"I know." Elijah rubbed the back of his neck. Clumsily, he walked down the stairs. His body shuddered as the aftershocks of rage quaked through him. Elijah had tried to do the right thing. He *tried* to walk away.

Hudson continued as if their minds were in sync. "But you did try to walk away, something I definitely have never seen you do before. Everyone in there was confused as fuck. The looks on their faces were priceless." Hudson slapped Elijah on the back and chuckled. Elijah winced, raising a shoulder.

"Sorry, crap. Didn't mean to do that."

"No. *I'm sorry*." Elijah spun his bracelet around his wrist instinctively, making sure it was still there. "I just ..." Elijah rubbed his left shoulder and noticed a scrape on his right elbow where his tattoo was. "Shit."

"Between you and me, man, he asked for that shit." Hudson pointed to the house. "He's lucky I pulled you off him."

"Thanks." Elijah sighed.

"Riley looked like she was turned on as hell when you tried to walk away, though."

"Whatever, man ..." Elijah smiled and dabbed blood from his bottom lip. His scab from his beating at the bar had been savagely ripped and the wound dripped blood down his black Aerosmith T-shirt. "You got any TP?" Elijah pointed at his throbbing cut.

"Yeah, be back." Hudson walked back toward the house, and Riley passed him, charging toward Elijah, her curvaceous hips jostling in all the right places. Hudson turned toward Elijah, walking backward after she passed, and pumped his eyebrows, giving him a wink and smile.

Freakin' Hudson.

"Why the hell did you have to do that?" She threw Elijah's camo hat at him, hitting him in the stomach. Elijah attempted to catch the hat, and it landed in the tall grass near his boots. He laughed, annoyed, and pinched the bridge of his nose.

"What's so fuckin' funny?" She planted her hands on her hips.

"You! We're not even together anymore, and you *still* blame me for shit that's not my fault." Elijah picked up his hat, and he paced through the thick, dew-covered grass. Thunder rumbled in the distance. A sheen of sticky sweat coated his forehead and temples, stinging the scabbed cut on his cheek from Allison. Reminding him that they would be coming back, and he was running out of time.

"Why did you come here?" Riley leaned in toward Elijah, studying him.

"It definitely wasn't because of you." Elijah raked his fingers through his dark hair and slid his hat back on his head.

Riley's eyes narrowed. Her voice softened, and she moved in close. "Then why?" Her nimble fingers were tender as she inspected his lip, and it caused a longing to surface in Elijah that he thought was gone. A longing for him radiated from her, and it tore at his defenses.

"That's none of your damn business." His voice lowered, the way his guard always did when she was close. The floral scent of her perfume was magnified in the heat of the night. Sweat trickled down her golden-tanned neck into the crevice of her collarbones.

"How are you doing?" Her raspy, southern voice dipped with concern, and her soul-piercing eyes flicked to his, then back to his swollen lip. He stayed quiet, and she sighed. Her breath smelled like rum. Secretly, a part of him took pleasure in the minuscule moment they were sharing. An aching emerged in his sensibilities, reminding him that she was no longer his to love.

They hadn't talked about Owen's death, and he knew eventually, if he saw her, the painful subject would arise. Riley attacked obstacles and problems at full speed. He couldn't recall a time where she'd beat around the bush. Except, for once, when it came to Owen.

Elijah swiped her hand away, wishing an energetic barrier would materialize, protecting him. Her lack of consideration was one of the reasons for the turmoil that destroyed their relationship. Shaking off the brief spell she cast on him, Elijah spun away, turning his back to her. The last thing he wanted to do was discuss Owen's suspicious death with the woman who had ripped his heart out. She'd caused an emotional civil war inside him between his heart and mind. After the last few months of isolation, the battle had spread to his soul—shredding him to pieces. Riley wasn't good for him, and he knew it. Love wasn't what he felt for her; it was the convenience of the temporary distraction she provided. His heart and logical mind were constantly in a knock-down-drag-out fight over how he felt about her. Her love had damaged him. They were over, she'd moved on, but he was still trapped in the ghostly confines of their toxic love.

"I'm not talking about that." Elijah's tone deepened and slowed, warning her to stop before she crossed a fine, complicated line. "Especially with you." His southern accent thickened. "It's been six months, Riley. I've been over you for about ..." Elijah rubbed the back of his sore neck, turning his attention back to her. He flipped his hand back and forth as if weighing out the time frame. "Six months of it. I have other thoughts than what the fuck you're doing with your newest piece of ass." Elijah eyed the house, then took stock of Riley's face. She was wounded, and it was an expression that Elijah knew well while they were dating.

"You're such a dick. I have no idea why I felt bad for you."

"I never asked you to," Elijah snapped disdainfully. "I don't need your pity."

"Why do you do this?" Riley crossed her arms defensively, and her face tightened.

"You'll have to be specific because the last time I checked, according to you, I did a lot of things wrong."

"Put up armor when someone gets too close." Her tone shifted from stern to soft. "Why do you push people away that care about you?"

Elijah spun away from her, darting toward his car door. He removed his keys from his pocket, then turned, marching back to her.

"Because eventually, they all *leave*. Shit gets hard, and they leave," he said with conviction.

"Did you ever consider that people *leave* because they give up?" Riley pointed at him with a shaky finger. "Because trying to get through your walls is impossible?" Elijah narrowed his eyes at her and opened his mouth to respond. Dylan stuck his head out of the back door.

"Babe, come back inside. I'm sorry." Dylan caught sight of Elijah, and his hand tightened around the edge of the door. For the first time, Elijah saw it—the way he acted in someone else. It was a horse-sized bitter pill to swallow. Riley kept her back to Dylan, and for a second, disappointment appeared on her face. Their conversation was over.

Flipping his keys around his finger, Elijah walked back to his Nova, trying to escape the primitive impulse to demolish everything around him. If he'd stayed much longer, the savage monster inside of him would subdue his rapidly fading civility. He opened his car door and paused, pointing to Dylan, who was now on the back porch.

"Your boyfriend needs you; you better get back in there, *babe*."

Riley bit her bottom lip and rocked from one foot to the other as if deciding whether or not she wanted to leave. Elijah watched as she strode back to the house. Dylan mumbled something into her ear as she went up the steps of the deck, and he wrapped his arms around her, hugging her tightly.

Elijah knew it hadn't occurred to Riley that he *had* let his guard down. And all it took was that one time for her to ruin his life and steal the last remaining moments he had with Owen. It was time to let go of his anger toward her and move on. But it was going to be a long road.

8

IT WAS MIDNIGHT BY the time Elijah arrived at Seven Sisters Road. Rolling down his window, he inhaled the musty scent of wet earth. Gnats swirled in like heavy snow through his open window, and he cursed, squishing one with his hand. The wind and rain from earlier were gone. The creepy stretch of coastal wetlands was filled with the harmonizing of crickets and toads. He could hear fish jumping in the water off the shore. The thunderous, swollen clouds had cleared, and an enormous moon illuminated the rocky road, swamp, and dense marshland like a massive spotlight. He angled his classic Nova in the direction of the crime scene tape that quartered off the section of land where the police department found Owen's body. A barely visible, makeshift path tagged with neon orange tape marked the way up to the tree where he'd been found hanged.

The old live oak branches were bent and broken at sharp angles and reminded Elijah of contorted limbs draped in ivy. Elijah was clueless about what the hell he was searching for or why he'd decided to torture himself by staking out the location. There was something about the land that caused a stirring in the shadows of his mind. He found himself willing memories to reveal themselves, except he had no idea what or where the memories were from.

Detective Bohannon called Elijah twice that day, making his homicide inquiry sound casual on his voicemail. There was nothing casual about any part of Owen's death or the fact that this location called to Elijah. His mind drifted to Shelly and how she would find out about Owen's drug association. Everything that's buried comes back to the surface, eventually.

Including our sins.

Elijah flipped open Owen's journal, reading through notes on one of his past life regressions.

Samuel's blood was everywhere. He'd weakened and was dying. Overwhelming sorrow took over my faculties, and I was unable to think clearly. Florence was by his side, weeping. The flow of death rushed around us, and it was then that I saw the evil beast outside the window, its piercing red eyes burning in the dark like two pieces of brimstone plucked straight from hell. Stalking and manipulating us all like prey. I cast a circle of salt and silver around Samuel, hoping it would protect him and help him last the night.

Regret surged through Elijah at the thought that he hadn't told Owen about his psychic abilities, and he slapped the book closed. Plopping the journal down on the seat, Elijah sighed. There was no action or movement. He glanced at his gas gauge. After he left, he needed to stop and fill up. The Nova's tank was almost empty. Elijah checked the time on his cheap sport watch and leaned over, pulling a flask out of his glovebox. Taking a sip, he winced as the burn of the whiskey traveled down his ragged throat. He replaced the cap and slapped it down on the black-leather bench seat. There was something he was missing.

His stomach growled, and he opened a Slim Jim, taking a bite. The steamy, Lowcountry night was still. Elijah's phone vibrated in his back pocket, and he lifted his butt up, pulling out his cell phone, giving a groan.

"Hey."

"Are you alright? Riley called me and said you got into a fight."

Shelly's concerned voice was soft. He knew she probably had already been in bed since 8:30.

"I'm fine."

"You don't sound fine. Did he hurt you?" Her tone shifted from concerned to protective. "She needs to dump him."

"You have to stop talking to my ex-girlfriend." Elijah rubbed his forehead, then gripped the steering wheel, turning his tanned knuckles white.

Shelly still spoke to Riley, even though six agonizing months had passed since their break-up. He'd tried to explain how weird it was to Shelly that they still shopped together and had lunch once a month. He was pretty sure that they met more than that. Getting over Riley was impossible; she blocked every attempt Elijah made to heal. It was torture.

"We've gone over this. Who I spend my time with is none of your business." Her voice was firm.

Elijah's exhausted eyes examined the shadowed forest line, and his throat tightened. A silhouette shot through the trees and high grass. The unknown being raced through the crime scene tape and paused at the tree where they'd found Owen's body hanging.

"Elijah, are you there?"

"Yeah, I'm here." Elijah was transfixed on a shimmering, translucent curtain in the dense marshland. Waves of rushing energy rippled into the atmosphere. His stomach cramped, and he exited his car, pressing the door gently until he heard a soft click.

"We're all having a hard time. Riley, well ... she's one of the good ones." Elijah could hear the hopefulness in her voice. She'd loved Riley. He knew it broke Shelly's heart when he cut Riley loose. Shelly had no idea of Owen and Riley's decisions that had torn Owen and him apart, and Elijah intended to keep it that way.

A heart-stopping, half-human, guttural scream reverberated from the depths of the dense, ominous southern woods.

"What was that?" Shelly said quickly.

"I'll call you later, okay?" Elijah lowered his voice to a whisper. "Stop gossiping about me with my ex. Love you." Elijah clicked end and slid his phone into his back pocket.

He tugged on the collar of his shirt, evaluating whether or not he should cross the road. Everything logical inside of him told him to leave. But his intuition told him to sprint into the unknown darkness. Elijah clenched his jaw, fighting back the acid rising from his stomach.

"Holy fuck. I'm gonna regret this." Elijah shook out his hands, darting across. Each thud of his boots against the mud made his face and side ache. Mud splattered on his jeans, and water soaked into his boots. A sweltering, savage wind tore around him, tousling Elijah's thick, deep-brown hair. The high grass rustled as if a feral animal was blindly wading through, searching for prey.

There was *something* in the spirit world connected to him, screaming for him to run for his life. Strangely, that same something anchored him to the area, making it impossible for him to flee. Elijah nimbly weaved through overturned tree trunks and branches, keeping his eyes on the silhouette that evaded him.

Elijah halted at the crime scene tape as if an invisible brick wall prevented him from continuing. The location was exactly like his dream except for Owen's dangling corpse. Elijah's body shook with a blend of fury and fright as he recalled the straining of the swinging rope. He knew the only thing preventing him from opening his mind enough to embrace the supernatural evidence that Owen was murdered was his denial. Because that meant that there was a chance Owen's spirit was genuinely trapped on the cursed land where they had all died before. And despite their rocky relationship as of late, Elijah never would have wanted that for him. Not for anyone.

Elijah knelt and pinched dirt between his fingers. There were granules mixed in with it. There was a white substance that formed a circle around the tree Owen was found hanging from. A makeshift altar made out of branches and moss dominated the middle. He wheeled around in all directions, searching for the mysterious figure. It had vanished into the shadows of the night.

A bellowing animalistic call, followed by a terrifying scream, echoed from deep in the marsh. It sounded like a woman dying; the weight of her suffering was heavy on his soul. Anger, anxiety, and rage seeped out of her tortured spirit and into every centimeter of the surrounding area. Elijah's head jerked in the direction of the horrifying cacophony. His shoulder muscles twitched, and he rolled them both back, keeping them from cramping.

There was a foreboding that exploded through Elijah's spirit as he tuned into the ghostly radio waves around him. The reverberation of a growl came from before him, and two blazing, ruby canine eyes flickered through the darkness. Goosebumps formed on the nape of Elijah's neck, and his throat tickled with a burn.

Elijah's cell phone rang, and a shock of terror jolted through him as he yanked it out. He kept his eyes locked on the beast; it eased toward him with murderous grace.

"Cam, this isn't a good time." Elijah glanced at his phone and notice the battery was dying; it was just full.

"I'm at the office. Someone has been living here. I found a duffle bag and some personal items." There was a deadbolt sound in the background, clicking.

"I'll be there soon. You need to leave." Elijah lowered his voice to a whisper. "Don't stay there by yourself. I'll text you when I'm on my way." Elijah's panicked eyes searched the forest. The massive animal was gone. Elijah jogged to a tree, hiding behind it, and even though his back was pressed to the trunk, he could feel its eyes on him.

"It's off Cawthorne road. You should be able to see the steeple."

"Steeple?" Elijah's voice shook.

"I'll explain when you get here. Are you alright? You sound—"

"I have the—" The phone beeped. It was dead.

Elijah twirled to leave and was met with a horrid face of death. A woman's pale, white skin emanated decay, and her eyes had a milky film. Her hair was ink-black and tied back in an intricate style bun with ringlets flowing over her shoulders. She wore a degraded, sapphire-colored, satin dress. Elijah assumed it was from the 1800s and could tell that it must have been beautiful and expensive when it was purchased.

The corpse gripped his arm in the same spot as the singed handprint he'd received from the ghost at Shelly's house. Time slowed around them, stopping.

The world around them faded—it was only the two of them, captured in a gruesome, intimate standoff. She hissed "Mary," and her rancid breath wafted against Elijah's cheeks, burning his eyes. Before Elijah could sift through his overloaded psychic senses, she disintegrated.

The world resumed spinning, and his ears rang. He wasn't in the same location; it was somewhere different in the forest. Elijah stood in the middle of the Shaw family graveyard. Overwhelming sadness conquered Elijah as he stood over a grave marked *Benjamin Jake Shaw*. Disoriented, he leaned against a tree trunk. He noticed a carving in the bark out of the corner of his eye. It was the shape of an upside-down triangle. Elijah grazed his fingertips over it, and a rapid succession of other symbols flickered in his mind's eye. Suddenly, Elijah was in someone else's body.

A man's Fingers trailing over different triangles in a spellbook, then herb jars. Someone furiously writing down a spell. An unknown man wailing, misery engulfs him at the sight of five women hanging from trees. The man's throat crunched and popped. It was being crushed, and he couldn't breathe.

Gasping for air, Elijah frantically clutched his chest as the pressure in his neck disappeared, and his breathing returned to normal. Pungent incense floated through the air. Multiple people were running in different directions. One was in front, and two were behind. Breaking out in a sprint, he followed the sound in front. A petite silhouette emerged through a shroud of leaves and branches as it hurdled over a fallen tree. Sweat poured from Elijah; thunder rolled in the distance. Elijah broke free from the forest, following the figure. It leaped onto a motorcycle, speeding off.

Elijah bent over, resting his hands on his knees, catching his ragged breath. "Fuck. What just happened?"

He spotted his car down the dirt road about a mile away, its beautiful silver body shining in the moonlight. Death marked the end of Owen's journey, but Elijah knew it simultaneously launched a crusade in his.

9

SEARCHING THROUGH THE KEYS that Shelly gave him, Elijah finally found the one that fit the lock. There were no front porch lights on, and it was near impossible to search for the keys while using his phone as a flashlight. High foliage next to the window blocked a dim glow from inside, darkening the doorway. The abandoned church on the edge of town that time had forgotten wasn't what Elijah would call an "office." The long dirt road leading up to the church was pitch-black and surrounded by high grass. If Camilla hadn't told him where it was, then he would have never guessed where to look. The map Owen left Elijah in the journal was anything but straightforward. Although, after the few experiences Elijah endured over the past few days, it was understandable. On the other hand, it also wasn't unexpected. Owen had talked about finding a church and converting it into a loft home.

Elijah's fingers numbed, and he dropped the keys, quickly picking them back up. Every layer he peeled back of Owen's complicated existence was filled with pain and anguish. He knew behind the large oak door, once he unlocked it, there was another secret waiting. Elijah wasn't entirely sure he could withstand the blow it would inflict.

Dread made his hand tremble, and the door handle rattled. Something evil was watching him, lurking around in the tall grass, stalking every unsteady step he made. Waiting to devour him. It was the crow and wolf that had been following him. He was sure of it. Their presence penetrated him like arrows to his psychic senses. That's how he knew they were around—they invaded his most private space, his mind. Elijah unlocked the door and hurried inside, twisting the deadbolt with frenzied anxiety.

"Elijah, don't move." Camilla's quiet voice was drenched in terror.

Frost crystals rippled up Elijah's arms; it felt like early winter. The pungent aroma of wet dog whirled through the chilly sanctuary, clinging to the inside of his nose. Threatening to leave him in pitch-black, the lights inside dimmed, giving an electric buzzing noise as they struggled to stay lit. An angry, primal growl rumbled through the church. A surge to flee took over his rational thought. Elijah held his hands out in front of him, the keyring wrapped around his right middle finger. Slipping a key between each finger, he formed a fist, creating a vicious right hook for the beast.

Cautiously, he turned to face Camilla, and two rabid wolves were dividing them. The beasts were in the middle of a sanctuary packed full of bookshelves. There was an open space in the middle with a round table. Hundreds of files looked like they had exploded and were scattered on the floor. Books lay open on different surfaces. It appeared that Allison and Landon had already found the office.

The smaller wolf watched Camilla. She was standing next to a bookshelf, her body trembling. It was the same one out at Seven Sisters Road only an hour before. How could this animal get here before him? The better question would be, how the hell did it follow him? The wolf facing Elijah was the same wolf that stalked him outside Owen's window. Now that it was closer, discoloration in the fur on the wolf's lower back caught his attention. The symbol was in the form of three swirls that connected, forming a triangle. The symbol appeared to be black, like the surface of the fur had been singed. The wolf's massive pupils watched him. The canine inched toward Elijah, holding its ground.

Elijah's eyes flicked to Camilla's, taking stock of her emotional state, then around the immediate area for anything he could use to kill the beasts if needed. There was a pink and purple duffle bag in the corner with woman's clothing neatly folded inside. That must have been what Camilla referred to on the phone.

The wildebeest-sized wolf trotted toward him, challenging Elijah for power of the room. *This is the alpha.*

He didn't recognize the second animal; it was smaller, had no mark but striking copper-colored fur.

"Here's—"

The alpha snarled, baring its jagged teeth, interrupting Elijah. It was like the sound of his voice angered the animal.

Elijah lowered his voice and tried again, speaking slower. "Here's what I'm gonna do."

The alpha let out a growl, baring its fangs, and lowering its snout to the ground, getting ready to pounce. The beast squinted, waiting for him to finish the sentence.

It can understand me.

Elijah slid out his phone and texted Camilla. *I'm gonna run out the front door.*

Camilla vehemently shook her head in disagreement. "I'm not gonna let you do that."

"I'm gonna jump out the window. Then I want you to lock yourself in the bathroom."

Elijah turned and unlocked the door, texting her again. *Don't listen to what I just said. I want you to lock the door behind me.*

"That's out of the question," Camilla said, answering both comments.

"Will you stop being freakin' stubborn for one second? Just do what I tell you."

Elijah furiously texted on his phone. *I'm pretty sure these damn things understand me.*

Camilla swallowed heavily, and a tear rolled down her cheek. Her perfectly shaped eyebrows pinched together. "Fine," she shot out, bewildered.

"I'm gonna run to my car, grab my gun, and come back in the front door and shoot the dogs." Elijah's fingers trembled.

Alpha savagely grated its claws against the wood floor like a bull getting ready to charge. He had a problem with this whole shit plan. His car door was locked, and it was a classic car. Back in 1968, the doors didn't unlock with a key fob. He had to open it manually.

"Fuck," he mumbled. He slipped his car key out from Owen's massive key hoard that he'd acquired.

"Well, can we get on with this terrible confusing plan then?" Camilla asked. Elijah could tell she was preparing herself mentally.

Elijah steadied himself; he clenched his jaw at the thought that he might die in less than thirty seconds. "Please don't let them eat me alive. One, two—"

He swung open the door and sprinted into the night toward his car door, jumping over the rail of the front porch. He landed heavy, and a jolt of pain shot through his knees. The scrape of their razor nails as the wolves redirected themselves toward Elijah answered his question. They *could* understand him. He heard the door slam behind him and lock. Elijah's heart pounded in his throat as he slid to a stop before colliding with his car door.

His window was down. He slid through the open window and thanked God for his bad habit. Frantically, he rolled up the window as they nipped savagely at his face, their rancid breath causing him to cough. Elijah's phone buzzed, and he slid it out of his back pocket.

"Sup."

"Well, you got them out of the office. You can shoot them now."

Elijah glared at the dog, then turned away and whispered. "That was kind of a lie. My gun's at home." Elijah felt like a jackass for not carrying it, but with drug dealers after him, he decided to leave it for Hudson. "I wish it wasn't. They seem pretty damn hungry."

"Are you safe?"

"Yeah, for now."

The Beta dog sat patiently as the other trotted off behind the car. It was the quiet before the storm.

"Owen has a shotgun in here somewhere. He told me about it." Camilla's face peeked out one of the stained-glass windows as she locked it, too. Her eyes were fixed on the colossal monster guarding Elijah's driver's side door.

"You couldn't mention that before?" Elijah's voice was scornful, and his breaths were shallow.

"I don't know how to use a gun."

"Cam, seriously?" Elijah threw up his hand so she could see it through the windshield.

"What?"

Elijah studied the Beta, curious where the other animal had disappeared to. There was something familiar about the wolf's energy.

"Elijah. Your trunk popped open."

Spinning around, Elijah saw the top of his trunk bobbing. His classic car rocked. The back seats rattled.

Bang. Thunk. Something tried to ram through the back seats. Elijah slid across the bench seat to escape, and the Beta was on the other side before he exited.

"Cam. I think you need to hurry and find that damn gun."

"What's wrong?"

"The rabid wolf is in my trunk."

"It can't get through to you."

"Umm—" Elijah's voice caught in his throat. "It's a classic. There's no metal separating the trunk. Just board and cushion. Find the gun *now*." Elijah recalled what Harper, Owen's neighbor, said about the crow and the wolf. They were omens of death. "I'm pretty sure these assholes want to kill me."

The back seats jolted. Elijah saw a lump get more significant and more prominent in the center of the seats with each impact. The beast was making a hole.

"For crap's sake. I'm gonna put you on speaker." Camilla's tone was shaky. She disappeared from the window. Crashing burst through the phone as she searched the church. He could hear Cam breathing heavily as she hurried. "What are you doing here?" Camilla's uneasy tone startled Elijah.

"Who's there?" Elijah's heart thrashed against his ribcage, threatening to explode. "Cam, what's happening? Are you alright?"

Elijah jammed the key into the ignition, attempting to start the car. The Nova made a sad, winding noise, refusing to start. A small hole appeared in the back seat, and the Alpha's snout poked through, sniffing the air of the car, ravenous for Elijah's flesh. Knots formed in Elijah's stomach, and acid rose, burning his throat.

"Shit, shit, shit." Elijah pumped the gas with urgency, and the engine sputtered, then died out. He'd forgotten to stop and get gas after leaving Seven Sisters Road. "Cam, it's starting to get through." Silence. "Cam?" The call dropped. "Holy hell." Elijah's heart sunk with uncertainty, not knowing whether Cam was alright or not. She was his only hope.

Giving up on starting the car, Elijah braced himself, pressing his back to his steering wheel. The Beta disappeared behind the car. Stabbing pain shot through his ribs, and he grunted. He made a fist around the keys once more. Metal dug into his palm.

The ground next to his car exploded. Quinn came marching up like a pro, the gun stable in her hands and her toned legs flexing through her tight jeans as the sawed-off shotgun recoiled. Her red, curly hair waved in the wind. She had a badass resemblance to Mila Jovovich from Resident Evil. She slapped open the gun, took shells from her leather jacket pocket, and loaded in two more. Whipping it shut, she aimed, waiting.

Quinn whistled a high tune. "Olly, olly, oxen free, ya bastard," she said, dangerously sweet.

The ravenous wolf in the trunk stopped. Elijah's car rocked as it leaped out, charging toward Quinn. Muzzle flare flickered burning Elijah's eyes. She shot at the alpha, and it yipped, springing back. Human-like shock clouded the wolf's demeanor as it frantically searched for the Beta. The Beta was nowhere to be seen and had vanished into the forest. Elijah hoped it wasn't making its way behind Quinn, creeping up for the kill. Blood dripped from Alpha's right hind leg, saturating the ground.

Elijah tried to open the door, and Quinn kicked it back closed with her foot, keeping her eyes on Alpha the whole time.

"Stay there." Quinn's voice was firm and commanding.

Knowing it had lost, the alpha eased backward and limped off into the woods, growling—disappearing into the darkness of the early morning.

Elijah observed the shed behind the church in silence. The post horror tremors that engulfed his muscles during the attack faded as he roamed through it. The rage that Alpha harbored for him was still thick, lingering in the air, keeping him on edge. It reinforced to him that even though the beast was physically gone, it still could invade his most private moments.

It was strange; Owen had all the tools to make his own bullets. It was a skill they had both learned at a hunting camp the summer of their junior year of high school. Rows of herbs and other plants with labels Elijah had never seen were growing in a connecting greenhouse. Elijah found it challenging to take his eyes off Quinn, watching her graceful moves. Her curly, crimson hair flowed over her shoulders, and was tousled by the coastal breeze. Quinn's arms were crossed, and her defensive stance spoke volumes about how much she trusted the two of them.

"There's a crapload of silver here." Camilla opened a crate that was filled with silver bars, then dropped the lid. Elijah recalled Owen's entry about the use of silver and killing a skinwalker.

Quinn took off her leather jacket, draping it over the back of a chair. "We needed it to take care of a few things. That's what the bullets are made out of," Quinn tapped a rack of homemade bullets. "And so is the shotgun."

"That shotgun is made of silver?" Elijah said, curious.

"Every part except the butt and the forestock," Quinn said, tapping the gun.

"Firstly, what the hell is a forestock?" Camilla was looking at Elijah now.

"It's where you pump or cock the gun." Elijah made a pumping motion with his hand, mimicking a shotgun.

Camilla laughed, directing the conversation back to the silver part of the gun, touching the barrel. "What were those things? Werewolves?"

"No, if they made it past the circle Owen and I set, they're something far worse. I haven't confirmed it yet." Quinn's face was stone.

"Oh, come on, seriously?" Camilla raised an eyebrow.

Quinn crossed her arms, leaning against a workbench. Elijah caught sight of a dirty, pink-camo water bottle. Quinn had been working in the shed right along with Owen. An image of them laughing and drinking beer on a steamy night flickered in his mind's eye. Quinn's eyes fell on Elijah, studying him intently. She read him like a book.

"What's the etching on the barrel of the shotgun mean?" Elijah asked.

"It's a protection spell, keeping the gun safe from anyone who might want to steal it." Quinn picked up the shotgun and a rag, then rubbed down the beautiful exterior.

Elijah walked out the door, waited for Camilla, then took off toward the church. He didn't want to spend another minute in that shed. Quinn followed them out and locked the doors behind her, carrying a small tube of dirt she'd collected with Alpha's blood in it.

The church was so much more than an office. It was a research center for the paranormal, and Seven Sisters Road was the main concentration. Bookshelves filled with scientific encyclopedias and research topics on parapsychology took up one-quarter of the shelves. Subjects ranging from secret societies, psychics, hunting ghosts to scientific studies on the use of channeled energy and telekinetic abilities took up the rest.

The walls were covered with theories about a vortex in the forest of Seven Sisters Road, leading to another dimension. Numerous ghost hunters, religious fanatics, and scientists had published articles about the magnetic polarity of the area. Elijah saw specific passages highlighted. Most referred to the physical and emotional effects of the land on the psyche.

Pictures of the graveyard and historical photos of the mansion in its glory were pasted on the walls. Elijah passed a picture of the same house burned to the ground. For a split second, the licks of the flames brushed against his neck, sweat trickled down the crevice of his back, and he could hear distant terrified screams. Red strings ran from one document to another. Connecting them all in a supernatural web of mystery.

"How come Owen never said anything about this place?" Elijah studied the high ceilings and the aged wood flooring, taking in everything around him, doing his best to stay focused.

All the pews had been removed, and the entire inside had been converted. A queen mattress and box spring were in the back corner, and a stack of books on the bedside table had colorful tabs staggered through them. Humming came from a retro fifties refrigerator in the back next to the bathroom, which contained a toilet, sink, and shower. In a nook near the bed, a hammock made of material similar to a parachute rocked with the whirling wind of the ceiling fans next to Quinn's duffle bag.

"From what he said, it grew over the past two years." Camilla paused, brushing back her bangs from her sweaty bronze skin. "He should have invested in a damn AC unit." She unbuttoned her white dress shirt, exposing her white tank top underneath. Slipping off her black heels, she dropped them next to the bed. She brushed off the dead grass and dirt from her jeans and sighed.

Elijah wondered if Riley knew about the place. If Owen shared it with her. There was no telling who he'd shared it with and who he'd kept it from. Elijah walked to a window and found a grainy, white substance. He sniffed. It was salt mixed with some herb he couldn't identify. He took a pinch and studied it between his fingers. It was similar to the substance that surrounded the tree where Owen was found.

"It's graveyard dirt, eggshell, and salt. It's supposed to keep out anything that has any kind of ill intent. Dead or alive. Looks like the circle needs a recharge." Quinn's cat-shaped, evergreen eyes watched him intensely. "Don't worry, no one else knows about this place." Creeped out slightly by her accuracy of his thoughts, he wandered down one of the aisles. He slid a book off the shelf that read "Psychic Abilities." Elijah tucked it under his arm to take with him and read later.

"*I* had to follow him here to find out about this place. LoJacked his cell phone after him and Riley …" Camilla's tone dipped, wounded. "Well, I didn't trust him much after that. It was *one* of the reasons, out of many, why we didn't work. He kept a lot of secrets. And apparently, family members hidden." Camilla shot Quinn an untrusting glance. "This is my first time being in the building longer than fifteen minutes."

"I thought you said that this is where he came with the crew to work on the documentary?" Elijah asked.

Quinn walked to the fridge and took out water, cracking it open. She chugged for a moment. "Jesus, this is gonna take forever to clean and organize," she mumbled and collected papers from the floor, putting them neatly into a file.

Camilla squinted, biting her bottom lip. "I lied. Sorry. This place was the reason why the crew stopped working on the film four months ago. He would never let them come here. He always insisted on doing all the editing himself. Wouldn't let anyone go through the dailies."

Elijah picked up a hint of the same earthy smell that emanated from Owen's journal. Spotting a small desk next to the bed, he imagined Owen writing furiously at all hours of the night. Authoring the pages of his legacy.

"Dailies?" Quinn said.

"The raw shots that were filmed that day," Elijah explained.

"He never told anyone because he knew no one would understand," Quinn said defensively. "What we do here isn't exactly received well in the general public. People have a hard time believing in things they can't quantify." Quinn picked up a few books, placing them back onto the bookshelf.

"But he shared it with *you*." Camilla motioned toward Elijah. "Not his best friend or girlfriend?" Camilla's body tensed.

"He didn't share everything with me," Quinn said.

Elijah stopped at a wall lined with open and messy file cabinets, changing the subject. "What is all this?" Elijah whirled his finger around in the air.

"It's a collection of folklore, paranormal, and metaphysical volumes. Owen acquired every religious text as well. Some spellbooks, and he has small amounts of historical documents about the Shaw family and the city of Beaufort."

Slapping his hand on the top of a file cabinet that looked like it had exploded, Elijah nodded to the floor.

"Hasn't he heard of a computer?"

"Computers and USBs can be stolen. Cabinets and files are much harder to search through and steal." Quinn leaned against a towering, oak bookshelf. "We've acquired a bit of information that would be useful to a lot of dangerous things. I hope who came through here didn't find what they were looking for."

"*Things*?" Camilla's eyebrows raised.

"Yes. Things. And one of them murdered my cousin. I'm gonna figure out who it is. No matter what it takes. Those *beasts* outside were just the beginning." Quinn crossed her arms, leaning against a green, beat-up file cabinet.

Elijah leaned against the wall, stunned, and Camilla stayed silent somewhere deep in one of the aisles. The silver bars and extensive library were confirmation Owen dealt drugs. If the camera and filmmaking equipment weren't before.

Elijah nodded in the direction of the open church. "The guy that built this place is not the person I grew up with. I don't know the person who made this place."

Camilla rounded the corner of a bookshelf, leaning on a battered filing cabinet next to Elijah. "So, what's the damn deal?" Tightening her expression, Camilla's eyes narrowed at Quinn as she waited for her response.

"Owen shut me out, went rogue about two weeks ago. There's a lot more happening out at Seven Sisters Road than anyone understands. Those ghost stories are cute fairytales in comparison to the real thing. Owen had started to unravel centuries of lies. Things that went farther back than the 1800s and black magic." Quinn brushed back her curly hair from her shoulder. "I saw two shady guys hanging around his dorms. I started asking questions, and he shut down after a few times."

A ceiling fan stirred loose herbs from broken glass jars across the floor and wafted Quinn's scent around the room. It was the earthy incense from the woods. She was the one he had chased and the one who escaped on the motorcycle. Quinn roamed down one of the aisles, picking up books and paperwork, walking away from Elijah and Camilla.

Elijah nodded to Camilla to follow him in the opposite direction. Camilla kept her eyes on Quinn, expertly studying her every move. "I don't trust her … I just … there's something she's not telling us."

Turning his back to Quinn, Elijah considered Owen's entries about skinwalkers. She *had* been gone for quite a while. It was convenient she happened to be in the same location as the wolves that were stalking him, not once but *twice*.

"What have you figured out about the drive?" Elijah kept a watch on Quinn, checking her location. His voice lowered to a whisper, "We need to find out where he put those drugs—and quickly."

"I went back to the sorority house and tried to open it, but it's encrypted, and we need the passcode. So, unless you know *what* it is, we're kinda at a standstill."

"Put that second major of yours in computer code to work, or find someone that can help you." Elijah leaned into her ear. "I don't want them to come after you too."

"I'd appreciate it if you didn't keep secrets at a time like this." Quinn's voice hardened, and her shoulders tightened.

"Whatever you and Owen were into …" Camilla strode to Quinn, inches from her face. "It caught up to him, and now your choices are about to catch up to us." Camilla flicked her finger between her and Elijah. "What we were talking about is none of your damn business. For all we know, you could have been the one to kill Owen."

Quinn's face flushed with rage, her shoulders stiffened, and her hand swung quickly. Camilla's head jolted to the side, and a booming *smack* reverberated through the church.

Stoic, Camilla rubbed her cheek, turning away from Quinn. "Maybe we shouldn't do the Turner deal." Her cherry red lips pressed tightly together. "We should pass. I have a horrible feeling about this." Camilla walked to the bed, slid on her high heels, grabbed her shirt, and then walked next to Elijah.

"Shelly needs the funds. Not to mention if I don't find some money, I'm gonna be dead soon."

"I don't know if I can go out there. I miss him so much. I never got to tell him ..." Camilla's sorrow seeped into him; it was overwhelming. She put on an excellent front to protect the fractured and broken soul underneath. And right now, she was raw and exposed.

"What happened to your arm?" Quinn motioned toward the handprint.

Elijah gritted his teeth in memory of the poltergeist. "Surprise visit from the otherworld."

The group went silent. Elijah and Quinn locked eyes, and she took a drink of her water, observing him and Camilla.

"You put your hands on her again, and I'll make sure you never get to come back to this church," Elijah jabbed an angry finger at Quinn.

Ignoring Quinn and Elijah's conversation, Camilla focused on the current immediate threat. "We'll get it figured out." Camilla sniffled, her voice muffled, as she pressed her face into her hands. "They aren't gonna take you too."

"Who?" Quinn asked.

"Nothing, don't worry about it," Elijah snapped. There's no way, especially now, that Elijah could tell her about Allison and Landon. He wasn't sure he could trust her yet.

Elijah wanted to show Camilla the journal and show her precisely what it is they faced. He could already see the change in her and the damage Owen's death caused. It became apparent he wasn't the only one under rapid emotional metamorphosis. Elijah could sense that Camilla was about to break. And allowing her to discover that Owen believed she was his soulmate was a devastating pain he wasn't ready to inflict.

10

IT WAS A ROUGH night and an even harder morning. Elijah's reeling mind kept him from napping before he got up at 4:30 for work. He spent the few hours he had reading about skinwalkers from different volumes in the library. They could change into whoever and *whatever* they wanted, man, woman, fox, wolf, or crow. The only thing actually needed was the flesh of the victim they wanted to turn into.

The skinwalker legend was a Navajo tradition and considered dark magic among *some* other Native American tribes. Throughout ancient history, various countries worldwide, such as Ireland and South American cultures, also recorded instances of evil beings who ate human flesh to change forms. It was vague at best on how a person became one and if they were malevolent after the transition. In most of the reports and eyewitness accounts Elijah read, it was difficult to separate false statements from the truth. There was never any physical evidence left behind from the creatures.

War, mob mentality, anger, and hate that spread like a disease through massive populations infecting even the most logical, level-headed individual was rationalized through these cultural beliefs and myths. They weren't myths, just a more profound soul-searching way to ponder our primal DNA. The shadow self, the darkness within, was a landscape the human race had explored since the beginning of time. Acts such as murder and revenge were innate and hidden capabilities of every human being. Elijah knew many had committed these atrocities for millennia while ignorant that it would change their soul forever. The crimes committed would follow them, waiting for the perfect time to strike, silently stalking them like a Great White shark waiting to devour its prey.

The hostility in the church was palpable, and Camilla was back to her old stoic demeanor a couple minutes after her exchange with Quinn. Quinn knew more than she said. Camilla's intuition wasn't wrong about that. Elijah was positive she knew about the drugs. There's no way she hadn't questioned where Owen got the money from or the large amounts of silver. Elijah was torn between wanting to trust her and knowing that she was one of the last people to see Owen alive.

A blanket of gnats covered the farm. Sporadic, tiny pinches covered Elijah's body as they ate the dead skin from his shoulders and arms. He'd forgotten his bug spray, and the bottle that was in his car was completely empty. The mountainous stacked bales of hay he worked his way through didn't show any signs of ending. And the moist hay was a magnet for the tiny pests.

Elijah's neck was stiff, and his broad back stung from the morning sun. His injured ribs popped every now and then with a wrong twist. The bruise that covered the right side of his abdomen had faded from purple to green. Mr. Nolan had offered to give him the week off from his duties, but Elijah needed a constructive distraction from the past few days. He needed something to do with his hands.

Working with his hands on the farm and digging them into the earth was cathartic and relaxing for Elijah. It gave him an understanding of life at the fundamental level. More importantly, it developed his accountability and work ethic at a young age.

After Elijah's crappy week, the physical work was what he needed to get his mind off of his expanding, arcane clairvoyance. There was something about getting his butt kicked at work that gave him a sense of accomplishment at the end of the day. Elijah took in a deep breath, savoring the woodsy-soil fragrance of the farmland. The sandy Georgia clay was still damp with heavy rain from the past few days.

Fatigued, Elijah's muscles weakened, threatening to give out, and he paused, wiping his forehead with a hand towel. A nap on the hay in the barn sounded like a perfect way to spend his lunch, regardless of the bugs that would feast on him.

He shook his head, talking himself out of the idea. When Elijah had started working on the farm at fourteen, he learned it was easier to push through the exhaustion. The heat was rising, and the crispness (what there was of it) from the morning was wearing off. The last of the morning, Georgia dew glistened like diamonds on the vast farmland. He procrastinated, wiping the back of his neck, then tucked the towel into his back pocket. Pressing forward, Elijah continued heaving the hay into the bed of the old, beat-up Ford truck.

"Elijah." Mr. Nolan limped over as Elijah chucked the next bale of hay. "Take a break, kiddo. There's two detectives here for you." Mr. Nolan handed Elijah a cooled bottle of water and leaned against the open tailgate.

Sweat plastered Mr. Nolan's wiry, gray hair to his head. Oil and dirt covered his stained overalls that hung from his frail shoulders. The collar of his white T-shirt underneath was damp with sweat. During the Vietnam War, Mr. Nolan stepped on a landmine, blowing the back of his leg off. The tendons hardened after it healed, stiffening his joints. He proudly showed the shrapnel scars on his back and arms one night to Elijah after drinking whiskey and playing checkers.

Elijah never knew the details of how he was injured or what happened to his life afterward. Mr. Nolan was never keen on speaking about the war. However, the injury never slowed Mr. Nolan; he ran the farm after his father died until he was sixty. Mr. Nolan often reminded Elijah of Clint Eastwood from the movie *Unforgiven*.

"What're they here about?"

"Didn't say. Everythin' okay, sport?" Mr. Nolan's usual hard and wispy southern accent softened.

"Yeah. I'm sure everything's fine." Elijah gave Mr. Nolan a squeeze on the shoulder and an unsure smile. Cracking open the water, Elijah zeroed in at the opening of the barn.

A middle-aged, bald, male detective and a young, blonde female detective were waiting patiently. A faint vibration tickled the surface layer of skin where the ghostly handprint was covered with a bandage. Elijah rubbed it, swallowing heavy. When he examined it the night before, there hadn't appeared to be any damage to his tattoos. Which was a relief.

Snatching his black T-shirt draped over the bed of the truck, Elijah pulled it over his head. Striding to the detectives, a throbbing formed between his eyes. Elijah hoped they weren't going to give him indisputable evidence that Owen had been murdered. Because if someone *had* killed Owen, the bastard who committed the crime would end up in pieces, spread across the wetlands, and devoured by an alligator. No one would find them, not even a psychic.

"What can I do for you folks?"

Elijah wiped the sweat from his forehead and took a swig of water. The cut on his cheek burned; oil and dirt were caked in the crevices of his skin. His busted bottom lip throbbed with pain each time he pressed the water bottle to it.

"Elijah Ward?" The bald man turned to him, sweat beading his ebony skin.

"That's me, sir." Elijah removed his leather work gloves from his sweaty hands and shoved them in his back pocket.

"This is Detective Jensen, and I'm Detective Bohannan. We work with the Homicide Division at Beaufort PD."

Elijah wiped his hands on his jeans, then courteously shook theirs. Quickly scanning the two of them, he noted that Detective Bohannan was a force to be reckoned with, possibly ex-military. He had wrinkles around the eyes, gray hairs in his eyebrows, and was muscular. Elijah could tell he was probably more fit than men half his age. However, Detective Jensen had a naïveté that oozed from her perfectly ironed gray pantsuit and the glinting Beaufort PD badge that hung around her neck. Her eyes skimmed over him, and she tucked her short hair behind her ear.

"You're a tough kid to get ahold of." Detective Jensen added.

"I've had a lot going on in the last week. What can I help you with?"

"We're here about a pal of yours named Owen Percy?" Bohannan's southern accent was thick, and Elijah made a guess he might originally be from Alabama. "We wanted to offer our condolences to ya'll."

"Thanks." Elijah sighed, and they both watched his reaction.

Bohannan took out a notepad, flipped it open, then wrote something. He searched through scribbles, flipping numerous pages. Apparently, he'd done his homework before coming to Elijah.

"His mother, Shelly, told us you were his best friend?" Bohannan looked up from his notepad, raising his thick eyebrows.

"I've known Owen my whole life ..." Elijah paused and rubbed his temple. "... sorry. *Knew* Owen my whole life. My dad and Shelly had been friends since they were in elementary school. Shelly adopted me after my dad died."

"Was there anything odd you noticed about Owen's behavior in the last month or couple of days before he killed himself?"

"Honestly? We both had gotten busy with our lives and saw each other maybe twice in the past six months. His master's in filmmaking kept him pretty busy all the time, and I'm working toward opening my own bar."

"We're following some leads at the college." Detective Jensen stuck her hands in her pant pockets and watched Elijah with scrutiny. Something sinister about her gaze gave him déjà vu. He wondered exactly how much they knew and if they'd figured out that Owen dealt drugs.

"Leads? Like what?" Elijah stared at Jensen, and she locked eyes with him.

"What do you know about his girlfriend ..." Detective Bohannan flipped back a few pages, ignoring his question. "... Camilla Lewis?"

Retracting a bit, Elijah rubbed the back of his sweaty sunburnt neck. "She's his *ex*-girlfriend and a royal a pain in the ass." He chuckled, trying to shake off that he'd become closer to her in the past twenty-four hours than he'd expected to.

His patience grew thin, and talking about Owen with two strangers giving him plastic smiles with suspicious eyes wasn't exactly how he wanted to spend his afternoon. Especially two detectives who were ogling him like he was their prime suspect.

"Then why did you talk to her three times yesterday?" Jensen gave a half-hearted smile.

Dismissing the conversation, Elijah strolled back toward the truck and twenty hay bales he was stacking. "I need to get back to work."

"Doesn't she stand to make a decent amount of money from the Turner Deal?" Bohannon adjusted the badge on his belt.

Jensen interjected, "On a documentary based on the murder of five sisters?" Something in Jensen's tone told Elijah she knew more than she let on. Elijah saw Mr. Nolan doing busy work next to the barn out of the corner of his eye, making it seem like he wasn't eavesdropping.

"Camilla and Owen had *both* been working on it, and Shelly needs money to pay off some bills from the funeral. Camilla's doing it as a favor," Elijah said sharply. He didn't like what they were implying; it was insulting. He paced the area they were chatting in and kicked a rock.

"You get roughed up?" Detective Bohannan's eyes lingered on Elijah's cheek, then he scribbled on a notepad. "Was it before or after you found out Owen and Riley had a one-night stand?"

Stopped in his tracks, the water bottle in Elijah's hand crinkled as he squeezed. Elijah's eyes shifted suspiciously back and forth between the detectives. His chest was on fire with the thought that complete strangers knew such intimate details of his life.

Keep your cool. Keep your cool.

He thought desperately about Shelly, trying to talk himself out of getting arrested. Too much was on the line, and going to jail for assaulting a police officer would seriously screw his *to-do* list. He had watched plenty of Investigation Discovery shows with Shelly, and he knew that no matter whether you were telling the truth or lying, they would use your anger against you.

Taking steady breaths, Elijah broke away from them, wandering to tools hanging from the rafters of the barn, tapping a dangling sickle. "I found out about ..." Elijah paused, considering his words. He walked close to the detectives.

"That happened six months ago. About the time I stop talking to Owen. Got my ass kicked in a bar fight the day Owen was found." He was genuinely astounded at how casual his voice sounded. The anger dissipated, and an unusual calm rushed over him.

"I bet that hurt, Owen betraying you that way," Jensen pressed, prodding his open wound. She had gone straight for his jugular.

"I'm aware where you're going with that." Elijah waved his finger back and forth between the detectives. "If you have any questions about the bar fight, call the owner, Matt. It was at the Thirsty Parrot."

"Isn't that where Riley works?" Bohannan asked.

Elijah's hands shook, and he did his best to hide his anger by running a hand through his thick hair. Clenching his jaw, Elijah stayed silent.

"You know what I find most interesting?" Detective Jensen eased in toward Elijah.

Staying stoic, Elijah planted his feet, keeping his ground, waiting for her to get to her point.

"You haven't asked us once about *why* we're doing an investigation."

An epiphany exploded through Elijah: *They had no leads*. Elijah decided he didn't owe them an explanation; he hadn't done anything wrong.

"No, because I've already spoke to Shelly. She told me you were investigating Owen's death. But if it'll satisfy you ... *why* are you doing an investigation?" Elijah gave his most arrogant smile. It was a protective measure he started as a child while under emotional pressure after his father's death.

"Well, we found abrasions on his back that suggested he was dragged." Jensen closed the space between them. She stood inches from him.

"When was the last time you spoke to Owen?" Bohannon asked.

Elijah's voice lowered. "He called me on July seventh. Except I didn't answer. It was weird talking to him after the whole sleeping with my girlfriend thing."

Saying that Owen and Riley slept together made his throat close. He decided that he needed to buy another bottle of whiskey on his way back to the apartment.

"Wasn't that the day he died?" Jensen pointed out. "What's with the bandage on your arm?"

"I hurt it while working with the tractor. Burnt it on the engine."

"Do you mind if we take a look at it?" Jensen went to grab his arm and remove the bandage.

Elijah swept his arm away. "You'll have to get a warrant for that. Have a good day, detectives." Escaping, he turned and swiftly walked back to the truck.

"Talk to you soon, Elijah." Detective Bohannan's voice was strong and sure. They had a suspect list, and he was number one.

Sharp awareness rolled through Elijah, cutting him like a knife: Owen could have been calling him for help, and Elijah might have been able to prevent his death. There was no way to know—not now. The possibilities of what might have been were lost to the southern winds. The guilt that consumed him wasn't something he wanted to discuss with two officers that were marking him as a prime suspect.

The world crushed his shoulders as his mind raced through every experience he'd had in the past few days. Elijah pretty much already knew what happened, he didn't have to ask, and all they did was solidify it for him.

Someone murdered Owen, and now I have to find the bastard.

Parker's forest green Toyota 4-runner barreled past the detectives' gray cruiser, bouncing on the rocky driveway. He parked in front of the barn. Elijah made his way back to the work truck and hopped up onto the tailgate. He watched as Mr. Nolan wobbled his way back to the farmhouse's front porch and eased himself into a weathered rocking chair. He tended to watch over Elijah the way he imagined his father would have if he were still alive.

Mr. Nolan had a quiet concern that Elijah admired. He always reacted *just enough* in every situation and never once let his temper take over. Elijah had been working for Mr. Nolan ten years, and he knew he would still be working for him after he owned his own bar.

Parker hopped out and jogged to Elijah, his shaggy, blonde hair flopping as he took each step. He bent over and placed his hands on his knees.

"Holy crap, I need to work out more." His fair-skinned cheeks were blotched with rose as he overheated.

Elijah cracked a smile. "What's up?"

"I've been trying to call you all morning." Parker stood and placed his hands on his hips, huffing like he'd run a marathon.

"I forgot my phone at home," Elijah said with a lilt. He hadn't really forgotten it. He just didn't want to deal with anyone. Ever again.

"I wanted to tell you I'm in ... for the docuseries." Parker whirled his finger around in circles in front of himself.

Elijah had finally gotten some good luck. He smacked the tailgate next to him, and Parker clumsily hopped up, snatching Elijah's water out of his hand.

"Jesus, dude." Elijah chuckled. A cross between a pinch and an itch on the back of his hand caught his attention, and he smacked a gnat, squishing it.

"Do you have any idea what running in the heat will do to a guy like me? My lungs could collapse."

"Or it could be you smoke too much weed?"

"Says the functioning alcoholic over here." Parker jabbed his thumb at Elijah.

"That's fair. I only have a couple more minutes unless you want to work," Elijah said.

"Those detectives came to question you too?" Parker chugged the rest of Elijah's water.

"Yeah." Elijah batted away a mosquito that buzzed around his ear.

"That's crazy they think Owen was murdered." Parker's shoulders slumped.

Elijah's face dimmed, and he rubbed the back of his neck. "Yeah, that's pretty crazy."

"I know I didn't know him that well, but he had mad skills. I saw a lot of his work." Parker batted away a gnat, "Damn gnats. Anyway, meet me after work at the library on campus. How's seven?" Parker handed back the empty bottle. Elijah threw it into his backpack.

"I can make that happen. Camilla says it's pretty much finished."

"Camilla, huh?" Parker's eyebrows pumped as he smiled. "She is fine as shit."

"You have a girlfriend, don't you? Chelsea? Focus." Elijah nudged Parker. "Don't get all horn dog on me."

"No, fo sho. We'll get this done." Parker swung his feet and opened a half-eaten bag of sour gummy worms.

"Like I said, though, I'm not sure about compensation." Elijah grabbed his camo hat and slid it on.

"Don't worry about that. If they pick it up, having my name on it will be enough. Also. Side note ... sorry about Dylan last night, dude." Parker shoved a gummy worm in his mouth. Parker and Hudson were stepbrothers, and they were both the sincerest people Elijah had ever met.

"Eh, he's a douche," Elijah said. He knew Dylan's type because he used to be and still partially acted like him.

"The only reason I let him come over is because of Ri."

Elijah smiled at Parker and chuckled. "That's funny ... 'cause that's what I used to say. *Because of Riley*."

"It's been six months, man, and I admire your loyalty, but ... seriously, when you gonna move on?"

Elijah sighed, patting Parker on the back. "Soon."

11

THE BEAUFORT CITY LIBRARY wasn't that far away from the University of South Carolina's small extension campus library. The location where everyone would be meeting soon to discuss the production of the documentary.

Beaufort County Library was where Elijah spent most of his time in kindergarten with his MawMaw before she passed. As a librarian, MawMaw Ward would bring discarded books home for Elijah to read, and he devoured them in a couple of days. The building had become a sacred space for him. Books were a sort of religious effigy. His MawMaw used to always tell him, "There's power in knowledge and compassion in understanding. Books give us different points of view that allow us to experience the entire world." He could still hear her gritty smoker's voice. Spilling out wisdom like she'd invented the concept.

Elijah smiled; he could still smell the stench of her Pall Mall cigarettes and hear the creaking sound of her wooden rocking chair. She sat in it every night on the tiny front porch of her shotgun house, drinking a glass of moonshine, telling him stories. After the last two weeks, Elijah needed something comfortable and familiar that still held light and love for him. So, he decided to make a stop and research the references Owen made in his journal.

Tucked in the back of the book, Elijah found the charcoal rubbings of nine basic geometric symbols in a small pocket. Some labeled and some not. Something was haunting about them; Elijah had seen them before.

Subjects of the occult were stacked, covering his favorite plywood table in front of him. There was an unspoken rule that the table in the back corner was his.

He'd made notes in Owen's journal, adding to the comments and observations his brother had made about the paranormal. From what Elijah understood, Owen had connected the concept of past lives to physics and energy transfer. There were sloppy scribbles next to the notes about String Theory and Relativity. The messy handwriting often flowed from Owen while he was in the creative zone. Elijah had read that scribbling several times in the short stories and screenplays he'd read for Owen. Owen told Elijah it was because his brain moved faster than his hand could, and the muse waited for no one.

Owen noted in one of his entries that because energy never died or ended, only changed form, it was a possibility that ghosts were on another plane of existence within our own. Owen referred to it as *the first law of thermodynamics or conservation of energy.* He theorized that Samhain, the Wiccan holiday of Halloween, was the day when the veil between the dimensions was at its thinnest. This was usually due to the energies of the universe and planetary placements. Owen believed it was an ancient holiday that marked a deeper scientific meaning. He thought that Wiccans, Pagans, and Buddhists truly understood how energy flow and the law of attraction worked within our world and universe.

Elijah never knew that Owen had such a profound intrinsic thought process about the spiritual realm. Grazing his fingertips over the words, Elijah could sense Owen's presence. The musk of Owen's scent surrounded Elijah, and he instinctively relaxed.

> *There's a darkness that resides in the woods. It calls to me. Swirling energy conjured from the earth has opened a vortex, portal, or gate to another dimension where the dead reside. I can sense it and, on occasion, see it. The energy field appears, rippling like the waves of heat radiating from hot cement. Something was started and never finished, and when it finally comes to a close, my greatest fear is that others will suffer.*

It made sense that Owen had cut everyone out of the production. He thought people were in danger and tried to protect them. Owen hid this part of himself from Elijah, and he'd wished they had discussed it before he died. Like always, they were more in sync than they knew. Elijah would have loved to have someone to talk to about his personal struggles with his psychic abilities. Owen would have been the one to support him. Letting him know he hadn't lost his mind. Elijah's foolish pride had, yet again, come between him and his brother.

Elijah still hadn't found the passage about how all the members of the group were connected. The ghostly hissing of the name Mary had been rattling around in his subconscious. The name bothered him and made him physically uncomfortable, and he had no idea why. He hadn't seen anything about the name Mary in Owen's writings. He'd kept a detailed list of the Shaw family, including the three sisters that were murdered, and figuring out how they each were connected to those people in a previous life would have been daunting.

Regardless, the journal that Owen left him was a gift and was something that would connect them, even with Owen's death. If Owen was right and souls were energy that merely changed directions, then Owen could still be drawn to Elijah. Nothing would sever their connection, not even death. The thought comforted Elijah, but that comfort diminished when he recalled the vision of Owen's apparition in his bedroom. The possibility that he could be stuck in paranormal limbo, wandering through another dimension trying to reach Elijah, caused his chest to tighten. Shooting a glance over his shoulder, he wondered if Owen stood over him now, watching Elijah read the words he authored, hearing what Elijah said about him to others.

Immediate throbbing pulsed through his temples. Elijah knew he had to help Camilla finish this project. He couldn't leave it unfinished like Owen's life. Not with what it meant to Owen. He'd been murdered trying to uncover the truth of who they all were, and Elijah owed it to him to find his murderer.

"Elijah?" A soft hand touched his forearm from behind. Elijah slapped the journal shut, clearing his throat.

Quinn held old newspapers to her chest and carried two boxes of microfilms labeled "Beaufort County 1870-1900" and two books on historical cartography. Gray circles were under her eyes and clashed with her milky skin. Quinn was depressed and anxious; it radiated from her.

"Quinn. Hey."

Quinn sat next to him. "How are you? I know last night was a lot to take in." Her voice was soft, and there was an unexpected comfort with her presence. Quinn's sorrowful energy transformed into a warm, peaceful wave that flowed through him. The tension in his muscles melted.

"You mean the part where you assaulted Camilla for saying what any normal person would have said?" Elijah grabbed his Slim Jim, taking a nibble.

"I'm not going to apologize for what I did. She had no right to accuse me of killing my cousin."

"You're not the only one grieving or trying to make sense out of Owen's death. Just remember that," Elijah said, stilling his movements for a moment.

Quinn tucked back a curly lock of her red hair and touched the large pile of books in front of Elijah. "You could've used the church to research in private."

"I needed a change of venue." Elijah turned the bill of his camo hat around, so it faced the front. He had a tendency to turn it to the back when he read or ate.

"Mmmhmm." Quinn crossed her legs and adjusted her cutoff jeans.

Silence grew between them, and she changed the subject.

"Did you know there was a family of four attacked? Two sisters in the neighboring town went missing, and their parents were murdered a week before the Shaw family? The parents were murdered by being hacked to death, and the sisters were never found. Their family name was Reynolds."

"I didn't." Elijah slid Owen's journal toward him, tucking it into his black backpack.

"Was that Owen's journal?" She smiled, and electricity shot through him, awakening passion he thought had died. "I've been looking for that." She raised an eyebrow.

"Well, right now, it's mine. He left it to me," Elijah said bluntly. "He didn't leave it to you for a reason."

Quinn turned her attention toward the stacks of books, changing the subject. "Past lives, shapeshifters, spell casting, the science of ghosts, psychic phenomena, and mediumship. Just your average light reading for a Friday."

Elijah's shoulders loosened. "I see you're reading about cartography."

"Yeah, I've had a small voice nagging me to study rose compasses and the history of the true north." She rolled her eyes and smiled.

"Just some light reading for a Friday," Elijah said sarcastically and smiled, remembering the sticker he'd seen only two days before at the Thirsty Parrot of True North Trading Company.

"I like your shirt." She tugged at the bottom of his Mumford and Sons T-Shirt. Elijah could tell she was trying to extend an olive branch, and he sighed.

"Thanks. I saw 'em last year." Heat flushed through his cheeks at her touch, and he rubbed the back of his neck. There was an uncontrollable urge for him to ask her about the symbols he found in Owen's journal. "You worked with Owen a lot. Can I talk to you about something?"

"Sure, anything." Quinn played with her necklace. Her penetrating eyes watched him.

The teardrop-shaped stone changed colors as she flipped it through her fingers. It reminded Elijah of the beauty of the Northern Lights. Her demeanor was completely different from earlier that morning at the church. He was unexplainably drawn to her. It felt like he'd spent his entire life with her. Never missing a day.

Elijah's fingers hovered over the folded papers. He studied her face, judging what her reaction would be or if he could even trust her. "Do you know what these symbols mean? Some were labeled, and some weren't." Elijah unfolded the rubbings and slid them to Quinn.

Her rosy cheeks flushed white. She cleared her throat and bit her bottom lip. "Yeah, actually. They're elemental symbols. Mixed with some others." She pointed to an upside-down triangle that had a line sideways through the tip.

"This one's Earth," Quinn sat the boxes and newspapers down on the table. "And these are Air, Fire, Water. Owen started studying elementals about five months ago. Asking me for help when he got stuck. Were these in Owen's journal?"

"Yes. I was trying to understand how they related to his notes."

"Do you mind if I read his journal? I might be able to help." Quinn adjusted her violet T-shirt and reached out her hand.

Elijah slid the symbol paper away from her, folding it back up. "You said you hadn't seen Owen recently. Why?" Elijah took another bite of his Slim Jim.

Quinn's emerald eyes saddened. "We had a disagreement."

"About what?"

Quinn played with the newspaper. "It's none of your business."

Elijah leaned forward onto his knees, playing with the Slim Jim wrapper. "Sorry I asked. If you don't mind, I need to get back to work."

"Look ... no ... I'm sorry. I just ... don't want to talk about Owen right now. He stirred up all this crap, and now I'm stuck in the middle of it all. I'm completely alone and isolated. My Nana won't speak to me, my aunt won't either, and the only person who accepted me for who I was is dead. I have no idea who I can trust."

Groaning under his breath, Elijah slapped down his jerky, knowing that Camilla would murder him later.

"We're going to the campus library tonight to work on Owen's documentary, finish it for Turner, and get some money for Shelly. You can come if you want."

All the contents took about an hour to organize. Elijah glanced down at his phone, unsure where Quinn had disappeared to. He kicked himself for not getting her phone number like a jackass. It wasn't like he could call Shelly to get the information. Owen's filming logbooks were incredibly accurate, and the group had every piece of information technically they needed—right down to which lens and aperture.

The group had separated all the investigation notes into three piles and all of the footage into another. Elijah hadn't found much that would be useful in answering questions about Owen's death. Most of it was run-of-the-mill research that was needed to accurately write the screenplay. Owen had always been obsessive about using correct facts in his writing. He reminded Elijah frequently (and with what Elijah knew about him now—ironically) that it was the reason he never wanted to write science fiction films.

"Elijah, sorry I'm late." A voice broke out behind them. Quinn walked out from between two towering bookshelves to get Elijah's attention. "I'm Quinn, Owen's cousin," she addressed Parker and Hudson with a smile.

"Sorry, sweetie, this is a closed meeting," Camilla said sharply. After their fight at the church, Camilla had understandably hardened her shell again.

"Hey … um, no worries. I saved you a seat." Elijah stood, pulled out her chair, and the group watched him collectively. They shot glances at each other, giving mixed reactions at his instant fluster.

Quinn's beautiful hair was now down and tousled. Elijah couldn't help but wonder if that's what her hair looked like in the morning after she got out of bed. "Sorry, didn't mean to interrupt." She set her backpack down on the table. "I tried calling you a few times." Quinn turned to the group. "I just thought I'd try and help with the film."

"Oh, no, we don't need any help. Thank you, though," Camilla answered for the group.

"Sure. Yeah. Of course. I'm sure there's something you can do," Hudson said and leaned back in his chair. He shot a cutting glare at Camilla, and she mouthed, "What?" Hudson turned back toward Quinn as he fiddled with a pen in his hands. "We have a short amount of time to get it done." Hudson gave her an unsure smile. "Although, it's a horrible idea to go out there, and I still think we should pass." He added.

"If they want the shots, we go and get the shots. We *do* need someone to hold the boom," Parker said firmly.

"If I weren't helping Shelly and Owen, I wouldn't even be going." Hudson shot a glance at Parker.

"She worked quite a bit with Owen at the office. So, she has a pretty good idea about Seven Sisters Road already," Elijah said.

"What the hell is the office?" Parker adjusted his Atlanta ball cap.

"That's a conversation for another—"

"Fine," Camilla cut off Elijah and scanned Quinn with catty eyes. "I'll try to ignore that Shelly ran her out of the funeral. Looks like you're in on the project."

"We were just going through the research Owen and his original crew collected." Elijah's heart rate quickened, and his eyes lingered on Quinn's. "I'm glad you made it."

The scent of earth and sea emanated from her clothes. It intermingled with the familiar Lavender and Vanilla scent he'd noticed when he saw Quinn at the funeral.

There was something peculiar in the way Quinn mirrored his reaction that instantly destroyed his defenses. The confidence and grace she carried was comforting and familiar. She was a long distance from the shy, lanky ten-year-old that used to pelt him with nerf darts.

Elijah lost track of time while he studied Quinn. However, the room had noticed every second of his lingering gaze. Quinn shifted in her seat, her cheeks blotching with red.

"Anyway," Camilla interrupted, and Elijah turned his attention back to her at the front of the room.

She gave him a 'How could you bring in an outsider?' glare.

"The lowdown on *The Seven Sisters Road* story. For those who don't know." Camilla plopped down in a bean bag, cross-legged, and fiddled with her messy bun. "The *legend* is the Shaw family lived out on Seven Sisters Road between 1850-1869. At the time, it was called Shaw Road after the family. There were seven sisters, one brother, and a Mom and Dad."

Camilla paused. She stared out the picturesque window at the twinkling campus lights. Camilla's face tightened with frustration, and Elijah knew in that instant she was struggling with the realization of what the detectives spoke to her about. If it were a suicide, it would have been open and shut. With it being declared a murder, that left no closure for the foreseeable future.

Quinn took over for Camilla. "There were only three sisters that were in recorded history. Three birth certificates and three death certificates. The number seven appears to have evolved over time. In that time frame of history though without a local town hall to keep accurate records or census' it's a possibility the birth or death of another sister could have gone undocumented."

Hudson flipped through a binder. "Owen figured out that the theory of seven sisters started spreading during Samuel's trial. He believes it was a case of misinformation on the media's side. Due to lack of literacy. So, there isn't any true way to know that correct number of sisters." Hudson plopped down the binder with a sigh, leaning back into his chair.

"According to death records, there were *two* brothers. The second was Benjamin Shaw, who rallied for his brother. He claimed it was someone else, and he saw the perpetrator on the property that night but couldn't name who it was. All the sisters were hanged on the property and buried there. Samuel Shaw was convicted of the crimes, given the death sentence, and hanged and buried on the property in an unmarked grave." Quinn leaned back in her chair, studying Elijah. There was a strangeness about the way she watched him; it was unsettling. Like she thought he was the one hiding something from her.

Camilla took a drink of water from her purple water bottle. "Owen believed that there was a wrongful conviction in Samuel's story. Owen did as much research as he could to prove his theory. He became obsessed with it, going out multiple times to the location. Doing ghost hunts to speak to the sisters, requesting documents from the county, and hunting down any ancestors he could find. He became pretty close to the owners of the property, who are ancestors of the Shaw family."

"Emma and Jerome," Quinn said.

"They're the last two remaining survivors of the Shaw family and made some trips out here from Oregon for on-camera interviews," Camilla added. "But their knowledge is limited. The incident was considered a black stain on the family's legacy. So, no one talked about it."

Elijah flipped through one of Owen's binders. "It says in his notes he found a historical police report. He thought it was something that pointed to the Shaw parents; one of them had an affair—"

"Owen said something about treasure. Or Civil War Bonds," Quinn interjected and leaned back in her chair, making herself at home. "There was a possibility of an estimated two million dollars in today's money out on the Shaw property that Samuel had acquired in bad investments. He had a lot of enemies. Owen thought that the sisters were murdered for the location of the money."

"There's also a theory that there were *no* bonds. It was just a business deal gone bad that Samuel was responsible for," Camilla said, disagreeing, taking lip gloss out of her pocket. Quinn's shoulders tightened, and she gave a forced smile that looked like she was in pain.

Elijah was only one man, and there was no way he could figure out a crime the cops assumed he committed or find forty grand in drugs in six days. The solution might be right under his nose, in the form of silver bars in Owen's shed behind the church. Elijah rested his forehead in his hand, and sighed in thought. *Hidden treasure unearthed that time had forgotten would be enough motive to murder someone.*

The list of suspects was exhaustive. The only person Elijah knew for sure that didn't murder Owen was himself. Owen's life was far more colorful and complex than Elijah imagined, and there were many darkened corners. One of those shadowed and malevolent corners was where he'd find the murderer.

Parker's phone beeped. "Aww shit. This had a full charge when I came in. My battery sucks." Parker tapped his phone, then shut it off.

Spooked, Elijah's eyes bounced around the room as Camilla and the rest of the group discussed possible scenarios. One of which was witchcraft. Quinn surveyed the group intently as they discussed the supernatural possibilities. Their voices muffled as they had the intense conversation, and a growling boomed in Elijah's ears. The sinister energy that had visited his room from a week before manifested, emerging from one of the aisles. As if he called it into existence with his melancholy thoughts, the baseball-sized mist expanded to the size of a beachball. Hovering silently, the entity rippled like waves in a lake. Strikes of electricity shot through its vicinity. The lights flickered above them, darkening the room for a moment. A collective gasp reverberated through the library.

Elijah clenched a fist, digging his nails into his palm. There was a warmth on his fist that grounded him back into reality. Quinn had wrapped a gentle hand around his.

There was a rising memory inside him, surfacing out of the murky depths of his soul.

A flash of Quinn's face as she danced in an elegant, eggplant-colored gown from the 1800s. The breathtaking vision of her sent a wave of passion intertwined with longing through his heart. It wasn't her same physical face or body, but he could read the energy of her soul and knew intuitively it was her. The scene faded and replaced with a forest—him and Quinn were lovers playing hide-and-go-seek like children, weaving in and out of trees. Elijah found her behind a laundry line of drying clothing and linens. Her beautiful blond, wavy hair was adorned with a crown of pink, white, and purple wildflowers. A muggy southern breeze blew the fresh scent of laundry into his face calming him as he kissed Quinn intensely and passionately.

Static rolled from Quinn's fingertips, shocking and yanking him from his retrocognition. Elijah instinctively jerked his hand away from her, spooked by the memory her touch drug up from inside him.

"Sorry I didn't …" Quinn bit her bottom lip. "I didn't mean to …" Her emerald eyes bore into Elijah with concern. She scooted her chair away from him, giving him space. "Are you alright?"

"No, it's okay." Elijah hoped that wouldn't be the last time she touched him. His reaction was less than receiving. "I'm fine. I haven't been sleeping lately." He rubbed the back of his neck, watching the still loitering spirit out of the corner of his eye.

"Me either." There was a flash of understanding in her expression. Quinn leaned into his ear. "You look like you saw a ghost."

"Yeah, I guess you could say something like that." Elijah gave her an unsure smile.

He had no idea what the hell was following him. Its energy was powerful, and he could sense it trying to invade his thoughts. He looked over his shoulder and watched as the fog dissipated into the ceiling of the library.

Elijah turned his head away from everyone else, closer to her ear. Energy pulsed between the two of them, potent and intoxicating. The intense beat against his psychic senses caused him to lose focus as it thumped against his soul in steady waves. There was something about Quinn's presence that temporarily calmed the storm inside him. The note Owen had left at the beginning of his journal made a tiny bit of sense now.

"No. It's ... thanks for being concerned." Elijah adjusted the bill of his hat and smiled.

They *could have lived and died together before*, in a previous life. His intuition gave him a warm, gentle message letting him know that at one time, long ago, Quinn had been so much more to him than his best friend's cousin.

12

AFTER A TUMULTUOUS NIGHT'S sleep on the crappy queen bed at the church, Elijah spent the morning going through the archives Owen had amassed. He'd learned that the Shaw family graveyard was built after the townsfolk had burned the plantation to the ground. Even though small amounts of evidence supernaturally and in reality were surfacing, it was still unclear how it all connected to Owen.

Elijah had spent the afternoon with Camilla at Monroe's, eating hash browns and planning how to film the last few scenes needed for the documentary. They spent the evening trying to log into the external hard drive Owen had given Elijah. After a few hours, Elijah and Camilla were grateful to gain access and discover every minute of footage Owen had amassed for the documentary, as well as recordings from Owen's hypnotherapy sessions. However, they were met with another file that required a password to open. After a quick call to Camilla's friend in computer programing, they learned it was a type of protection that would erase the entire hard drive if too many guesses occurred. So, Camilla and him decided to wait and process everything else on the drive first. Elijah made a mental note that after this week was over he needed to make a list of all of the passwords he thought Owen would choose.

Seven Sisters Road had an undercurrent of grim determination that night. The land was saturated with evil. Something inside those woods wanted him dead, and it wanted everyone to suffer. Elijah had put Owen's silver shotgun from the church under his seat to take home and clean and considered taking it into the woods. It would be the ultimate test, shooting the beast with silver home forged bullets. He also decided it might be a good idea to invest in a holster for his handgun. If this was his life, for the time being, he needed to start carrying protection.

The burn from the ghost on his forearm was healing, and his sleeve tattoo was still intact. Elijah had no idea how he was going to figure out who Mary was. With all the information spilling out at him, he was lucky he hadn't drowned yet. He studied the stillness of the towering cypress and live oak trees.

Elijah cracked the window in his car for fresh air. The world around him was still, and the sound of silence resounded profoundly, buzzing in his ears. There was no sign of any wildlife or insects, except for mosquitos—there were always mosquitos. Whirling mist with faint glowing colors of gray and blue flowed between the trees, fading as it reached the road. He turned on his radio and pushed in a mixed cassette tape. It was the 80s tape his father had left in the glove box. Elijah had amassed about ten more he'd found at random thrift stores along the coast from South Carolina to Florida during summer vacations. Being in the car and listening to his father's favorite music was Elijah's safe haven. Although AC/DC's "Highway to Hell" couldn't have come at a worse time.

Quinn sat across from him, monitoring the woods through her open window, and drummed her hot pink fingernails on the outside of the door in thought. Quinn lived at the church, so Elijah had spent most of his time in the last twenty-four hours with her. They were the first to arrive for the investigation that night. All-day, she had insisted on arriving at the forest before everyone else.

"You notice there's no sounds of wildlife?" Quinn broke the silence.

She angled herself toward him and leaned against the door, making herself comfortable. His dash lights illuminated her face in the darkness, and beads of sweat had collected on her forehead and chest, sparkling like glitter.

"Yeah, actually I did," Elijah affirmed.

Pulling at her black V-neck, Quinn straightened her stone necklace. The stone's beautiful colors of sea-foam green and dark purple were swirled together, glistening with a pearlescent sheen. Her eyes lingered on him.

"There's something about this area that's seductive," Quinn said. "I could feel it when Owen and I came out here last time to do an EVP."

Elijah was caught off guard and chuckled awkwardly. "What?"

"This area's dark … something twisted happened here," she said flatly and honestly. Quinn's eyebrows pinched together in thought. She paused. It seemed like she was checking with herself for confirmation. "Yep, that's what it is." Quinn sat forward, removed a lip balm from the pocket of her worn jeans, and then put it on. "Owen was on to something."

"On to what?"

"He thought there was more to this place than hauntings."

"You don't have to do this, Quinn. I know it must be hard … to be *here*."

Quinn played with her lip balm before shoving it back into her jacket pocket, considering her words. "This must be hard for you too." She reached out and grabbed his hand. "Besides, if my best friend slept with my girlfriend, I'd have kicked his ass." Quinn chuckled. "He was a good guy and one of my favorite people, but man, was he a sucker for a pretty face."

"Yeah, he sure as hell was." Elijah smiled, and for a moment, the stress faded away. "Despite what happened, he was my *brother*. No matter what," Elijah tilted his head to the side, "even though I wanted to beat the crap out of him."

"He loved you. You know that, right?" Quinn scooted in toward him and crossed her ankles, placing a hand on the back of the seat. Elijah remained quiet, and he turned away from her. "It's okay, I understand. You don't have to talk to me about this. I mean, you barely know me." She scooted back.

"No." Elijah put his hand on her thigh, stopping her. "I just … it's not that. Weirdly enough, you're the only person I feel comfortable enough to talk to about this right now. It's strange." Elijah squinted, gripping his steering wheel. "I don't normally talk to anyone."

"Well, that sounds awful." Quinn rolled her eyes, smiling. "Everyone needs someone to vent to. Even the strong, silent type." She winked at Elijah, and heat spread across his chest. "Life's hard." Her voice cracked with exhaustion. She had been helping with research all night long. Elijah was pretty sure the only reason Camilla tolerated her was because she was helpful.

A breeze came through the open window and blew her long, curly hair from behind. Vanilla rushed into Elijah's nose. He took a deep inhale, and the terrible week he endured faded. Frightening as it was for him to admit, it wasn't lust. There was something more drawing him toward her that he couldn't explain. A craving for her swelled in his chest to the point he thought he was going to combust. It felt like he was seeing her for the first time but had known her his entire life.

"There's something I need to talk to you about." Elijah straightened his shoulders.

Quinn turned her attention solely to him. Elijah rubbed the back of his neck, taking a sip of his energy drink. "I'm psychic, I think ..." Quinn squinted, watching him with curiosity. "I've seen ghosts since I was twelve. I've never told anyone, not even Owen. I'm telling you now because I need to tell someone before we go into that den of hell over there." Elijah pointed to the woods. Quinn adjusted herself in her seat, tucking one foot behind the other. Her face was unreadable, and Elijah couldn't tell if she was judging him or intrigued. A long silence engulfed the Nova.

"I need to show you something." Quinn reached into her backpack and pulled out two pictures. "Do you believe in reincarnation?"

"At this point, I'm kinda convinced anything is possible." Elijah leaned into her, curious about where the conversation was going. The judgment Elijah expected disappeared. He raised an eyebrow, recalling Owen's journal entries.

"I personally believe we *choose* the lives we reincarnate into so that we can learn specific lessons. Sometimes along the way, we meet people from what is called a soul tribe."

He scooted away from her, turning toward the window. The beginning of Owen's journal was so much more than what he'd expected. A whole new world was unfolding for him, and he wasn't going to be able to share it with his brother. Elijah froze, and for a moment he thought he could hear Owen's distant voice whispering from deep in the woods. Elijah stayed silent and his desire to conversate diminished.

"There sometimes can be people who we're *drawn* to that can't be explained. The connection they share can't be severed through space or linear time. Souls that are woven together through dimensions." Quinn paused, scooted in closely, and inhaled deeply. He could tell she was taking in his scent. Elijah took the two photos from her hand. They were inches from each other, and the urge to caress her lips with his caused his thighs to tingle.

"People, or souls, that never connected or were betrayed by their soulmates or soul tribe are subjected to severely horrific future life experiences. It keeps them from enlightenment—the whole group. They transform into ghosts, poltergeists, and dark energies, to name a few. The longer they stay stuck, the darker more twisted they become. They have to be forced to move through the gate."

"Like purgatory?" Elijah said, locking eyes with her. He noticed the iris of her eyes had a brown ring around it.

"Yes, they're blocked from becoming a higher consciousness. They have to let go of the energy that put them there or is trapping them there."

"So, they have to forgive?"

"Exactly." She spoke slower now. "Someone has to help them cross over and raise their vibration." Quinn swallowed heavily. He could sense her longing, her need to touch him. Elijah smiled, and his eyes skimmed over a cracked and aged photo. He flipped it to the back and saw a scribbled date of *1865* and then flipped it back over, examining the scene. Elijah peered at a young man standing in front of a tent proudly, holding a rifle. His military uniform was caked in mud, and his brown hair was disheveled under his hat.

"Was this you?" His eyebrows pinched together, and he gave a curious smile.

"No, you jackass, that was Benjamin Shaw. He was Samuel's brother." She slid the photo out of his fingers and placed it on the bench seat. The second photo underneath was a closeup of a red silver dollar-sized birthmark inside of a wrist. It was a circle with a line through it. The lines of his birthmark were so deliberate that it could have been a tattoo to the untrained eye. "You see this on his wrist? There?" She pointed to the historic photo, and Elijah squinted. She waited for the light to go on.

"Whose wrist is this?"

"It's Owen's. It's why I got thrown out of the funeral."

"Owen didn't have a birthmark on his wrist."

"I know. The birthmark didn't appear until after he died. The person you chased through the woods at Seven Sisters Road the other night ..." She bit her bottom lip. "Was me. I was trying to get dirt from where Owen was killed. So, I could contact him and put a protective circle around the tree to protect his soul from whoever killed him. To make sure that I was safe, I cast a summoning spell ... on you."

"That's ... how is that ... you could have asked me to help you." Elijah's raspy voice dipped. "You didn't have to manipulate me."

"Owen's obsession with Seven Sisters Road was on a scale we could have never imagined. I had no idea what I was facing, and I knew he loved and trusted you."

Elijah pinched the bridge of his nose, reached over to his glove box, and grabbed his flask. He took a furious sip and shoved it back in, slamming the glove box shut. He started to say something, then paused.

"What is it?" Quinn said.

"Did you ... did you ever fully contact Owen?" Elijah stuttered, doing his best to stay calm.

Quinn raised her eyebrows, then stared at her hands. "Oh. Well, I didn't get a chance to collect everything I needed."

"So, you were saying ... Past lives?" Elijah said adjusting his hat and getting them back on track.

"I've heard of them, but neither my Nana nor her coven has witnessed anything like this." Quinn held up the picture. "From what I know, anyway."

"You're part of a coven?"

"Was. We're called The Sisters of the Waking World," Quinn said proudly.

"After I started helping Owen, I was excommunicated for helping an outsider."

Elijah picked up the picture of Owen's wrist. "That symbol." Elijah squinted in thought, then reached underneath his seat and took out Owen's journal. He unfolded the rubbings. "Look." Elijah took the photo and placed it next to the symbol. "It's the same."

"Holy shit. It's the magic circle marking. I can't believe I missed that," Quinn said disappointed.

"I was thinking about this earlier. The rough texture around the rubbings could be bark," Elijah said, tucking it carefully back into the journal. "The last time I was out here," Elijah pointed to the woods, "I saw the water symbol carved into a tree." Elijah was so involved in the conversation; he hadn't noticed Quinn was resting her hands in his lap. Elijah's eyes shot down, and Quinn cleared her throat, removing her hands. She put the pictures back in her bag and grabbed a piece of gum, popping it in her mouth.

"We need to go out there and find it again. Owen thought you were psychic. He said he caught you a couple of times with information you couldn't have known on your own. Owen never knew how to ask you. I told him to talk to you; I kept pushing the issue. We could have used you for the research. That's *why* we stopped talking. I wanted him to bring you to the church and get your reaction. But after Riley, I don't ... he ... Shelly ... that's why I summoned you."

Jumping headlights appeared at the end of the narrow dirt road behind her head, and Elijah checked the last message on his phone. Camilla texted him five minutes ago and said they were fifteen minutes away. He had no idea who it was.

An orange Honda with an extended tailfin parked next to them. The high-pitched sound of the modified muffler choked off. Two men jumped out; it was Allison and Landon. He wondered how they found him and if there was a LoJack in his car. He made a mental note to check under his Nova later before leaving.

"Stay here." Elijah's face turned to stone. "No matter what you hear, don't get out of the car."

"What's the matter?"

"Stay here." He grabbed her hand, squeezed. "Please?"

Elijah got out of the car and met them on the other side of theirs, drawing them away from Quinn. The last thing he wanted was for them to do anything to her. It would weigh on his conscience for a while if they did, probably until he died. Which, if he kept going at this unfortunate fateful rate, it wasn't going to be much longer until Elijah himself was in a casket.

"How's it going on the funds, Elijah?" Allison put his hands on his hips and narrowed his beady eyes. Elijah was able to tell in the dark that he wore a concealed weapon under his shit-green, button-up Hawaiian shirt. Elijah wondered if he had a closet filled with blood-stained, Hawaiian button-up short sleeve shirts. One for each day of the week and each of his violent moods.

"I'm working on it. I couldn't find the money or the product."

"Well, you're gonna have to work faster 'cause boss says there's no exceptions," said Landon. He pulled out an old coin, flipping it back and forth over the back of his fingers in one fluid motion. "And he's not giving you an extension." Landon flipped the coin extravagantly and caught it behind his back, sticking it in his pocket.

"Do we need to give you a push to get your ass into motion?" Allison raised an eyebrow. Landon and Allison closed in on him like rabid dogs.

"Maybe we should tell the boss it ain't gonna happen and save ourselves some time." Allison jabbed a cigarette-stained finger in Elijah's face, and Landon pumped his eyebrows with vicious excitement. They were gonna kick his ass *again*, for Christ's sake.

"No, I'll get it. I said I would, and I will."

"Josiah knows what you're doing out here. We have people watching the place, and since Owen's been such a pain in the ass, he wants a cut of the documentary *and* the forty grand. If there *is* treasure, you better not hide it." Allison's face hardened, and it was apparent that it wasn't only Elijah who was having a rough week. By the way they were crowding him, he could tell that they were both two seconds away from shooting him in the head, shoving him into a garbage bag, and tossing him into the marsh.

"We have no control over how soon Turner pays. We also have no proof there is treasure. It's a legend."

Ignoring Elijah's comment, it was clear they didn't give a shit about what he had to say. "He wants three-quarters of whatever you find. Since Josiah's money funded most of the project, it's only fair," Landon added.

"Either way, Owen worked for that money, and your boss *already* made his share." Infuriation took over Elijah, and before he knew what he was doing, his fist connected with Landon's face, and a crack echoed through the silence. Landon stumbled back and caught his footing, leaping forward and tackling Elijah into the car. Alison drew his gun, pointing it at Elijah's face. Landon maniacally laughed; there was something different about him, but Elijah couldn't put his finger on it.

"What Owen did with what he earned has nothing to do with your asshole boss," Elijah said, furious.

Elijah's neck and back twisted as he was tossed to the dirt road, and Landon kicked him in the ribs. Mud caked his face. He rolled onto his stomach to save his head and side.

"You're a waste of space, and both you and your friend deserve what you get," Landon said furiously.

There was a hidden resentment for Elijah and Owen behind his soulless eyes. Elijah was unsure what had happened to Landon in the last day, but his energy had changed from light to heavy. He had been broken during the previous twenty-four hours. Elijah hoped that by some miracle, Quinn was facing the other direction. He might even welcome the freaky ass wolf that was following him.

"Ummm, gentleman?" The two goons turned their attention to Quinn.

Elijah's heart sank. She didn't stay in the damn car like he asked. His eyesight wavered, and Elijah sat with his sore back against the ridiculously tricked-out Honda. Elijah clenched his eyes shut, hoping that they would work. Throbbing formed behind his right ear as his eyes refocused. Quinn was pointing a handgun at the angry drug dealers.

"Ooooh. Allison. It's a girl with a gun," Landon said, taunting Quinn. Her eyes darkened with displeasure, and she stared him down with a frown. She trained the barrel of her handgun on his chest. Landon lunged toward Quinn, and she fired a warning shot next to his foot, stopping him in his tracks.

"I'm not a girl; I'm a woman, you jackass, and my daddy was a Marine and a sharpshooter. I started shooting a gun at ten. Don't test me 'cause my next shot won't miss. Back away from him now." Her voice was steady as a rock. Shocked, Allison and Landon backed away from Elijah and turned their full attention toward Quinn.

"Damn, sweetie, too bad you aren't workin' for us. Redheads are hot." Landon gave a slimy smile and bit his bottom lip.

"We weren't gonna kill him or shoot him. He's no-good dead." Allison nodded his head toward the crime scene tape. Quinn's finger tightened around the trigger of her handgun, and a hatred formed in her eyes with the mention of Owen's death.

Allison's tanned and wrinkled face lit up. "But how 'bout this: Either you guys get us the damn money, or we kidnap your girlfriend." He winked at Quinn. "Who is way hotter than Owen's ex."

"You'd be dead before you get your hands on me. Now that you assholes are done asserting your pathetic dominance take your piece of crap fast and furious wagon and get the fuck out of here. I'm not gonna ask nicely again." Quinn flashed an annoyed but smooth smile.

Two headlights appeared at the end of the roadway, and Elijah knew who it was immediately. Parker's old 4-runner was hard to miss. The engine had a distinct winding sound, and it reverberated all the way down the road.

Allison holstered his gun, and they both jumped back into the car, speeding off, splattering Elijah with mud. Quinn walked to the Nova and tucked her handgun under the seat. She rushed to help Elijah, but he waved her off dismissively.

"I could have taken care of that, my damn self."

"From where I sat, it looked like you couldn't," she snapped.

Elijah leaned against his car, rubbing his left cheek where he'd been punched. Elijah had the distinct sensation that everything awful he'd perpetrated in his life was returning back to him this month. Every nasty comment, ass-kicking, wrongdoing he'd committed was sucking the life out of him.

"What was that all about?" She bore her eyes into him and clenched her jaw. The moon behind her lit up her hair like a halo, and Elijah pinched the bridge of his nose. He shook his head, and she stopped him.

"Don't you *dare* say nothing. If it's about my cousin, I want to know."

Elijah grabbed a shirt from the back seat, took off the dirty one, and threw it in the car. "You mean you don't know who they are?" Quinn's eyes widened for a split second at the sight of his bare chest, and he grinned, pulling on the semi-clean one.

Quinn cleared her throat. "I feel like this goes without saying, but, duh?"

"What are you doing carrying a gun! You shouldn't have ..."

Parker pulled into a spot next to them, and Elijah stopped mid-sentence. His stomach churned at the thought that he would have to end this whole shit storm even faster—and keep Quinn safe at the same time. Anger and resentment pulsed through Elijah, and he felt like he was on fire. The decisions Owen had made affected everyone around him after his death. Either way you considered the situation, both the survivors and Owen were incredibly screwed.

"Hey, guys, ready to go do some ghost hunting?" Parker asked cheerfully, snacking on flaming hot Cheetos.

"Who was that?" Hudson jabbed a thumb down the way Allison and Landon had exited.

"No one. Some people that got lost," Quinn said quickly. Her eyes snapped to Elijah's face as he walked around his car and turned off the radio, which played an ominous 90s version of "Don't Fear The Reaper."

"Then why do you look like you got the shit kicked out of you?" Hudson asked.

Camilla jumped out of the back and paused, watching Elijah and Quinn. "What the hell is goin' on with you guys?"

"Nothing we just ... it's this place," Elijah said, rubbing the back of his neck, doing his best to keep it together.

Camilla waved him over, and they walked away from the group. "Who was in the car?" She raised an eyebrow. "Don't give me no Sunday school version." She poked Elijah's chest. "Or try to protect me."

"It was the drug dealers. They found out about the Turner deal and gave us five days. They want a cut of the Shaw treasure that most likely doesn't exist. Be careful they threatened to kidnap people."

"Jesus." Camilla grabbed Elijah's wrist and squeezed gently, her eyes wide.

"You wanted the truth."

13

ELIJAH'S SIDE ACHED, AND his face throbbed. Sweat trickled down his back as he scanned through the trees with his camo flashlight. Elijah had no idea *how* he and Quinn had strayed so far from the group. It seemed like they were all together one second, and the next, the mist that blanketed the forest had swallowed them whole.

Owen's silver shotgun was strapped to Elijah's back in his favorite holster. After Allison and Landon's visit, there was no way he was leaving it behind. Camilla objected to bringing the firearm but was outnumbered when it came to the vote on whether to bring it.

Quinn and Elijah were in the Shaw family graveyard. It's where he'd found himself only two nights before when he'd encountered Alpha. The scorching temperature from the day dissipated, and there was an uncharacteristic chill in the evening air. Quinn and Elijah were standing so close that the heat from Quinn's body warmed Elijah's forearm.

"Camilla said something about finding the location of the house based off of the location of the three hangings," Elijah said. He unfolded the map of the area and stopped, leaning against a dampened tree trunk. "Finding the remnants of the house is important to the end of the documentary. This is also where I saw the symbol on the tree." The smell of rotting wood drifted through the air on a light breeze. Swelling gray clouds collected above them, and Elijah glanced toward the sky.

"It's gonna start raining again," Quinn noted, reading Elijah's mind.

Elijah was starting to believe they were searching for a needle in a haystack and that it was useless to keep trekking through the foggy night. He wasn't entirely sure that it would contribute much, but what Turner wanted, Turner would get at this point.

An owl hooted in the distance, and the sound of an animal moving through shallow water came from the shoreline. Flapping wings and a screeching crow startled Quinn, and she spun around. For a second, Elijah thought she hesitated, waiting for something.

"You expecting something to happen?" Elijah asked.

"No …" Quinn stuck her flashlight in the side pocket of her backpack, raked her hair back with her fingers, and tied it into a messy ponytail. Quinn slipped her flashlight back out, skimming over the gravestones, then swept it across a perfect line of rocks. "These stones form a perfect circle around the graveyard, connecting to the trees."

They were standing in the center of the circle.

"Here." Elijah held back Spanish moss and chipped away caked-on mud. "Someone tried to hide it." Quinn joined him, and they studied the symbol etched into the bark—the same one on Owen's wrist. "Benjamin Shaw's grave is right there." Elijah pointed at the headstone. The overgrown grass of the graveyard rustled in the breeze with the utterance of Benjamin's name.

"It's at the center of the circle," Quinn observed.

The trees around them creaked as they rocked in the wind. The sounds of the night were distorting, mixing with the wind and sounds of nature. It blended like multiple voices speaking at once, playing tricks on Elijah's mind, manipulating his reality.

Elijah traveled to each massive oak tree, checking for symbols. He ran his fingers over the weathered, etched symbol he'd come to know as Earth.

"They're here, and they all match the rubbings."

Elijah walked back to Benjamin's grave, kneeling. Touching the weathered granite, something inside him awakened. The weak spiritual pulse of a life from one hundred and eighty years ago started to strengthen. Entities that resided within the shadows were beating against the doors of his psyche, asking to be invited in like a psychic vampire waiting to suck his life force dry. The atmosphere around Elijah and Quinn was thick with sorrow. It took every ounce of emotional strength he had to keep them at bay. Elijah swore he could sense someone watching them as they journeyed through the graveyard, creeping behind them.

There was something about the ground that was familiar; Elijah knelt, digging his hands into the clay dirt. The energy was different than the rest of the forest. It whirled around him, causing a nauseating cramp in Elijah's stomach. The graveyard was drawing him in like a fly to a Venus flytrap. A golf ball sized light flickered into view hovering in the forest, catching his attention. Energy waves rippled out of the light like the surface of a lake.

It could be the gate. It's starting to open.

"This was a bad idea." Quinn veered to the left, stopping, trying to decide on a path to take from the graveyard. Mud squished under her feet. "We need to get back to the car."

Quinn spun, then traipsed into the woods away from the graveyard—bewildered Elijah trailed after her.

The world around Elijah closed in with each cursed step he took deeper into the hellish woods. "We haven't found what we're looking for."

"You getting any impressions?" Quinn changed the subject.

"Impressions?"

"Psychic information from the area, or messages from the dead," Quinn clarified.

"I have no idea how to actively do that. It kinda just happens," Elijah said.

With the heavy rainfall over the past few days, the forest had turned to mud and swamp. Elijah smacked at mosquitos that kept buzzing around his ear, searching for dinner. He cursed at himself for not bringing bug spray.

You figure being psychic, I might have seen the bugs coming. But, if my abilities did include precognition, then maybe I might have seen Owen's death coming, and he'd still be alive.

"There's nothing telling you what might have happened to Owen?"

"No." Elijah's voice lowered. He had no desire to witness that again, and everything was unfolding so quickly that he hadn't even considered the possibility. "Those are visions I can do without."

Quinn stopped, pointing her flashlight at the ground. "I'm sorry, that was ..."

Elijah rubbed the back of his sweaty neck. "Don't worry about it."

They continued moving through the forest. Elijah could sense eyes on him, not only from one entity but from multiple spirits. They were wayward, not original to the land. Prickling spread through Elijah's legs, and anxiety spread in his chest, causing sweat to trickle down his neck.

"You realize you made it worse right?" Elijah kept a diligent eye on their surroundings, expecting the wolf that had been stalking him to leap out and devour his flesh.

"I don't remember any of this. I've been through these woods multiple times with Owen."

"Don't ignore my question." Elijah adjusted the strap of his holster.

"You've been evading mine all night," Quinn retorted, and her eyes were locked on his. "I have no idea *what* I made worse. You won't tell me. So, no, I didn't know that."

"I asked you to stay in the car. That's all you had to do." Elijah glared at her, annoyed by her lack of obedience.

"You're not my damn father." Quinn turned to him, beelining through the fog and forest, closing the gap between them. "Don't tell me what the hell I should and shouldn't do."

"I *knew* the dangers, and you didn't. There was no time to explain. All you had to do was trust me."

"We barely know each ..." Quinn choked on the words and paused. Elijah knew that she felt the same pull toward him that he felt for her—it was written all over her face. "Never mind. We need to find a way out of here. Quick. I have a bad feeling about this. We've gotten plenty of EVP questions on this recorder. With no answers from spirits or Owen." Quinn powered down the recorder and tucked it into her back pocket. "You think the treasure exists?"

"The jury's still out on that." Elijah's doubt was transparent, and she gave him a glance of disapproval. "There's something on this land. Except, I don't think it's treasure. I'm pretty sure it's something of personal importance."

"Knowing what I know about Samuel … or you …" She paused like she had something else to say but decided against it. "Let's say it's a possibility."

"There was something else you were gonna say. What was it?"

Quinn shot Elijah a warning glance; the topic was sensitive. He continued with the task at hand and decided to pry later—at the church, maybe. Quinn's face ashened, and her eyes brimmed with tears. Her breath turned to steam as it left her mouth. Frost crystals formed, biting Elijah's lips.

"Listen," Quinn whispered.

The sound of heavy breathing came from all directions. Quinn raised a frightened finger, pointing past Elijah, and he whirled around. A gray smoke crept through the trees and rose above them. The entity hovered silently. It was intelligent and studied them like easy prey; Elijah had no idea how he knew. *He just did.*

Elijah could hear the entity's thoughts drifting on a frigid gust that cut through him. Disembodied whispers carried through the night reverberated in surround sound. The shimmering, gray wisp closed in on them both like a cobra, waiting for the perfect time to strike. Quinn wrapped her arm around Elijah's, and he pointed the flashlight at the massive ball of smoke. The flashlight shorted and blackened.

Quinn's voice was tense with terror. "Elijah, we need to go." She stared directly into the spectral mass, transfixed, and swallowed heavily.

There was something that Quinn *knew,* and he didn't. He could see it echo in her terrified response. Elijah threw the useless flashlight to the ground and blocked her. The malicious entity eased through the trees, foxfire flashing within it. An animalistic wail boomed from deep inside of it, and the anomaly paused, centimeters from Elijah's face. It huffed like a bull, and its hot, rancid breath blew off Elijah's hat, ruffling his hair. He turned his head to the side, hoping it wouldn't possess him.

Leaning in, Quinn pressed her chest to his back and her lips to his ear. Her heart raced so intensely, Elijah could feel it beating against his shoulder. "When I squeeze your hand, start running, and don't turn back."

Unsure, Elijah squeezed her hand in affirmation. Quinn intermingled her fingers in his and squeezed. They broke into a sprint across the forest. Elijah scooped up his hat, and Quinn gripped his hand so tightly his fingers went numb.

Escaping the monster, the atmosphere of the forest transformed from sizzling to icy in an instant as the demon pursued them. The rage emanating from the mysterious anomaly beat against Elijah's back, and he pushed himself harder. Both he and Quinn weaved through obstacles, and the moon strobed through the branches of the trees as they raced to escape the inescapable. Winded, Quinn stopped and leaned against a tree; Elijah tugged her hand and drug her.

"We ... can't ... stop."

The ravenous snarling of a dog echoed through the night, and they simultaneously paused. Quinn shot Elijah a glance of terror, not sure if running was the right thing to continue. Cautiously, they turned, and the alpha wolf from the church bared its long, jagged teeth.

Quinn patted the empty holster at her side. "Shit, my gun's in the car."

"Get behind that tree. Take my phone and call Hudson, then go to them." Elijah drew out the silver shotgun and cocked it.

"I'm not leaving you out here." Her voice was desperate and frightened. "That isn't *any* wolf, Elijah."

"Just do it," he said firmly.

Exasperated, Quinn grabbed his phone and tucked herself between two closely grown trees. Her worried eyes shifting between Elijah and the horrendous canine with feverish anticipation. Elijah wasn't entirely sure of the grim events about to unfold. It appeared that Alpha was going to get him after all.

Quinn clutched the stone on her necklace and started whispering, staring directly at the hungry wolf. Elijah couldn't tell what Quinn was saying, but it was audible enough for him to hear a rhythm. She was chanting.

The angry canine turned its attention to her, and its eyes blazed with crimson. Enraged, it trotted toward Quinn with menacing grace. It launched toward her, and Elijah intercepted the monster slamming it to the ground. He leveled the barrel, pressing the silver to the wolf's neck. Its skin sizzled, and the beast yelped, writhing in pain with the touch of the metal. Furious, the creature found the strength to nip at his neck, fighting to free itself. Elijah punched the beast in the raw shotgun wound it received from Quinn earlier that day. Alpha thrashed in pain, becoming more infuriated. The beast's muscles shuddered under its skin with rage. A blood-curdling scream echoed through the depths of the pitch-black forest, and Elijah's head instinctively jerked toward the sound.

"Camilla!" Panic and adrenaline ravaged him. "Hudson, Parker!"

The massive creature took advantage of the distraction and clawed its way loose, kicking dirt into Elijah's eyes. Searing pain shot through his arm as the dog sunk its razor teeth into Elijah's flesh. He catapulted the beast, and it tumbled across branches and fallen leaves, colliding with a tree trunk. Determined, Alpha recovered and charged at him. Finally, clear of Quinn, Elijah shot, missing the wolf. A tree trunk exploded, sending wood chips flying.

The Beta appeared out of the fog, intercepting and protecting Elijah. Its beautiful copper fur with golden highlights sparkled in the night under the moon. The two animals fought for footing as they threw each other around like rag dolls.

A woman's menacing ghostly voice in the woodland sang the name *Samuel*. It was a tone that let him know the spirits were searching for him, and they wanted to take him to the dimension in-between. They wanted to drag him to hell. Elijah lost control of his mind, and multiple images flickered through like an out-of-control movie reel. His consciousness was being forced from his body.

Elijah hovered above the forest. A billowing cloud of black smoke rolled into the sky from a fire, then in an instant, there was nothing. The rhythm of archaic drums assaulted his ears, blasting him awake. He was on the ground huddled next to a tree, at the edge of a marsh. Murky, brown water soaked Elijah's grey wool pants. He patted his chest and noticed he was wearing a grey vest, red tie, and white dress shirt that were all in tatters. He instinctively knew it was clothing from a past life. His past life. Elijah's vision blurred; he looked down at his bloody, dirty hands; they were the hands of another person. Elijah noted the bite mark on his arm, still fresh. It was in the exact same spot as the one he'd just received. Pain radiated through his arm from the wound, spidering outward into his body. It stung and made his body feel like it was on fire. Confusion clouded his mind. The individual he'd inhabited had no idea how they arrived at the location. The only thing Elijah could decipher was that he'd been summoned there beyond his control.

He clenched his eyes shut and reopened them, hoping they'd regain focus. The flickering light of orange and yellow from a massive fire danced across the dark forest. The unsteady glow allowed his eyes to adapt to the night. Two trees came into view, and he immediately identified them as ones around the Shaw family graveyard. Mud squished under his feet as he wriggled his way up a tree trunk to stand.

"Hello?" Elijah's voice was different—thin and deeper. It wasn't his. Elijah's heart thumped so rapidly he could hear the pulse in his ears. Firelight flickered, illuminating the dark woods, and the smell of smoke burnt his nose. He followed the scent, stopping ten yards away, watching a figure placing rocks next to each other to make a circle around a blazing mansion. Elijah recognized the ring of stones, it was the one that was around the Shaw Family graveyard. The cloaked figure stopped, standing still, raising its hands to the fire, and the rigid form rocked back and forth, chanting.

Elijah, compelled, continued cautiously, and the branches under his feet cracked. The being never moved at the sound of Elijah's steady progression.

The chanting intensified. "I give this offering to appease the gods and ask you to open the gates."

A bare, dirty foot nudged his elbow as he paused next to a tree. Elijah saw the corpse of a golden-haired woman dangling from a thick tree branch. In shock and disgust he backed away and noticed one of the symbols from Owen's journal etched into the tree trunk—Water. Mania overtook Elijah as he witnessed a total of five women hanging from separate trees surrounding him. Each tree had a triangle symbol carved into the bark.

The malicious being turned to Elijah with its hands raised. It was a man, his blond hair wild and his face covered in mud. He wore a tattered gray suit. The man's round eyes were deep with rage and anger, blazing like the alpha's. He rushed at Elijah, gripping his forearm, and chanted under his breath, penetrating him with his anguish. Dull throbbing traveled through Elijah's forearm and through his torso to the back of his head. The fire flared behind him, and the home collapsed in on itself. Elijah writhed in pain, fighting to loosen the man's deathly grip. When he looked back at the attacker, his face had morphed into Elijah's.

A thump and a dog yelp sucked Elijah back into the damp forest. The glow of flashlights appeared deep in the fog. Sensing the approach, Alpha disappeared into the night.

Time skipped, and before Elijah knew what happened, his face was in the mud, and the taste of metal filled his mouth. Someone was restraining him. Whatever that *thing* was, it had overpowered him; it penetrated his mind and took his memories. Fighting, Elijah's ears rung, and his earlobes burned. His eyesight wavered, and he squinted, barely making out pearlescent energy that surrounded him like a compact dome. Elijah was weightless and being lifted off the ground.

The clicking metal of handcuffs wrapping around his wrists brought him back into the full swing of reality. Two officers were arresting Elijah. The ringing in his ears subsided. Frantically searching the trees, he saw that Quinn was gone. The Beta that had been protecting Elijah hid behind a tree, then vanished into the shadows.

With the way the evil entity could travel and the way he pissed off Alpha, he wasn't sure sending Quinn out into the forest on her own was a good idea.

14

ELIJAH HAD BEEN SITTING in an interview room at Beaufort PD for two hours. The bite wound on his arm had been stitched and bandaged. The localized anesthesia wore off, and it throbbed, but the bleeding had stopped. Something felt different to Elijah, like a bit of the skinwalker had injected itself into him. His skin was tender, and sweat coated his forehead. Guilt about leaving his friends seeped through Elijah's consciousness like a disease.

The vision of the burning mansion from his retrocognition haunted his senses. With the acrid odor of death still clinging to his nose, Elijah wondered if Samuel had murdered his sisters. The thought that he might have murdered his siblings in another existence made him feel disgusted with himself. His mind raced, searching for the memories from the time loss he'd suffered. A flicker of a memory traveled through him, and white-hot, poisonous, saliva coursed through his veins.

What did the Alpha do to me?

Elijah had been booked and fingerprinted for trespassing. He had no idea why he was still in the station and not in a holding cell. His hand on his bitten arm shook uncontrollably, and he couldn't decide if it was from damage or nerves. He still had Quinn's firearm in his vehicle. They already didn't like him, and trying to explain two guns, one of which belonged to his dead brother, would have been impossible.

Studying his reflection in a two-way mirror, Elijah noticed the wounds on his dirty face were at different phases of the healing process. His brown hair was filled with sand and soil, and his clothes were caked in dry mud. His chin was scratched from the rocks of the forest floor, and the abrasions burned. When they arrested him, his body had been numb with terror, and he had no idea that he was injured. He wondered what happened to Quinn and what the hell she chanted behind the tree.

Digging his hands into his hair, Elijah rested his elbows on the table. What the hell was happening to him? *This all has to be some bad dream I haven't woken up from.* He leaned back into his chair in disbelief and rubbed his wrists where the skin had chafed from the handcuffs. Elijah rubbed his leather lion head bracelet with his thumb, relieved it hadn't fallen off. Elijah dropped his hands to the table and stared vacantly. He ran his fingers over the dents, studying the imperfections in the metal, wishing he could change lives with someone else at the moment. Any life with far less colorful friends and less grim, complicated fates. Muscles in his legs and back spasmed with exhaustion.

Owen's aftermath *was* slowly sinking into Elijah's reality like larvae, morphing into a parasite within him. The way the alpha wolf's saliva had in the forest. The problem was he had no idea why Beta had protected him. No matter what, Elijah was grateful for the interruption.

He pinched the bridge of his nose as his patience threatened to dissipate. He was exhausted, and the two hours he'd been sitting in the cheap brown office chair felt like years. There was an abundance of things on his supernatural to-do list. First and foremost, get his damn gun and holster.

Detective Bohannan entered the room with a determined walk. He slapped down a file on the table, planting his palms firmly on the edge, invading Elijah's personal space.

"Why'd you run from the cops?"

"What are you talking about? I didn't ..." Elijah paused. Telling the cops the truth would only make him appear bat-shit crazy. "I didn't realize it was the cops. It was pretty foggy, and being out there by myself kinda freaked me out. I did get bit by a rabid dog." Elijah raised his arm, flashing the bandage.

The air thickened as Jensen walked into the room and took a seat across from Elijah. The smell of cigarettes wafted toward him, and the scent of the woods emanated from her white collared shirt.

"The wolf was probably angry you were encroaching on its territory,"

Jensen's eyes darkened.

An image of the black smoke that chased him and Quinn through the forest flashed like lightning in Elijah's mind. His shoulders tensed, and his breath shallowed. *They hadn't found the rest of the group or Quinn.* Elijah was caught in a dangerous dance between relief and concern. There was no telling *where* they were or if they were injured. Or dead.

"Where's the shotgun?" Bohannan stood, his legs wide, taking up most of the room.

"I'm sorry?" Elijah swallowed heavily.

"We found a fresh shotgun blast in the side of a tree near where you were found." Jensen folded her hands on the table in front of her.

"I didn't have any shotgun."

Jensen gave him a glare and leaned forward, keeping her eyes locked on him. "You're lying."

"Why were you out there?" Bohannan walked closer to the table, closing in, catching Elijah's attention.

Elijah focused and steadied his breath. "I told you the other day there was a docuseries Owen was working on, and it was about Seven Sisters Road. I was out there doing some scouting for filming." Elijah kept his voice steady and maintained eye contact with Detective Bohannan. He'd heard enough 'film speak' from Parker, Owen, and Camilla to know what terms to use. Elijah was relieved he'd paid attention.

"At nine o'clock at night?" Bohannan asked, crossing his arms.

"Kinda sick you guys are still going through with the filming. I mean, you're going to be in the place your brother allegedly committed suicide." Jensen's voice was thick with judgment.

"With the way you're digging into this case, I highly doubt you believe he committed suicide." Elijah locked eyes with Jensen, then leaned forward. The assumption that he was helping for some sort of sick kick infuriated him. "His mother needs money for the funeral. The only way to get it for her is to finish Owen's work, so that's what I'm doing." He paused, considering telling them to fuck off, but quickly weighed the consequences. Elijah kept quiet and leaned back into his chair, breathing deeply through his nose, settling the flames of anger growing.

Jensen flipped open the folder and removed a picture of Allison, setting it in front of Elijah. Allison was younger in the photograph, but his hair was the same length, and he was wearing a Hawaiian T-shirt.

I guess variety is the spice of life.

"You know this man?"

Elijah looked at the photo and shook his head. "Nope, sorry. Should I?"

"Well, for a second ... you know what, never mind." Jensen gave a sly smile. She slid out a picture of Allison and Elijah at Monroe's. "'Cause I'm pretty sure this is you talking to him at the diner after meeting with Camilla. The one you called a pain in the ass."

"The guy asked me for some change."

"You said you didn't know him."

"Exactly, you asked if I knew him, not if I'd met him. I *don't* know him," Elijah said quickly.

Bohannan cracked a soft smile; his rough voice interjected Jensen's attempt at games. "He's a drug dealer. Works mainly out of the Savannah port. Some of our colleagues in narco have been trying to prosecute him and his boss, Josiah, for a while." Bohannan walked across the room and leaned against the wall. "They've been connected to six murders that we know of and multiple disappearances," Bohannan added.

Elijah's throat closed as the threat Allison gave Quinn earlier stirred in his mind. He shouldn't have sent her out alone. She could still be out there lost in the woods, trapped with a paranormal killer or a drug dealer that could rape and murder her. Elijah bounced his feet, leaning back in the chair. Growing up with a lawyer for a short amount of time, Elijah knew he should be asking for one. He was also aware that it would be used against him, making him look more guilty.

"Elijah, did you hear me?" Detective Jensen stuck her face in front of

Elijah's, regaining his attention. "Why you sweating?"

"It's hot in here?" Sweat trickled down Elijah's temples, and it felt like he was sitting under the sun. Hot, muggy air from the vent above beat down on him, and he noted how odd it was to have the heat on instead of air-conditioning.

"We have Landon on video talking to Owen before he died." Jensen slid out a time-stamped video surveillance picture and placed it on top of Allison's. "That's his sidekick, Landon, but I'm sure you knew that."

Elijah remained quiet and adjusted himself in the plastic chair. His side ached, and the bite wound on his arm throbbed. After the week he'd had, his fragile body couldn't find any comfortable position. Every inch of him stung. He licked his dry lips, and the scab on his bottom lip cracked.

"Look, kid, I'm gonna be honest. I liked you for this in the beginning. I still haven't completely ruled you out. You *know* something, I could tell the moment I met you." Bohannon gave a classic Dirty Harry, thin-lipped smile, angling away from Jensen.

Jensen's eyes narrowed in response to his defensive body language, annoyed. It was clear that Bohannon didn't care for his partner either.

"Sorry, can't help you. I have no idea why Owen would be talking to him. It must be a misunderstanding." Elijah clenched his jaw and wondered if Shelly knew what happened if the detectives told her what they'd learned. He needed to get the hell out of the police station.

Elijah hadn't gotten a useful call. The only phone number he remembered was Camilla's, and he had gotten her voice mail. It would be just his luck that the only phone number he remembered was of someone who never really liked him. He was waiting for someone, anyone at this point, to come and save his ass.

Jensen eased in closer like she was having an entertaining conversation with a friend. "Come on, you think we were born yesterday?" Jensen gave him a soft smile that he knew was practiced. Something bothered him about the way she smiled. It was familiar. Elijah was unsure why, but there was something about her that rubbed him the wrong way.

Elijah knew that if he told them what he knew, there was a chance that Josiah would send more people after him and anyone else he cared about. After he left the damn police station, he was going to get a fucking drink.

"You dealing drugs, too? You guys get into a fight about the money?" Jensen pressed him, and Elijah's hands trembled with fury.

"What are you talking about?" Elijah's chest felt like someone crushed it with a vice.

"Allison and Landon, they've been sighted at the Thirsty Parrot a few times. That's your hangout, right?"

Elijah shifted in his seat, his comfortability shaken. Vulnerable and exposed, he etched his confident expression in stone, not wanting to give them anything to use against him.

"Once again, not sure what the hell you're talking about."

Bohannan stomped across the room and pounded a fist on the aluminum table. "I'm tired of the games. Give us an answer, or you're goin' to jail for accessory."

Elijah stared him down, leaned in toward him. "I have no idea what you're talking about," Elijah maintained. He leaned back into the chair, keeping his eyes on Bohannon, not blinking once. The detective backed off.

"We're processing everything in his dorm room, all his financials and phone records. It's only a matter of time before we find what we need." Bohannan shoved his hands in the pockets of his gray slacks.

A light knock echoed from the door, and Jensen answered it. There was furious whispering between her and another woman that Elijah strained to hear. From the tone of it, the other voice was an authoritative one. It was Jensen's boss.

Jensen moved out of the way, allowing the door to swing further open, and walked to Elijah. "You're free to go."

A tall woman with short, brown hair observed her detectives with disapproval, standing firm in the doorway of the interrogation room.

"What do you mean?" Bohannon's eyes narrowed at Jensen, then he turned to the woman in the doorway, pleading his case. "We haven't even got a chance to search his car."

"And you won't." The woman walked into the room, turning her attention to Elijah. Her short hair was sleek, and her smile genuine. "I'm Captain Hersh. I apologize for any inconvenience this might have caused you. Owen's death was ruled a suicide by the medical examiner. I have no idea why my detectives are bothering you right now." She extended her hand, shaking Elijah's. Captain Hersh dropped a plastic bag with Elijah's wallet, hat, pocketknife, and dead flashlight onto the table. She seemed nice, but Elijah got the sense that if you crossed her the wrong way, she'd put you in a hurt locker.

"I'm free to go?" Elijah grabbed the bag and took out his wallet.

"It seems as though the trespassing charge was a misunderstanding. A legal waiver was signed by the property owner a year ago, allowing the crew of the production clearance to be on the site. You are a part of that crew. You haven't committed any crime." Captain Hersh raised her eyebrow at Jensen, then her disappointed eyes shifted to Bohannon.

Jensen sighed and begrudgingly smiled. "I apologize, Mr. Ward. We made a mistake."

Bohannon crossed his arms defensively, and his angry eyes were fixed on Elijah. "Cap. If you let him go, he's gonna destroy evidence." Bohannon's scowl caused Elijah to clear his throat.

"What about my car?" Elijah put his hat on and slid the flashlight into his pocket.

"It's on the side of the building," Jensen's words brimmed with bitterness.

"Thank you, Mr. Ward. Have a good evening." Ignoring her detectives, Captain Hersh waved him out the door.

Elijah escaped the intensity of the room—hurrying down the hall. The captain's voice boomed from behind him, "That was a rookie mistake, Jensen. You're lucky I don't fire you both. Are you trying to get us sued?"

The tension and shaking in Elijah's hand subsided when he dashed out the front doors. They hadn't had time to search his car and find the journal or the firearms. Quinn must have been the one to get him out. She *knew* Emma, the last living heir to the Shaw property. He reminded himself to give her a big, fat kiss when he saw her at the church.

Those hopes were dashed when he walked out the front door of the police department and saw Shelly standing there, her arms pinned across her chest, more pissed off than he'd ever seen her before. Binx, restless, moved around her white Volkswagen Jetta parked in front of the police station, whining out of the cracked window.

"What the hell were you doing out at Seven Sisters Road? I had to call William to get you out."

Elijah winced. He knew that calling her lawyer ex-husband for a favor was less than enjoyable. They hadn't talked in twenty years until recently at Owen's funeral. "Well—"

"You shouldn't be out there, Elijah. It's morbid." She pointed at him furiously, moving down the stairs so quickly it looked like she was hopping.

"There's a good—"

"Don't go out there again," Her weary voice shook. She stopped at the sidewalk; her face twisted with fury.

Thunder rumbled off the coast, and a warm wind gusted through the barren city street, whipping around old Memorial Day banners that were clanking against the streetlights.

"I wasn't trying to upset you, but if you'd let me talk, I'll tell you why I was out there." Elijah stuck his hand out, trying to calm her.

"If you continue to act like I'm *overreacting,* I swear to God." She raised her eyebrows and pursed her lips in frustration.

It was a manipulation tactic that William frequently used while they were married. Elijah knew he always gaslighted her into believing she was overreacting. In reality, she was spot on about her assessments and should have never doubted herself. He *was,* after all, having an affair.

"Camilla said that Turner still wanted to purchase the docuseries for one-hundred and fifty grand. At first, I didn't want to do it, but she said she wanted to give you seventy-five grand. I was trying to solve the money problem for Owen's funeral. Even get you a little more." Elijah's tone was soft and raspy.

The soothing sound of a rustling palm tree filled the silence between them. Shelly's shoulders dipped, and then she sighed. "Elijah, I don't care about that money. I care about *you*. I'll figure out Owen's funeral costs later. Remember, I'm the parent. I don't need you to fix things. Just be here for me."

"William should be paying for half. It's the least he could do." Elijah said, annoyed. Rain sprinkled, tapping the concrete. A warm, nutty aroma floated past Elijah from the candy shop a block down.

"I don't want his damn money. I didn't need it when he left us to start a new family, and I don't need it now," she said quickly. Her face softened, and she gently examined his arm. "Are you alright? They said you had to get stitches."

"I'll be fine. I mean, it hurts like a son of a bitch ..."

"Watch your language." She released his arm. "Well, you need to tell your little ghost crew that you're out of the filmmaking business. Camilla can sell it *as is* or do the rest of the damn work herself. Owen gave enough of himself already."

"Thank you for your help. I know you hate talking to him."

"I hate talking to him, but I love you more."

Elijah followed Shelly down the rest of the way, escorting her to the driver's side door, and Binx growled at Elijah through the half-open window.

"Binxy, what's the matter with you? For criminy's sake." Shelly waved him back away from the door. "Do you need a ride home?" Shelly hugged him once more.

"No, my car's here."

Binx scratched at the window, violently trying to escape. A protective ferocity burned in his eyes. The mild-tempered dog turned into a rabid beast in one minute and was ready to defend what it loved. Elijah looked down at his fresh bite wound, then up to see Jensen standing on the stairs.

Elijah opened Shelly's car door, helping her in, then shut it, squeezing her shoulder gently through the open window and smiling. The skies opened, and heavy rain poured, drenching both him and Shelly. It appeared that Quinn and Elijah's weather predictions earlier in the evening were correct. There was a storm moving in.

15

USING HIS TRUNK FOR cover, Elijah cautiously slid Quinn's handgun into his gym bag, surveying the street for Jensen or any other officer that might be watching. He patted around the trunk and checked under the seats. No sign of Owen's shotgun.

Rain fell sideways, and the streets were flooded. Elijah raced to the front door, his body aching and his muscles burning. The newly placed, hanging Boston ferns were sitting on the floor inside the lobby door, and he quickly maneuvered around them to avoid tripping. Wiping the rain from his face, Elijah cursed himself for not paying extra for the covered parking garage; he was drenched.

The back of his skull had a slow throb. His forearm pinched and burned where Alpha had gnawed. The wound was deep; he was gonna have one hell of a scar. The emergency medical technician informed him of how lucky he had been that the dog missed all his tendons and there was no major damage. He'd received the first of his rabies shots in his shoulder, and his muscle was sore. Elijah was relieved it hadn't been on the arm with his sleeve tattoos. Each work of art that created the sleeve was a labor of love. They all meant something to him.

A heaviness plagued his steps as he strode through the narrow, dimly-lit hallway of his apartment building. He leaned against the wall, catching his breath. Flipping the keys around his middle finger, Elijah contemplated drinking himself to sleep again. Stale cigarette smoke and mold irritated the back of his throat, a natural byproduct of living in a historic building in Savannah. Everything was either from the colonial period or from post-Civil War.

The hallway was silent except for the buzzing of fluorescent lights and the sound of Mrs. Steever, the manager, two doors down, guessing incorrectly at Jeopardy. Alone for the first time in two days, Elijah thought about the night, the wolves that had materialized, his vision, and Quinn.

I know she's hiding something.

Thunder cracked like a sonic boom, and the hallway lights flickered. The fixtures popped. Elijah had learned from Mrs. Steever when he moved in that they were bronze and from the late 1930s. The crimson hallway carpet was worn, stained, and needed to be replaced. Elijah had only lived in the apartment for a year, but he'd observed at least two spirit orbs in the hallway.

When Elijah entered, Parker was sitting in the massive, chocolate-colored, and battered chair next to the couch. His bouncing knee bumped the cheap, wooden, Ikea coffee table. Blotched red rings circled his eyes, and his gray T-shirt was damp around the collar. His hands trembled as he lit a joint. Smoke furled into the modest, open apartment, instantly drifting into the kitchen. Camilla and Hudson were sitting on the couch with Chinese takeout and two bottles of whiskey. Elijah knew from experience that if Camilla drank whiskey, it had been a night of Earth-ending proportions. The last time he'd seen her drink whiskey was when her grandfather died and when her dog Rosey was hit by a car.

They must have experienced something too.

"Jesus Christ, there you are." Hudson's words were tinged with hysteria. He took a shot. His reddish-brown skin was covered in a sheen of sweat, and his hair disheveled. A street light from the kitchen window trickled through the blinds creating uneven lines across his relieved face.

"They finally let you out?" Camilla placed her hand on her chest, grateful. "I'm glad you're alright." She bolted to Elijah, hugging him. He squeezed her back with one arm.

Soothing guitar notes of a John Mayer song hummed in the background. Elijah dropped his duffle bag, and it landed with a thud against the wood floor of the modest apartment. She handed him a shot of whiskey, and he downed it, setting the shot glass on the coffee table. Burning spread in his throat.

"What the fuck happened to him?" Elijah threw a hand at Parker, whose eyes had turned vacant. Electric trepidation overwhelmed the room; despite everyone's attempts at keeping their shit together.

Elijah could only recall two times in the last year that this type of energy had registered to his psychic senses. The first was the night that Hudson got into a car wreck and was in the hospital. The second was when they found out Owen and Riley were sleeping together. It was as if the universe tried to warn him of imminent tragedy in the only way possible, through the energy of the atmosphere.

"You need to sit down." Camilla took her seat on the green leather couch, patting the space between her and Hudson.

"What the fuck happened?" Parker repeated Elijah's question as if he'd been so lost in disillusioned terror, he'd only now just processed what Elijah had said. "Shit straight out of a horror film. That's what." Parkers voice was raspy as he leaned back into the oversized chair. Then he sat forward, pointing at Elijah. "That place is crazy. I'm not going back there." A large puff of pot smoke exited Parker's mouth. Elijah walked to a window and cracked it open. Rain tapping on the inside windowsill sprinkled onto the kitchen floor.

"Do any of you know what happened to Quinn?" Elijah rubbed the back of his neck, an acidic sour taste attacked his throat.

"She called us from your phone and told us what happened with the cops." Hudson pulled out Elijah's phone from his front pocket and set it on the coffee table. Elijah snatched his phone; it was dead. "We met up; she caught a ride with us here, then took off. We haven't heard from her since."

A sharp knock at the door made Elijah spin, and he peeked through the peephole. The sight of Quinn's heart-shaped face sent a wave of relief over him.

Elijah swung open the door, ushered her in, and then locked it behind her. "We were just talking about you."

"Glad you made it out." Quinn had changed her clothes and now wore black jeans, teal converse high-tops, and a gray hoodie.

Elijah's relief was immediately replaced by a dread that blanketed the room. The lights flickered through the apartment.

"What the hell is wrong with the electricity tonight?" Camilla took a shot of whisky and winced as she swallowed. "What did they ask you?" She continued through a cough. "What the hell happened to your arm?"

"They asked me about the drugs." Parker and Hudson stopped, staring at Elijah, dumbfounded. Elijah had forgotten neither Parker, Quinn, or Hudson knew. "Shit." Turning away, he faced the door.

"You can't say some shit like that and then not continue," Hudson said quickly.

Elijah glanced over at Camilla, and she nodded in confirmation. He rubbed the back of his neck and turned toward his friends. Elijah could sense Quinn's eyes boring into him.

"The guys you saw leaving earlier tonight were drug dealers."

"I knew it!" Parker slapped the chair. "I told you they were shady." He pointed at Hudson.

"Owen owes them forty grand in cocaine *or* money, but since he's dead, they came after me. They told me that if I didn't get the money, they would go after Shelly. I didn't tell her because I was hoping in some way I could protect her." As the words left Elijah's mouth, a throb formed between his eyes. "But that didn't happen because the cops already know about Allison and Landon. They showed me pictures tonight of Owen and them talking. I'm pretty sure if I don't get that money, Allison is going to murder me."

"Jesus. Why didn't you say anything?" Hudson sat on the edge of his seat, his eyes wide.

"I didn't want to get you guys involved. I talked to Camilla about it because she was the only one I could think of that would know anything. Camilla, a wolf bit me, and I had to get stitches to answer your other question. It was the same wolf that Quinn shot out at the church. And it was pissed off."

Elijah observed Quinn with his peripheral vision, waiting for her reaction. Quinn gravitated toward Elijah. He wasn't sure how to ask her about the chant.

"Well, I can tell you one thing, bro. They're not gonna kill you." Parker coughed and snubbed out his joint. Quinn observed Parker and stayed silent, her gaze unwavering.

Elijah leaned into Quinn's ear, "I have your gun in my bag."

"I grabbed the shotgun before I left," Quinn's lips were next to his ear, and her breath brushed his neck, "you passed out when the cops found us."

The tenseness in Elijah's shoulders melted. It helped knowing where the shotgun had gone.

"What happened to you guys?" Elijah said, pulling out a chair for Quinn, and she sat.

Elijah took a seat across the room in his brown recliner. His mind was muddled with all the puzzle pieces of the evening, and he needed space from everyone's chaotic energy to organize his thoughts. Hudson stopped the music. Camilla picked up a silver handheld voice recorder from the coffee table, biting her bottom lip. Hudson and Parker were both watching her as she prepared herself for the story she was about to tell. In the silence, the air-conditioning unit clicked on and vibrated the windowsill.

"Before I play this, you need to know it was completely silent in the forest, no animals, *nothing*."

Elijah recalled the moment right before the wolf materialized and how he and Quinn were in a paranormal vortex.

"Alright," Quinn said as she kept a vigil on Parker and studied him; her eyes shifted to Elijah and then back to Parker.

She knew information about Parker that Elijah didn't. Something was terribly wrong.

"I also need to tell you I've done a lot of research with Owen. The concept of the afterlife was always fascinating to me. All of the evidence that we collected could have been interpreted as several things." Camilla hesitated, then pressed play on the recorder, setting it down on the coffee table with a shaky hand. Parker laughed in the background, and Camilla abruptly told him to shush. Then she asked a question. "Who lives in these woods?"

A distorted sound blasted from the speaker, and Elijah clenched his jaw. The static faded, and a hissing, sinister voice surfaced. "Those who have hanged." Unaware at the time and unable to hear the answer, Camilla asked another question. "How did you die?" A mixture of voices came through; this time, the answer was only half audible. "... murdered ... sacrifice ... Samuel ... sacrifice. Mary."

Elijah's head dropped, and he rubbed the back of his neck, turning away from the group. His heart sank at the solidification of the name Mary from another source. Camilla swiped up the recorder, clicking it off. Composing himself, Elijah turned his attention back to the group. Silence fell over the room, and Camilla gripped the recorder so tightly the plastic made a cracking sound. She clenched her eyes shut, breathing deeply to soothe herself.

"Was that a mixture? That sounded like different voices." Quinn scooted forward in her seat. "The last one—"

"Owen's voice." Camilla took another shot and dug her face into her hands. Her chest shuddered, and a small sob escaped into the room.

Hudson rubbed her back, and he wrapped an arm around her in comfort. Hudson's troubled eyes shifted back and forth between Quinn and Elijah as his knee bounced nervously. Hudson continued, nodding toward his brother.

"Shortly after these questions, we witnessed something, but it's probably better if you watch it on camera." Hudson clicked on the TV, and Camilla stood abruptly.

"I can't watch this again." Her strained voice faded as she escaped to Elijah's room, shutting the door.

Night vision appeared on the screen, and Hudson laughed in the background. Camilla made a statement about the air chilling. Quinn and Elijah watched the screen with anticipation. A woman's blood-curdling scream boomed from the TV and reverberated in the room. Terror shot through them, and Quinn jolted in her chair. The camera caught the vision of a woman swinging from a tree. The dead woman was dressed in nineteenth-century clothing. The dead woman was solid and not opaque like you'd expect a ghost to look.

Elijah recognized the woman's clothing; it was the woman he'd seen in his vision in the graveyard. Parker was so close with the camera that it vibrated when the woman's foot hit the lens. Parker gave a guttural, primal scream, and Elijah heard Hudson calming Camilla.

The camera angle widened, and there were five women all in the same area. Limp and dangling from the trees. Elijah's stomach clenched, and he ran to the kitchen sink, heaving drunken whiskey along with his Slim Jim.

"You alright, dude?" Parker was turned toward Elijah and got up walking to him.

"I'm fine." Elijah waved him away, directing him to sit back down.

Elijah wiped his mouth with a napkin and observed Parker exhaustedly plopping back into his seat. There was something that was *off* about his energy. Elijah leaned his back against the counter—it was only there for a split second on the screen—but he saw it.

"Did you see that?" Elijah pointed at the screen.

Quinn's face turned grim, "I did."

"See what?" Hudson asked.

Camilla strode back out and sat on the couch, doing her best to act composed, the way she was taught.

"That right there ... go back." Elijah made a backward motion with his hand.

"I'd prefer him not to," Camilla snapped.

"Just do it," Quinn demanded.

Elijah took the controller from Hudson and backtracked on the footage.

"There." Elijah paused the video and walked to the screen, tracing a faint outline of a symbol with his finger.

It was carved into the trunk of the tree where the spirit hung. It resembled a stick figure fish. It was a different symbol than the one in his vision. However, it was similar to one on the list of rubbings in Owen's journal. Quinn shot a frantic glance at Parker and then back at the screen.

"Holy hell," Quinn said and took out her phone, taking a picture of the frozen TV screen.

"You guys were in the graveyard?" Elijah said.

"Yes." Hudson's eyes were on Elijah, syncing with his paranoia.

"Elijah, isn't this one of the symbols on the rubbings?" Quinn asked urgently.

"Yes, it is." Elijah grabbed the journal from his bag and slid out the rubbings, placing the same symbol next to it, matching them up.

"When Owen and I were doing research into runes, I saw this symbol in a book."

Quinn rushed to Parker and knelt in front of him. "Parker, how are you feeling?"

Concerned by Quinn's reaction, Hudson bolted to his brother and was now standing on the side of Quinn and Parker.

"I'm fine. Just a little freaked out." Parker wiped his forehead of sweat. "Which you're making worse, by the way."

"Parker. This is important." Quinn's voice was more desperate this time.

Alarmed, Elijah was now standing behind her.

Camilla stiffened in her seat, tapping her fingers on her knee. "Quinn, he said he's fine. You're freaking me out."

Quinn went to check Parker's eyes, and he swiped her hand away. "Dude."

Elijah grabbed Quinn's arm. "Start talking. You're freaking everyone out." His eyes narrowed, and the muscles in his jaw twitched.

Quinn shook off his grip, scowling at him. He kept his position next to her and watched her intently. Shocked, Camilla and Hudson took their seats on the couch, and Quinn bit her bottom lip—trying to say something that Elijah was confident would blow out of the water what they'd witnessed on the screen only minutes before.

Quinn sighed in defeat. "That symbol is either associated with attachments or possessions. Since the entity showed itself to Parker, there's a good chance it connected itself to him."

Camilla's face hardened, unamused. "This is hardly the time for jokes."

"It's not a joke." Quinn's eyes narrowed, and she clenched her jaw. "I know because, well, my mother and father were witches, my grandmother's a High Priestess, and ... well, I'm a witch."

"Shelly's not a witch," Elijah said firmly.

"No, she kinda renounced Wicca for Christianity. When she met William. Before that, she practiced for twenty years." Quinn sat in a chair, then stood again. Vulnerability covered her face. "We don't tell too many people because they have an overactive imagination based on media and movies."

Camilla's nose wrinkled, and her lip curled in disgust."You're a devil worshipper?"

"No," Quinn said, clenching her hands. "I don't believe in the devil. I believe in good and bad energies. Every religion has them. It's about the intent of the individual. I'm a white witch, I practice light working."

Hudson, still stuck in shock, shook himself out of it, and finally asked a question. "So ... you're a nice witch?"

"Yes, that's exactly what I am." Quinn smiled.

"What's wrong with my brother?" Hudson's tone shifted into solution mode.

"Is no one listening to me? I fuckin' said I'm fine." Parker ran a hand through his blond hair.

"The symbol on the tree is possession. If a Shaw sister was hanged from that tree, he could be possessed by the entity that showed itself to him." Quinn paused, deep in thought. "I've never seen an entity bound to a symbol before. This is uncharted territory and very advanced witchcraft. It's too early to tell if she's attached herself to him. But there were multiple voices, which means there were multiple spirits. There's a possibility he's not the only one in this room that could be possessed."

"Okay, so what the hell *can* you tell us?" Elijah's tone was clipped with annoyance.

"What I do know," Quinn paused, glaring at Elijah, "is his condition will worsen. The effects of this, if the connection isn't severed, could lead ..."

"Could lead to what?" Elijah urged, tense with frustration.

"His death. They'll drain his life force, prey on his weaknesses, and cause depression, delusions, and anxiety."

"I'm not listening to this." Parker walked to the kitchen and poured himself water.

"You don't actually believe this, do you?" Camilla stood in protest, annoyed.

"Are you kidding me? You were *there*, Camilla," Hudson snapped and turned his attention back to Quinn. "What do we do to find out if this is a *thing*. If she's attached to my brother and maybe to us?"

"I have to make a call. Let me see what I can do." Quinn pulled her phone from her pocket and walked into the bathroom.

"There has to be some explanation. We don't have some stupid sister from the 1800s attached to us." Camilla said, annoyed.

Elijah's lower back ached, and his stomach churned. "What if that's what happened to Owen?"

Hudson's eyes widened, and he stiffened in his spot. "You mean ..."

Camilla stood and grabbed her car keys. "I'm going home."

"You shouldn't be by yourself, Camilla," Elijah protested.

"I'll do whatever the hell I want."

"Fine." Hudson stood exasperated and padded into the kitchen, standing next to his brother. Their judging eyes watched her, and the brothers whispered furiously to each other. Elijah could tell that Parker was losing the disagreement.

"This is crazy. If you guys want to buy into this crap, fine. But there's no such thing as possession or witchcraft." Camilla's face was tight, and her hands were balled into trembling fists.

Elijah walked over to Camilla and lowered her next to him on the couch. "With all of the information Owen has in the church, our experience at

Monroe's, what we just witnessed … you can't tell me you don't believe any of it."

"The church was Owen's need to understand things he couldn't find an explanation for. Plus, I have no idea what's in the church, except for research." Her eyes softened, and she whispered, "Or maybe his ideas were just drug-induced ramblings."

"You don't think Owen was murdered." There was a rageful essence behind his words.

"I have no idea *what* to think. No matter what, he made a selfish decision to drag us all into this crap, then leave it for us to sort through." Camilla's hands shook, and her face drained of color. "I don't feel good." She covered her mouth.

The air around them chilled. Camilla took flight through the living room; her limbs flailed as an unseen force catapulted her into the wall. She tumbled to the floor, rolling like a log across the wood. Quinn came charging out on high alert in time to witness Camilla being drug by a violent, unseen force. Camilla crashed into a dining room table. Glasses shattered, and bills scattered.

"Something's wrong with Parker." Hudson's panicked voice caught Elijah's attention.

Quinn rushed to Parker. He convulsed on the floor, and his eyes rolled into the back of his head, only the whites of his eyes showing. Slashes appeared across Parker's right cheek and neck, dripping blood down to the floor. The rancid scent of burning flesh filled the room, and Parker bellowed in agony. An archaic symbol shaped like a fish sprang up in welts, then transformed into blackened, singed, open wounds on his forearm. It reminded Elijah of the brands they put on the horses on the farm.

"What's happening?" Hudson's voice was strained. His hands hovered over his brother, afraid to touch him.

"He's being marked," Quinn's voice was shaky with horror.

Elijah scrambled to help Camilla but was blocked by an invisible wall. Camilla hungrily gasped, her lips turning pale-blue as a phantom rope drug her into the air by her neck, her legs flailing under her. She swung her fists frantically, trying to free herself from the attacker, then clawed at her neck, trying to loosen the invisible ligature. Elijah could see the muscles and tendons compacting in her neck as if a rope were tightening. Camilla suffered stigmata as the flesh on her arm was singed, too, with the symbol Elijah recognized as *Earth*.

Quinn threw her hand in the air. "I call on the protective divine Goddess to save us. All evil, seen and unseen, you are banished from this place. I protect everyone in this room from harm physically and mentally. This I make true three times, three times, three." Quinn yelled the chant once more, the vein in her neck pulsing as she fought against the poltergeist. A warm, loving wind whooshed through the room. In an instant, the chaotic scene ended.

Camilla, suspended in midair, fell and then crashed onto broken glass. She gasped and backed herself into a corner like a battered child fleeing their abuser. Blood flowed from her cheekbone under her left eye. Her body shook violently as Elijah wrapped his arms around her, holding her tightly, protecting her from the Shaw family demon tormenting her. He could hear her wheezing and knew the evil son-of-a-bitch had injured her throat. Her palms bled from embedded glass.

Elijah saw the ghost in the center of the room. It was the same entity in the forest with black hair and a white face. Two more stood behind the black-haired woman. A familiarity about their faces gnawed at him. Elijah had seen them before somewhere. No one but Elijah saw them, but they could hear their evil laughter, which whirled around them in stereo. The three women flickered like a hologram and then disappeared into another dimension. It hit Elijah where he'd seen them; they were dangling from the trees in the video. And they were in a photograph in an old newspaper he'd seen at the library when they were sorting information. The tortured souls were undoubtedly the murdered Shaw sisters.

It took about two hours to calm Camilla. She reluctantly rested in Elijah's bed, her breathing shallow and quick. Whimpering and trembling, she rattled Elijah's metal bed frame. She was buried in his blankets. Surprisingly, the neighbors hadn't called the cops. It was a feeble victory for the day. The last thing he needed was Bohannon and Jensen getting wind of a domestic disturbance at his residence. They were already circling around him like vultures.

The rain slowed, and Elijah opened his bedroom window, letting in a cool breeze from the bay. The seagulls squawked, and the occasional car driving by splashed through puddles.

"We need to talk—right now." Elijah grabbed Quinn's hand.

"I'll stay in here and watch her." Hudson took Elijah's chair next to Camilla and sipped on a cup of coffee.

Elijah yanked Quinn into the living room that was now empty. Hudson had already cleaned up the mess and vacuumed the floor. If you were to show up for a visit, there would be no way to tell such horrific, supernatural violence had occurred only a short time before. Parker laid in Hudson's bed, sleeping. The group was unsure if they should take them both to the hospital. Camilla refused to go, unsure how to answer the questions that would follow from the officers and her father. Parker passed out at the exact same time Camilla was released from the malevolent being that held her captive.

"What the fuck was all that?" Elijah said. "You show up in my life, and in less than twenty-four hours, I'm attacked by a phantom wolf, and my friend is torn apart by a poltergeist, and the other is possessed. When we went out into those woods, did you know this could happen?"

Quinn stilled, and guilt clouded her features. "I ... this wasn't supposed to happen."

"Are you fucking kidding me?" Elijah said furiously.

Sighing, she turned away from him, shame heavy on her shoulders. "I can't

... you wouldn't understand. Owen was right to not get you involved in all of this."

"That in there," Elijah jabbed a finger toward Camilla, "is all your damn fault, isn't it?" His voice deepened, and a vein throbbed in his neck.

Quinn's eyes narrowed, and her lips tightened. "Don't act like you wouldn't have gone out there without me. I've been going out there alone for weeks. Nothing's happened."

"Yes, we would have, you're right. But there's a difference between *knowing* there's a shark in the water and having no idea. You knew the dangers and didn't say anything."

Elijah guided her further away from the bedrooms and into the kitchen. "You could have said something, at least to me, when we were sitting in the car." All the lights were out, and the streetlamp from outside accentuated her defined cheekbones, casting shadows across her face. Quinn's energy shifted in confusing ways and became difficult for Elijah to interpret. "Why do I get the feeling there's more?"

"I didn't know *that* would happen. I thought we'd get some shitty EVPs and be on our way."

"Well, we're in the deep end *now*. Either you tell me the truth, or I'll get answers another way. I'll go to Shelly."

Quinn leaned against the windowsill, pinning her arms across her chest, sighing. She surveyed his face. Elijah knew she must have been contemplating whether or not he was bluffing. Finally, Quinn gently grabbed his hand and guided him to the front door.

QUINN SAT ACROSS FROM Elijah in her beat-up Ford truck. Explaining who and *what* she was would be tricky; there wasn't really a manual on how to tell people that you could read auras. Quinn had honed her ability to see energy fields around people when she'd moved in with her Nana. Defining and explaining the idea of spiritualism from her experiences was difficult. Truthfully, it would depend on how open Elijah was to the concepts.

Stalling, Quinn played with the Fluorite stone hanging from her rearview mirror. Elijah was studying her with those intense eyes of his; they changed color from hazel to dark gray within a matter of hours. It reminded her of the mood ring her Nana Evie bought her at a psychic festival when she was ten, right before she took her to her first Samhain. She cracked her driver-side window, hoping mosquitos wouldn't start to eat her alive. Heavy rain was still cascading from the sky, and a light spray tapped on the inside of her door. The air in her truck was thick, and the humidity made her skin sticky.

Earlier in the evening, after she made it home, she saged herself, using every protection chant she knew, covering every possible dark energy. She could use the help of her Nana Evie, but at this time, Nana wasn't speaking to her. Because of Nana's avoidance of her, Quinn had to search for her own protection chants. She'd learned specific protection chants by heart when she was a child, but this situation was far more complicated than protecting herself from an eight-year-old schoolyard bully. A need to cleanse her energy was strong and came on quick. And after getting to the apartment and witnessing the poltergeist attachment to the others, Quinn knew her intuition hadn't failed her.

Nana made it clear to her when she first started learning the craft that cutting connections to evil entities pronto was imperative—'life or death,' she'd say. Quinn's spellbooks were still scattered and opened on the floor of her apartment, on the off chance she might need them again. She cast a circle and closed it, but the black salt was still in its perfect shape, waiting for her to return.

Since Owen's death, she'd been carrying an Apache Tears stone, which was good for helping those who were grieving over the tragic loss of someone they loved. The rare volcanic stone also helped to ground her in the energies of the earth. Quinn could rely on the crystal's powerful vibrations; it would keep her safe from those who wished to harm her in her vulnerable emotional state.

Quinn rested her back against the door. Elijah smelled like Old Spice, laundry detergent, and whiskey, and she couldn't decide whether it was the odd scent or him that made her worries melt away. His rugged, defined jawline and rough exterior had developed after she saw him last, twelve years ago. Messy, his dark-brown hair was being ruffled by the warm breeze from outside. His broad chest was tense, and his shoulders rigid. She could tell he was pretty pissed off at her, and he had a right to be. She'd made a terrible decision. Directing her attention back to the topic at hand, she cleared her throat.

"Alright, let me start by saying this ..." When she exposed herself to people about her belief system, they had a tendency to do one of three things. Give her a glare like she was insane, stop talking to her, or continue being her friend. Usually, the latter resulted in Quinn having conversations about ghosts, magic, and mythical beings that would make others believe she was certifiable.

Quinn tapped her fingers on the steering wheel, weighing out what his reaction would be. She took in a deep breath, asking the universe to assist her in seeing his aura. Beautiful flickers of aqua and lavender flashed like lightning bugs around his torso and head.

She smiled, "I'm an organic witch."

"You were saying Shelly was raised a witch?" Elijah's thick eyebrows pinched together, and he turned to her, leaning against the door.

"Yes. My mom and dad were too. There are about seven generations that we can trace."

"What does *organic witch* mean?"

She smiled. "We're born with natural abilities to cast spells and connect to the universe around us. We're highly in tune with the ebb and flow of energies. Owen's natural ability was extremely advanced. He was awesome at elemental magic."

Elijah rubbed his forehead, then shifted in his seat, staying silent.

"I don't *fully* consider myself a witch; it's easier to tell people that because they need a label. I subscribe to my own mixture and style. I take the good from everything I study and apply it to my magic. My grandmother isn't elated about the concept. The reason I was excommunicated and kicked out wasn't only because I was helping Owen. I was also helping grow his abilities against his mother's wishes."

Quinn wanted to tell him everything she knew, but she had no clue if she could trust him. For all she knew, he could've been the skinwalker and the one who murdered Owen. But, after the shapeshifter bit him, that was highly unlikely. There was a spiritual war on the brink of erupting, and she needed to make sure she chose the correct side.

"What does that have to do with anything?" Elijah said impatiently.

"Give me a minute. This isn't easy to explain," Quinn said, holding up a hand.

Quinn had felt drawn to him as a child. Every time she visited (which wasn't much), her dreams for weeks afterward consisted of a man and a woman on a riverbank making love. As a ten-year-old girl, that gave Nana Evie some interesting breakfast conversations, to say the least. She could still smell the warm scent of cinnamon pancakes Nana made as Quinn sat next to her on the counter, dangling her feet, heat spreading across her cheeks as she explained the lovemaking. Quinn couldn't tell him she'd used him as bait to draw out what she thought killed Owen.

"I'm pretty sure what killed Owen is trying to kill you too, and that you used to be Samuel Shaw, Benjamin's brother." Quinn braced herself for Elijah's skeptic reaction.

Seconds seemed like decades as they ticked by, and silence fell over the cabin of the truck as she waited for his response.

I can't tell him I used him for bait.

Don't do it.

You can't do it.

"I used you as bait." Quinn blurted out, and short bursts of red sparks flashed in his aura.

Shit.

"In the woods, you said it wasn't a normal wolf. What the hell was it that you drew out?" Elijah's voice shook, and she could tell he was doing his best to keep his calm.

"The dirt and blood I took the other day after I shot the wolf, I used it to summon skinwalkers."

"This is insane." His tone was soft and shocked. "What is it with your family making bad decisions and making me pay for them?" His voice shifted into a coarse and furious tone she'd never heard before.

Heat spread through her body, and on some level, it was predictable that he would have that reaction. There was a long silence. Elijah turned his head, staring out the windshield.

"I'm gonna go now." She nodded to the door behind him. "If you don't mind?" She took her keys out of her pocket and put them in the ignition.

"No, wait. Let me process this." Elijah said and took one of Quinn's hands that gripped the steering wheel into both of his. He scooted in closer to her, and her focus wavered. All the muscles in her body relaxed with his touch, and her anxiety faded. His soothing energy pulsed off of her sweaty skin, and droplets from the storm tapped the back of her hot neck. Steam fogged the windshield and passenger windows.

"You used me as bait to prove what?"

"Owen's theory is that there was a skinwalker, and it used Samuel's identity to murder his family. Witness testimonies place Samuel in the city at the bar, but servant testimonies place him at the plantation at the same time. Which is impossible, unless—"

"A skinwalker committed the crime. Owen wrote something about those in his journal." Elijah spoke slowly, and she could tell he was thinking through what he was going to say. "I *have* had a wolf and crow stalking me. There was a crow at Owen's funeral. Then, of course, the two wolves at the church."

"Owen wanted to clear all past life karmic debt. He was trying to right a wrong by letting the world know the truth." Quinn slid out her lip balm and put it on.

"He wasn't only trying to clear the family's name; he was trying to clear Samuel's name. He was trying to prove *I* was innocent? What makes you believe it's a skinwalker?" Elijah swallowed heavily, and fidgeted with his leather bracelet. Quinn wondered what his psychic abilities consisted of and if he could sense whether she was telling the truth or not.

"A witch can only become a skinwalker if they murder a close member of their family. Which means a member of the Shaw family murdered Samuel's three sisters. And that someone is a skinwalker."

"*Is* ... that would make them one hundred and eighty years old. How do you explain the Reynolds? The family in the neighboring town."

"It could have been a practice run. Testing out the ritual."

"Or there could be more than one that changed around the same time." Elijah raised an eyebrow and sat back into the seat in shock. His shoulder rubbed against hers.

"I think Owen figured out *who* the dark witch was. The cops are searching for a killer they'll never find. They can change into whoever they want," Quinn said, and a pang of guilt rose in her stomach.

"That also means it could be anyone." Elijah flashed his bloody bandage at Quinn. "And I'm next."

Quinn slammed her hands on the steering wheel rapidly, and a shot of pain traveled through her wrist with each slam, cursing herself silently for her inability to think about others. "What the hell ... did ... I ... do ... to ... you?"

Tears brimmed her eyes, and she rested her forehead on the steering wheel.

"That thing started stalking me at Owen's funeral. It would have gotten to me one way or another. You just made it a little easier. The poltergeist of a very pissed-off woman has grabbed me on more than one occasion, leaving a handprint right here." Elijah pointed to his bandage. "I saw the ghost for a split-second upstairs, then she disappeared." He tore off the massive Band-aid and showed her the singed handprint and bite wound that somehow ended up in the same spot. The jagged savage tears were still covered in an anti-bacterial salve.

Quinn grazed her fingertips over the edge of the wounded flesh, careful not to touch. A pit of despair bloomed in her chest, and an agonizing sensation branched from her subconscious that she'd lost something. Except, she had no idea what it was, and it made her feel hollow. Tears rolled down her cheeks. She'd made a disastrous mistake, and there was no way for her to take back what she'd done to Elijah or Owen. Elijah's touch was unexpected but felt like home when he wiped away her tears with a gentle hand.

"We have to sit down and write out everything we know so far." Elijah withdrew her from her self-pitying thoughts, his tenor voice soft.

"He came to me for help the day he died." Quinn's bottom lip trembled. She cleared her throat, holding back her guilt.

Elijah scratched his chin, lowering his gaze. "He did?"

"I was pissed off at him about not telling you about Samuel, or in other words, *about yourself*. I told him to let you go and move on if he wasn't going to involve you. That you two were never going to be the way you were before. He was having nightmares of Benjamin's memories and your—or Samuel's— hanging after the crimes. There's something seriously evil in those woods that was tormenting him, and it's not a ghost." Quinn pointed in the direction of the Seven Sisters Road. "There are signs of necromancy and black magic. Whatever is out there—it's hungry for souls and its controlling the dead. That's why Parker and Camilla were attacked."

"What were you saying in the woods? When you were behind the tree?"

"It was a protection spell … for you. I also kinda called the cops."

"You fucking what?" Elijah's voice lowered as if he was trying to keep a secret. A crimson and orange-colored energetic dome pulsed around his head.

"Don't be mad." Quinn put both of her hands up, calming him. "It was the only way I could ensure you'd get out of there safely."

"Do you have any idea what you did? I went to jail." Elijah hopped out of the truck, slammed the door, and bolted toward his apartment. Drenched in seconds, he stopped, his head dropped, and he spun around. Elijah got back into the truck, slamming the door again, shaking the cab.

"I didn't have time to explain. You should trust me," Quinn snapped, throwing Elijah's words back to him from earlier in the evening.

"I did, apprehensively, by the way, and you've gotten me bitten and cast a summoning spell on me." His voice was heavy with frustration. Water rolled down over his defined nose and cheeks from his hairline. "I don't like it when people keep secrets. Although, it seems like everyone around me I trust has been keeping them from me lately."

Elijah rubbed the back of his neck, and she saw pain cross his face. Quinn could tell by how he turned away from her that he was talking about Owen and Riley. After a moment, his anger faded.

"This whole situation sucks," Elijah said, his voice tainted with regret.

"My parents died. They both did," she said quickly.

Elijah's eyebrows pinched, "when?"

The muscle in Quinn's temple twitched, and she clenched her jaw. "About ten years ago."

"Shelly never said anything about it."

"My mother's death hurt her. Quite a bit. They were close."

Elijah scooted closer and watched her with sad eyes. He was inches from her face, and she bit her bottom lip. "Are *we* connected somehow?" He asked.

"I'm still trying to figure that out, but if Owen was Benjamin, there's a good possibility that we're all connected, or at least *you* are." Quinn played with the Labradorite stone that dangled around her neck. It was the best gift

Nana had given her, and the stone protected her on most occasions.

"I'm not going to be able to tell Shelly any of this, am I?"

"She doesn't particularly care for Nana or me. It's been a while since Nana and Aunty spoke." Quinn's face flickered with disappointment.

Trying to escape the intensity, Quinn exited the truck, closing the door behind her, leaning against it. The warm rain drenched her, and she wished it could cleanse away the heartbreak of her cousin's death, as well as the isolation and depression that haunted her. Quinn did her best to keep her head in the game, and as far as she was concerned, she deserved a medal.

"What do you think is wrong with Parker?" She watched Elijah back away, deeper into the truck, giving her space. The rain lightened, and Quinn turned around, speaking through the partially open window.

"One of the sisters is attached to him, or maybe something darker. Witch legend around here says that there were six sisters. One was unaccounted for and removed from historical records. From what Nana said, they all practiced white magic. Except for Olivia. She practiced black magic." Quinn slid into the truck and squeezed Elijah's wet hand.

"Well, it's time to figure out who Olivia is then." Elijah grazed his knuckles over her chin, and pink sparkles flickered around him, just out of her peripheral vision.

Something was irritating about the name Olivia that stoked a fire of fury in Quinn that threatened to burn her alive. Stirring from deep in Quinn's soul, an ominous warning blasted through her thoughts: the woman behind the name Olivia would lead to her death.

Again.

17

HUDSON SLEPT ON THE couch, cocooned in a plush, black throw blanket when they made it back upstairs. His phone was tucked in his hoodie that was draped over the recliner, vibrating the chair. A light flickered under the blue fabric, and then the phone went silent. Elijah guessed it was Jess calling to see if Hudson could come to the bar.

Quinn's fair skin glowed in the dancing light from the late-night infomercials on the television. The air inside the apartment was suffocating and smelled like stale marijuana. The terrifying energy that consumed the room earlier faded, and Elijah was relieved that it no longer affected his thoughts. It made him happy to know he wasn't going crazy, that his whole life wasn't a colossal joke. Elijah peeked through his bedroom door. Camilla slept soundly on his bed. He checked on Parker, who was also still sleeping, in Hudson's bed. Parker panted, his chest rising and falling in quick movements—the symbol burnt onto his arm was covered with a bandage.

Parker's phone lit up in the corner on Hudson's nightstand, and the light on the back strobed. It was something Parker put on his phone to help him answer his phone at parties and clubs. In the pitch-black of the room, the dancing light stung Elijah's eyes. He walked over to the face-down phone and pressed the ignore button on the side.

Elijah guided Quinn to the back of the apartment and into a cluttered office. Elijah clicked on a lamp in the corner and then turned on the ceiling fan. He set a book on a stack of old newspaper clippings to keep them from flying around the room. The walls were covered in seventies wood paneling and reminded Elijah of the classic men's studies that were commonly designed into historic homes. An old fireplace was in the corner, and the iron door handle creaked as he opened the closet.

"This is all of the information we got from Shelly and Camilla. We can pack it all later today and take it to the church. That way everything, will be in one location. You might have a better idea of what to look for since you were working with Owen on aspects he wasn't telling anyone else about." Elijah paused, wondering if he should show her the journal.

Quinn's eyes scanned through the room, going over all the boxes and piles of information. "The protection spell I cast around the two of them will only last for a short while. Whatever entity that was in this apartment tonight will be back. We need to take them to the church. Having the least amount of interfering energies around is the most ideal. We need to create a circle of protection, then find a severing spell to help them separate themselves. We also need to find out if the poltergeist is connected to Hudson too. But, at this point, if it was, I think it would have made itself known," Quinn said matter-of-factly. "I'll go search the library when we take them there and see if there are any spells that might help."

"Owen came to me too. On the day he died. He tried to call me like you told him to. I was too much of an asshole to speak to him." Elijah rubbed the back of his neck and sighed in regret.

"He hurt you, Elijah, in the worst possible way. Don't sell yourself short. What he did was beyond unforgivable. He made choices too." Quinn hopped up, sitting on the desk in the middle of the room and rubbed her forehead in disbelief, then wiped her eyes. "You're a good friend."

"You were a good cousin. You sacrificed a lot to help him."

Quinn sighed and crossed her feet at her ankles, leaning back onto her hands. Elijah eased in closer to her, sitting next to her on the desk. His shoulder naturally gravitated toward hers. "When we were being attacked by Alpha—"

"Alpha?"

"That's the name I gave the wolf that's been following me. Or now the skinwalker. Anyway, something happened I never experienced before."

"What's that?"

Elijah told her about his vision and the blond mystery man's face. Goosebumps formed on his arms when he told her the last part. "It was my face. I saw the symbol on the tree. The Shaw mansion was on fire in the middle of the circle."

Quinn's eyes widened with excitement. "That's amazing. That sounds like astral projection and retrocognition at the same time. You need to write down every detail." Quinn snapped her fingers. "We need to go back out there. There's something those spirits wanted you to find."

Elijah stood, turning toward Quinn, easing his hips between her legs. He rested a hand on her knee, testing the waters.

"I'm jealous, by the way, that you have those abilities." Quinn smiled.

"They aren't as awesome as you might think. What's it like doing magic?"

"You have to be confident in what you're doing. *Believe* in the universe. Attune yourself to its positives and negatives. You also need to pay attention to the details."

Elijah drug his fingertips along the outside of her leg, stopping at her hip, and he could hear her breath catch in her throat as he pressed his hips against the inside of her thighs.

There was something complicated and familiar about being in her presence. He wanted to move away, knowing he shouldn't be touching her, but at the same time was inexplicably drawn into her. His lips were close to her ear, and he inhaled the earthy and floral scent of her skin.

The worries that plagued his mind vanished, and he struggled to focus. Quinn had *definitely* cast a spell on Elijah, compelling him to absorb the surge of intoxicating adrenaline and craving for her that spread through his body with her closeness like an addiction. He wrapped his free hand around the back of Quinn's neck, leaned into her, and his cheek brushed hers. For some reason, the action was natural, like they'd done it a million times before.

A driving desire to taste her skin teased him like nothing he'd experienced before. Licking his lips, Elijah's hand trembled on her hip as they remained quiet, sharing an intimate moment in silence, drinking in each other's presence.

His full lips brushed her soft cheek, and she closed her eyes, longing. Quinn's body melted into his. The pressure of her curvy form against him awakened a desire that he knew would never fade. Déjà vu engulfed him, and his logical mind fought with him, telling him to back away. Quinn's breath grazed over his lips, and he closed his eyes, waiting to taste her.

The high-pitched sound of his phone ringing in the quiet caught him off guard, and he pressed his forehead into her cheek. Elijah groaned, and Quinn rested her forehead on his shoulder.

She pressed her hand against his chest, smiling. "Your heart's beating so fast."

Elijah wrapped his hand around hers, holding it against his chest. He bit his bottom lip, sighed, and yanked his phone out. Riley was calling him.

"You've got to be kidding me," he mumbled. Hesitating, he considered turning his phone off completely. There was a lot of work to do, both research and magical protection wise. But, making out with a hot redhead was now on the top of his list. He growled, annoyed with his need to be loyal to *everyone*. "I have to take this. Stay right here." Elijah backed toward the door, keeping his eyes fixed on her, and tripped on a box.

Quinn giggled and rubbed her bottom lip with her thumb. "You might want to watch where you're going."

"Don't go anywhere," he said, pointing at Quinn.

She smiled and winked, and he bolted out of the room and shut the door behind him. Elijah hurried into the living room and through the back door, being careful to leave it cracked. The door locked automatically, and neither he nor Hudson was given the key from Mrs. Steever, even after one year.

"This better be good. I'm busy," he said, annoyed.

"Elijah?" Riley's voice was thick with distress, and he heard her take a ragged breath. She'd been crying. "I've been trying to get ahold of someone to come get me, but no one is answering."

"What's the matter?" His voice softened. He knew *that* tone because he'd been the cause of it more than once.

"I need someone to come get me. I'm at the Thirsty Parrot."

Elijah meandered toward a balcony window and looked in on Quinn, who was flipping through a file. "I'm kind of busy right now. You can't take an Uber?"

"I tried, but Dylan put a block on my credit card and our bank card."

Elijah sighed, knowing he was going to regret getting involved in her relationship with Dylan. "I'll be there. Give me a couple minutes." Elijah clicked end, racing back into the apartment.

"She's gonna kill you, man." Hudson was awake but still had his eyes closed, and Elijah strode past him and back to the office.

"Yeah, I know."

Riley was always able to yank him back into what he knew was a disastrous liaison. Elijah wasn't entirely sure how this would go over, and he was hoping Quinn didn't want to go with him. The last thing he wanted was Quinn and Riley in the vehicle together. It was a level of drama he wasn't prepared for.

"Hey …" His voice was soft and low.

"I heard." Quinn nodded toward the cracked balcony window, turning her back to him. "Go. I'll stay here and go through all this stuff."

"You want to go?" Elijah said, striding to Quinn, placing his hand on her lower back.

"No. I have reading to do." She walked away from him to the desk, flipped through a file in her hand, and removed certain pages, setting them on the desk.

Hesitantly, Elijah kept his eyes on her, judging whether or not she was frustrated with him. He grabbed his backpack from the floor next to the desk and removed Owen's journal.

"Here, maybe this will help." Elijah handed it to her, then gripped the book as she tugged. Apprehensively, he let go.

"You can trust me, Elijah."

"I want to. I do."

Shifting gears, Quinn set down the journal on the desk, her demeanor lightening. "We have to figure out how to check to make sure there's a poltergeist connected to Parker and Camilla before we do a spell we have no time for."

"Let me help then. Hopefully, you can fill me in as to what's going on." Hudson peeked through the door and rested his head on the doorframe. "There's apparently more to Owen's story than we all are familiar with."

Elijah gave Hudson a smile of encouragement. "We'll get it all figured out." He walked toward the door, then paused mid-stride, turning to Quinn. "I'll be back. And when I am, we *all* need to have a talk."

Elijah didn't want to leave, certainly not without the journal, but they were running out of time. He knew that whatever they were all going through would change the course of their lives forever.

THERE WAS A TREMENDOUS amount of information to go through. It was nearly impossible for Quinn to concentrate, knowing that Elijah had so easily left her to rescue his ex-girlfriend. Quinn had thought that everything Owen collected was at the church. His search for the truth and passion for knowledge had no boundaries. That was clear to Quinn after uncovering the treasure trove of research at Elija's house. Quinn had no idea Owen would turn into a hermit and cut off his family once he discovered their origins. A pang of guilt pulsed through Quinn as she thought about his last moments alive and the way she'd inadvertently helped him get to the noose. Giving him information about spell casting he wasn't ready for was her first mistake among many. The second, not calling Shelly and telling her what he was doing. Quinn picked up Owen's journal and flipped through his notes.

Hudson sat in a chair chugging an energy drink, quickly flipping through files, writing notes. Quinn was familiar with silence when people first tried to figure out how to ask about the paranormal. She'd helped her Nana on some protection spells and banishments of harmful energies a hundred times since she'd been eleven, and regular everyday people always responded with the same hesitant reaction. Her Nana used to tell her to be patient and keep in mind that most individuals new to such experiences are having a dramatic shift in their reality and fundamental belief systems.

So many things were encompassed by the unknown. The Earth was ancient. Control of its vibrations and manipulation of its elements was a practice that had been in use for millennia. Ironically, those unfamiliar with the teachings called it "New Age." despite some metaphysical belief systems predating Christianity.

Surprisingly enough, Hudson showed no signs of judgment; his expression was more of curiosity. He ruffled his short, ebony-colored, curly hair in thought, glancing at Quinn out of the corner of his eye.

Finally, Hudson stood abruptly and walked out of the room, then a couple seconds later walked back in and set a bottle of whiskey on the desk. Hudson put two shot glasses in front of Quinn and himself, then flipped the chair around backward; he straddled it, facing her. He filled both glasses and slid one toward her. Quinn set the journal on the desk.

"Here's the deal. I know what I saw, and I know what you did, but if we're gonna do this, I need to have a few drinks first." Hudson watched her closely, waiting for a response.

Quinn took the shot, shaking her head as the liquor burned its way down, warming her chest. "I don't like to spend a bunch of time explaining shit that will make you feel like you're on a bad drug trip, but here's the short. I'm a witch, ghosts exist, different dimensions do as well, and I have a tendency to kick the ass of evil supernatural entities with my Nana. I'm still relatively new to hunting and tracking. Owen and I are both descendants of a long line of witches." Quinn paused, evaluating whether or not she should continue, tucking a curly, red lock of hair behind her ear. "Owen was the reincarnation of Benjamin Shaw. We both believe," Quinn hesitated, doing her best to contain the pain of the correct past tense term concerning her cousin. "Sorry, Owen *believed* Elijah is the reincarnation of Samuel Shaw, but now it's up to me to prove it."

Hudson laughed and gave a "holy shit" expression, then took another shot. "Did you know what was out there?"

"I had an idea."

"You could have told us."

"Think about what you just said," Quinn fired back quickly, keeping eye contact over the whiskey bottle as she poured them both another shot.

"Fair enough, this is kinda a 'gotta see to believe' type of deal." Hudson took another shot. "Now to the million-dollar question, how do we fix whatever is going on?"

"Honestly?"

"I'll do whatever's necessary to protect my brother."

Quinn tossed Owen's journal to him. "Those are Owen's most recent notes. We have to make a list of the *entire* Shaw family. Even extended family. We need to find someone named Olivia Shaw." Quinn whirled her finger in the air. "Our problem right now is we have a rapid-fire of paranormal shit coming at us and no organization of information."

"I have no problem with organization. This whole mess was driving me insane. Elijah has a way of … well …"

"He's a mess overall." Quinn smiled at the thought of him.

"Yeah, you could say that." Hudson laughed. "But, I guess that's one of his many charms, at least that's what the ladies say."

Heat rose in Quinn's cheeks at the recollection of the intoxicating scent of Elijah's sweat blended with aftershave, the warmth of his skin. Quinn cleared her throat. "We each need to write down notes and experiences, then compare them." Quinn leaned over and opened the book. "This part of the journal says that Samuel was buried in an unmarked grave, and his body was stolen later that evening. From what I know, their father, Edgar, was an amateur cartographer. According to Owen's past life hypnotism sessions, he has memories of Benjamin and Edgar moving Samuel's body. According to these notes, they did it to protect him from grave robbers. Edgar marked Samuel's final resting place on one of the family's property maps." Quinn tapped a box labeled "maps" and unloaded its contents, then unfolded a copy of an old map and pinned it to the wall. "This is one Owen got from Emma, a distant relative of the Shaw's."

Quinn studied the map. A familiarity about it called to her. The map had nothing more than a basic depiction of the Shaw land, there was no indication of where the mansion had resided. The only directional markings on the map were a rose compass. East, South, and West were labeled. Quinn ran her fingertips over the spot where "North" should have been marked. The paper was rough, and she could see grooves where someone had removed the prominent N symbol. The map was messy and different from Edgar's other pieces of work she'd seen.

This had to of been made in a hurry. Edgar's other works are beautiful. This one is sloppy.

Silence fell over the room as they both worked intently. Quinn took out a newspaper article from a large envelope about the murders; there was a black and white picture of Samuel Shaw at the top. His shoulders were square, and his blond hair was shaggy, he was dressed in elegant clothing, and his almond-shaped eyes had a hidden despair behind them. An almost overwhelming need to retch all over the desk made her jaw clench. Out of all the research she'd done with Owen, she'd never seen a picture of him. Samuel Shaw was the man she dreamt about as a child. The one she'd been making love to on the shore. She'd seen his face too many times to forget his intense, passionate energy, and even now, it seeped out, wrapping around her from the image. She skimmed over the article.

SAVANNAH, GA - 1896
Since the horrendous murder of the beautiful Shaw sisters, their brother, and murderer Samuel, a demon and fiend still stalks the beautiful streets of our beloved city, unchecked and unscathed. When will this madness end, and when will he be punished? Miserable—lamentable—horrible is the handling of this travesty by the courts.

Quinn slapped down the newspaper, despair filled her heart, and an urge to rip the article to shreds filled her. Instead, she sighed with exhaustion, turning her attention to Hudson.

"What do you think Camilla knows?"

"Honestly? Nothing. I'm pretty sure she's only continuing this because of her career."

A broken, hoarse voice interjected, "Is that what you think?" Camilla's bottom lip trembled. Cascading rain beat against the windowsill in the silence.

Camilla rubbed her temples, clenching her eyes shut. A thick, scabbed rope burn marked her neck the color of dried blood and grave dirt. Tears brimmed in her eyes, and she brushed her bedhead hair from her face.

Guilt overwhelmed Quinn. She knew it was a poltergeist of one of the Shaw sisters, possibly all three, that had come back to the apartment. Attaching themselves to Parker, Camilla, and Elijah. Figuring out which one was attached to whom so they could sever the chords would be the tricky part.

"Camilla? I didn't ... I wasn't trying to sound ..."

Camilla fled into the living room.

"Excuse me." Hudson went after Camilla, and Quinn followed. "You can't leave. You shouldn't be alone right now. None of us should."

Camilla ignored Hudson and gathered her belongings, furiously shoving them into a pink overnight bag. She swiped up her keys.

"He's right," Quinn added, doing her best to support her new acquaintance.

Hudson placed a hand on Camilla's shoulder, and she shoved it away. "Don't you touch me. I should have listened to my father when he told me you all were trash."

"Fine." Hudson's shoulders stiffened. "Go." Hudson motioned toward the door. "I don't give a shit." Hudson turned his back to her.

Camilla glanced at Quinn and then left, slamming the door behind her.

"Is she gonna be ..." Quinn stopped mid-sentence, her stomach was doing flips, "alright?"

The hair on Quinn's arms stood on end, and vertigo whirled through her. Quinn stumbled, her vision blurred.

Something evil is coming. I can feel it in the air.

"She need ... don't let her leave." Quinn stuttered, unable to speak.

Cold sweats spread across her body, and her knees weakened, giving out from underneath her. Quinn collided with the floor, her right shoulder cracked, and pain exploded through her back and chest. She scrambled to stand, but her legs were too weak. Quinn yelped in pain.

"Holy shit, are you alright?" Hudson hurried to her, placing a tender hand on her cheek.

Thickness spread through her throat, and the putrid scent of damp ashes caused her eyes to water. She searched frantically to find out where the phantom smell emerged from. The color drained from Quinn's face as she fought to breathe. A terrifying realization crashed its way into Quinn; it wasn't a phantom odor from an angry spirit. Quinn huffed the scent of ashes out from her lungs. Hudson pulled her into his lap and cradled her.

Acid and a thick substance crept up her throat, coating the base of her tongue. Quinn coughed, and ashes spurted from her mouth, scattering across the floor. Hudson, shocked, held her tightly as she threw up messy chunks of grey and black ashes that were dry as a bone. Quinn's body convulsed, and she grunted in pain as a symbol singed its way onto the flesh of her left forearm.

A woman's disembodied whistling reverberated through the room. Unable to speak, she thought to herself desperately, reciting her personal protection spell.

Goddess Hecate, I call upon you to help protect me from evils seen and unseen. I cast out all uninvited souls, human and inhuman, fighting for control of my consciousness.

19

ELIJAH ADJUSTED HIS STILL damp camo ball cap, and clicked the glow button on his black sports watch, checking the time. It was a quarter past one when he had arrived at the Thirsty Parrot. Riley sat at a patio table, texting furiously when he slowed to a stop. Her brown, wavy hair was tied back in a messy bun, and loose tendrils framed her face. Rain poured over the umbrella she sat under, thunder cracked and boomed, rattling Elijah's windshield. Instinctively, Riley smiled when she saw him, and Elijah noticed for the first time that his heart hadn't skipped a beat like it used to. She slung her purple backpack over her shoulder, dashing away from the bar. Elijah could tell she was eager to leave the whole night behind her. He reached over and unlocked the door, shoving it open. Riley tossed her bag in the back seat. Her floral perfume wafted into Elijah's face and he took in a deep breath savoring the scent. Recalling the still-raw pain she caused him, he sighed, emotionally exhausted. Riley shut the passenger door and got comfortable in her seat, adjusting her Thirsty Parrot T-shirt.

Despite the weather, the historic Savannah streets were bustling. Numerous night owls strolled through the dank cobbled streets, laughing. A group of seven college men stumbled into a 1920s diner half a block down River Street. The sweet aroma of pancakes drifted through his window and made him long for hash browns from Monroe's. A horse-drawn carriage carried a group of tourists down the street. And the voice of a ghost-tour guide from a trolly boomed over a speaker as it passed, then faded into the distance.

A flickering neon pink and white sign with "24 Hour Tarot Readings" caught Elijah's attention. His eyes gravitated toward the darkened window of the fortune teller he'd noticed while Allison kicked his ass two days ago. The window was opened slightly now, and smoke flowed out from underneath the curtains. There was something about the mysterious woman that called to him on a psychic level.

Two drunk girls whizzed by on beach cruiser bikes, blaring rap over a blue tooth speaker, jolting him from his thoughts. The two rain-drenched girls splashed through mud puddles and narrowly missed Elijah's Nova as they passed. He was still trying to process what Quinn had explained to him only twenty minutes ago, and after replaying it a few hundred times, he *knew* somewhere inside she wasn't bullshitting him. Quinn hadn't meant any of them harm. She was only trying to figure out who killed her cousin. Her reasons for not trusting Elijah were sound. He could have been the skinwalker for all she knew.

There had always been something different about Owen that Elijah could never put his finger on, and there was an ongoing joke that Owen had an old soul. The consideration of it made him curious about how old his soul was. He was Owen's blood brother at another time, so Elijah's connection to him was unbreakable. Benjamin and Samuel's existences were intricately woven together by love, anger, forgiveness, and loyalty.

"Elijah, did you hear me?" Riley's tired voice drew Elijah back from his spiritually consuming contemplations.

"No, sorry."

"Are you alright? You've been staring at that tarot reader's window for a minute."

"Yeah, I'm just tired." Elijah rubbed his eyebrow, trying not to look annoyed.

"What the hell happened to your back seat?"

"That's a long story." Elijah squinted at the thought of the cost of fixing his damaged baby, then sighed at his current reality. Adjusting to the massive transformation in his belief system was taking its toll. He'd trusted every step he made his whole life, but now the ground was too shaky. His foundation was crumbling, and it was only a matter of time before a crevasse opened and swallowed him whole.

"Thank you for coming to get me." Riley smiled sweetly and twisted a silky strand of hair around her finger. Elijah couldn't help but chuckle. She appeared innocent, but she was most definitely anything but. She must have thought he was born yesterday. He knew right away she wanted something.

"You're welcome," he said quickly. "You want me to drop you at home? Or at your mom's?" Elijah knew the twenty-minute ride would be a test of his will.

"Actually ..." Riley hesitated and continued playing with her hair. Red and blue strobing lights from the bar window illuminated the car, and two middle-aged drunk guys walked out the heavy wooden door, laughing and stumbling down the narrow sidewalk. "I was hoping I could come to your place." She gave a hopeful smile.

Elijah raised his eyebrows and gripped his steering wheel. "Oh. Uh ... no, not tonight. Raincheck?" He knew what she was trying to do, and he didn't want to be the backup fuck or the make your boyfriend jealous fuck. Riley's smile vanished, and she instantly yanked on her lap-belt and turned toward the window.

There was a shit show to take care of at his apartment already, and there was no way Riley needed to *find out* about any of the supernatural crap going down. Regardless of whether Owen thought she was a part of their "Soul Tribe." Not to mention he was still trying to figure out how to wrap his head around all the information himself. Trying to sift through supernatural occurrences at that magnitude was maddening.

"You have someone over there?" Riley's face hardened, and she straightened her skin-tight, yellow, Thirsty Parrot T-shirt.

"Kinda, yeah," he said sharply.

"Huh ..." Her hazel eyes narrowed at him thoughtfully. "Who is it? Jess. It's Jess, isn't it?"

"It's someone you don't know."

She rested her chin in her palm and her elbow on the door. "So, this is the end?"

Staying silent, he made the decision for her. Elijah turned down the block and headed to the outskirts of town toward her mother's house. Taking her back home to Dylan would be a colossal mistake. Elijah needed to get back to Quinn and help her go through the files and information. He had to find a treasure that didn't exist—before he or anyone else he knew was abducted and murdered by drug dealers. The pressure of the last week closed in on him, and a throbbing pain spread through his forehead. There was still a poltergeist, past life mystery, and a damn Skinwalker to sort out as well. Elijah rolled his shoulders and thought about the comfort of his bed.

"Elijah, maybe we should get back together. I miss you, and I made a huge mistake." Riley scooted closer to him.

Heat surged through Elijah's neck, and his hands trembled with anger. "You *did* make a mistake. A *couple* of times." Elijah turned on his radio to stop the conversation, but it failed.

"I understand I've been fucked up to you, but you weren't that great to me either. We both did things that we shouldn't have done to each other." Her voice was firm but pleading at the same time. She stopped herself in the middle of the leather bench seat, watching him seductively.

Elijah straightened his shoulders, keeping his eyes on the road, and turned the radio up. Riley turned it back down. "I'm trying to talk to you."

"I'm trying to listen to Foreigner."

Riley's lips set in a hard line.

Elijah rubbed the back of his neck and fell into an old familiar role. "I don't have anything to say."

"After everything that's happened? With Owen dying ..."

"Don't you say his name," Elijah said firmly, pointing at her but keeping his hand on the large steering wheel.

"I started reflecting on my life and what I'm doing with it," she continued. "The one good thing I had was you, and we both ... well, at least *I* have learned a lot. We could make it work. Life's too short not to try." She placed her hand on his thigh, and he swallowed heavily. Riley was using emotionally torturous warfare; she was wholly aware of what that spot did to him. He took off his hat and raked his fingers through his dark, messy hair. He slid his hat back on and cast an uneasy peek at her, doing his best to keep his attention on the road. Her hazel eyes were full of innocence, and she gave him a sexy smile, attempting to reel him back. It spoke volumes about how desperate she was. Elijah knew that if he gave in to his desire for her, the next morning would be a disaster. Shutting out Quinn before he could find out where it was going would be stupid. He wasn't entirely sure Riley *was* what he wanted anymore, and giving her false hope the way she'd done to him numerous times would be cruel.

Elijah adjusted his position in his seat nervously, and then eased to a stop at a red light. Now that his dream of working out their problems came to fruition, it didn't feel right. He'd changed, but she was still the same. He removed her hand from his leg and set it on the seat.

"He cheated on you, didn't he?"

Riley's eyes teared, and she covered her mouth.

"Well, how about that?" Elijah raised his eyebrows. "We're toxic for each other. Our relationship destroyed friendships and families. That's a place I'd rather not go back to." There was a finality to his voice that even he didn't expect.

Tears welled in Riley's eyes, and she bit her bottom lip. "You're an asshole, you know that?"

"You're not the only one who's been changing, Riley, and repeating the same shit over and over is tiring. What I've been doing with my life isn't working, and it's gotta stop."

"It's because of this *other* girl, isn't it?" Her voice was rigid with disdain.

"Actually, no." Elijah raised his eyebrows, then smiled at her accurate assessment of his desire to make everyone happy. It even further solidified his belief in her manipulation. "I started considering a change way before her. What I *do* know is I'm not doing this with you again. It's not good for either of us." Every time she gave him hope and took it away, it destroyed him. The excruciating pain had happened so many times that he was numb to the destruction it created in his life. He was a glutton for punishment, but even Elijah had his limits.

There was something on a grand spiritual scale happening to him. The bizarre events unfolding in Elijah's life at such a rapid pace told him things were never going to be the same. Quinn's presence unearthed buried intuitions within him, and after the unexplainable things he'd witnessed, it was freeing to know he wasn't alone. There was information on the edge of his consciousness, clawing to free itself from the pits of his subconscious. Maybe even from past lives. And he wasn't too sure if he wanted to find out what hid there.

Elijah turned down a country road, and the city lights faded away as he drove into the darkness. Raindrops on the hood of his car sparkled like diamonds in the intermittent passing streetlights. The high-pitched ringing of his cell phone withdrew him from his thoughts, and he snatched it from the seat, relieved it was Quinn. "Hey, what's up?" he said sweetly. Riley snuck a glimpse at the screen and scooted away from Elijah when she heard the soft tone.

Hudson's frantic and breathy voice burst through the phone. "Elijah, you need to get back here, man. Like fucking yesterday." The sound of him drinking came through, and Elijah knew he was downing a shot.

Elijah straightened his shoulders, panic setting in. "Why are you calling from Quinn's phone? Is she alright?"

"My phone wouldn't wor—"

"Is she alright?"

"You need—"

"Are Camilla and Parker okay?"

"What's wrong with Camilla and Parker?" Riley interjected, sniffling and wiping her nose with a napkin from a fast-food restaurant. Elijah pinched his phone between his shoulder and ear, then gave her a dismissive wave, telling her to be quiet.

"I'll tell you if you let me talk." There was a brief silence then Hudson continued. "Quinn collapsed and passed out. She started coughing up ashes. And the symbol of Fire appeared on her arm; it's singed into her skin."

"Are you serious?"

"She's in your bed right now. She told me she was fine and to not call an ambulance. She's asking for you, though. Just ... back ... now ... before."

"Hudson ... you there?"

Elijah held his phone away from his ear and saw a pixelated screen. Static shot through his hand, sending a searing pain like an oil burn through his fingers. He dropped it onto the seat. Then the screen went black.

"Shit. Shit. Shit. This isn't good."

A disembodied voice hissed through his phone and then his radio.

"What ... what was that?" Riley choked out.

The dashboard lights flickered, and Elijah recalled his flashlight in the woods. His heart sank, and the long bench seat under them vibrated as the engine stalled.

"What's happening?" Riley wiped tears from her cheeks, sadness turning to alarm.

"I have no idea. I wish I knew." Elijah shot her a glance, and a pang of guilt filled him about their conversation. He was blunt sometimes, and it was both a blessing and a curse.

Panic surfaced in Elijah when he cranked the engine and pumped the gas, and the engine sputtered, refusing to turn over. "Not ... fucking ... again."

A chorus of clicking and buzzing from Cicadas outside in the trees surrounding them came in through the windows, breaking the swelling tension in his car.

"I've told you, I don't know how many times, that you needed to get rid of this thing," Riley scolded.

"It was my father's. I'm not getting rid of it," Elijah snapped, resting his forehead on the steering wheel, continuing to turn the engine over unsuccessfully.

Icy air settled in his car, frosting his windows. "Paint it Black" by The

Rolling Stones played over the radio, and goosebumps spread across his arms. The hairs on the back of his neck stood.

"Why is it cold in here?" Riley's breath steamed the passenger window, and she wrapped her arms around herself. The dim lights of the dashboard cast shadows over her high cheekbones and narrow nose, and she glanced around as if sensing someone watching them.

Glass exploded into the car, and she shrieked, reaching for Elijah. Before he could grab her, Riley folded in half and catapulted out the passenger window onto the grass. Elijah shoved open the passenger door and scrambled across the bench seat to get to her. The headlights from the Nova lit up the marshland and Riley's horrified face. Her voice shook with terror as she screamed and was violently dragged across the muddy grass toward the water. Clawing at the ground, she desperately called for Elijah.

Elijah sprinted after Riley as she kicked, fighting against the phantom attacker. Before Elijah could get to her, she was in the murky water of the Savannah marsh. Elijah charged into the water, diving in as Riley's head submerged, and her screams turned to watery screeches. His eyes burned as he fought to find her under the murky marsh water. Cattails and grass wrapped around him, restraining his movements, and dirt stirred, forming an underwater tornado, making it difficult for him to find her. His chest ached with the need to breathe, and he swam to the surface.

Gasping, he spotted her thrashing under the surface of the water fighting the unseen devil. Elijah dove again, this time wrapping his arm around her waist, but something tugged at her, pulling them both deeper. The water began to cool, and Elijah's chest tightened. His mind was tired, and his legs burned. He recalled the protection spell Quinn had said earlier to protect Camilla and thought it to himself with desperation.

I call on the goddess to protect ... shit, what was the rest? To protect us from evils seen and unseen.

In an instant, the struggle ended, and tension under the silty water released. Elijah towed Riley to the surface, his lungs burning. She was limp with exhaustion, and if he hadn't felt her heart beating on his chest, he would have thought she was dead. As if the universe was listening to his troubled mind, Riley coughed out water, gulping hungrily for air as he swam her to shore. The wounds on Elijah's face stung from the algae-filled water, and stabbing pain radiated from his ribs. He did his best to block out the debilitating fatigue that rushed over him, his body weakening with each stroke of his arm. The freshwater and dirt felt like acid on his skinwalker bite.

Elijah reached the shore and laid Riley down on her back. She rolled to her side, clinging to him. Elijah wrapped his arm around her protectively and scanned the now serene waters. He didn't have the slightest clue what he was searching for, but he had the undying sense that something sinister was out there watching him. The evil entity wasn't only waiting to destroy him. It was *punishing* him.

20

RILEY SAT IN THE living room with Hudson, and they were quietly exchanging details about their personal experiences of the night. Hudson had loaned Riley some dry clothes, and she gratefully sipped on a hot cup of chamomile tea. Her fingertips were scratched, and two handprints, like the one on Elijah's arm, were burned onto her ankles. An upside-down triangle had appeared on her right forearm. Elijah was able to discern it as the runic symbol for Water, also another one of the symbols on the trees in the graveyard.

Besides being visibly shaken, Riley appeared to be processing the whole experience surprisingly well. Elijah tried calling Camilla after learning about her departure, but there was no answer. Parker was asleep in Hudson's bed, and Elijah could sense an entity weighing heavy in the room. The air felt like soup as he walked through it and hovered over Parker, who was breathing steadily and drooling on his brother's pillow. Parker's eyes shifted furiously under his eyelids. Hudson said he'd woken for about twenty minutes and then fallen back asleep. Elijah half expected a poltergeist to jump out of the darkest corners of the room and pull him into hell-filled oblivion.

Elijah shut Hudson's bedroom door, and quietly padded across the hall to his room. Quickly closing the door, he tried to block Riley's view from behind him. Elijah gently sat on his bed next to Quinn, studying her as she slept. Her beautiful, curly red hair was messy and spread out over his pillow like a halo. A confusing longing for her stirred in his soul.

Quinn's cheek was warm in the palm of Elijah's hand, and the softness of her skin removed him temporarily from the chaos of the past few days. His clothes were still damp, and his black T-shirt clung to his chest. Elijah's muscles burned every time he moved, and it reminded him of his freshmen year on the football team.

"You're back." Quinn's eyes fluttered open.

Elijah brushed a strand of her curly hair away from her soft face.

"Sorry, it took so long. Are you all right?" His fingers lingered on her face, and he skimmed his thumb across her jawline. He picked up her arm, studying the scabbed fire symbol wound on her forearm. Elijah's heart sank, knowing that she wasn't immune and that she was now attached to the same unknown fate as him and his friends.

Quinn groggily lifted herself, resting her back on the headboard. Elijah slipped off his shoes and gave a tired grin. She was wearing his Beaufort High football jersey. The window above his bed was open, and a humid, warm breezed drifted in, as insects bumped against the screen. The scent of wet dirt and seawater wafted through the open window, instantly relaxing him as much as possible after the hell he'd gone through in the past twenty-four hours.

"I'll be fine. We'll talk about that in a minute. I should be asking you that question. Why are you wet?" She raised her eyebrows, and the light expression from her face disappeared. "You were attacked."

"I'm not even gonna ask how you know that, but it wasn't me. It was Riley." He pointed to his jersey, and she shrugged.

"I hope you don't mind."

"No, it's fine." He pointed to his wet shirt. "Do you mind? I need to change."

"Not at all." She turned toward the open window.

Elijah tossed his damp hat across the room and slipped off his shirt, putting a dry one on.

"I'm gonna have to go by Camilla's sorority. I want to make sure she's alright."

"She probably needs time to herself right now to process everything. A lot has happened in the past few weeks. Plus, she's in a house full of people." Quinn said, pointing at him assuringly.

"You're right." Elijah sighed.

"But, we should find her as soon as humanly possible. That protection spell I cast will only last so long." Quinn raked her fingers through her messy hair.

"Hudson said he called her sister, she's going to go by and check on her. If she's not back or doesn't call by tomorrow morning, I'm going to find her." Elijah said firmly.

"I'll go with you. Is Riley alright? What happened to her?"

"She's as okay as she can be." He slid off his pants and grabbed a pair of sweats from the top of his cluttered dresser. "It was crazy—she was there one minute, then the next she was being dragged from my car and getting drowned in the marsh. It's probably better that we all stick together because whatever's happening, it's gonna get worse. I can sense it."

He turned around just in time to catch her sparkling emerald eyes on his butt, and pink spread across her face, hiding her freckles. He cleared his throat, pushing back the thought of making love to his dead best friend's cousin. He pulled on the sweats and sat next to her on the bed. The whole interaction was surreal yet natural.

"When I blacked out, I'm pretty sure I had a past life memory. It was after looking at a picture." Quinn leaned over and grabbed a copy of the front page of a historical newspaper.

Elijah turned to her, fascinated.

"Here." Quinn tossed the newspaper on the bed. Elijah picked it up. "It's Samuel Shaw." She bit her bottom lip. "It says he was survived by his wife, Temperance Shaw."

"This is the man I saw until his face morphed into mine." Elijah raised his dark eyebrows and tossed the newspaper down onto the bed. Quinn placed it on a bedside table, and Elijah grabbed lotion from his dresser, squeezed it into his hand, and rubbed it all over his sleeve tattoo. "So, maybe your past life theory has some substance."

Quinn started to say something, then stopped. "Okay, this is gonna sound weird." Her voice lowered to an unsure tone.

"Weirder than a skinwalker, past lives, and magic? Can't wait to hear it." Elijah set the lotion bottle back down, returning his attention to her. Quinn studied him, glancing at his chest and abs. "I'm up here." Elijah pointed to his face, chuckling.

"Fine, but it's incredibly intimate, and I've only told my Nana."

"Mmmmk," Elijah gave a mischievous grin. "Now you've got my attention." He picked up his book, *Hamlet,* from the side table, opening it to the bookmark.

"After every visit I had with you as a child, I would go home and have dreams about making love to a beautiful, handsome man on a shore. It was *always* the same man." Quinn waved the paper. "This *is* the man. If Samuel is one of your past lives, then ..."

"I don't remember making love to you or marrying you."

Quinn's eyes widened, and she smacked him playfully. "You don't seem like the type to read Shakespeare." She slapped the top of the book, almost whacking it out of his hands. He could tell by the glint in her eyes that she was dying to change the subject.

"I'm a bundle of surprises." Elijah flipped to the next page, half-listening and half-reading. Deciding to let the conversation about their one-hundred-and-eighty-year-old marriage pass, he zeroed in on Shakespeare's words for the time being.

"After reading Owen's journal," she dropped the leather-bound diary on the bed between them, "it's a possibility that the symbols from the rubbings are one small piece of a *larger* spell. Which would make sense if it was a skinwalker."

"You're relentless, aren't you?" Intrigued, Elijah tucked a finger between the pages and set the book in his lap. Quinn flickered a quick smile of affirmation, and Elijah continued. "Owen did mention something about the possibility of a portal being out there. A gateway."

Quinn sat and crossed her legs, pulling his black and white comforter over her knees. "But how could a skinwalker kill their family after they had *already* changed? Whatever Samuel—or, in other words, *you*—did, you pissed off the wrong witch and a massively powerful one, but there's no way to tell *who* it is in the family." She stopped and swallowed heavily. "We need to go back out there in the morning and figure out if the graveyard was built on the location of the Shaw family home. We have to find out if that part of the story is urban legend or fact. Let just say it is true. Maybe there was something left behind in the ruins that could help."

"What about Emma, the relative that was helping Owen?"

"Most of the Shaw family's belongings were destroyed in the fire, and she's only a distant relative. From what I know, she has limited knowledge. It was a large black mark on the family history. The remaining relatives were either lost track of or killed."

"Well, If we're going back out to hell street, can we get some sleep first?" Elijah scratched around the fresh bandage on his skinwalker bite, then closed his book, placing it on his side table.

"Yeah. That sounds amazing." She smiled and then got up from the bed.

"Where *you* going?" Elijah reached for her while snuggling with his pillow.

"I'm going to the church."

Elijah grazed her wrist, trying to pull her back to the bed. "No, you're not."

"Excuse me?" Quinn's mouth set in a hard line, and she adjusted the stone around her neck.

"Not after Allison threatened you." Elijah's voice was firm and steady.

"I'm not afraid of him," Quinn said sternly.

"Well, you should be."

"I'll be fine. I need access to spellbooks and historical information," Quinn said dismissively.

"If I promised to get you all the help you need to go through all the information, would you stay here, please?" Elijah sighed and rubbed his heavy eyes. The cut on his face burned, and the scab cracked. "You can even have my bed; I'll take a cot in the office."

She hesitated, and then her expression softened, showing a transparent weakness for him he'd never seen in anyone else before. "Fine. Only because we should all stay together right now." A rush of satisfaction filled Elijah as she sat on the bed. "I'm not gonna make you sleep on a damn cot, though." She slid underneath the covers and made a line with her finger. "You stay on that side of the bed, and I'm staying on this side," she said ruefully.

Elijah chuckled. "Absolutely. I did just meet you again for the first time in twelve years." He pumped his eyebrows as his eyes traveled from her legs to her face. "I'm aware of your reputation from your aunt. I have no desire to be taken advantage of by such a temptress."

Quinn smacked him playfully. Lying down, she pulled the comforter to her chin and rested her head on the pillow next to his. Her floral, intoxicating scent wafted into his face, and Elijah rubbed his forehead, darting his eyes away from her. He knew if he continued to watch her, it would become impossible to keep his hands to himself, as well as stay on his side of the bed.

The last thing Elijah saw was Quinn's face lit by the sunlight that streamed through the curtains. The golden hues engulfed the room, bathing the two of them in warmth. Her calming energy wrapped around him like a safety blanket, lulling him into a deep sleep. It was the closest Elijah felt to serene in years. And for the first time in weeks, his mind relaxed enough to allow the anxiety and depression that consumed him to fall away. Even if it was only for a moment.

IT BARELY HAD BEEN A second between the time Elijah closed his eyes and the restlessness that consumed Quinn. Elijah's breathing was steady, and his dark hair clung to his forehead. His expression was soft and serene; watching him sleep made the whole night worthwhile. She could still smell the coastal saltwater on his skin. An intense craving to kiss him and press her body against his made heat rise on the back of her neck.

Quinn brushed his fine, shaggy hair back from his forehead and ran a gentle thumb over his bruised and scabbed cheek. Slipping from bed, Quinn pulled on her jeans. Elijah's whole room was a mess, and it drove her insane, but on some level, she knew in the future, his messiness would be what she liked the most. What the messiness told her was that he was too busy helping others to stay long enough in one place to clean. She stopped on her way out the door and pinned the corner of his *Walking Dead* poster back to the wall.

You can learn so much about a person while observing their bedroom, the most intimate of all places.

The apartment was silent, peaceful. It was a drastic comparison to the evil that had made itself known the night before. The wood floor in the historic home creaked with each step as she made her way down the hall to the office. The smell of coffee filled her with a deep warmth as she paused, watching Hudson sleep on the couch. His rich, reddish-brown skin was silky in the morning glow, and she smiled. Elijah and Hudson were great friends, and she could tell he would be instrumental in Elijah's recuperation after Owen's death.

Hudson's aura was a spectacular blend of lilac and turquoise, and in that second, her intuition told her that Hudson must have been a part of *their* soul tribe. Quinn hadn't said anything yet, but she knew without a doubt that they were all together once long ago. She wanted to make sure before she said anything to them because connecting people to the wrong soul tribe could have devastating consequences.

Quinn eased into the office and quietly shut the door behind her. She hadn't smelled it at first, but there was a lingering mixture of faint aromas. The smoke from the fireplace and Elijah's aftershave.

After her latest romantic disaster, dating wasn't entirely on the top of her list, but she knew what Nana would say. *You find the best gems when you're not looking*. Quinn rubbed her forehead in exhaustion as she observed the piles of research. Owen was always thorough in everything he did, but to Quinn, the mounds of information he'd left were a reminder of all the sleep she wouldn't be getting any time soon. They'd spent a lot of time at the church, but it wasn't doing research. It was spent teaching Owen the craft.

She took a seat at the desk and started sifting through a stack of maps, trying to find schematics of the house at Seven Sisters Road. She'd seen a historic blueprint when she was digging through everything with Hudson. Suddenly, the door swung open, and a wavy-haired girl walked in carrying two coffee mugs. Her eyes were wide, and her expression full of love until she saw Quinn. Stopping short, her eyes glanced to Elijah's football jersey with annoyance.

"You must be Riley," Quinn said.

Riley wasn't what Quinn had expected. After all the drunken confessions from Owen, Quinn had built up a seductress image of Riley. That predatory image certainly didn't match the simple, southern woman standing in front of her.

"I'd like to say I know *your* name, but I don't. Whatever bar he picked you up at, he'll never go back." Her eyes were cutting, and she gave a plastic smile.

Quinn remained silent, unimpressed by Riley's juvenile emotional warfare. Riley glared at her, and she raised her eyebrow, judging. "I thought you were Elijah; this was for him. I'll just take it to him." Riley turned to leave.

"You know—he just fell asleep, and the last week's been pretty hard for him." Quinn strode briskly to her and wrapped her hands around the mug, stopping her. She felt Riley pulling the cup away, and she tightened her grip. "He needs to sleep. I'll drink it," Quinn said, clenching her jaw.

A splash of the coffee dripped onto Riley's hand, and her lip twitched. She released her grip on the mug, "It's black. You don't want to drink that. I'm sure you'd probably want something more *complicated*." Riley's eyes narrowed, and her face flooded with judgment. Quinn could tell Riley was sizing up her competition.

"I love black coffee, it's perfect." Quinn gave the best smug smile she could muster and took a sip of the coffee. "Mmmm, delicious. Thanks for giving *it* to me."

Riley's face turned red, and Quinn stuck out her hand. "I'm Quinn, by the way, Owen's cousin. The white daisies you sent to his funeral were beautiful." Riley's hazel eyes averted to the floor in embarrassment, and Quinn pulled her hand back, wrapping them both around the "My mom went to Vegas and all I got was this lousy cup" mug.

"You mean the funeral that you weren't invited to?" Riley bit back.

Shelly had always been a gossip. She was sure that her aunt most likely talked crap about her. Quinn took note of the upside-down triangle on Riley's forearm; it was the symbol of Water, one of the elemental symbols used in spell casting.

"Hey? You need some help?" Hudson gave a broad smile and shuffled between the two girls, doing his best to break the tension. His long, red silk robe dusted the floor.

Quinn kept her eyes on Riley, and the two were now staring each other down with a fury that could have taken down kingdoms. Quinn broke eye contact first, bored of Riley's games. "I would love it, actually." Quinn tucked the jersey into the front of her jeans, set the coffee cup on the desk, and tied her long crimson hair back in a ponytail.

"How you doin' after last night?" Hudson leaned back in the office chair and put his hands behind his head, angling himself toward Quinn.

"Fine, just a little tired. My mind won't let me sleep right now." Quinn took a sip of coffee and set it on the desk.

Riley flickered an uneasy smile, kicking his chair. "Hudson, you didn't tell me that Owen's cousin was here."

Hudson raised his dark eyebrows. "Oh, yeah, it was a long night, and I was exhausted, sorry." Hudson shrugged and started flipping through files. Either oblivious or tickled by the current girl drama, Quinn couldn't tell. "She's helping us figure out some stuff about Owen. Plus, she has superhuman powers." Hudson pumped his eyebrows.

Quinn chuckled. "Hardly, I just know a few things that will help. Things that might even help *you*." She waved toward Riley.

"You have powers?" Riley grunted, apparently entertained, and shot her some, 'great, Elijah likes a crazy girl' looks. Riley's skepticism oozed off of her, and Quinn knew any help they got from her would be purely because of her desire to get Elijah back.

"Not powers, just an ability to work with energy." Quinn thumbed through the pages of the file.

Hudson laughed in wonder. "Did you know Owen and Quinn come from a line of witches?"

Redirecting the conversation, Quinn put the focus where it should be. "According to town records, the plantation and mansion were torched after the sisters' deaths. It doesn't say by who or how it happened. I have an inkling there might be something of use on the property." Quinn paused, "if there's anything left." She said doubtfully.

"I'm aware of the history. I helped Owen film at the location." Riley's steps were swift as she crossed the room to a stack of files. "The house was supposedly located where the graveyard is, but there's no remnants of the foundation. There's over twenty acres out there. It could be located anywhere."

Ignoring the bitchy tone in her voice, Quinn turned to Hudson. "Elijah and I were talking about the symbols being a part of a bigger spell." Quinn looked up from a map she inspected. "If you want to join us, you can." Quinn flickered a smile.

Riley eased further into the room, her shoulders slumped in defeat. "What can I do?"

Damn, she didn't say no.

"You can take that pile over there; we need to find all maps of the area or historic plot documents." Quinn thought about telling them how she knew for sure where the mansion was, but Elijah's abilities were his to share, not hers.

The front door slammed, and steady footsteps beat against the hardwood floor. Camilla strolled into the room with a file tucked under her arm and a Starbucks venti in her hand. Her ebony-colored hair was tied up in a messy bun, and perfume wafted into Quinn's face. She'd gone home, showered, and changed into torn designer jeans and a comfortable-looking Alabama Football tee. Camilla slapped the file onto the hardwood desk in the center of the room.

Secretly, Quinn gave an internal sigh of relief that Camilla was alright. She'd been worried all night that something terrible might have happened to her. Allison's threat about a kidnap sounded legit, and it scared her more than she wanted Elijah to know. Quinn felt guilty for letting her leave but was good at hiding her concern.

Quinn had always been good at controlling her emotions. It was something she learned from a young age after moving in with her Nana. Her Nana had short patience for emotionally vulnerable people. She said it made them weak and left them open to the dark energies they worked with. Their coven The Sisters of The Waking World, left little room for rebellion or mistakes.

"I contacted a connection I have at the medical examiner's and got Owen's autopsy report." Camilla's voice was still hoarse. The rope burn around her neck was scabbed, and Quinn was amazed she hadn't made an effort to conceal the wound. Her face was absent of any makeup, and her flawless caramel skin made Quinn slightly jealous. A thick scab had formed over her eye wound, and the minor lacerations from the glass on her hands were bright red.

Camilla tapped the file, then picked lint from her shirt, and dropped it to the ground. "I'm not only in it for me. Despite what you might think." She gave Hudson a cold scan.

"You mean you snuck in and stole it," Riley snidely remarked, keeping her eyes on one of Owen's cinematography logs she was flipping through.

"Riley can't say I'm glad you've joined our pathetic little club," Camilla said, raising an eyebrow, unruffled by Riley's catty tone.

Quinn could tell that the deep, heart-breaking wound Riley played a part in hadn't healed for Camilla. "She have to be here? I'm sure there's a frat party somewhere that's missing its slut doing a keg stand."

"First of all, fuck you. And trust me, it's hardly by *choice*." Riley exposed two scabbed handprints around her ankles. Camilla cocked her head to the side, glanced at the wounds unimpressed, and rolled her eyes.

"At least you didn't get hanged." Camilla pointed to her neck.

Annoyed, Quinn interrupted, "You both are still *alive*. That's what matters. This isn't a contest."

Riley scowled at Quinn as if it was her fault she was attacked.

Camilla nodded in agreement. "I'm here for Owen *and* Elijah." The whole room knew what Camilla was dying to say. "I mean, it *is* your fault that—"

"You *all* are here for Owen and Elijah, just like me ..." Hudson paused, his tone soothing. His eyes surveyed the two women as they stared at each other with contempt.

Quinn went to speak and decided to stay silent. She could tell Hudson was taking in the emotional temperature of the room.

Hudson picked up the file and flipped it open, breaking the silence. "What does the report say?"

Camilla pointed to the page. "There was petechial hemorrhaging in his eyes and—his hyoid bone was fractured. According to my contact, that's all expected, except they found drag marks on his back. There was an attempted bite from a dog on his leg. There were no signs of scabbing; the skin had barely been torn. There was a burn mark on his forearm in the shape of a hand."

Quinn took the file. "Jesus." She picked up a photo of his leg. Everyone gathered around and saw a oval jagged bruise on his calf.

"Whatever Owen was looking for out there he found it, or knew its location, and there's a good chance he pissed off one of the spirits while he was at it," Camilla said flatly.

"The Shaw family demons definitely have *something* to do with it," Quinn stated with finality and took a seat in one of the chairs. A melancholy silence settled through the room as everyone took a moment to think. Quinn's eyes surveyed the group, studying their reactions. Any one of them could be the skinwalker.

"What the hell is going on?" Hudson's eyes widened.

Quinn saw Riley's fingers twitch at the question. Her eyes darkened. A flicker of orange and red pulsed from Riley's aura and out into the room. Quinn had never seen the colors mixed that way. The unresolved anger between the two women was more than she could take. Quinn leaned against the wall and flipped through the file, silently reading the notes. A scribble caught her eye that Owen had written about Hellhounds and the possibility of Underworld Greek mythological creatures being present out at Seven Sisters Road. Quinn gave a soft smile and an internal chuckle. It was genius and not an avenue she would have even considered. He'd always been the one to think outside of the box and go against convention.

"How's Parker?" Camilla's voice softened. The tenseness in her stance melted, and she played with the lid of her coffee cup.

Hudson paused, setting down a pile of papers. "It's hard to tell. He's been in and out of sleep, but he's doing a *little* better. Thanks for asking," Hudson smiled.

"Hey. Glad you're back." Elijah rubbed his eyes and wrapped his arm around Camilla's shoulders.

Heat shot through Quinn, and she scratched the side of her nose, stretching her neck. She diverted her eyes, focusing on the medical examiner's report.

I'm not jealous. I'm not jealous. This is not happening.

"You're supposed to be sleeping." Riley took a sip of her coffee and batted her best bedroom eyes.

Quinn aggressively flipped through the autopsy.

"I got a short nap. We have a lot to do." Elijah rested his hand on Camilla's shoulder. "Maybe we should take everyone to the church. With what's happened—"

"I agree," Quinn said. "We can take all this stuff and make it a hub. Try and get Parker, Riley, and Camilla's situation straightened out. Get everyone to search through the office for the drugs." She smiled at Elijah, and he smiled back, his eyes lingering on hers for a moment.

"Wait ..." Riley kept her eyes on Quinn, annoyed. "What drugs?"

"I'll explain it when we get to the church. There's something I need to do first, though." He turned to Camilla and squeezed her shoulder. "Can you take them out, and I'll meet you there?"

"Yes, for sure." Camilla smiled, taking a sip of her Starbucks.

"Ahhh. What's the church?" Hudson leaned forward onto his knees in the chair, holding a map.

"In due time. Right now, I need to speak to Elijah." Quinn waved him out of the room.

They walked into Elijah's bedroom, and she handed him the folder. "It's Owen's autopsy. Look here." She pointed at the picture of the bite bruise.

"The skinwalker bit him."

"Notice something?" Quinn's finger traced the circle.

"It's the same size as mine."

"Alpha tried to bite Owen first."

"But, why?"

Quinn took back the file and slapped it shut. "Owen figured out what was happening with the skinwalker too late. If the fucker *has to kill him* and eat his flesh ..." Quinn paused, fighting the overwhelming guilt. "He tried to talk to us and ask for help. Instead of listening, we turned him away. He was up against them alone."

"Now I feel like shit," Elijah said. He ran a hand through his dark hair and leaned against the wall.

"Yeah, you and me both." Quinn's words were clipped as she did her best to fight tears. Despite her efforts, one slid down her cheek. Elijah wiped it away with a tender hand and pulled her in, wrapping his arms around her. Quinn rested her cheek against his shoulder.

If there was anything in Quinn's life she regretted most, it was the loneliness, helplessness, and terror that she allowed her cousin to feel while he hanged in the woods, the life slipping from his body. But unfortunately, now, it was written in the stone of the past and something she could never rewrite.

22

FLICKERING PINK AND RED lights stayed with Elijah. The buzz as they clicked on and off echoed in his ears. He couldn't get the image of the illuminated tarot sign from River Street out of his mind. The woman's cold face as she stared down at him while Alison and Landon kicked his ass haunted him. There was an uneasiness nagging at him that told him that he would regret it if he didn't stop by and visit the psychic. Besides, he could use all the help he could get to find the drugs at this point. It was the only thing he needed to know, besides whether or not he was going to die.

If I don't check this out, I won't be able to sift through hundreds of years of past lives.

Elijah parallel parked in front of the psychic's building then turned off the Nova. "I'll only be a moment."

"What's the point of coming here?" Riley said from the back seat, her annoyance transparent.

"Don't worry about it. Will you both, please, stay here?" Elijah glanced at Riley in the rearview mirror. Both Quinn and Riley answered simultaneously.

"Okay," Riley said.

"No." Quinn's tone was firm as she slapped down Owen's autopsy file.

Elijah raised an eyebrow, trying to conceal a smile. He was drawn to Quinn's fire like a moth to a flame.

"He wants us to stay here." Riley leaned forward in her seat. "It's not *ideal*, but it's what he wants." Riley gave Quinn a thin-lipped flicker of a smile and crossed her arms.

Ignoring Riley, Quinn opened her door. "I have some questions for her." She hopped out and shut the door, leaning her back against it.

He turned to the side, nodding toward the door. "You might as well come too. I don't want to leave you alone right now." Elijah hopped out, pulling the seat forward. The berating sound of construction and the scent of freshly laid cement wafted through his broken window. The shattered glass from the night before had taken Elijah about an hour to clean. He hoped that it wouldn't rain before he bought a piece of clear plastic to put over the passenger window. Sitting, Riley thought it over.

"Come on, Ri, we got stuff to do," Elijah said, ushering her out of the seat as she played with yellowed cotton sticking out the massive hole.

"I don't have time for this," Quinn mumbled under her breath, walking toward the psychic's door.

Riley hopped out, dangerously close to Elijah's face. For the first time, he hadn't thought about kissing her. His residual emotions over the last couple of days were starting to fade, finally. It occurred to Elijah that he'd been desperately grasping onto a memory of what their relationship used to be. That memory was skewed by his emotions and pain. The delusion of their relationship had been more potent than the truth for quite a long time.

They made their way through a tall, thin door between two restaurants and up a set of narrow stairs. Elijah took the stairs two at a time, stopping in front of a door at the top. The old building smelled of mold, and the historic, floral tile mosaic on the bottom floor was visible from the staircase. A sign on a purple, heavy oak door read:

Kiren Avalon
Tarot Reader and Intuitive

Elijah's heart raced, and he hesitated, holding his fist in front of the door. Quinn knocked for him, her hits hard and loud.

She shrugged, "This was your idea."

A tall woman with dark blonde, straight hair opened the door. Her smile was welcoming and warm. The tall women's blue eyes traveled to each of their faces. She took in a deep breath and shot it out quickly.

"Well, come in. Don't hover. I won't bite. Much." Her Irish accent was thick and melodic. "I'm Kiren."

She guided them into her sacred space. Quinn moseyed in as if she was at home, her shoulders relaxed. Riley shut the door and leaned against it, rigid. A calmness rolled over Elijah. Ribbons of smoke flowed from a wrapped bunch of light-green leaves in the corner.

"What's that?" Elijah leaned into Quinn's ear, pointing to the herbs burning. Riley's eyes watched him closely.

"It's sage. It's used to clear out negative energy and raise vibrations." Quinn was so close to him that her knuckles brushed his.

Elijah's fingers twitched, and an urge to grab her hand and experience her touch dazed him.

"Everything in our universe has a vibration." The woman smiled, drumming her fingers against a deck of well-worn Tarot cards, her many stone rings shimmering in the daylight.

He heard Riley sigh sarcastically behind him. Kiren set down her tarot cards and picked a new one.

"Sorry about this one." Quinn jabbed a thumb toward Riley. "She hasn't *awoken* yet."

Kiren studied Riley, walking in close to her. "Now, darlin', where's ye manners? Spirit guides us to awaken on our path in our own time."

Riley crossed her arms. "I'm standing right here."

Kiren's round eyes surveyed Riley as if she was examining a precious jewel, estimating whether or not it was genuine.

"Personal space ..." Riley backed away from Kiren.

Beautiful pillars of stones were placed through the room. The colors were vibrant reds, yellows, blues, and purples. There was a sign that blocked a back-hallway reading, "Employees Only." Elijah guessed that it's where Kiren lived.

Breaking away from his observations, Elijah noticed the woman's eyes lingering on him. She shuffled a deck of colorfully designed tarot cards, squinting at Elijah. He could sense her reading his soul, trying to decode his secrets.

"Why are ye here?" Her flowing, purple sundress flared out as she turned toward her chair.

"I have a question. Elijah here …" Quinn nodded toward him. "He's got something he needs to ask you too."

Tapestries with green and gold Celtic symbols decorated the modest space. A short, multicolored bookshelf with what Elijah guessed was at least a hundred different tarot decks lined the wall across from a table with two chairs.

"Have a seat." She pointed Elijah to the worn, wood chair in front of her. "Cost is sixty dollars an hour. Thirty for thirty minutes."

An arrogant grunt came from Riley, who appeared more than eager to bolt out the door. "That's a ridiculous amount to have you flip out some cards." She waved her hand nonchalantly. "And make some guess—"

"She's worked years to hone a skill and gift from the universe that people make fun of and undervalue." Quinn's tone was defensive and deep. "Yet, they come to her anyway when they're desperate …" Quinn shot a cutting glance toward Riley. "And are at their lowest points spiritually. *Paying* is the least we can do. People pay *you* to bring drinks to their table."

Riley mumbled, and Elijah couldn't hear what she said. Her face was blotched red, and her lips were turned down in a frown. He could tell she wanted to pounce on Quinn.

Kiren flicked her eyes out the window, then gave a tight-lipped smile. "Is that beaut' of a car yours?"

Elijah sat and scooted his chair toward the table. "Yeah, my father gave it to me. He got it while he studied abroad—Ireland, I think." Elijah's eyes scanned the street until he found the spot he'd been only days before when Allison and Landon attacked him. He still had no idea where the drugs were. He was secretly hoping he'd find them stuck in a small, obscure crevice of the church.

Raising an eyebrow, Kiren shuffled the cards. "Is there any way these two can step out into the hallway? Having too many energies in one room tends ta muck up the readin'. Especially when they want ta throttle each other." Kiren chuckled, shaking her head.

Elijah turned to Quinn. "Will you stand in the hallway with her, please? I'll come get you when it's your turn."

Quinn reached for the door handle, but Riley blocked her from leaving. "*Now* you want to listen? We should have stayed in the car." Riley opened the door for Quinn, waving her out. Annoyed, Quinn pointed Riley through it first. Riley darted out the door, mumbling, and Quinn followed, shutting the door quietly behind her.

"Those two are a handful, eh?" Kiren set the deck in front of Elijah, swiping her hands across a silky, black tablecloth with stars.

"I've never experienced them at the same time. Things happening lately have made that impossible to avoid. Which is why I'm here."

"I got a sense you guys have known each other for a while. What's your name, son?"

"Elijah. I'll do a half-hour."

Kiren shifted in her seat. "'Tis a solid name. Well, Elijah, outside of knowing yer name, that's the only thing I require. Don't tell me anything else. It tends to influence the readin'. I want you to concentrate on your question, then go ahead and cut the deck."

Cutting the deck in silence, Elijah noticed her eyes on his car again.

"You like my car?"

"Had a beau that owned one when I was younger." She fanned the deck on the table, then pointed. "Pick out ten cards, no more, no less. Don't flip them over; I'll do that."

"How long have you been in Savannah? If you don't mind me askin'?" Elijah skimmed his fingers over the worn edges of the cards and slid one out. The image of her performing another reading flickered in his mind for a millisecond.

"Oh, about twenty-seven years. I've kinda been all over but always came back. For the beau, of course. It never worked out. After a while, I stopped hearing from him."

"Twenty-seven years is a long time to be dedicated to someone." He slid out number three, then four.

"He's my twin flame. I made a few mistakes the way we all do. It's been about fifteen years now since I last saw him. We'll come back together eventually."

"What's a twin flame?"

"It's believed by some spiritualists that we're created as one spiritual energy. When we choose to be in a solid human form to learn certain divine lessons, on some rare occasions our ethereal body is split in two." She put two fists together, pulling them apart. "We come to Earth entering two different bodies. Both parts of one energetic whole. And no matter what we do, we are drawn back. Because we essentially are drawn to the other half of our self. Quite romantic." She grinned. "Their purpose is to challenge us and make us better. The traditional idea of romance is quite different from reality. It's not supposed to be daisies and easy goings."

Elijah picked the last card, and the deep tone of her Irish accent made him smile. The thought of having another half of ourselves out in the expansive universe was endearing. It meant none of us were ever alone. What Quinn had told him about Samuel the night before caused heat to rise on his chest.

"This tattoo, where'd you see it?" Kiren pointed to a complicated Celtic knot on Elijah's forearm, nestled in among his sleeve tattoo.

"My father had one. I think it's considered a love knot."

Kiren's face was unreadable momentarily as she studied the tattoo, then gave a warm smile. "It's beautiful. Well then," Her eyebrows pumped. "Let's get started," She collected the remaining tarot cards and put them back into a pile, setting them to the side. Kiren took Elijah's first card and flipped it over, placing it in the center of the table. It was a woman covered in a cloak standing atop a cliff. The title read Hermit.

She smiled, "My dear, you have the sight. I could sense it from the moment you strolled in the door."

"The sight?" Elijah leaned back in his chair.

"You're one of *my* kind, dove." Her eyes twinkled with recognition.

"How did you—"

"See this lantern the woman is carrying? It's a light that only she carries. It allows her to look down from the cliff, giving her the bigger picture. This staff she holds represents the fire of the mind. You have an old soul; your intuition and psychic abilities have evolved through your lifetimes. In this particular life, the activation of your psychic sight was inherited. From a parent, maybe?"

"Neither of my parents mentioned they had them. Well, at least not my dad."

"Just because he never told you doesn't mean the connection doesn't exist." She popped her finger up, her eyebrows pinched together. "You've been resistant to your abilities. Afraid of what others will think of you. And you shouldn't, you're a natural, and they are a gift from the Universe." She thoughtfully tapped the card. "There's a darkness attached to your gift. Someone wants to manipulate your abilities. It's someone you've known for quite a while."

"I'm not sure what you mean." Elijah's shoulders tightened. He scoured through his mind trying to think of *anyone* he told.

Ignoring his denial, Kiren went forward with the reading, flipping over another card, laying it across the first. The picture of a woman with swords sticking out from her back made his breath catch in his throat. *The Ten of Swords.* "You've experienced a lot of loss in your life, grew up at a young age. You've dealt with the fallout of others' actions and choices around you." Kiren paused, and Elijah thought he saw her eyes darken.

"There's a brother around you right now. He's recently crossed over and wants to get you a message. This *brother* is where you'll find the answers. And solidification." She hovered her hand over the cards. "The sun rising in this card represents a karmic cycle that is about to come to a close for you. The sun is rising in the darkness. It's going to be a long process in this life. But I have a sense you'll make it through. You're not only changing the course for yourself but others around you as well. You're changing the course for your entire soul tribe."

Elijah hadn't expected to be emotionally violated. He cleared his throat, turning his head slightly toward the door, wishing Quinn was standing next to him. He pushed her forward, stuck halfway between terror and curiosity. "What else can you pick up?" Scooting forward, leaning on his elbows, Elijah tapped the toe of his boot.

Revealing another card, she laid it above the cross that the other two made. *The Sun.* "The rejection of your intuition will end with the emergence of someone tender and supportive. She's your twin flame. You've known her for a while in this life. An internal switch will flip, and how you perceived her will change." Kiren smiled sweetly. "Isn't love grand?" She refocused on the cards. "Although you might not recognize it, your connection to her is strong. It's lasted over lifetimes."

Elijah was astonished. It was the most amazing thing he'd experienced. "What's my brother trying to tell me?"

"He's showing me there's someone around you who's pretending to be someone they aren't. I'm being given a vision of someone taking off a mask. Like this ... " She wrapped her hand around her face, then swiped it down. "How strange." Kiren closed her eyes, concentrating. A moment passed, and she lulled herself into a trance. She turned her ear toward the ceiling like she was trying to hear someone speak behind her. Her eyes bolted open, and the color drained from her face. "You need—you—leave now." Kiren struggled to speak. She stood and pointed him toward the door with a shaky hand.

Shocked and confused, Elijah eased out of his chair. "What about payment?"

"This one's on me." She ushered him to the door, opened it, shoved him out, and slammed it shut behind him.

23

THE THREE OF THEM were now driving out to the church. Quinn sat silently in the front seat next to Elijah, and played with her teardrop stone necklace, deep in thought. The silver chain glinted in the sunlight as she leaned on the door handle. Humid wind beat through the broken window against her face, and sweat dampened a small spot on the chest of her gray T-shirt. Her beautiful, curly, red hair whipped around, and Quinn's lavender scent drifted around the car. It drove him crazy with desire.

Riley was in the back with her earbuds in and music on, her head bobbing on the duct-taped seat from the uneven road as she rested with her eyes closed. Elijah knew she was probably listening to something from the 80s like "Leather and Lace" by Stevie Nicks and Don Henley. It was her favorite era to listen to when she was stressed.

Elijah was having a difficult time understanding what had happened at the tarot reader's. Guilt waved over him. Kiren could have witnessed the visions that perturbed him as of late. Possibly a cannibalistic vision of the future, were the skinwalker was eating him. If energy could contaminate other energy, it was possible she had sensed Riley's experience from last night. Elijah's mind raced through what Kiren said. Trying to catalog and commit to memory every second of the interaction was impossible. And still, Elijah found himself grasping for Kiren's words before they faded into the vastness of the universe. Elijah wondered if Quinn was the one she was referring to as his twin flame. How was it possible for someone to read his life from a deck of cards?

Explaining to Quinn what happened with Kiren was challenging, to say the least. Quinn was pretty firm about storming the office. She became enraged when Elijah told her about the mask part. Infuriated, Quinn demanded he go back. Holding his ground, Elijah insisted they be respectful and give Kiren the space she requested.

For Quinn, it confirmed that they were looking for a skinwalker. She was eager to get more answers. Elijah told Quinn they could always go back the next day after Kiren had some time. As a psychic himself, Elijah knew other people's emotions had a tendency to be incredibly uncomfortable and overwhelming at times.

"I've seen my Nana do a million readings. Never once have I watched her push someone out in the middle of it," Quinn said, startling Elijah out of his thoughts. He gripped the steering wheel. The muscle where Alpha bit him was sore, and the fresh scab pinched.

Elijah turned down a narrow dirt road, then reached back and tapped Riley's leg. "Hey, Ri, we're almost there." Elijah could see the steeple of the church poke out the top of the trees.

Riley sat up, pulling the earbuds out of her ears, and raked her hand through her wind-blown hair. "What's with this place?"

"It was Owen's. Quinn lives here. No one outside of Quinn knew it existed except Camilla. And that wasn't until recently." Elijah glanced at her through the rearview mirror.

"Why are we coming here? What does it have to do with anything?" She impatiently brushed hair off the sleeve of her shirt.

"This is something you would have to see to believe. Be careful; there's been wolves hanging around," Elijah said. His shoulders tightened at the memory, and he clenched his jaw. He and Quinn were gonna have to explain their skinwalker theory. "Camilla is supposed to be going over Owen's past life regression recordings that we found on the drive he left me."

Quinn's eyes were locked on Elijah, and a tightness formed in his throat. "What?"

"How come you didn't mention the drive or the recordings last night while we were talking in my truck?"

Riley leaned forward. "Because, honey, this is what Elijah does. He doesn't communicate." Riley chuckled, leaning back and crossing her arms. "Until it's too late," she mumbled. "Good luck and Godspeed." She patted Quinn on the back.

Quinn's eyes shifted from Elijah's face, and she shot Riley a warning glance to keep her hands off her.

Elijah parked next to Camilla's black Toyota Camry. "I wasn't entirely sure I could trust you yet. You *did* use me as bait. Plus, I'm telling you about it right now." He turned off the nova and shoved his keys into his pocket. Cautiously, he scanned the area searching for Alpha and Beta.

Parker's 4-runner was parked next to the church's back door, and the trunk was still open. Elijah could see a few boxes from the apartment still stacked inside. Elijah slid out Owen's journal from under his seat. Quinn went to open her door, and Elijah stopped her. He jumped out of the car and sauntered to the other side, opening it for her.

"I could have opened my own door," Quinn said with a tinge of frustration in her voice. Elijah helped her out of the car and then pulled the seat forward for Riley. Quinn walked toward the front porch of the church.

"Yes, I'm aware of that." Catching up with Quinn, he beat her to the front door, blocking her. "Let's wait for her," Elijah heard the car door slam. He turned back to see Riley with crossed arms and a sullen expression, taking quick strides.

Quinn sighed, "Is this necessary?"

A pang of guilt hit him, and his chest tightened. "Yes."

On some level, he was doing the same thing to Riley that she'd done to him. Except, what Riley and Owen did was far worse. Two months of sneaking behind his back were unforgivable.

"We gonna go over *everything* in there?"

Elijah gripped the journal, keeping the loose papers from falling out. "Yes, we *all* need to talk about what's in there together."

Quinn spun around, leaning over the railing, turning her back to him. The need to wrap his arms around her from behind was maddening. The desire to touch her intensified with every passing second.

Riley finally made it to the bottom of the stairs, and Elijah swung open the door. Quinn took the journal from him, unhappy. Walking down an aisle, searching for a book, Quinn watched Elijah and Riley out of the corner of her eye. Riley stopped in the doorway, observing. Confusion clouded her features.

Elijah waited for Riley to process what she saw. His weak spot for her and Owen bordered on absurdity. His desire for Riley made him prideful and blind. That was the reason Elijah forgave Riley sooner than Owen. Except, in his soul, Elijah was aware that the betrayal hurt him more from Owen than it did from Riley. It took six months and the death of his best friend to figure out that it was okay to forgive, but it didn't mean he had to forget.

"This is amazing." Hudson came around the corner of a bookshelf, digging his fingers into his ebony hair. Hudson's face was covered in wonder. Like he'd opened the best supernatural Christmas present he never knew he wanted.

"We all need to discuss something. Go get Camilla and Parker. Meet me at the desk in the back."

Quinn followed Hudson to the back. Elijah turned to Riley, who was still on the front porch, leaning against the railing.

"You need to hear this too," Elijah waved her inside.

"I can't. I'm not ready for this." Riley sniffled, wiping her nose.

Cicadas were singing an afternoon song in the trees, and grass swayed in the warm breeze. Elijah joined her on the front porch and leaned on the railing next to her.

"I know this is hard. But, the attack on you isn't the last of things. Actually, I'm pretty sure things are about to get way worse before they get better." Elijah's head dipped, his hungry and bleeding heart pounded. "That journal, besides this church, was the last thing that Owen left us all."

Riley crossed her arms, cradling her elbows in her hands, and Elijah waited for her response. Her hazel eyes turned distant. "He loved you," Riley's voice was low. "And regretted every second. He told me. When you stopped talking to him ..." Tears welled in her eyes. "Something inside him broke. He told me it was like losing a part of himself. His *brother*."

Goosebumps formed on Elijah's arms, and heat raced across his chest. There was no doubt that Benjamin and Samuel *were* the connection between him and Owen. They were brothers in that life, this one, and possibly many more. His wounds ached at the tormenting thought, and the cracked ribs he'd thought were healing shot pain through his back.

Riley smashed her lips together. She choked out a sob and stared at the weather-worn porch, avoiding eye contact. The emotional dam she was desperately working to keep intact crumbled. Riley's grief-riddled wails bellowed through the rural land. Elijah wrapped his arms around her, holding her close. A pang of guilt struck his conscience.

She never got to say goodbye. Not like everyone else did. Because I couldn't let things go.

"I have to live the rest of my life knowing I took those last moments from you and from him. I'm ... I'm ... so ..." Riley exhaled a ragged breath, calming herself. "I'm so sorry, Elijah." Riley nuzzled her cheek into his shoulder, wrapping her arms around him.

Elijah pushed her away gently, keeping a hand on her shoulder. "I made a choice not to talk to him," Elijah said. Riley looked at the floor, avoiding eye contact, and Elijah continued. "It's something I regret every day." Elijah dipped his head to get her attention. "We all make bad choices. In the end, it's what we do in the aftermath that makes us better people."

Elijah spent the first thirty minutes explaining his paranormal abilities. The ones he'd kept secret his whole life. His friends watched him intently. Surprisingly enough, he wasn't met with criticism. Elijah explained his experiences since Owen had died and his astral projection out on Seven Sisters Road.

"You can see ghosts, hear them, and travel through space and time?" Hudson asked, his face filled with wonder.

"I'm still learning about it myself, but yes."

Hudson smiled, "Dude, that's badass—"

Parker pounded his hand on a desk, his face cherry red. "Can you see the fucker that's attached to me? Cause I'd appreciate it if you told them to leave me the hell alone," Parker said, his voice rough.

The room went silent, and Elijah could only assume everyone was trying to make sense of what was happening to them all. Parker grazed his fingers over the scabbed long slices on his face and neck in thought. Parker's eyes dimmed with sadness, and he glanced at the bandage that covered the seared symbol on his arm.

"You're not the only one," Camilla said, breaking the silence. Sweat was beaded across her forehead.

Her body had weakened, and Elijah could tell it was hard for her to move around. The rope burn on her throat was bright red against her beautiful brown skin, and the bruising was rich, blended shades of plum and forest green. Her voice was still hoarse, and she winced while swallowing. Elijah could tell she was getting worse.

"They're drawing on your energy, using it to complete the tasks they need," Quinn explained.

Elijah pulled out the journal and showed them the sheet with the symbols. They each found their corresponding symbol, and the light in their eyes dimmed. The group stood in silence, studying the passage on soul tribes, each taking in the information ambivalently. Elijah had no idea if it was because they were processing a shift in their reality or if they were pissed off at him or Owen. Quinn was leaning against a tall, gray file cabinet, away from the huddle, with her arms crossed, observing. Elijah could see her out of his peripheral vision as thoughts stormed behind her troubled eyes.

Parker's face had paled and thinned since the attack the night before. His fingertips tapped the large oak desk impatiently. "There's no way this is possible. This would mean that we were all together before in a previous life." His voice was raspy and low. Parker's long blond bangs were stuck to his sweaty forehead, and he brushed them out of the way, rubbing his brow.

"Quinn showed me a picture. You have it?" Elijah extended a hand to Quinn.

She raised an eyebrow. "Yes, actually, I was gonna show it to the psychic." Quinn slid them out of her back pocket and handed both to Elijah. They were damp with sweat.

"This is Owen's wrist after he died. This is Benjamin Shaw. Look. Here." Elijah pointed to an enhanced close-up of the old photo.

"Holy hell." Hudson's wide eyes shot toward the ceiling. "Sorry, God."

Camilla was sitting at the desk, flipping through the journal. She stopped in the middle, reading. Her beautiful, brown eyes saddened, and she slammed the journal shut. Camilla shoved it away furiously, banging her hands down on the wood. Tears streamed down her face, and Riley handed her a ball of toilet paper.

"Owen was my soulmate, and now he's dead. I'm going to spend the rest of my existence in this life without the one person that makes me whole? The other half of myself?" The room stayed silent. Riley walked over to the other side of the desk, guilt covering her face.

"From what you've said, this means *we all were and will always be connected in every life*?" Hudson asked.

"This is insane. No fucking way." Parker's eyes narrowed, and he turned away from the group, escaping down an aisle. He pivoted, turning around, and walked back. "This is impossible; this can't be true." His blond eyebrows pinched together, and his nostrils flared.

Hudson glared at his brother. "This you can't believe? Psychics, black magic, and poltergeists devouring your soul till you die are fine," he tapped the journal. "But soulmates and soul tribes is going *too* far?" Hudson's southern accent surfaced for a split second, and Elijah flashed a smile.

"I have commitment issues. What can I say?" Parker said quickly.

Camilla chuckled, then coughed. "So, who were we to each other in past lives?"

"I haven't been able to find that in Owen's research notes yet. I think he was killed before he could answer that question," Quinn answered.

Riley cleared her throat and adjusted her yellow Thirsty Parrot T-shirt. "That means everything that unfolded in our lives wasn't an accident. Parker and Hudson's parents getting married and them becoming stepbrothers, Shelly raising Elijah ... us all meeting, taking the same classes, being in this room together at this moment. This was all planned somehow?"

"That's not all." Elijah shot Quinn an uneasy glance. "We think the *thing* behind all of this is a skinwalker, and there's two of them."

"What the hell does that even mean?" Parker's eye twitched.

"Slow down," Riley stammered, darting from outside of the circle of friends. "It's a pretty big leap to go from ghosts and poltergeists to sinwalkers, or whatever the hell you just said. Which, by the sounds of it, is something weird."

Quinn gave Riley a dirty look, correcting her word. "*Skinwalkers* ... are rooted in Native American beliefs. They are Shaman's who practice black magic and necromancy. But, there are other cultures that have recorded similar creatures. In Ireland they're considered púca's and Germany Doppelgängers."

"Camilla, you remember the wolves from the other day?" Elijah asked.

"How could I forget?" Camilla crossed her arms and straightened her shoulders.

"The larger wolf is the one that bit me out at Seven Sisters Road. They're supposed to be able to shapeshift from human to animal, and even into the form of other people."

Quinn walked down one of the aisles. Elijah heard her pluck a book off the shelf and walk back. She leaned against a file cabinet and flipped through it.

"I need some fresh air," Parker hurried through the church.

"I'm gonna go with him," Hudson walked backward, keeping his eyes on Elijah. "We need to figure this out." He spun around and jogged after his brother.

Camilla stood silently next to Quinn now, both scanning a reference book about shapeshifters. "They frequently use necromancy to control spirits. The attacks are being caused." Quinn flashed the book, confirming their suspicions. "The only question is ... what the hell did we all do?"

"If we're a soul tribe, and Owen was Benjamin, and you were Samuel ... " Riley paused in thought, glancing up at the ceiling.

Elijah stared down at the rubbings of the symbols, wondering what significance they played in the larger picture.

Quinn continued her line of thought. "That means each one of us could have been present at Seven Sisters Road. Or knew the people murdered,"

"Maybe even been the *ones* murdered," Riley added. "I can't believe this."

"From what I know, this exact scenario, in one way or another, will play out in the next life too unless we figure out how to break the cycle," Quinn said, flipping through another page.

Camilla's face flushed white.

"What?" Elijah rested his hand on her shoulder, doing his best to be comforting.

"That means the skinwalker that took a bite out of him is ..."

"Related to him somehow. Elijah and I *thought* that could be the case, we discussed it last night, but now I'm positive." Quinn snapped her fingers in thought, keeping her eyes on the book. "Riley, you look for everything you can on the genealogy of the Shaw family. I'm going to do a search for more skinwalker information. I need to figure out how the spell works."

Riley scanned over the labels of the filing cabinets as she passed. "Will do."

"He put the historic files in cabinet number four," Quinn said, guiding Riley. "Owen had a theory that whoever killed the Shaw family could have done it looking like Samuel. That's why he was convicted."

"Camilla, have you listened to any of Owen's past life regression recordings? We have to find out who each one of us was. *If* we were present."

"I haven't. But, I'll get on it." Her voice was steady, but she crossed her arms and sighed at the thought.

"We need to find out who Olivia Shaw is," Elijah added. "Quinn said, according to one of the *many* legends, there were six sisters and one of them was written out of history. We need to find out if Olivia Shaw was the sixth sister. Also, look for the name Mary. Spirits have repeated that name a few times."

Elijah opened a file cabinet drawer. He moved slowly, sighing from the aching and popping in his joints. Terror-filled screaming for Elijah came from outside. The high-pitched sound caused his flesh to crawl. Elijah's mind raced with thoughts of the ravenous wolves appearing and attacking Hudson and Parker. Ripping their entrails out. Before he knew what was happening, Elijah was hurdling over the porch railing, landing on his knees next to Parker's convulsing body in the high grass of the yard.

Hudson's firm hand stabilized his brother's head, and the other was planted on his chest.

24

THE TERROR IN THE air was palpable. Elijah assisted in pinning Parker down to keep him from injuring himself. Quinn sat at the top of Parker's head and placed both of her hands on his crown. She closed her eyes and inhaled through her nose, exhaling steady meditative breaths. Hudson yelled at Riley to call nine-one-one. Camilla stood on the porch, observing the horrific scene.

"My phone's dead," Riley said.

"Mine too," Hudson's voice was breathy and terrified.

"The entity is draining the battery life out of everything," Quinn said. Electricity surged through the exterior light fixtures, making them flicker.

"Elijah, I need you to concentrate. Put your hands on his chest." Quinn's voice was firm. Elijah did what she said. "I want you to call forward the entity in your mind. *Now*. Before he dies."

"I can't—"

"Elijah." Hudson's face was deep with fright, and he nodded toward Parker, who was now foaming at the mouth. Already knowing what it was like to lose a brother, it was the last thing Elijah wanted for Hudson.

Doing what Quinn ordered, Elijah pressed his hands to Parker's chest. Hateful energy engulfed him, making Elijah's throat close, and he coughed. He continued focusing, asking the entity to show itself. The physical world disappeared, and the name *Helen Shaw* flashed in his mind's eye.

"Helen Shaw," Elijah stuttered.

"Are you sure?" Quinn asked.

Elijah opened his eyes and saw the solid figure of a corpse standing over Parker, laughing. Helen's face was sunken, and her eyes clouded and milky. The rancid smell of decay burnt Elijah's nose. Helen's tattered sapphire dress blew in the coastal wind.

"Helen, leave him alone." Elijah's angry voice boomed and he narrowed his eyes at her. Tunnel vision took over as Helen raised her open palms toward him. Pure hatred tainted Helen's eyes as an tempestuous gust blew her hair into a flurry.

Remain steadfast in your belief, trust the universe.

A bad feeling squirmed in Elijah's stomach. He had no idea what was about to happen, only that he would be paying a hefty price. Quinn's muffled voice caught his attention.

"Camilla, go to Owen's bedside table and get my Book of Shadows; it's a black, leather-bound book. Grab nightshade from the greenhouse; it's labeled, and there's a bottle of graveyard dirt on the shelf next to it. Go, bring it now." Camilla sprinted into the church.

Helen rushed Elijah, and he collided with a tree trunk. Pain exploded through his back, making his lungs temporarily seize.

"Ugh, son of a bitch." Elijah rolled onto his side, then sat back up.

"Jesus. What the hell just happened?" Hudson turned to Quinn.

"It's who's killing your brother. I gave her a distraction."

"Don't hurt him." Riley raced to Elijah—pleading, her face coated in anguish. She drug him into her lap, wrapping her arms around him defensively. Elijah was torn from Riley's grasp, and the bite on his arm bled profusely. It felt like acid was burning his insides as a handprint materialized on his neck.

"Elijah!" Tears filled Riley's eyes. "Stop. You're hurting him." Riley screamed at Quinn. "What are you doing to him?" Riley's panicked voice lowered to a growl, and Quinn ignored her question. She bolted to Quinn, grabbing her arm. "I asked you a question."

A low humming sound, followed by the spontaneous popping and shattering of glass caught Elijah's attention. The light fixtures and bulbs on the outside of the church had exploded.

Quinn yanked her arm free. "I bought Parker some time," she yelled back with unsteady determination.

Elijah's legs thrashed against the ground as he was drug across the dirt and up the side of the church. Helen pinned him by his neck, pressing his back against the jagged siding. He fought against his attacker, and the more Elijah struggled to free himself the tighter her grip closed around his neck. Camilla ran from the back of the church, standing next to Quinn.

The world around Elijah blurred, and darkness spread across his vision. Panicked voices around him muffled. The vertebrae in Elijah's neck crunched and popped. A primal need to breathe took him over, and Elijah fought with all his strength to free himself. Unsuccessful, Elijah tried something different.

I call on the gods and goddesses to protect me from evils seen and unseen.

Helen laughed at Elijah as if she could read his mind and knew the pitiful attempt he was making. The painful pressure released, barely, allowing his vision to return. Elijah's arms became heavy, and his eyes surveyed everyone as he took stock of the situation, hoping he wasn't going to die. Elijah blacked out, then came to.

"... to say the chant out loud and put my name into the slot needed. Hand me the nightshade and graveyard dirt." Quinn's voice shook, and she took a deep breath calming herself, then snatched the ingredients from Camilla. "Okay, let's do this."

Camilla's eyes shot to Elijah and Parker, then she backed away, terror covering her face. Quinn tucked the nightshade under Parker's head. She took the graveyard dirt and sprinkled it over herself, then she gently grabbed Camilla's hand. "Now. No time for doubts. You can do it. No matter what happens ... don't stop reading until you've reached the end."

Helen's grip tightened again around Elijah's neck. He shoved down his fear and looked straight at the corpses rotting face. An epiphany hit him. Helen was torturing him and savoring the act of strangling him.

She's enjoying trying to kill me.

The two other apparitions of women from the apartment appeared behind Helen again. They flickered out, then flickered back into view like a distorted hologram. Elijah's eyesight faded as he struggled to breathe. His head felt like it was going to explode.

The poltergeist loosened her hands, and Elijah was so dizzy he almost threw up. He blinked several times, attempting to regain focus through the chaos and through his torture. Elijah noticed five women now, each separately standing next to Quinn, Riley, Parker, Camilla, and Elijah.

"Now would be a good time—five pissed-off poltergeists are standing here," Elijah coughed out. Instinctively, Elijah knew these two new women were connected to the Shaw sisters and this wasn't all of the them, one was missing. Six was the correct number not just five.

Camilla's voice was loud as she called out the Shaw sisters, yelling the spell like Quinn had asked. The poltergeist attached to Camilla squeezed her chest, and she fell to the ground, uttering the spell. Quinn grunted in pain as the fire symbol on her arm burned, glowing like an ember.

Riley stood next to Elijah, sobbing, her expression helpless. "I'm sorry." She grabbed his hand, holding it comfortingly.

Elijah's eyesight faded; the back of his head throbbed. Helen's decomposing nose was inches from Elijah's. The black pits of her eyes penetrated him with evil. His ears rung, and Camilla's terrified voice faded in and out as she battled to finish the spell like Quinn instructed. Then blackness.

Samuel was dying. Sweat poured from him, soaking the fainting couch where he rested. A beautiful woman held his hand tenderly, her blonde hair cascading over her shoulders in tousled ringlets. He looked down at her as she knelt next to him. Her eyes were filled with desperation. Samuel looked up to see a Native American woman with a kind face mixing a potion. She worked her calloused hands over the bottle, mumbling to herself.

"Here, drink this." The medicine woman's tone was soft and kind.

"No, just let me die." Samuel said weakly.

"You're not thinking this through, Samuel. Please?" The blonde woman

pleaded. *"Will you please quit being so stubborn?"* Her eyes rounded, and a tear rolled down her pale cheek.

"I'm not changing into one of those things. This whole mess is my fault. I deserve to die." Samuel said, his breaths labored.

"You're a good person, this isn't your fault. It's the skinwalker's." The medicine woman replied.

Heat surged through Samuel. *"I killed my family."* Samuel's voice was drenched in guilt, and the blonde woman wept.

The gentlewoman sat next to him. *"Samuel, what she did was her own hate and anger. She's responsible for her own actions, no one else. But if your final decision is to not transform, then I have no other choice than to leave you. I respect you too much, Samuel, to go against your wishes."*

The Native American woman packed up her belongings, and the beautiful blonde woman grabbed her arm.

"You can't let him do this. Please. Johana, I need him. I can't lose him. Isn't there a way to do a reversal?"

Johana gently touched her face. *"I'm truly sorry, dear, but the spell is too far along."* Johana turned her attention to Samuel. *"You're a fine young man. I hope your soul finds peace after it leaves."* Johana's beautiful ebony hair was wild, and the firelight flickered across her reddish-brown face. *"I should have never taught her my customs."* Her eyes narrowed, regret raw in her expression. *"She wasn't ready."* Johana squeezed his hand, *"I'll miss you, my friend. You've been good to me."* Johana stood hesitantly, made her way to the door, quietly shutting it behind her.

The blonde woman knelt beside him, sobbing and struggling to speak. *"This is Temperance's doing. She doesn't want us together."*

Despair consumed Samuel at the thought of leaving the beautiful woman behind and alone.

Samuel's throat tightened, and nausea churned in his stomach. *"I knew I'd hurt her, but I'd never thought she'd kill me. We both know that even if I do survive this spell, they will still hang me. Either way, I'm going to die."*

Burning spread across the back of Elijah's head. Out of instinct, he shot up, swinging at Helen. His lungs burned from sage as he gasped, grabbing at his throat. There was a dull, slow throb in his body from the fading physical pain of his past life memory.

"He's awake." Riley sat next to him on the queen bed, calming him, and began cleaning his bite wound.

"Where's Parker? Is he okay?" Elijah's voice was hoarse. It hurt to speak. There was a clicking noise when he swallowed.

"He's fine." Riley pointed to Parker, who had removed wood flooring from the church and sat cross-legged next to a small hole. He chowed down on a sandwich. Parker clumsily waved and smiled with a mouth full of food. "Looking for the drugs, haven't found anything yet."

Hudson was behind him, his thick, ebony hair disheveled. He was still wearing his basketball shorts from the night before and sipping on an energy drink. Elijah's friend buzzed around, connecting all the organized articles and pictures about the Shaw family from the apartment with a red string. Numerous ceiling fans in the office whirled, making harmonizing whooshing sounds complimenting his anxious energy.

Darkness had fallen, and Elijah's eyes burned. "How long have I been out?"

"It's been about five hours."

"Where's Quinn?"

"Hey." Quinn came around the corner. Her voice was raspy and exhausted. She took a sewing kit from the side table and shoved it in the drawer. "I'm glad you're alright."

"I think I experienced another memory of Samuel's."

Quinn, intrigued, moved closer. "What was it?"

"He was dying, and a kind Native American woman was tried to help him, and a blonde woman cried and fought to keep him alive. I need to find everything I can about the Shaws and who that Native American woman was."

"Tell him what you did." Camilla came charging from a desk where she had hooked up Owen's external hard drive to a laptop.

Quinn's smile faded.

"Tell him, or I will." Camilla threw a pissed-off hand at Elijah, her voice tinged with sadness. She mumbled furiously in Spanish, waiting for Quinn to answer.

"I'm gonna go get you some water," Riley strode off.

Quinn stayed silent; she bit her bottom lip. Easing away from Elijah, she sat at the bottom of the bed.

"Somebody better tell me what the hell is going on. Now." Elijah sat, his weary eyes shifting between Camilla and Quinn.

Quinn hesitated. "I transferred Helen's connection."

"To who?" Elijah hesitated, scared to ask the next question. "To me?"

"To her," Camilla answered for Quinn. "She didn't just transfer Helen, she took the connection from me, Parker, you, and Riley. And she used me to do it. As of now, both of you are marked to die. And we have to watch the whole thing unfold." Camilla took five deep breaths, then held up a photocopy picture of the woman with the dark hair who had attacked him. "Meet Helen Shaw. Your and Owen's lunatic sister." Camilla slapped down the old picture on the bedside table next to Elijah. "Right now, you and Quinn are the only ones standing in the skinwalker's way."

"What are you talking about?" Elijah's breath thinned.

Quinn spoke up from the end of the bed, gently touching Elijah's foot. "We found what we were looking for. The spell needed to create a skinwalker. The flesh of a loved one, graveyard dirt, a sacrifice. The spell has to take place in a familiar location to both the skinwalker *and* the victim. There's a new moon tomorrow, which would be ideal for the skinwalker rite. I hate to state the obvious, but the skinwalker already bit you," Quinn said.

Elijah stared at her, confused. "You guys aren't making any sense."

Camilla closed her wounded eye for a moment and gently rubbed the cut on her eye socket. "That handprint that Helen left on you is used to mark sacrifices. The symbols on the trees have the same purpose, one for each victim. *The sacrifice*. Those poltergeists must have been the last victims. The thing is, there were only three Shaw sisters on record that were ever born. So, where'd the other two come from?"

The handprint on Elijah's forearm was gone, completely healed. Quinn held out her arm, showing Elijah that the handprint was now on her forearm—along with the five symbols. He squinted, examining her bare ankles, and noticed burn marks in the form of handprints.

Astonished, Elijah directed his attention back to Camilla. "You saw them?" Elijah raised his eyebrows, leaning against the headboard. His back throbbed.

"All five crazy-ass bitches?" Camilla's Puerto Rican accent thickened. "Yes."

The light in Quinn's eyes faded. "The only scenario I can come up with is the skinwalkers trying to survive. If it's been alive for this long, the only way to do that would be to kill who it was closest to. Our soul tribe, *if* we are all connected, have lived through this story before ... that skinwalker keeps sending us through the same lessons over and over so *it can* stay alive. I'm pretty sure you're the main ingredient, but it's only a theory."

"You're telling me this thing is killing us because it loved Owen and me one hundred and eighty years ago?" Elijah ran his fingers through his thick hair.

"Yeah, pretty much." Quinn laid down on the bed next to him. "I need to rest a minute."

"Where's your necklace?" Elijah asked, brushing her bare collar bone with his thumb.

"I took it off. If I hadn't, Helen wouldn't have been able to connect to me. It's a protection stone." Quinn yawned.

Elijah was pretty sure she'd been wearing it when they were going through the chaos.

"How do we get rid of it? Is there a way to sever the connections? Reverse my bite?"

"There should be a way to sever the connections. I've watched Nana Evie do it before. I called Shelly. She's on her way here." Quinn brushed her messy hair away from her face and covered herself with a gray sheet.

"Fuckin' great." Elijah shoved back the blankets and swung his feet out of bed. "I need to listen to Owen's recordings. Maybe there's something in there about the identity of the skinwalker."

Quinn grabbed his hand, keeping her eyes closed. "Don't be mad at me. We need help, Elijah. We're out of our depth right now."

25

THE CHURCH HAD MINIMAL lighting, and mostly all the fixtures inside weren't large enough. The light from the ceiling fans that spread through the sanctuary's vaulted ceilings was barely enough to see by. The group decided to close all the windows on the off-chance Alpha, and Beta wanted to reappear. Elijah wasn't sure what to make of the Beta. He hadn't seen the wolf since the night prior. He had no clue as to why the animal had turned against its partner to save him. Elijah had listened to some of Owen's past life regression recordings, and nothing of use was revealed. Elijah did his best to make it through the information, but his mind immediately blocked out anything that could have been useful. Hearing Owen's voice was too agonizing. Not enough time had passed to allow him to objectively listen, and he wasn't sure that there ever would be a day when he could say that it had.

The humid and warm air in the church caused the porous wood of the structure to give off an aroma of damp cedar. Sweat trickled down the back of Elijah's neck, and his black T-shirt stuck to his skin. Elijah decided the first order of business (if he survived) was to get an air conditioning unit for the church. He'd been walking around in his bare feet for a few hours, going through all of the books on necromancy and shapeshifting. There was little information about his rival, but something was better than nothing. The hardwood flooring creaked under his toes as he hurried through the aisles, finding books and setting them on a desk. Elijah paused, grabbed a pencil, and scribbled a possible password on a notepad for the secured file on Owen's hard drive. He'd amassed a list of twenty in less than an hour to help Camilla. He'd also simultaneously searched through every genealogical file Owen had compiled on the Shaw family.

There wasn't *one* mention of *anyone* named Mary or Olivia. The names both disconcerted him in a way that told him they were just a sliver of glass in a larger shattered reality. Bewildered as to why Elijah's obsession to uncover who the names were connected to caused anxiety to surface. Elijah's intuition told him that he was running out of time.

He did discover that the Shaws only had three daughters: Louisa, Sophia, and Clara. They were the top of society and had been quite nasty to other girls within the city. Looking at their death photos, Elijah could tell they were the same ghosts outside of the church earlier that day and now attached to Quinn. He found a marriage photo of Samuel and a woman named Temperance. She had long, curly, blond hair and delicate features. Temperance's smile was wide, which Elijah noted as unusual for a photograph in that time frame. Temperance was in love.

Something about the photo piqued his psychic senses, so he tucked it in his back pocket. Temperance *wasn't* the woman he saw in Samuel's vision; the woman Samuel was madly in love with. There also was no mention of any Native American woman in Beaufort. He hadn't the slightest clue who the mystery medicine woman could be.

Digging deeper, Elijah found where Owen discovered the affair between Edgar Shaw and Phoebe Reynolds, both respective pillars of their vastly growing communities and patriarch and matriarch of their families. They'd written love letters.

Elijah took a break when Shelly arrived, full of rage, her face covered with confusion at the sight of the church. He explained to her what was happening, and she quieted for about fifteen minutes as she glared at Owen's journal, furiously flipping through the pages, getting angrier with each flip. Riley stood next to Shelly, rubbing her back. Binx was curled into a ball on Owen's bed, snoring. The anger he had witnessed from Binx at the police station was gone. The only thing he could guess was the Binxy didn't like Jensen.

Hudson was hiding in the corner with Parker quietly discussing historical maps of Seven Sisters Road, both of them making their best effort to avoid confrontation. Camilla sat quietly in the corner, shifting her eyes between everyone, watching the scene play out. She cursed in Spanish under her breath as she turned her attention back to the computer, paused the documentary footage, wrote a note, and pushed play.

Elijah knew she cursed because she'd done it before when she and Elijah found out about Riley and Owen. Earlier in the evening, Elijah had found Camilla hiding behind the shed by herself, sobbing. The only thing he could think to do was to hold her and let her cry. Listening to Owen's voice on the past life regressions and seeing him in the videos was torture. And Elijah knew out of all of them, the pain Camilla was enduring watching and listening to him was far worse than anything anyone else in the group would have to suffer.

"It's most likely those poltergeists are going to kill you unless we can kill the necromancer that cast the spell. It'll take five days to complete a sever spell, and from your state right now, I can tell you have three days less than *that*. We have no idea what *type* of spell was cast." Shelly was red in the face, and her whole body was stiff. "But you knew that, didn't you?"

"If I hadn't transferred it, three people would have died," Quinn said tiredly, leaning against a file cabinet. She'd stripped down to green sweat-shorts and a white tank top.

"You transferred five centuries-old poltergeists from three people into *one*."

Elijah could sense Quinn's energy diminishing with each passing second. Shelly might be angry, but he knew her assessment was on target. He rubbed the back of his neck, a wave of uncertainty crashed over him. Elijah had no idea if he or Quinn were going to survive the night.

"Let's say you guys are right, and that skinwalker has been alive for almost two centuries. If we're going to kill the creature, we'll need the original incantation, silver, and its given name at *birth* for a reversal—or there's a more savage way. Ripping out its heart and burning it."

"There's a crapload of silver in the work shed," Camilla yelled from the back. She typed busily on her laptop, keeping her eyes on the screen, pausing only to take a drink of coffee.

Shelly ignored her, too blinded by her fury. "Information that old is going to be impossible to find. It takes weeks of preparation to properly complete and execute a reversal spell of that magnitude."

"Nana's done a sever spell for a poltergeist in a day." Quinn was annoyed now.

"We're talking about *one hundred and eighty years* of connections, cords, and emotional energies that are complex and complicated *through dimensions*. A mixing of spiritual and magical practices with the Navajo, Necromancy, and Wiccan. You can't undo everything in a day. Those spells Evie created were used for the *recently* dead." Shelly yelled, and she turned away. "I can't even look at you right now."

Elijah understood why Quinn had made the decision to transfer the poltergeists. She already *knew* what was happening, and she didn't want anyone to stop her from saving them. It's the same thing he would have done.

Shelly turned back around, her arms swinging. "Also, if this skinwalker is manipulating the dead, robbing them of their *free will*, this witch is *evil*. I can't believe you did this to him." Shelly pointed furiously at Elijah. "This is why I'm against practicing magic. Because of this right here." Shelly's tone was rich with disdain.

Elijah stepped between the arguing women. "She was trying to find out who killed Owen."

"*You*." Shelly pointed a finger at Elijah, and her eyes narrowed. "I told you to stay away from her. Now, look at you! You're gonna die."

"I just have to ride out the next two days. The spell will fade. She's the one that has less time," Elijah said flatly.

"No. You can't just ride out the next few days. It's eaten your flesh. The first phase of the spell has already passed. At most, you have two days after it takes a bite out of you, unless you find a way to reverse the spell. If it doesn't eat all of you, you have to either eat the flesh of someone you love and turn into one, or you get sick and die. There's no in-between. I have never heard of anyone in history recovering from a skinwalker bite." Shelly swiped her hand through the air. "Let's hope for your sake there's a loophole we haven't found yet."

Elijah's breath left his lungs, and everything he never did with his life flashed before his eyes. "I'm gonna die?"

Shelly reached for Elijah, and he turned away from her, walking down one of the aisles. The realization of his own impending doom whirled around him, and for one minute, the rest of the world stopped existing.

Camilla stopped what she was doing in the corner and joined the group conversation. Her onyx-colored hair was pulled back in a messy bun, and her black tank top was damp with sweat on her chest. Her eyes shot to Quinn and then back to Elijah. She turned away, placing her hands on her hips, cursing furiously in Spanish under her breath.

"Not to mention Camilla." Shelly turned to Quinn. "If you die, she's gonna have to live the rest of her life with the guilt that she helped you kill yourself."

Quinn's eyes gravitated away from Shelly's face, landing on her hands where she picked at her cuticles. "There's a balance to everything. You know that. The skinwalker controlling Helen will get the evil energy returned to them three-fold. What you put out is what you get back." Quinn's tone was steady. "Everything has a yin and yang. It's one of the first things we learn as children in the coven." Quinn looked up from her hands, walking toward Shelly.

Shelly tried to find her way around Elijah, and he blocked her. She leaned, looking around him at Quinn. "You did something incredibly irresponsible, and now I might lose the only family I have left. I'm going to lose both of you."

"You had no idea your own son was practicing elementals. If you hadn't turned into such a bigot, he could have come to *you*. You would have known." Quinn tried to maneuver around Elijah and get to her aunt. Elijah blocked her, and she gave him a cutting glare.

"Hey. Chill out. Don't talk to her like that." Riley narrowed her eyes at Quinn. "We might not be in this situation if you'd respected her wishes."

"Don't get me started on you," Quinn said, jabbing a finger at Riley, then turned back to Shelly. "Owen was already working spells on his own before I came into the picture. I have no idea how he got started, 'cause he wouldn't tell me. If you hadn't lied to him and told him his whole family was dead or lost touch, he might have had somewhere to turn."

"After your mother died, everyone else *was* dead to me. Did you tell Owen?" Shelly waved his journal. "About my mother and his lineage?"

Quinn sighed, and stared at the floor. Sweat beaded on her chest, and there were gray rings under her eyes. "I told him about all of us."

"That's why he started pushing me away? Well, that's fitting. Did you tell Elijah about his father too?" The words had escaped Shelly's mouth in an angry flurry. As soon as they left, her remorseful expression told him she'd wished they hadn't.

Elijah crossed his arms, and his eyes hardened. "What about my father?"

"You told Owen when it suited you, but not Elijah?" Shelly jabbed a thumb in Elijah's direction.

Quinn backed away, wiping her sweaty palms on her shorts. "He didn't die in an accident. Your father—"

"Was a Medium too. He died when he was helping two witches, Kathrine and her husband Gregory, perform an exorcism on a home to save a little girl. Who were those witches?" Shelly glared at Quinn.

"My mother and father ..." Quinn paused. It was apparent the words hurt her to say.

An overwhelming desire to run and an engulfing need to stay disoriented him. His emotions were sent into an upheaval, and Elijah wasn't sure he wanted to be privy to the truth. His head whirled, and acid bubbled in the back of his throat, coating his tongue. Quinn had known about his abilities the whole time. That's why she'd summoned him out to Seven Sisters Road and used him during the ghost hunt.

Quinn continued, "My Nana Evie sent them there, knowing the risk."

"That right there ... is why I officially left the coven. They were irresponsible too." Shelly slapped down Owen's journal on the desk. "Messing with things you don't have a full understanding of is dangerous. One of the first things we learned in the coven as children." Shelly spat Quinn's words back at her.

Shock and betrayal ravaged Elijah. "You knew the truth about my father this whole time, and you, of all people, let me believe a lie?" Elijah did his best to control his tone, but as his eyes shifted from Shelly to Quinn, his patience fluttered out. "You both fucking lied to me."

Shelly's eyes brimmed with tears, and she pointed a finger at Elijah "Don't you curse at me again, Elijah Ward. I don't care what the circumstances are."

Elijah turned to Shelly, the muscles in his arms twitching. "You lied to me my whole life." Prickles spread through Elijah's legs. He placed his trembling, clammy hands on his hips to keep himself from throwing something. "You have any idea how long I've dealt with this ability on my own? Believing I was crazy? You left me vulnerable to destructive energies as a child? And you could have helped me?" Elijah's voice was stern, and his shoulders tightened.

The room fell silent, and it sounded like the group had collectively stopped breathing as if they were all interconnected, waiting to see how his anger would unfold. The weight of their collective gazes caused the back of his neck to heat.

Shelly leaned against the desk. "I was trying to protect you—"

"The way you protected Owen?" Elijah's tone was bitter and cutting.

"Elijah, com'mon man," Hudson said softly from the corner. He slapped a book he held onto a desk and walked to where Elijah stood.

Frustrated tears rolled down Shelly's face. "I tried to stop your father from going to that house, and he wouldn't listen." Her voice was strained as she threw an angry hand at Elijah. "The way you're not listening now," Shelly sniffled. "He had the same stubbornness you do. There was more to that haunting. Something wasn't right about the whole situation."

Elijah's hands ached to hit something, so he turned his back to her, taking long, deep breaths. Parker joined his brother next to Elijah, as if they were a bomb squad trying to diffuse him from exploding with rage. Elijah's brother had died, now he was going to die, and so was Quinn.

All because of disagreements and a lack of communication. I'm going to die.

The ridiculousness of pride and old principles in the Ward men not only cost Elijah's father his life, but they were also now going to cost him his own.

"Detective Jensen and Bohannon came by and showed me the pictures of Owen with the drug dealers. When were you going to tell me my son was involved?" Shelly folded her arms across her chest, waiting for Elijah to turn back toward her.

"I didn't want to stress you out. I was trying to take care of it on my own. They were threatening to kill you *and* me." Elijah kept his back to her, his heart in a million pieces. The sight of her made him want to escape to his car and leave Savannah in his rearview mirror.

"You still should have told me!" Shelly's voice strained. "He's my son."

Elijah walked toward the back door. He could hear Hudson's raspy voice behind him.

"I hate to break up this heartwarming family moment, but we're running out of time. The new moon energy starts tonight." Hudson turned to Shelly. "The truth is Quinn tried to right a wrong and saved my brother's life. *Knowing* there was a massive chance she'd die," Hudson said firmly. "We need to put our minds together and figure this shit out. Did it occur to anyone that this is exactly what these bastards wanted? To divide us?"

Elijah shoved the already open door, slamming it against the wall as he walked out. "Don't worry, I'm done." He stopped on the back porch, kicking the side of the church repeatedly, then sat on a step, digging his hands into his hair.

Binx startled Elijah, trotting out of the church with his ears tucked back and laid halfway in his lap, pushing his snout under Elijah's hand, asking sweetly for affection. He stroked the spot between the dog's eyes with his thumb. The soft golden fur of Binx's head and back was relaxing; unconditional love was a comfort Elijah needed. The warmth of Binx's companionship had helped him many nights when it felt like his life was falling apart and he was losing his mind. His canine companion was always there to bring him back from the edge of madness. Elijah scratched behind Binx's ears, grateful for his support.

"You'll never lie to me. Will you Binxy?" Elijah whispered, and Binx raised his ears, crawling further into Elijah's lap.

Elijah could hear Shelly's voice through the door as he studied the inlet. "Hudson's right. We need to figure out our plan of action. If this skinwalker's going to do anything, it would make sense for it to be under the new moon. All spellwork for new beginnings is usually cast at that time."

The divination Kiren made was accurate—Elijah *did* inherit his abilities from a parent. He needed to speak to her again. She was the only one who'd given him any kind of truth. It became clearer that his mother might have left because she couldn't deal with the dangers of the paranormal lifestyle. It made him a tad less angry toward her.

Quinn walked up behind him to talk, and he escaped from her into the greenhouse. Elijah had thought the connection to her was real. But, as it turned out, there *never had been* one. She'd only used him to find a skinwalker.

THE FURY INSIDE ELIJAH calmed, and the time for him to brood about things he had no control over had passed. Someone was waging war against his soul tribe; they wanted to destroy him *and* them. There had to be a reason why this particular Shaw family member had changed into a skinwalker. As far as their research showed, there were nine immediate family members. They were able to rule out four of them: Helen, Benjamin, Temperance, and Samuel.

The only curious thing about Temperance is that after the burning of the Shaw plantation, she seemed to disappear into the world. There was no death certificate, proof she'd received any funds after Samuel's death, or any documentation showing she had been remarried. Emma and Jerome, the last living descendants of the Shaw family, said she vanished.

Binx was in the tall grass near the back door of the church, chasing crickets. Soft rain tapped on the modest greenhouse glass as Elijah brushed his fingertips over aromatic sage leaves, trying to decide the best part of the herb to pluck. The exterior lights of the church filtered in through the limescale windows, dimly illuminating the aisles and the labels on the planter boxes. The pungent smell of earth and mildew burned his nose and made the back of his throat itch. Steam and humidity in the greenhouse dampened Elijah's shirt. The timed watering system clicked on, and mist sprayed from the hoses that lined the greenhouse ceiling. A large fan oscillated in the corner cooling the water on his hot, sticky skin.

Elijah was searching for the herbs that Shelly had put on a list. They had all decided to create an *effective* protective circle around the church and its grounds. Elijah suggested using silver shavings intermingled with salt based on an entry in Owen's journal. It was supposed to specifically target skinwalkers.

Elijah slid out the picture of Samuel and Temperance from his back pocket, studying their faces. Her blond hair was in a high up-do, and ringlets cascaded over her shoulder, and her 1800s style wedding dress was extravagant. Elijah rubbed a dirty thumb over Temperance's face.

I betrayed my wife. What did I do to my family?

Overwhelming sadness and guilt took hold of him, and Elijah shoved the picture back into his jeans pocket. Staring at her face caused a melancholy to rise in his soul. The contents of the journal and the information in the church were proving to be invaluable. The lush and beautiful plants filled every aisle and hung from the ceiling. Each was labeled with its scientific name and description of its magical uses. He was unaware that Owen had a green thumb.

"What we need to ask is what these rune symbols, Navajo traditions, and the necromantic magic can tell us about the witch. The spells are unique to the caster. So, where did they learn these abilities and spiritual beliefs? Why did they use them together? What was their motive to *become* a skinwalker?"

Elijah could hear Shelly from behind him at the greenhouse doorway and the crinkling of Owen's rubbings in her hand. She wasn't wrong, and the questions were valid. There was a *human* reason behind the killer's motives, no matter how skewed they might be—the basics of what we all were, was emotions. This killer had a background, and they needed to search for things that matched what they knew.

Keeping his eyes locked on the plants, Elijah plucked what he needed and dropped it into a mason jar. There was a new level of mystery to his life, not everything was so black and white anymore, and Elijah wasn't sure he liked this new mixed color of grey.

He heard Shelly walk in behind him and lean against a wooden greenhouse shelf, waiting patiently for his response. In truth, Elijah had no idea how to respond, and his mind was flooded with confusion.

Did his father know what would happen to Elijah? Was his *MawMaw* aware of his and his father's gifts? Were they genetic? How come they never told him about his *possible* abilities? Sorrowfully, Elijah would never have a chance to find out. An aching to find his mother waved through him.

"Elijah, did you hear me?" Shelly gently touched his arm, her hand trembling. "I can't deal with you being mad at me. Especially not right now." His head dipped, and he pinched the bridge of his nose, staying silent. Shelly turned him toward her. There were red rings around her eyes, and her blonde bangs clung to her sweaty forehead. "It's not her fault. Quinn's. She lost *both* her parents. You *both* were orphaned at the same time. Quinn was right. If I'd told you and Owen, he might still be alive. I'm a horrible mother." Shelly caressed a velvety leaf of one of the flowers.

"Owen should have come to you. No matter what you thought." Elijah's raspy voice was sullen but firm. "You were only doing what you thought was right."

"He did always have a way of shouldering things alone." Shelly cracked a half-smile at his memory. Her steel-blue eyes filled with tears. "What have I done to my family?"

"I need to tell you something," Elijah said. "I went to a psychic. She told me that Owen's spirit was trapped in the afterlife. Someone's keeping him captive."

"What psychic?"

"A woman who has an office next to the Thirsty Parrot. Her name's Kiren."

"How do you know you can trust her or her visions? Not all psychics are genuine." There was something about how Shelly recoiled at the mention of her name that was a little strange.

"I saw Owen the night of the funeral. I'm pretty sure she's right. I have a feeling it's the skinwalker controlling him."

Wails of guilt reverberated through the greenhouse; tears cascaded down Shelly's cheeks. Elijah witnessed her broken soul shatter more. The trace amounts of remaining rage inside him diminished. No matter how mad he was, nothing was more painful than Shelly crying and Elijah being the cause. Elijah engulfed her in a hug as raw emotions of Owen's murder reeled through her. It was as if she was reliving the pain of identifying Owen's body in the morgue all over again.

"Me being mad will pass. It's just gonna take some time. We need to find out if Owen is trapped in between dimensions. Being controlled by that thing. I'll do whatever it takes to fight for Owen," Elijah's tone was gentle.

"I know you will. Your dad didn't want this for you. A life filled with death. I did my best to keep it away. I cast protection spells on you daily, trying to block as many visions as I could."

"You did?" Elijah raised his dark eyebrows in acceptance of her answer and wiped away her tears.

"I still do. You're my son."

Elijah squeezed her tighter. His whole body relaxed, and it occurred to him after reading Owen's journal that this was one of those moments he was supposed to relearn from his past life. His intuition was screaming that he was on the right track. Elijah was supposed to learn how to *forgive*.

"It's gonna be alright. I'm gonna be okay, so is Quinn."

He wanted to believe it would be, that they would have the fairytale ending they so desperately wanted. His psychic awareness was growing. The precipice of everything he was born to become had arrived. Shelly did her best to protect him and Owen. In the end, it wasn't enough. She was only one person like he was only one man.

"You know Nana excommunicated Quinn. For helping Owen. She doesn't have anyone." Elijah kept Shelly locked in a bear-hug and rubbed her back.

Shelly sobbed into Elijah's chest, then quieted, attempting to talk. "What she's battling is intense. My granny used to call it ghost-fever. As a white witch, Quinn's energy is lighter. The multiple angry ghosts vibrate at lower frequencies. The two different energies are fighting for control, and she's outnumbered." She held him as if it might be the last time, clinging tightly, afraid to let go. "The constant exposure of multiple lower energetic frequencies is causing her physical body to break down. Camilla, Riley, and I are doing our best to help and hold it at bay, but if it keeps building ... even if we stop the entities, the damage to her physical body will be irreversible."

Sorrow and hopelessness rolled over him. Elijah cleared his throat, resting his cheek on the top of her head. Tears welled in his eyes and rolled down his cheeks.

Shelly sighed, "Quinn's not gonna be able to hold on for too much longer. Her soul *is old*, and she's strong, but each of us have our breaking point."

"Hey, Hudson says he found something." Riley's exhausted voice startled Elijah. Her bloodshot eyes studied Elijah and Shelly. Riley walked over and turned Shelly toward her, holding her gently in her arms. Riley observed Elijah, her eyebrows pinched together as she tried to keep herself from crying. She used one hand to wipe away Elijah's tears while still comforting Shelly. Riley swallowed heavily, then mouthed the words, "*I'm sorry.*" She grabbed Elijah's hand and squeezed.

"I'm so glad I have you, Riley," Shelly coughed out.

Binx's low, protective growl, and sharp bark tore them from their moment of grief. Shelly wiped ribbons of tears from her cheeks. The scrambling of Binx's claws against the wooden back stairs of the church warned Elijah that the dog was charging for a threat. An unknown malicious predator ready to devour them all. Riley grabbed his arm; the evil radiating from the forest was on her radar as well.

"Binxy, No. Come back." Camilla's voice echoed through the rural land.

"Hello, hello, my friends," Owen's voice boomed from the darkness.

Camilla tripped over her own feet in shock, then quickly regained her balance. Before Elijah could process what was happening, Riley dashed from the greenhouse, joining Camilla. "Bix, for god sake, come back!" Riley's voice was strained with worry.

Binx's angry barks faded as he charged into the woods. Elijah's stomach flipped, and his hands balled into fists. The bite on his arm throbbed, and his mouth watered. Owen's voice echoed again.

"I know you can hear me. I'm watching you right now."

Riley looked at Elijah through an open window of the greenhouse, and her eyes widened with fear. Shelly trembled, and tears brimmed her eyes.

Shelly spun toward Elijah, a shaky hand covering her mouth. "That's not, he's—"

"It's the skinwalker. They mimic voices." Elijah moved to the window, meeting Riley, who was on the other side. "Go get the shotgun."

"You don't have to tell me twice." Riley sprinted into the church, hurdling over the back stairs.

"You stay in here." Elijah kept his eyes on the woods. The energy stirred a hunger in his primal senses, and it was intoxicating.

"No, you can't ... don't go out there," Shelly pleaded.

Elijah jogged out of the greenhouse shutting the door behind him. Riley stood firm at the top of the stairs next to the church's back door with the shotgun pointed toward the forest. Binx went quiet, and a pain-filled yelp echoed through the night. Elijah fought the urge to run into the dark and save the dog. The whole group raced toward the back door.

Elijah threw his hand up, "You guys stay in there. Don't come out. You're protected." His voice was a blend of indignation and anxiety.

"I'm coming to help you," Quinn's tired voice pierced the night. Elijah heard her stumble, and Hudson's soothing voice calming her, telling her to sit.

Binx's bloody, limp body catapulted out of the forest and rolled, landing at Elijah's feet. The dog's chest rose and fell rapidly, and his beautiful golden fur was coated with blood and matted around his neck. Binx whined and his breathing shallowed. His jaw relaxed and his tongue rolled out onto the ground. The kind and loving dog stopped moving. Camilla shrieked as Parker and Hudson yelled obscenities. Elijah struggled to breathe and fell to his knees, hovering his shaking hands over Binx in shock.

The asshole killed my dog.

Shelly sprinted out of the greenhouse to see what was happening, and her horrified scream rattled the windows as she instinctively went to Binx. Before Elijah had the wherewithal to tell her to get back in, someone was holding a knife to her throat. Landon's face peeked out from behind her as he used her as a shield. His brow was thick with sweat, and he panted heavily. The stale scent of cigarettes drifted on the coastal wind, and Elijah narrowed his eyes, waiting for Allison.

"Allison isn't here." Landon grinned devilishly, and a dab of blood painted the corner of his mouth. His voice morphed from Owen's back into Landon's like a sound mix from a movie. "He saw me changing forms, so naturally, I had to feed him to the gators. Which is unfortunate. I kinda liked him." Landon smiled and raised an eyebrow, straightening his leather jacket. "Consider it a gift." He wiped the blood from his mouth with the back of his hand.

Shock rocked Elijah as he paused, trying to understand how Landon had run the length of half a football field in two seconds. Riley leveled the shotgun at Landon, clicking off the safety. Everyone inside crowded around a window, watching the scene unfold from behind her. Elijah didn't see Quinn. It occurred to him this could be a ploy to misdirect and kidnap someone. Elijah kept his eyes on Landon. "Someone go sit with Quinn. Lock all the doors, shut all the windows." Camilla and Parker disappeared.

"Sorry about the way I came into the property." Landon flickered an evil grin that showing that he enjoyed his lethal game of chess. "I didn't want anyone to follow me." His voice was light and playful, like he was enjoying a conversation with a friend, a *family member*. But it couldn't be Owen masking himself, he was dead. Elijah had seen his ghost. "I have to give you credit though, the protection spell you cast around the church is pretty solid." Landon's smile faded.

Shelly's continued silence made Elijah unsure if she was in shock or contemplating her death. She was stiff, and both of her hands were out to her side, trembling. Ice ran down Elijah's spine, the metal of the silver shotgun rattled in Riley's gloved hands.

"Let her go, and we can go talk alone, by ourselves." Elijah's voice was steady.

"How 'bout you kiss my ass." Landon tightened his grip on Shelly's arm and dug the blade of his dagger into her throat, drawing blood. It dripped down her neck, and Elijah felt an unfamiliar hunger surface.

There was a flash of light in Landon's eyes, the same fire that blazed in the alpha's.

"You're the skinwalker. The wolf." Elijah took a few steps, and his eyes narrowed. "My family."

Shelly whimpered as Landon wriggled the blade into her pale neck, and her fists clenched.

"You move any closer, and I'll slit her throat." Landon's eyes were wild with a contained homicidal urge fighting to be released.

Elijah had no idea how he'd made such a wrong judgment. When he'd first seen Landon, he could swear there was an innocence to him. Elijah's nostrils flared, and his hands shook. A surge of adrenaline pulsed through his veins and the need to beat Landon into oblivion threatened to take over his rational mind. Uncertain how to proceed, Elijah took deep breaths taking back control over his fight-or-flight urges. The last thing he wanted was to be the reason for Shelly's death.

"What do you want?" Elijah straightened his stance, standing taller, refusing to let Landon make him cower; he let go of his fear. Shelly needed him to be strong. Her life at the moment depended on it.

"I want Florence's grimoire, and you're gonna find it for me. I've been looking for one hundred and eighty years, but I finally got lucky. In this life, you all are smarter, and *you* have more knowledge of the afterlife, a special link."

"Who's Florence? What spellbook are you talking about?" The stirring of emotion at the unknown name made goosebumps form on his arms.

Landon clenched his jaw, annoyed. "Quinn," he waved to the inside of the church, "who was Florence, your mistress. You usually remember her sooner. But, past life indiscretions aside, it's time to get down to business. Either you get it for me, or all of you will die—again."

Landon's face paled, and his grip around the dagger tightened. Elijah could tell he wasn't well and that Quinn was right, the spell was fading, and the skinwalker was dying.

"Why should I do anything for you?" Elijah's hands were balled in fists.

"Are you deaf? I'm going to kill all of you." Landon's tone was arrogant and firm.

"You're sick and decaying. You've spent centuries trying to get revenge against me. Aren't you ready to die?" Elijah stood his ground, quickly taking in his surroundings for any other outliers that may be waiting to attack.

"This is your fault! You took him away from me, and now you have to give him back!" Landon's voice was desperate and resentful, but a woman's tone surfaced underneath. Landon's eyes widened, he took the knife away from Shelly's neck and pointed it at Elijah in rage. "You're the one who did this to me. Made me this way." Landon shoved Shelly out of the way, and she stumbled to the ground, crawling next to the church, holding her throat. Landon rushed toward Elijah, Riley took the shot, and before Elijah knew what was happening, Landon grunted with an inhuman, dog-like yelp. The gun was catapulted behind the church, and Riley was cut across her arm, screaming in pain.

Landon's eyes shifted to Riley, then back to Elijah. "I'm not dying. I've only been in this body for too long," he said. "You'll never kill me, Samuel. It's the only thing you've never been able to do."

A blur formed in the space between him and Landon, and Elijah was catapulted through the air. He collided with the greenhouse, and his back exploded with pain that radiated through his arms. Elijah's whole body ached as he lifted himself from the broken glass, rolling out onto the wet, muddy ground, blood flowing from the wound on his left shoulder. Before Elijah could reorient himself, Landon hovered over him with the point of his knife to his throat. Elijah noticed the initials TMD on the handle of what he was now able to tell was an antique dagger. Owen's matching leather bracelet Elijah had been searching for was around his wrist. Whether Landon was in his true form or not, Elijah had no doubt that the monster was Owen's murderer. Elijah searched the woods for Beta, hoping the dog would arrive.

"I'll give you a little motivation. If you want your soulmate, Quinn, to survive ... and for me to sever the connection with the sisters ..." Landon paused and gave Riley a curious glance out of the corner of his eye. Riley's shoulders slumped, her stoic stance temporarily rattled. She kept her eyes off Elijah, and he could tell she was avoiding looking at him. The mention of someone else being his soulmate had stung. It was written all over her face. "You'll get the book because if you don't, I'll change her." A gust of wind brushed Elijah's face. Landon now stood next to the church where Shelly rested. "It'll be nice to have a lineage witch, even if I can't have a psychic for eternity." Landon knelt, his nose inches from Shelly's cheek as he studied her like a fine specimen.

"Don't you touch her!" Spit flew from Elijah's mouth as he scrambled toward them.

Landon threw up a warning hand, ignoring his comment, turning back toward Elijah. "I knew Quinn would transfer the sisters to her to save the others. Especially *you*. You have until 3 am. If I don't get what I want ... I'll devour every single one of you. But by that time, Elijah, hopefully, you'll have already done it yourself." Landon's tone was grave.

"I have no idea what you're talking about." Elijah's back cracked as he sat.

"You can try to hide it from your friends, but you will only be able to resist the cravings for so long. It always takes over, and soon you'll be begging me to help save her from an eternity of horror." Landon raised his eyebrow as if to say, "checkmate." Then, as quickly as he'd arrived, like a phantom traveling on the wind, he disappeared into the steamy Lowcountry night.

"Elijah, are you alright?" Riley raced to him, and he stood, using the frame of the greenhouse to help him.

"Shelly, are you okay?" Elijah wiped off his pants. "Shelly?"

Camilla raced down the stairs, searching for her. Hudson and Parker searched the woods.

Tears brimmed Camilla's eyes. "She's gone. He took her."

Hudson stood in front of the group. They were all sitting except Quinn, who rested in her hammock with one leg over the side. Foreboding energy was palpable through the thick, humid air of the summer evening after Landon's visit. The toll the five poltergeists took on Quinn's physical being already showed after just six hours. Elijah stared at Quinn, mystified at how she was both mentally and spiritually keeping the angry spirits at bay. She vomited multiple times, and her eyelids were heavy. The sister's wrathful emotions teemed from Quinn, breaking her down from the inside.

"My guess is the symbols that afflicted you, and now Quinn is carved on all the trees surrounding the graveyard. And each of the poltergeists are connected to those runes. Since they are bound to the symbol, they are now bound to her." Hudson glanced at Quinn, "Using her life force like a battery."

"Ya'll better watch yo asses 'cause we figured out that even a momentary connection will open the gateway to allow darker entities to come through for a short amount of time. The ones that do come through can attach themselves to you." Parker pointed to everyone.

Hudson shot his brother a scathing glance, and Parker shrugged. "Do you mind if I continue?"

"Not at all, Mulder." Parker waved at him with nonchalance.

Elijah shot a glance toward Binx, who was doing surprisingly well and resting in the corner. His wounds were all superficial, and Camilla, visibly shaken, had dressed them.

"I got lucky somehow." Hudson's face flickered with guilt.

Elijah knew he felt awful for being the only one unaffected. It was in Hudson's DNA to be passionate about the details of anything serious that affected the ones he cared about.

"Now, if we mark the trees we've identified in the circle, along with two more, accounting for the other women outside of the Shaw sisters, look what happens?" Hudson took a swig of his energy drink and swirled his finger at the jagged and varying red strings. They crossed from one to another at different lengths, but all met in the middle, pinpointing a location on the map—Benjamin's grave. "This location here is where Samuel was reportedly executed." Hudson pointed to an area about a mile away from the outside of the strings. "The strange thing is there's a rose compass on the map next to it, deliberately painted in the center of the map with the North symbol missing. You can tell by the strokes that Edgar purposefully removed it from the drawing."

"It's a pentagram." Quinn's last word turned into a cough. Her voice was hoarse and thin. "The shape around the trees." Quinn whirled her finger in a star motion and then plopped her hand back down to her side.

A flicker in Elijah's mind—*stairs, a fireplace, stone walls.* Elijah walked to the map, touching the center in thought. "The trees encircle something, more than the graveyard and old property. Quinn, you said that you thought they were part of a bigger spell. What if the sacrifices weren't only to change a family member into a skinwalker but to open a gateway?"

"Mmmmhmmm is possi ..." Quinn's voice trailed off, and she coughed, then continued speaking with her eyes closed. "It would explain the other women. You could be right. Energies of that magnitude absorbed from another dimension would last for centuries. It could have been a twofer." Quinn paused, taking in relaxing breaths before continuing, "That's the weakness. From what I know, if they don't complete the ceremony every thirty years, they could die. Using the vortex would make them close to immortal. Renewing every two-hundred years."

"Wait, there's a theory that there was a vortex or gate there. That means that the gate had already been opened one hundred and eighty years ago."

"That circle of stones surrounding the house covers about a half-mile." Elijah shot Quinn a glance. "They were trying to keep someone *out*. Someone made a protection circle around it to keep out the skinwalker. What Landon needs is in that circle; it must be where Florence's grimoire is located, but where? And why does the skinwalker want to change me?"

"Maybe it's always been about changing you." Camilla touched Elijah's shoulder.

Confusion covered Riley's face as the words left Camilla's mouth. "That doesn't make sense," Her phone rang and startled her out of her thoughts. "I've got to take this. I'll be back." She answered quickly. "What do you need, Dylan? I'm busy." Riley hurried out the front door and onto the porch.

Stabbing cramps spread through Elijah's throat where Helen had strangled him. He winced and massaged the back of his neck. "All I know is Quinn and Shelly are running out of time. We can sit here as long as we want and theorize. I'm going out there. It's the only way I'll find the spellbook."

"You're not going out there, Elijah. That's what those damn things want." Riley's voice was firm. "There's two, remember?"

"Parker and I can go with the maps, sit in the 4-runner, and keep watch. Owen had some pretty good comm and walkie equipment. I'll hook you up to it." Hudson grabbed his boots.

"No, no way in hell am I going back out there. Have you all lost what's left of your minds?" Parker dropped a book on the table with a *plunk*. "We don't even know how to find what we're looking for."

"Quinn saved your life," Hudson said shortly, sliding on his boots. "Shelly needs us. It's the least you can do." His eyes narrowed as he grunted at his brother.

Parker paused, throwing his head back. "Gawwwd. I'm going only 'cause I don't want something to happen to yo ass. Mom and Dad would kill me," he grumbled.

"I'll go with you," Riley said, coming back inside. "I'm not gonna let you go out there by yourself."

"What if *you* don't come back?" Parker watched Elijah intently, his head dipping.

"Then I can die knowing I did everything I could to change the outcome not only for me but for all of you." Elijah smiled and turned back toward the room. "Before we go out there, I need to go back to my apartment and get my gun." Elijah walked to Quinn, who struggled to stay awake, laying in her hammock. He grabbed her hand and squeezed. "Did Owen make any silver bullets for a 9mm?"

"You can check. I know he bought a mold for them." Quinn coughed, then it transformed into a gurgle. She pulled her hand away from her mouth, blood spotting her fingertips. "That can't be good." Quinn rolled back into her hammock.

Camilla's eyes widened, and she bolted to Quinn's side. "Hurry. And be careful, please?"

Elijah clenched his jaw, and despair jolted through him. Camilla returned to the desk and impatiently typed on the laptop keyboard. "I'll keep working at this. I've got a whole list of possible passwords. Whatever is on this drive … there must be answers for us. Otherwise, it wouldn't be so well guarded."

A silence fell over the group, and an urgency flooded through Elijah. He needed to get to Shelly before it was too late. There was no way he was going to lose her and Owen. But, at the same time, he wanted to share the last moments he had with his friends and his soul tribe. They had all played a part in his current life. Their souls were all so familiar to him that it wouldn't surprise him to learn about multiple other lives where they'd fought, loved, and defended each other. The group was playing a supernatural Russian roulette by going out to Seven Sister's Road. Elijah hoped that for once, the psychic impressions he had received were wrong. Because those fragmented messages were telling him something he didn't want to be true—one of them was going to die.

27

THEY'D PUT TOGETHER A decent amount of ammo containing silver. Elijah had 9mm bullets that would fit his handgun, and Riley collected ample shells for the shotgun. For an added kick, they grabbed the mixture Shelly had created for the protective boundary of the church and loaded it into the shotgun shells. Riley went by her apartment and got her handgun. The two barn-sized doors to the workshop were open, and the songs of cicadas and toads filled the night. Light rain tapped on the tin roof and created a soothing sound. Elijah's favorite time was when the unbearable heat and stress of the day faded into cool, simple evenings.

Insects were beating against the bare bulb hanging above their heads. A small 70s style, silver FM radio played classic rock softly in the background. The music was interrupted by an annoying beep, alerting whoever was listening of an emergency weather alert. An electronic male voice came on, and Elijah glanced at the radio, noting that there was a warning for a severe tropical storm on its way to the South Eastern coast.

Elijah's intense eyes drifted over to Riley, and he analyzed her expression and body language in the steamy work shed. Riley's face was taut with determination as she wiped down the sawed-off shotgun with an oily rag. Beads of sweat marked her forehead and neck. Stray, wavy strands of her brown hair stuck to her face.

"You can ask me what you've been dying to ask me, Elijah." Riley kept her eyes on the shotgun as she wrapped a small piece of fabric around the tip of a cleaning rod and shoved it down the barrel, twisting it around. For an added measure, Shelly had etched a protection and banishment spell into the barrel's exterior, adding to the existing writings. It reminded Elijah of a prop from a supernatural-horror film.

"Which is what?"

Her round eyes locked on his. "If I knew about all of this."

"*Did* Owen bring you here?" Elijah finished loading the bullets into the second ammo box he was packing.

"I already told you he didn't." She set down the weapon, grabbed lubing, and squeezed it over the springs. "If I knew what was going on—*the truth of it all*—I would have told you." She put on her work gloves, loading the shotgun shells filled with silver. Sweat rolled down her temple.

"Who makes a shotgun out of silver?" Riley smiled.

"I'm sure he had his reasons."

Elijah swore there was a flicker of light in her pupil but decided it was his mind playing tricks on him again. Exhaustion toyed with his mind. Combine that with his psychic abilities, it became almost impossible to separate delusions from reality. Riley's hair cascaded over her face, and the harsh light of the shed glinted against crimson strands Elijah hadn't noticed before. Riley pulled it back into a ponytail, then wrapped it into a messy bun.

"Why are you staring at me?" She raised an eyebrow, giving a half-smile.

"I'm not. It's just ... eight months ago, I would have never thought we'd be here."

"Yeah, me either." Riley took a swig of water. "Ghosts and necromancers."

Slinging his backpack over his shoulder, Elijah strode toward the church, then stopped, turning around. "I'm gonna go check on Quinn and get some water. You want anything?"

"A bottle of vodka?" Riley smiled. "Tell Quinn I'm gonna do my damndest to make sure we figure this shit out."

Elijah grabbed his camo hat from the workbench and slid it on, then readjusted it. He'd worn it so much the inseam was starting to poke him in the back of his head. "I'll tell her, and Ri ..."

"Yeah." She paused and sighed, looking up from the water bottle cap she was playing with.

"Thanks," Elijah's voice softened. He dipped his chin, playing with his backpack strap. It was the closest he'd felt to Riley in a while. "No matter what happens ... thanks."

She wiped sweat from her brow. "I'll always help you, Elijah. Always."

Cool air drifted across Elijah, and the hair on his arm stood; someone was watching him. Elijah turned, scanning the trees, hoping that Landon hadn't decided to return. Riley's chatting muted, and everything around him faded. Behind the shed, out of Riley's view, Elijah saw a mass of energy blended with mist form into a translucent image of Owen from the waist up. Elijah held his breath as he watched the spirit of his brother reach to him, terror on his face. A telepathic message waved through his consciousness. *Don't forget about me. Don't leave me here.* Owen's voice was a distorted whisper. Elijah was wrapped in warm, loving energy, and he fingered his leather bracelet, fighting back the tears he wanted to let flow.

"Elijah." Riley stood in front of him now. The world around him came back into view, and he watched as Owen's spirit dissipated. "Are you alright?" Tilting her head to the side, she asked, "Have you seen a ghost?"

"I'm fine," Elijah cleared his throat, staying silent, ignoring the second question.

Riley quickly changed the subject. "Here, it's Quinn's gun. Give it to Camilla." Riley set Quinn's handgun in his hand. "It's loaded with silver bullets, just in case."

The energy was heavy inside the church, and Camilla hovered over Quinn, who lay on the bed now. Camilla was burning sage, waving it over Quinn, and mumbling. Sweat poured profusely from Quinn; her face had thinned in seven hours. Her body spasmed as if she'd received quick bursts of electricity. Her eyes raced behind clenched-shut eyelids. Elijah's last sense of assurance rapidly disintegrated as the pain he'd felt throughout his life rushed over him like a tidal wave. The undertow swallowed him whole, sucking any thread of hope he had left into an abyss of despair. Lying on a blanket next to the bed, Binx whimpered as if he could sense Elijah losing his grip.

"Here." Elijah checked the safety and set the gun on a desk near Camilla.

"I have no idea how to use one of those."

"After all this is over, remind me to teach you."

"I suppose after the events of the last couple of days, it would be necessary." Camilla paused and set down the sage, snuffing it out.

Elijah played with his lion bracelet, twisting it around his wrist, then rubbed the back of his neck. His knees weakened, and he sat on the bed next to Quinn. He rested a hand on Quinn's; her fingers trembled under his, and there were fresh cuts on her face.

"Where'd the cuts come from?" Elijah grazed his fingertips over the lacerations on her nose and left cheek. The crimson of the cuts clashed with her fair skin.

"They just appeared. First, they were welts, then they developed into what you see now." Camilla's eyes were red, and she sobbed. "How did we all get here?"

Elijah brushed Quinn's hair away from her face. "She had a protection stone around her neck. Her grandmother gave it to her. Maybe that will help if you can figure out where it went." Elijah held his head in his hands, staring at the ground. It was torturous to watch her suffer. There was nothing he hated more than hopelessness. Elijah's shoulders were heavy, and the war Quinn waged inside seeped into him. The twin flame connection they shared was sending private messages. It rippled from her hand into his body. Elijah's psychic senses read it crystal clear.

There was no turning back from their fates. One of them was going to die.

Elijah walked into the bathroom, and he lost control plowing his fist into the wall. Sheetrock exploded from the hole, and the thud of his hand hitting a beam reverberated through the church. His knuckles bled, and his hand throbbed. He returned to the sanctuary, shaking out his sore fist. He knelt next to Quinn on the bed, sliding his hand under hers, intermingling their fingers. He leaned into her ear and whispered, "I'm here, Quinn, and I promise no matter the cost, I'm gonna save you."

Outside, Elijah heard a crow shriek in the distance. The familiar nauseating spinning in his stomach took over. It was Landon, the skinwalker, hovering, waiting to devour them all.

28

KIREN SAT ON THE floor, leaning against the outside of Elijah's apartment door, sleeping. Riley paused behind Elijah, grabbing his hand. He turned and cast a cautious glimpse at her, and in a split second, Elijah knew Riley was considering the same thing he was. Kiren could be a skinwalker. Riley grabbed the handle of her Glock in its hip holster. Elijah put his hand on hers, stopping her. Apprehensively, they approached her, waiting for her reaction. Elijah tapped the bottom of her foot with his boot. Kiren's groggy green eyes fluttered. She yawned, sitting up.

"Is there a reason you're in front of my door?"

"I needed to speak with ye." Her exhausted, raspy voice instantly relaxed Elijah.

"How'd you find my place?" Elijah asked, raising an eyebrow.

Kiren stood, brushing off her slim, black jeans. "I told the bar owner of the Thirsty Parrot you owed me money after walking out on a readin'. It wasn't too hard after that. He doesn't like ye much." She smiled. Her thick Irish accent reverberated through the hallway.

The sounds of Wheel of Fortune came from Mrs. Steever's apartment. It was Saturday night; her daughter Charlotte was over. Elijah could hear both of them guessing wrong simultaneously.

This honestly can't be one of the last things I hear before I die. Elijah rolled his eyes.

"Again, why are you here? We're kinda busy," Riley said.

"Mmmm, yes, *you*." Kiren squinted at Riley, pronouncing the full *you* this time—as if it was an insult. "I'm here because of the *busy* part. I have some information for you that couldn't wait."

"Elijah, we don't have time for this."

"Let me say first that I'm sorry about shoving ye out earlier. You're a powerful Medium. Well, a Medium, among many things. I was caught off-guard by your abilities, wasn't expectin' such gruesome information."

Elijah unlocked his apartment door, ushering Kiren inside. Riley came in behind him and locked the door.

"You've got my attention," Elijah said briskly.

"Good." Kiren played with one of her purple crystal rings.

"You were right. My abilities did come from a parent," Elijah said.

"What do you want? Why'd you come here?" Riley asked suspiciously.

"That car in the drive. The Nova." Kiren took off her red leather jacket, draping it over the back of Elijah's recliner.

"I'm not giving you the car." Elijah grabbed a handful of Slim Jims and two energy drinks from the kitchen, shoving them in his backpack.

"Ye said it belonged to your father?"

"Yeah, so?" Elijah set his backpack on the couch.

"Did he acquire it from someone else?"

"Could you get to the point? We're short on time." Riley impatiently walked backward, keeping her eyes on Kiren, then grabbed a bottle of water out of the fridge.

"I told you he got it when he studied abroad." Elijah paused.

He studied in Ireland.

Elijah got an image of his father with a woman on a green, rocky shore.

"Why? What about the car?" Riley asked.

Kiren ignored Riley, keeping her eyes on Elijah. "Is your father's name Noah Ward?"

"Alright, thanks for the help, but it's time for you to leave." Riley snatched Kiren's leather coat from the couch, holding it out to her. Kiren ignored her.

Elijah trembled, his breaths became labored, and each expansion of his cracked rib cage made his head lighter. He thought about the conversation at her shop. Elijah rubbed the back of his neck, clenching his jaw. A cold sweat broke out all over his quivering body.

Kiren smiled, extended her arm, a showed Elijah an identical Celtic knot tattoo matching the one in his sleeve tattoo. It was the first one Elijah had gotten. It was similar to the tattoo his father had since Elijah could remember.

"Noah and I got matching tattoos when I met him in Ireland. I knew you'd find me when the time was right. For years, my spirit guides told me it would be *that car* that brought ye and your father back. Elijah, I'm your mum."

Elijah's heart skipped a beat, and his breathing shallowed. He tried to speak, attempting to force words from his mouth. Instead, he stayed silent, and he shook his head in disbelief. Riley rubbed Elijah's back, and she shoved Kiren's jacket to her chest.

"Why'd you take off and leave him?" Elijah shot Riley a piercing glare. "What? You can't tell me you aren't wondering the same thing?"

"Is that what ye father says?" Kiren glanced at Elijah, wounded. She grabbed her jacket and put it back on, leaning against the arm of the couch.

"I'm not sure how to say this, but ..." Elijah's voice cracked, and his words caught in his throat. "Dad died over ten years ago."

Devastation clouded Kiren's face, her breaths quickened, and she turned away from them. Her shoulders shuddered as she silently sobbed. The heartbreak of hearing about his father's death was raw, and Elijah's unresolved emotional pain whirled through him. He was immediately sucked into the torment of that day and the words that tore his young life apart. Sharing grief and loss over his father's death with his mother was something he'd never thought would happen. Some part of Elijah had accepted that she didn't want him, and he would never know her. Riley took a couple steps toward her, then shoved her hands in her pockets. Riley hung her head and gave Elijah a sullen stare.

"I have and *will* always love your father. I'm so sorry you had to go through that alone," Kiren said, "no one told me."

"Some psychic," Riley mumbled to the floor. Elijah and Kiren glared at her. Riley raised her eyebrows, "what?"

Kiren turned her attention back to Elijah. "I was always afraid to ask my spirit guides that question." Kiren choked on her last words, holding her breath.

Elijah had an impulse to hold his mother, to soothe her anguish. His father was the twin flame she was referring to, and now he was gone.

There was a heavy knock at the door. "Elijah, this is Detectives Bohannon and Jensen. Open up."

"Shit." Elijah threw his head back. "You have got to be kidding me." Elijah glanced his sports watch. It was 11:30, an odd hour for detectives to be knocking at his door.

There was no telling how long they'd been standing and listening. Elijah grabbed Riley's water, took a drink, and handed it back. Another knock broke the awkward silence, and it was louder and aggressive this time. Kiren stood tall, wiped her eyes, then nodded at Elijah to open the door.

Annoyed, Elijah grabbed the knob and swung it open. Jensen muscled her way past Elijah and into the living room. Bohannon hesitated, scowling at Elijah as he tailed his partner.

"This isn't a good time, guys," Elijah said quickly, attempting to usher them back out.

The detectives stood with a wide stance in the center of the room, glancing around. He knew they were searching for evidence. Hopefully not evidence of drugs because he was pretty sure Parker had a stash of weed under the kitchen sink in a coffee can. Bohannan's eyes gravitated to Kiren, and he smiled. She flickered a smile back.

"We've been trying to reach you all day. You've made us chase you around for two days. When is it a good time?" Bohannon stuck his hands in his pant pockets.

"We're here because we found Landon's body this morning in an abandoned building. He's been dead for a few days. He's been eaten." Jensen's eyes were locked on Elijah's face, waiting for his reaction. "Allison is missing."

"You what?" Elijah closed the door and joined the detectives in the middle of the room. Elijah glanced at Riley. The Landon they had seen wasn't the skinwalker's true form.

Bohannon pinned his arms across his chest. "Since you've been connected to them, it wasn't that hard to get Chief to let us question you. We've been waiting here for you for a while."

Riley was now sitting in Elijah's brown recliner. Her face drained of color and she fidgeted with the water bottle, her feet bouncing. Uncertainty and trepidation settled over the room.

Jensen sniffed the air, and she smiled. "You been smoking weed in here, Elijah?"

"What? No. I don't smoke weed."

"We talked to Shelly. She was pretty mad when she found out Owen dealt drugs, and you didn't tell her." Jensen's suspicious eyes traveled to Riley and lingered on her. "Riley Evans. What a surprise. Shouldn't you be with your *boyfriend*?"

"We kinda broke up," Riley gave a catty smile to Jensen. Her eyes flashed with sadness. For a second, Elijah thought he saw a deeper hidden subtext in their exchange. Something far beyond a breakup.

"Where were you last night? At about eleven-thirty?" Jensen played with the change in her pocket. The clinking filled the room.

Elijah paused. He couldn't tell them about the church. Especially not now. He adjusted the bill of his camo hat, then stuck his hands in his jeans pockets.

"He was with me," Riley said.

"What were you doing?" Bohannon dusted lint off from his BPD-issued jacket.

"That's none of your business." Elijah pointed at Bohannon, then Jensen.

Bohannon closed in on Elijah, his eyes burning with frustration. "Well, it kinda is. Because we confronted you with pictures of notorious drug dealers that we have proof you knew. And now one's dead, and the other's gone missing."

"We have a vested interest in the one who's dead. He was an undercover narcotics officer." Jensen inched forward like a boa constrictor subduing prey.

"We were having sex. We met at one of our secret hideouts at our friend Parker's house. Drank a few rum and cokes, then made sweet love all night long." Riley walked over to the group, standing next to Elijah. "There might still be a condom on the ground somewhere." She bit her bottom lip and gave a cocky smile. "I have no idea what it is about him, but he always keeps me coming back." Riley's eyes were directly on Jensen's now. The room went silent as they stared at each other.

"Maybe it was the one that went missing?" Kiren said quickly. "That killed the other one."

"Who are *you*?" Jensen said quickly, turning from Riley, her eyes narrowing in annoyance.

"A friend." Kiren locked eyes with Jensen, letting her know she couldn't intimidate her. Elijah could tell Kiren was reading her energy.

Jensen gave a wicked smile, her eyes slowly moving from Kiren's face to Elijah's. She stirred the coins in her pocket, then pulled one out, flipping it over the back of her fingers. "People keep dying around you, Elijah. Even drug dealers. Maybe it's time to ask what you're doing wrong."

A spark of adrenaline surged through Elijah's veins, threatening to ignite and cause him to combust. A pounding developed in his ears as his heart thrashed against his ribs.

"It's time for you both to leave," Riley said. "If you don't have anything else, then you'd better spend more time building a case instead of stirring the pot and *attacking* people."

"Is there a reason you have a gun, Riley?" Bohannon rubbed the stubble on his chin.

"I have an open carry permit through the state." Riley's tone dipped to flippant. "And a concealed weapons permit. Now, if you're done?" She motioned toward the door. Bohannon crowded Riley, and she took a step back.

Bohannon stuck his hands in his pockets, grinning. "It's when you apply pressure that you find the answers you're searching for."

Riley stood her ground, spreading her stance. Her hands on her hips. She stared into Bohannon's eyes, her face hardened. Her stature gave Elijah déjà vu and had the patina of an old John Wayne movie. Resonating silence packed with frustration and arrogance took over the room. The uncomfortable showdown made Elijah clear his throat and break the standoff.

"You're wasting time. Instead of finding Owen's killer, you're standing here, harassing my friends and me." Elijah's level of infuriation was reaching a tipping point, and with his underlying supernatural change reaching its peak, he did his best to calm himself. Going to prison for attempting to eat a cop would top the charts for worst day ever. Precious moments were ticking away to find Shelly. The thought of the skinwalker torturing her made Elijah's body tense.

"You guys need to leave," Elijah said. "Now."

Jensen's eyes narrowed at Elijah, arrogance seeping off her and into the stuffy atmosphere of the apartment. Ignoring his order, they both stayed put, and she flipped a coin. Elijah caught it in mid-air, clenching it in a fist, furious at her casual response to his anger about the killer still walking free.

Ramming him into the wall, Jensen pressed her forearm against his throat. Her strength was overpowering. The scent of the woods and the earth wafted into Elijah's nose. She tore the coin away from him, then tucked it into her pocket.

"Catch you guys later," Bohannon tapped Jensen on the shoulder, breaking her intense glare. "Let's go." Bohannon nodded toward the door. Jensen stormed out the door, and Bohannon followed her.

"I don't like *that* Jensen. I couldn't get a read on her energy." Kiren's eyes were still on the door where Jensen had walked out.

Elijah shut the door and locked it. Walking to the kitchen, he grabbed a bottle of whiskey from the top of the fridge and took a long swig. "Jesus. Now they're saying I murdered three people. Not to mention if word gets around … Josiah, their boss or whoever the hell he is, will probably have me cut into pieces. If this fuckin' skinwalker doesn't kill me, he most likely will."

"What do you mean?" Kiren said quickly.

"Elijah was bitten by a skinwalker, they took his adoptive mother, plus Quinn, his friend, is dying." Riley turned away from Elijah and Kiren. She put her hands on her hips, then her head dipped.

"Well, that makes more sense. It's *planning* on forcing you to eat the flesh of someone you love. It's using your weakness against you. That's no good. Let me help."

"We don't need your help," Riley said.

"No offense, but I'd like to hear it from my son." Kiren turned to Elijah waiting for a response, and he stayed silent. "If you want me to go, I will," Kiren said. Her intense gaze caused Elijah to shift from one foot to the other. "You felt called to me for a reason. Let me help. Everything else we can work out later."

Elijah's stance softened, and he walked across the living room, breaking his silence. "What do you have for me?" He took a clean shirt from the laundry basket and shoved it into his backpack.

"Elijah. Are you serious? How can we trust her?"

"Just ... we don't have time for this. We can use all the help we can get."

"My spirit guides gave me the same message as before. *The answer you're searching for lays with your brother.* That's what they kept repeating."

"I've searched through everything, so have my friends. There's nothing else to find." The problem was that Owen left them *too* much information and no productive way to go through it all. Elijah walked back into his room, opened the safe in his closet, and grabbed his Smith and Wesson 9mm.

"This is going to sound awful, but what if it literally means, *lays*?" Riley asked.

Elijah walked down the hall to the office and opened the door, continuing their conversation from another room. "Like in Owen's coffin? With Owen?" Rifling through their camping equipment, he grabbed two flashlights, clicking them on and off, checking the batteries. Riley followed him, and her floral perfume wafted around the room. Elijah could hear Kiren mumbling in the living room. Her words became more enunciated the closer he got.

Kiren paused, listening to someone they couldn't hear. "Elijah, come here." She stuck her hands out, waving. The many stone rings on her fingers clinked as she moved them quickly. "I need you to help me receive the message. Hurry, he doesn't have a lot of time."

Elijah placed his gun in its holster and clipped it onto his belt. He walked to Kiren, who extended her hands, waiting for him to grab hers. Static tingled his fingers, and he instinctively closed his eyes. He could hear Kiren coaching him. "Breathe, go inward, call him forward."

"Who?"

"Your brother. The one who recently passed over. Owen. His ties are to you."

"Oh no. I can't ... there's no way."

"Elijah, you get to talk to him. He wants *you*." Riley touched his shoulder.

Elijah closed his eyes. His blood pumped savagely as his heart hammered. The sounds of the world around him faded, and then there was silence. An overwhelming unconditional love replaced the heavy atmosphere.

Owen, I'm here. What do you need?

Images flipped through Elijah's mind's eye. *Owen was sitting on Benjamin Shaw's grave. The letters TN scratched into a tree trunk.*

"He is me." Owen's voice boomed in Elijah's ear, and his eyes jolted open.

"Oh my god. Do you smell that?" Riley whirled herself around in circles of amazement.

It was Owen's woodsy aftershave. Elijah inhaled deeply, and his body relaxed. He was reminded why he was on *this* journey. Because he loved his brother, and Owen deserved justice.

Kiren gave a warm smile. "He's got beautiful energy. He's loved and protected you in every life. He misses you."

"You, my dear," Kiren kept her eyes closed and touched Riley's arm, "he said to stop blaming yourself for everything. You're only one person." Riley stood, staring at Kiren in shock. Speechless.

Kiren slowly opened her eyes, looking directly at her son. "You heard him? Didn't you?"

Elijah pinched the bridge of his nose and turned away.

She followed him, trying to get his attention. "It's called clairaudience. Being able to hear those who've passed." Kiren touched Elijah's shoulder. "The abilities you have are a gift. Noah knew that, but I was too stubborn to accept them. You can help those that others can't, my son. Noah did his best to pull away from them so we could be together. It was a part of him, and he was never going to be able to abandon that. I had no right to ask him. By the time I'd moved back, he'd moved on and told me there was no place in your lives for me."

"Elijah, what did Owen say?" Riley's bottom lip quivered.

"Benjamin Shaw. *He is me*. It's located with Benjamin Shaw. We have to dig his grave up. Can you do me a favor?" Elijah grabbed his phone, Handing it to Kiren. "Put in your number. I'm gonna send you coordinates. My friend needs you right now. If you could help her, that would be great."

"Elijah, for all we know, she could be the skinwalker." Riley nodded toward Kiren.

"No, she isn't." Elijah sighed. "She's something that I wasn't expecting, that's for sure. But she's not evil or a skinwalker." Elijah threw his backpack over his shoulder, adjusted his hat, and took his phone back. Heading for the door, he stopped, studying his mother, observing her fully for the first time. Elijah was both enraged and relieved. The blend of complicated emotions was something he would have to figure out at a later date. She was, after all, the only blood relative he had left.

Riley trailed Elijah. "Don't expect these couple favors to erase years of abandonment."

Elijah nudged her, giving her a glare. She brushed a wavy lock of hair away from her face and shrugged. "What?"

He smiled at her, not able to help himself. "I can take care of myself." He turned back to Kiren. "But yeah, what she said."

29

RILEY WAS QUIET IN the nova. Relief rolled through her expression as she watched the apartment building fade in the rearview mirror. There was something about Kiren that made her anxious in two seconds. Elijah called Camilla to update her about what was happening and tell her that Kiren was on her way. He decided to conveniently leave out the fact that it was his *mother* who was coming to help.

Camilla mentioned that Quinn had taken a turn for the worse. She was speaking in an unknown language, and they were doing their best to administer her fluids. Camilla had given her a muscle relaxer in hopes it would calm her. Elijah could hear the desperation in Camilla's voice as she told him to hurry. It was about an hour's drive out to Seven Sisters Road, and for the first thirty minutes, Riley was texting furiously on her phone with her boss.

"That asshole shouldn't have given out your information."

"We're on our way to kill a skinwalker, find Florence's book of shadows, locate and close a vortex to another dimension, and you're worried about that?"

"It's the principle of the matter." Riley's voice went high, and she sighed, slapping down her phone. "What if it was somebody far worse?"

"How did he even know where I lived?"

"He could have dropped Hudson off?" Riley raised an eyebrow, and her full lips pursed in thought.

"You don't have to do this. There's no telling what this *thing* could do. I don't want you to get hurt. I have no idea what's going to happen to me."

"The inevitable? Besides, I'd like to think there's a choice. You eat the person you love, or you die."

"You get to choose?" Elijah's voice lilted, and he gripped the steering wheel in thought.

"Silver lining. Am I right?" Riley smiled, and it instantly turned to sadness.

"Sure, cannibalism or death. The choices are fabulous," Elijah said in a singsong voice, and Riley smiled. It always made her giggle when he sang-spoke. "Despite what's happened, Ri, I still want you to be safe. Live a life filled with kids, a house, and all that." Elijah waved his hand.

Riley turned toward Elijah, resting her arm on the back of the seat. "Remember that trip we took out to the drive-in three years ago when we first started dating?"

"You mean the Starlight? Yeah."

"We saw that ridiculous B grade horror film? Owen was throwing popcorn at the screen, pointing out inconsistencies, and Camilla complained about getting mud on her wedges? The temperature was one degree below the bowels of hell, and I had to change shirts because I was covered in sweat?"

"What about it?"

"When I felt alone after we broke up, and sad when I didn't go to Owen's funeral ... that's the moment that comforted me. Despite the craziness of that night, it was perfect. *We all had each other*. But those moments don't last. The hard shit comes, and we make choices. I made bad ones, and instead of sticking by you, I bailed. I'm not doin' it this time, Elijah. This time I'm here till the end. I'm not making the same mistake." There was something in her energy drifting into Elijah that was broken. Something was ending for her; she *had* changed.

Elijah smiled, then reached over and grabbed a cassette tape from his glove box. "Here." He slid it in. Simple Minds "Don't You Forget About Me" burst through the speakers. "I made this 80s mixed tape after we split. You don't wanna know how hard it was to find a tape recorder I could use."

A silence grew between them, and Elijah wondered if Temperance and Samuel had shared a similar experience. His intuition told him there was a gruesome end to their story. There was no telling if Temperance's body was lying out in the marshland of Seven Sister's Road without a proper burial.

Riley smiled, rubbing his back. "I want you to be happy too, Elijah. Always." Riley eased back into the bench seat, resting her head, staring at the rapidly passing countryside, tapping the outside of the car door, singing along.

Thunder rumbled in the distance. Rain cascaded in sporadic waterfalls from the clouds that blanketed the ocean. Hudson and Parker texted Elijah saying that they'd set up base camp in their previously parked location. Thankfully, one of them had a couple plastic bags and tape for his window. If he lived through this night, he didn't want to have to spend his startup money for the bar on new leather seats.

The color had returned to Parker's face, but the thinning was still prevalent. The jagged scratches on his face and neck from the poltergeist clashed with his tanned skin in the stormy light. He was his perky self again. It made Elijah happy that something good came out of the last few days, but his happiness was destroyed in seconds when he remembered *why* Hudson was healthy.

"Anybody know how Quinn's doing?" Riley asked.

"Camilla said she's getting worse and that a woman you sent over there is helping," Hudson answered, raising an eyebrow, keeping his eyes on the comm equipment he was pulling out of a storage box.

"It's a long story. We'll talk about it later," Elijah said. "On another note, the real Landon is dead. And the skinwalker we saw wasn't in their true form."

"Jesus, how many people has this thing killed?" Parker stopped and rubbed his forehead.

Elijah's mind wasn't totally off Josiah, Allison, or Landon. There would be questions for him from Josiah, no doubt, about Landon's death and Allison's disappearance. Unfortunately, the skinwalker's interference with the drug dealers did give him a little bit of extra time to deal with finding the drugs.

Elijah was beginning to think that Owen had intentionally ripped off Josiah. The drugs were in the shed in the form of silver. If it came down to it, Elijah could repay the drug money in untraceable silver with interest.

"This is the norm now, isn't it?" Hudson leaned against Elijah's trunk, his Alabama hat turned backward as he checked the batteries on some equipment.

"For me, anyway," Elijah said.

"Here." Riley removed her gun and its holster from her belt, handing it to Parker.

Parker took the gun and holster. "This skinwalker thing can't suck out our brains or plant larvae in our body, can it?"

"It's not an alien, stupid," Hudson said sarcastically. "It's a shapeshifter."

Parker gave Elijah an uneasy glance, then rubbed his forehead.

"Right. Glad tonight's not a *full moon*." Parker smiled.

"They don't need a full moon to change forms. That's a werewolf. They can do it at any time." Elijah sprayed bug repellant on, avoiding the elephant in the forest.

Hudson searched through the tub. He pulled out a headset, turning it on. "This is so surreal."

Parker nodded to Elijah, then took the headset from Hudson and placed it around Riley's neck. "Great, all my friends are out at the beach, drinking and smoking weed. I'm here sober with some crazy-ass shapeshifters that were created by black magic. No offense."

"None taken, asshole," Elijah said, smiling.

"Gotta have goals." Riley grinned, slapping Parker on the back.

"If I'm doin' it with anyone, I'm glad I'm doin it with you crazy fools. Besides, after this, I'll have a ridiculous amount of horror film ammunition."

"Hopefully, after this, we can make a film together. Semi-autobiographical." Riley took a drink of water.

Ghostly whispering drifted from the woods, and everyone stilled. The voices called for Samuel, beckoning him into the darkness. Hudson grabbed Elijah's shoulder and squeezed, then took the GoPro and calibrated it for night vision, clicking it into the suction-cupped tripod on the hood of Elijah's car.

"Maybe we can get some footage that will help us."

"We're running out of time." The voices faded, and Elijah's hands clenched. He could feel his transition picking up pace, his six-senses sharpening.

Something hard poked Elijah in the back of his head. He took off his camo hat, running his fingers over the inside. He saw a lump at the back; there was hand stitching.

"What's the matter?" Riley asked.

"There's something in my hat."

"What?" Hudson was messing with tape that had gotten stuck to his finger.

"Something's been sewn into my hat." Elijah grabbed his pocket knife and cut the stitches. He pulled out Quinn's beautiful stone necklace. "It's Quinn's protection stone. She sewed it into the lining of my hat." Quinn was dying and still concerned about his wellbeing. Elijah slid the chain over his head and tucked the stone under his shirt.

The stone reminded him that he wasn't alone. Even though at times he might have thought he was. No matter the situation throughout time, his soul tribe and Quinn would always be there. There was nothing the skinwalker could do to take that away. Not in this life or the next.

ELIJAH AND HUDSON stood at the edge of the property, staring into the pitch-black abyss of the forest. Warm rain poured over them as lightning flashed through the swollen, gunpowder-colored sky. Death swirled through the air, and coastal storm waves pounded like war drums.

Parker and Riley talked next to the truck as she pulled on a blue raincoat. The one Elijah had bought for her birthday the first year they were dating. He smiled and tightened the straps on his backpack. Thunder cracked and vibrated in Elijah's chest. He knew that he was on his way to his death—metaphorical or physical is what he wasn't clear about. He'd failed to tap into Shelly's energy, and the unknown of what was happening to her squeezed his heart like a vice. The shame of not protecting her would stalk him into the next life like the skinwalkers.

The vibrations of the violent history of the land rippled through the ground and tickled Elijah's feet. The sorrowful winds off the coast of Beaufort were whirling whispers of dread around him. His stomach somersaulted and cramped. Numerous ghostly shadows flickered—weaving through the trees, and the memories of the events of his terrifying past life as Samuel weighed heavily on him. This cursed land was where he and many others had perished.

"Hold this until I get back?" Elijah said.

Hudson studied Elijah curiously as he removed his hat and handed it to him. Lit by the glow of the LED flashlight pinned to his hat, Hudson's face was covered in fear.

"What?" Elijah raised an eyebrow.

"Do you sense anything?" Hudson's raspy voice was barely a whisper above the wind and patter of the rain.

"There's *something* out there, several things." Elijah swallowed heavily, perturbed.

"I could tell you sensed something. It shows on your face." Hudson was soaked, and the bottom half of his jeans were caked with mud. "I never knew what that look meant, but now I do."

Elijah knew imposter Landon or the Beta was waiting to separate them, and if he was going to do any damage, it was essential to kill Alpha first. There was no telling the identity of Beta or how many skinwalkers there were, but the pack leader needed to be removed.

"I need you to promise me something."

"What is it?" Hudson slid on his raincoat over his already wet clothes.

"Things are gonna get crazy, I can sense it. If I say it's time for you to go, I want you to lea—"

"I'm not gonna—"

"Leave. Take Riley and Parker and leave. You guys are my family. I don't want to hurt you. I have no idea how this is going down. There's two of them, and there could be more." Elijah raked his fingers through his wet hair, and the muscle in his neck twitched. "I have no idea how fast my *change* will happen."

Hudson's eyes saddened and his jaw clenched. "I'll see you in a few. And by this time next year, we'll be opening The Raven, selling those crazy gothic specialty drinks you've been creating. Besides, you owe me free drinks, remember? *And* I could definitely go for a better paying job." A tentative silence grew as Hudson played with Elijah's hat in his hands, "She's gonna be alright, Shelly. You couldn't have protected her from that monster. It's been ahead of us for centuries."

Elijah kept his eyes on the forest, "I know, but it doesn't make this situation suck any less."

The tall grass in front of them swayed in a furious dance. Elijah's flashlight beam roamed over the shore, searching for a safe route through the wetlands for him and Riley.

Real-world threats such as alligators, snakes, and poisonous spiders awaited them, intermingled among possible skinwalkers and paranormal dangers. The odds were stacked high against Elijah in two different dimensions, and he knew there was a chance that everything from both his past life and current one would cave in and crush the breath out of him.

"Here, hand me your cell." Hudson tugged a plastic bag out of his pocket and slid Elijah's phone into it, wrapping it with duct tape. "Only pull it out and use it in an emergency. Here's the maps." Elijah was now holding laminated copies of the maps that they'd studied at the church.

"What's your plan?" Parker joined them, rubbing his forehead. Elijah knew this was the last place he wanted to be, but he sucked it up anyway, like a good friend.

"The plan is ... there is no plan, because every single one I've made has gone to shit," Elijah admitted, keeping his eyes on the forest.

"Fair enough." Parker shoved his hands into his pockets. The intermingled scents of stale weed and sea air emanated from him.

Silence loomed, filled with all of the unsaid words they wanted to say to each other. Elijah was aware that this could be the last time he would see Hudson.

"Well, we should probably get a move on. The weather service issued a severe tropical storm warning for Beaufort," Riley said, joining them as they stood staring into forbidding darkness.

"Radio back with your coordinates every ten minutes. Don't worry about the rain. It's weatherproof, but it *can't* be submerged in water any longer than two minutes."

Elijah blew out a long sigh, double-checking the walkie on his hip.

"I secured your headset lines with duct tape, so you should be good as far as your headset coming unplugged," Parker explained. "You've got brand new batteries, and I put an extra pair in your backpack in a sandwich bag. In case any ghosts drain them."

"This is your last chance to back out." Elijah turned to Riley with hopeful eyes. "You could stay here with Hudson and Parker," he suggested, raising an eyebrow.

Riley's hair was drenched, and the collar of her shirt soaked. "And miss all the good and gory fun? Besides, you need someone to help you dig into a grave and open a one-hundred-and-eighty-year-old casket in the rain." She adjusted the strap of her pink camo holster, carrying the silver shotgun on her back.

Elijah turned to walk away. Hudson stopped him, paused, and gave him a quick hug, slapping his back. Elijah pulled away and gripped Hudson's shoulder, smiling weakly.

"I know, man. I know. Stay safe," Hudson said. "Station four." Hudson raised the walkie, running toward Parker's truck. Elijah and Parker did the complicated handshake Parker loved one more time, and for a second, a smile flickered over Parker's face. He wrapped his arms around Elijah like a clumsy little brother and squeezed, then quickly let go.

Elijah strode to the woods and stopped, waiting for Riley as she hugged Parker goodbye. Elijah and Riley were on their own, venturing into the darkest depths of a nightmare become reality.

Parker watched them until they disappeared into the woods. Once they were out of his view, Elijah found a place to stop. He turned to Riley.

"I needed to talk to you away from them."

"Sure, what's up?"

Elijah paused; his shoulders slumped. "If that thing successfully changes me, I want you to kill me." Elijah's voice was muted by stirring trees and foliage, so he moved closer to Riley, leaning on a tree next to her.

"What?" Her beautiful hazel eyes were round with shock. "Elijah, I'm not gonna *kill* you." Her face twisted with disgust and confusion.

"I'd rather be killed by you than turn into that *thing*." Elijah jabbed an angry finger in the direction of the Shaw family graveyard.

Riley leaned on the tree next to him, its Spanish moss waving in front of her, blocking her face. "You can't ask me to do that." She ripped down the moss, throwing it to the ground, her voice shaking.

The air around them cooled, a vacuum shifted the atmosphere, and quarter-sized raindrops beat against the forest floor. The drops pelted against the wood and trickled from the branches above, soothing Elijah. He soaked up the moment; it was going to be one of the last genuine human moments he had left. The simplicity of an open window, going fishing in the rain, a warm summer breeze, the aching loss of his father, the taste of ice cream, the relationship with his mother he would never get to mend. The dream of owning a bar he would never get to open, the wife and children he would never have. The trauma of it all hit him and left him breathless.

Riley's attention shot to the tropical storm off the coast. She squinted, observing the swirling, angry clouds, and checked the time on her watch. "We've officially moved into the strongest new moon phase. If that gate is going to strengthen, it's right now."

Elijah ran his fingers down her arm, grabbed her hand, pulling her close to him, tears sliding down his face.

"Then promise me this ... you'll kill me before I hurt *you*."

Riley frowned, and she wrapped her arms around him, laying her head on his shoulder. "It's not gonna come to that."

His arms tightened around her. "That's a really nice thought. Hold on to it."

Sweat cascaded from every part of Elijah. His leg muscles were fatigued, threatening to give out, and the balls of his feet were numbing. Elijah's boots beat against the mushy ground, spitting mud onto his jeans. His chest heaved, and he saw Riley next to him out of his peripheral. She'd always given him a run for his money when it came to physical strength. But there was something about how *well* she was keeping up that caught his attention. Her breaths were steady, and she was barely breaking a sweat.

Elijah wanted to stop and rest, but he didn't want to give Landon (or whoever the hell it was) a single moment of vulnerability. The sight of Quinn's thinned and pale face before he'd left flickered in his mind. Her despair and relentless courage soaked into his soul, making a permanent imprint on who he would be in the future—if he survived. Quinn's talisman bounced around under his shirt, thumping his chest in sync with his heart. As he thought about her, his strides quickened. He stopped and checked the map for their location and then continued. Elijah's wet feet rubbed against the insides of his boots; blisters were forming on his toes.

The white ring of rocks around the massive graveyard appeared out of the stormy morning like a beacon. Lightning flashed, leaving phantom cracks across the sky. Hostile winds thrashed the trees, and the branches clacked and cracked like brittle bones. Elijah knew the storm was close because it was the only time the air cooled, and the pressure in the atmosphere shifted. He glanced down at his watch: it was 1:00 am.

They arrived at the circle, and Elijah strode across the protective stone line. Riley stopped, leaning against the tree with the magic circle symbol. Behind Benjamin Shaw's headstone, Elijah swore he could see a shadow weave in and out of the darkness. He checked each tree trunk around the graveyard and found the corresponding symbols to Owen's rubbings, including the ones Hudson had theorized in the pentagram.

Elijah's breaths were labored, and his throat burned. He grabbed a bottle of water from his backpack and took a swig. A growl reverberated from behind Elijah, sending shivers down his spine. Both he and Riley spun quickly in the direction of the sound, and the plastic bottle flung from Elijah's hand to the ground. He could picture fake Landon in animal form, stalking them in the comfort of the shadows, enjoying the torment he was inflicting. Their flashlights panned shakily over the forest. Elijah scanned the darkened trees, hopelessly searching for a hint of Shelly's life force.

Nothing. Please don't let Shelly be dead.

Riley stood next to Elijah now, and he could hear her huffing the air. She was trying to catch onto a scent. He turned away from her and pulled out his shovel, unfolding it. "We need to get to work. You take the protection mixture and make a circle around us. I'll start digging." Riley was concentrating on a particular space in the woods. Her eyes locked onto a black hole. "Ri, did you hear me?"

"Yeah, sorry." She set her flashlight down on Benjamin's headstone and grabbed the container out of a pocket on her shotgun holster. She coughed and rubbed her back.

"Are you okay? You drink enough water?" Elijah raised an eyebrow, studying her face, then dug the shovel into the ground.

"I'm fine." Riley ran a hand over her ponytail and wiped rain from her forehead. "Just worried about Shelly. I feel helpless right now."

Elijah kept his eyes on her, and in an instant, he knew she was hiding a deadly secret.

A secret she'd shared with the blood-soaked land beneath their feet. And it was only a matter of time till he uncovered the wreckage the secret would cause in his life.

31

QUINN HAD BEEN IN and out of consciousness. Her body throbbed, and her muscles were stiff. Every blurry and scattered moment she awoke, her mind went to Elijah. Something about the skinwalker didn't make sense. Her intuition had been repeating a specific narrative—there was a deeper meaning to what the skinwalker wanted. It wasn't only trying to survive. Quinn knew Helen's poltergeist had weaved its way into her unconscious thoughts, draining her life and soul essence.

The skinwalker's use of necromancy was skilled and formidable. This Shaw witch had done more than master the dark arts, she'd become one with the energy. Being able to shift at will from human to animal form took a tremendous amount of practice. Quinn could sense the hate and resentment the necromancer harbored for Elijah. The vile emotions were beating against her vulnerable psyche.

Quinn spent most of her time in a spiritual trance, speaking with Helen and figuring out her role. Quinn wasn't sure what universe or dimension she was occupying, and intuitively she knew her ethereal body had been separated from her corporeal one for far too long. There was no doubt in her mind if she didn't return soon, she'd die. The only information Quinn extracted from Helen is that she was a murdered member of the Shaw family. As a result of her probing questions, Helen forced her to view torturous memories of her and Elijah in their past existence. But, through the painful memories, Quinn learned that her name was Florence Knight, and she was Samuel's mistress.

In her astral haze, Quinn stood in a field, and a riotous, bloodthirsty mob cheered for Samuel's death. Sweat and the scent of earth drifted on the wind. The hateful emotions of the 1800s crowd tore through the tainted land like a hurricane. The executioner kicked the stool out from underneath Samuel, and his legs flailed. Instinctively, Quinn screamed for them to stop and to spare his life. She lost all hope when reality set in. He hadn't died instantly, he was suffering, and she could hear his neck bones crunching and popping. Quinn stood paralyzed with shock. She was nothing more than a voyeur to the past life horror, unable to save him. Samuel was innocent, and there was no way to prove it. She wiped away the tears of misery streaming down her face. Quinn's clothes stung her skin in the blistering sun, and she was certain she was about to catch fire.

Grief tore through her, ripping apart Quinn's spirit. Half of her fell away into the chasm of the universe the moment Samuel took his last breath. His body slowed to a stop and went limp after a short tremor of his muscles. A warm breeze blew over the shoreline, and the Shaw plantation home loomed in the distance, the site that would later become the graveyard. The shoreline instantly sparked a feeling of intense love in her soul. It was the location in her dream where she and Samuel had made love.

"You do this in every life." Helen materialized and leaned against the platform where they executed Samuel. "Watch him die." Her intricately sewn, sapphire-satin gown swayed in the coastal breeze. Her dark-chocolate hair was in a beautiful up-do, and a few ringlets cascaded down over her shoulders. "It's exciting to watch the horror on your face, repeatedly." Helen's eyes widened with enjoyment, and she tapped the bottom of Samuel's bare, dirty foot, making him sway.

"Why ..." Quinn wiped her tears, breathing deeply to calm herself. "What made you evil? Why do you do this? Why do you help the necromancer?" Quinn shuddered, her mind flooding with morbid, grim questions.

Helen vanished and reappeared, standing next to Quinn, crowding her, her nose inches from Quinn's face. Gritting her teeth. "At first, it was hell being controlled, but then I realized the necromancer was right. All of this started because of *you*, and you don't deserve him."

"You murder him in every reincarnation?"

"It's the only way to keep you separated. You *are* two parts of a twin flame, after all. Essentially, I'm protecting him from himself. That's what a good sister does." Helen played with a gold coin between her fingers nimbly, keeping her menacing eyes on Quinn.

Quinn's heart fluttered, and her chest tightened. Pins and needle tingling spread across the surface of her face, and stars formed on the edges of her eyesight. Quinn's neck erupted in a stabbing cramp, and her muscles spasmed in response to violent squeezing. A woman with frizzy, black hair straddled her, strangling her in a murderous rage. Fighting for her life, Quinn kicked wildly. The hysterical woman dodged her shots, her grip tightening like a boa constrictor around Quinn's throat. The woman was different; it wasn't Helen.

"You have the power to bring him back." Her face was a swirling mesh of anguish and rage. "Instead, you'd rather let him die." She jerked at Quinn's neck, wringing it like a wet towel. "If it were Samuel, you wouldn't think twice." The brunette terror leveled her weight on Quinn's throat. "Bringing him back is the least you can do since Samuel is the one who killed him."

Tapping into her last reservoir of strength, Quinn grabbed a nearby stone and hit the raging lunatic on the back of the head. Disoriented, she released Quinn from her death grip and rolled onto her back, groaning and holding her bleeding head. Quinn gasped, and icy air burned her throat. She stood, stumbling away from the woman, using the wall as her guide to put space between the two of them. Then, the stars in her eyes faded, and the warmth of a crackling fire warmed her toes through her beautiful, crimson, satin shoes. Quinn adjusted her skirts under her elaborate, amethyst colored, satin gown. She recognized it as a gift that Samuel had given her. The tightness in Quinn's chest lessened as she took steady breaths. Gazing around the room, she quickly realized that she was in a cellar, probably a servant's quarters.

Images flashed behind Quinn's eyes of her shoving a spellbook into

Samuel's hands and sending him away. Keeping her eyes on the woman, she eased her way to the door. The woman rolled onto her knees, her black silk dress stained with clay and dirt. She sobbed, tears of deep grief streaming down her face. The woman stopped herself and straightened her back, her bloody hands folded in her lap.

"I miss him, and I want him back," She whined.

Steady and firm, a woman's voice reverberated through the dank servant's quarters. "You know we can't do that. If we bring him back, he'll be something unnatural and inhuman. He won't be your fiancé; he won't be Thomas. We'd have to find a vessel for his spirit, and I'm not gonna help you kill anyone." Quinn paused, uneasy at the foreign voice coming from her.

Firelight flickered across the dark-haired woman's face, and in an instant, all emotion drained from her as fast as the fire danced. The woman stood quickly, stomping across the room, gripping her skirts in both her hands. The manic attacker stopped inches from Quinn's face, her eyes deep with hatred. "I'll tell Temperance about your secret love. I'm sure she'll be delighted to know her husband is fornicating with the *help*."

Quinn's face flushed with heat, and her hands balled into fists. "You're not going to manipulate me. I won't do it."

"Johana will help me. One way or another, I *will* get him back."

"Samuel had nothing to do with Thomas's death."

"He never stopped it either!" Mary's face contorted with fury, and her voice lowered. "You all played a part in taking my whole life from me, and all of you will pay. You're going to regret the day you turned your back on me."

"Florence? Mary?" A familiar and loving man's voice echoed above them; it was Samuel.

The woman's eyes narrowed. And like a switch was flipped inside of Mary, all anger, hatred, and fury disappeared. She smoothed her hair and brushed the dirt from her dress. "Yes, brother, we're down here."

Despair overwhelmed Quinn as she stared down at her hands in panic. They were covered in blood. Mary had gnawed at Samuel's arm and fled into the night. Quinn tore the bottom of her beautiful, plum-colored silk gown and wrapped it around his open wound. He was sweating profusely, and his dark-blond hair stuck to his forehead. He lay on a fainting couch, his beautiful emerald eyes half-open.

I'm at the Shaw plantation.

Quinn had no clue how she knew where she was, but she guessed it was because of the *universal consciousness* Nana Evie had told her about. She was connected to time, and most importantly, she was connected to her past life, Florence. Quinn instinctively knew Samuel was Elijah. His gorgeous, shimmering, lavender aura wrapped around her.

The esoteric knowledge Quinn obtained as Florence was surfacing from somewhere deep in her spiritual consciousness. Florence was quite skilled and passionate about her abilities.

The expansive plantation home around them was immaculate and shimmered with gold, luxurious furnishings. Candles flickered through a men's sitting room, and Quinn heard a crow screeching outside the window, its beak intermittently tapping on the windowpane. The bookshelves were filled with volumes of Shakespeare, Hawthorne, and Poe. A small, ornate, ivory fireplace crackled on the other side of the room. Winds raged outside the window, and a live oak's branches clicked against the glass.

"You have to go," Samuel coughed. "She's going to hurt you. She's furious with me. I don't know why she's doing this. I trusted her." Samuel had the same concern in his eyes she'd seen in Elijah's. The energy of his unconditional love radiated into her. No matter how badly they were torn from each other, he was her other half. Quinn wondered where the entity of Helen had disappeared to—her silence was frightening. She waited for her to appear and tear her from this tender moment.

"Who? Who's trying to hurt you?" Quinn said.

"You know who." Samuel swallowed, then coughed.

"I need you to say it. Please. It's important."

"Mary Olivia Reynolds. My illegitimate sister," Elijah coughed. "Either I hang for the murder of the Reynolds family and my own family, or I die from skinwalker sickness." The soft, gentle touch of his hand on her face filled her with hope. "She conspired with Temperance."

Quinn rested her head on Elijah's chest. "I can't leave you." She clung to him, gripping his shirt. A warm memory flooded through her; they were carving TN into a tree trunk on the shore where they'd made their lovers' escapes.

A tall man dressed in black trousers and a white dress shirt charged into the room. His brown hair was disheveled, and he was sweating profusely. Quinn knew who he was. It was Benjamin. "Florence, we must go, now."

"No, I can't. I'm not leaving him to die alone." Quinn sobbed uncontrollably.

"Go with my brother he'll keep you safe. I'd rather die than hurt you. I'll see you in the next life. I always do. You're my soul's *True North*. You're my home, Florence." Samuel gripped her arms.

A massive *thump* then *crashes* caught Quinn's attention. She glanced at the window and noticed black smoke billowing outside the plantation home, and flames rose quickly, catching like wildfire in the wind.

An aching engulfed Quinn's whole body. The scene around her faded, and she gasped for air. She was lying on a bed. Blinding light burnt her eyes, and she kept them closed as she coughed. The sounds of fans wafting and people frantically speaking were muffled.

"Oh my god, it worked!" Camilla's elated voice pierced Quinn's ears, and they popped. She covered them instinctively, wailing with discomfort. The pressure of Samuel's touch on her cheek was still lingering. Heat rolled through her, and adrenaline raged through her veins. She was caught between two planes of existence.

The mattress shifted as someone sat next to her. "Quinn, can you hear me?" A soft hand touched her face. She forced her eyes open and sat up quickly, leaning on her elbow. Her head whirled. Quinn laid back down, covering her mouth.

"I can hear you …" Quinn heaved into a trashcan next to the bed. "Where's Elijah? I need to talk to him." Her voice was raspy.

"He's gone out to Seven Sisters Road." A familiar Irish accent caught her attention.

Quinn opened her burning eyes, and the blurriness faded. Kiren sat next to her, and Camilla stood over her. Binx sluggishly braced himself on the bed, licking her sweaty face, ecstatic she was awake.

"Binx, stop." Quinn petted the wounded dog keeping her other hand on her churning stomach. Binx waddled to the end of the bed, plopping down with a huff through his snout. "Kiren? What are you doing here?" Quinn raised an eyebrow. "Can I get some water?"

"That's a story for another time," Camilla said, crossing her arms and glancing at Kiren.

"I need to get to Elijah." Quinn sat, swinging her legs over the side of the bed. "Where's Aunt Shelly?"

"Um, Quinn. I don't think you should go out there." Camilla blocked her from standing.

"Where's my aunt?"

"The skinwalker took her, and they demanded Florence's spellbook, or they threatened to kill her," Camilla said flatly.

Keeping her eyes closed, Quinn motioned to a table, "Hand me that spiral notebook, please."

Kiren grabbed it and handed it to Quinn. She flipped to the center, scanning her notes.

"The skinwalker is *Mary Olivia Reynolds*. She was helped by Elijah's wife, Temperance. Hand me the file from my backpack?" Quinn pointed to the corner near her hammock. Kiren walked swiftly to Quinn's backpack and took out a file, handing it to her. "Edgar Shaw, Samuel's father, had an affair with Catherine Reynolds, a socialite in a neighboring town. The last thing I remember is the love letters Elijah found corroborating that." Quinn unfolded a copy of the Reynolds family tree. "Mary was Benjamin and Samuel's half-sister." She set down the family tree studying its branches. "Her fiancé, Thomas, was murdered by a lynch mob because of rumors that he'd cheated a local man out of vast amounts of profitable land. His lynching occurred two years before the murders of the Reynolds and Shaw families."

"The skinwalker is his sister?" Camilla was stunned.

"Yes. I'm the one who taught Mary magic as Florence. The other two poltergeists, not related to the Shaw family, are Mary's sisters. They are *all* her sisters. The souls of the Shaw and Reynolds women are tied to one coin so she can control them. She used both families to open a gateway and to turn into a skinwalker. I have to get to Elijah."

"He called and said they thought the spellbook was with Benjamin in his grave," Camilla said.

"They're searching in the wrong place." Quinn rubbed her forehead.

"I'm gonna go call him." Camilla swiftly walked out the back door.

"How'd you get rid of the sisters?" Quinn asked, glancing at Kiren.

"It's a temporary Banishment Spell," Kiren said. "I studied for a short time with a Wiccan high priestess. I'm not sure how long it will last."

Sliding on her boots, Quinn examined Kiren, unsure.

"Elijah sent me to help you." Kiren smiled.

Worry for her aunt burned through Quinn. She'd listened to her Nana blindly for so long that she never considered Shelly was angry and grief-stricken, and that's why she'd left the coven. Marrying William and switching religions was a way to distance herself. Nana Evie made it seem like it should have been an honor for her mother to die, but now Quinn understood that it was only an honor if it was voluntary. Not if someone withheld information or forced you to play martyr.

Camilla strode in from the front porch of the church. "I can't get ahold of anyone." She shoved her phone into her back pocket, raced to the fridge, and grabbed a bottle of water, handing it to Quinn. "I'm going with you." Camilla's voice was firm, but her face showed uncertainty.

"Me too. If my son needs my help, I need to go."

Quinn's eyes widened. "You kicking Elijah out makes more sense now." She pulled a gray hoodie over her head. "Where's that shapeshifting book? The one with the reversals?"

"It's right here." Camilla went to hand her the book, but Quinn pointed to it.

"Rip the page out about reversal. We might not stop Mary, but at least we can try to slow the skinwalker spell down until we find a way to stop it from affecting Elijah. Go to my duffle bag. My *Book of Shadows* and a vial labeled Shifter Blood is in there—grab it for me, please."

Quinn's body was fragile, and her past life memories were beating at her delicate soul. She could detect Mary's sisters squatting inside her, waiting till they could resume taking her over. The only thing more potent than their hate was the torment of witnessing Samuel's murder. The surfacing of that memory lit a wildfire of ferocity inside of her. Quinn hoped silently that the other death's of Elijah's she'd witnessed would stay hidden in the vastness of the universe.

In that moment, Quinn made the decision, it was now written in stone. No matter what, even if it took her last breath, Quinn would get to Elijah and help him survive. In this life, it was time to reshape the mold of his destiny.

32

A CROW'S SCREECH FROM above sent adrenaline through Elijah, and he smacked a mosquito taking blood from his arm. He flicked it to the ground, annoyed his bug spray had already worn off. The winds were easing, and the rain slowed. Elijah knew it was the calm before all hell broke loose. Zeroing in on a flying silhouette in the sky, Elijah realized it wasn't a crow that had screeched but a vulture, barely visible. There were three circling overhead not too far from where they were. The muddy hole he was digging was only halfway down to the grave; that was his guess anyway.

"Do you see that?" Elijah nodded, pausing from his digging.

"Yeah, it's probably a dead deer or something."

Elijah's psychic senses pushed him to go and check it out. "Let's go find out what it is." He set down the shovel, darting toward the circle of vultures.

"We don't have time to do this. We're kinda under the gun here," Riley called after him. "Remember? Your life, Shelly's, and Quinn's are all at stake?"

Tropical winds blew through the trees, blasting leaves and moss in his face as he hiked his way across the highest ground he could find. Going over the maps, Elijah could tell it had been years since anyone had ventured into the rugged terrain. With angry poltergeists, vortexes, and suspicious deaths, it wasn't dumbfounding that no one wanted to spend their afternoons hiking through the freakish and haunted territory.

What sane person would want *to be here?*

Branches in the forest cracked as he walked through, his mind's eye focusing on the location the vultures were circling. Elijah's muscles were sore, and the cut under his eye from Allison stung with sweat.

It was about ten minutes before he found two more vultures on the ground, pecking at something that was buried. The putrid scent of rotting flesh drifted on the angry winds. There was a hand on his shoulder, and Elijah spun quickly. It was Riley.

"Crap. Don't do that. With what's happening to me right now ... just don't do it again."

"I wasn't gonna stay there by myself. Is that a shallow grave?" She covered her mouth and plugged her nose at the same time.

Elijah turned his attention back to the grave, and he saw hundreds of small movements under the surface of the dirt. He turned in the other direction, vomiting on a fern.

Fucking maggots.

"If someone had the wherewithal to bury it, then I'm guessing it's not a deer."

Elijah walked over, kneeling next to the moving mound. His eyes teared from the putrid odor of decay. The biological fumes burnt his raw, sore throat. Elijah rubbed his neck, remembering Helen's hands wrapped around it earlier in the day like a vice. The memory of her emaciated face was troubling and haunting. The hate Helen had for him in the depths of her pitch-black eyes made Elijah shiver. He found moss on the ground and used it to dust off a spot on the clandestine grave. A bloated, rotting face emerged under the dirt. Jensen —the detective he'd seen recently—was in the advanced stages of decomposition. Dumped like trash.

The lone murder of Owen was one thing, but now there were three more murders and a missing person as well. And not just any murders, the murders of a damn homicide detective, undercover narcotics agent, and a drug dealer. The killer had created the perfect storm to destroy him. Both sides would be coming for him, and there was nothing Elijah could do to stop the devastation it would cause in his life. Quinn's voice echoed in his head about the deaths of the Reynolds and the Shaws and how Samuel was framed and an innocent man. History had repeated itself.

Elijah mumbled to himself. "The flip of the coin. Shit. Landon had a coin the other night when he kicked the crap out of me. And Jensen had a coin at the apartment when we saw her. They're the same person. The *same* skinwalker. There must be importance behind the coin. Did you see the way she freaked out when I touched it?"

"We need to get back to digging," Riley said, attempting to refocus Elijah.

"You know what this means, right? The skinwalker conveniently buried the detective investigating me, where, thanks to Quinn, I got arrested. Owen was found dead out here, and Shelly ... if Shelly ..." Elijah rubbed the back of his neck. "If she's found out here too, plus Landon's death ... This skinwalker wanted to make sure I wouldn't say no to *turning*, so I could disappear before being sent to prison as a serial killer."

Riley's face twisted in confusion, her flashlight on the bloated, purple, and brown face of the corpse. "That makes no sense. Why does it need you to change so bad?"

"Fuck. I forgot to turn on my walkie." Elijah put his earbud in and clicked on the walkie. Riley reached down and clicked on hers as well.

"... hear me?" Hudson's panicked voice scratched through the earpiece.

"I'm here."

"Jesus Christ, dude, you gave me a heart attack. I was about to come out there."

The spirits around Elijah were whispering warnings of death. Emotions of dread were devouring his mind. With every shovel of dirt he heaved out, the sandy earth around him seemed to pour back in. Elijah was drenched in sweat, and the heavy blanket of humidity was smothering him. It was always muggier after heavy rain. The sweltering tropical coast and insects hungry for his blood were diminishing his ability to focus.

Elijah's ribs popped with each extension of his arms. Exhaustion and worry were setting in; the strength he had a few days ago was gone. The bite mark on his arm throbbed. Blood had coagulated around the jagged edges of the scab and stitches. The sight of it caused him to dig faster and quicker. Time was running out.

He paused, sticking his head out, and leaned against the dirt wall. Riley had propped herself against Benjamin's gravestone, keeping guard with the shotgun and picking at the end of her dirty leather gloves. She turned to look at him.

"Can I ask you something?"

"Sure." Elijah took a drink of water.

"What is it about her? Quinn."

"Honestly? I wish I could tell you." Elijah wiped his brow and resumed shoveling. "The only thing I know is that she's different. She isn't like any other person I've met."

The spade hit something solid. A hallowed thud echoed under the ground.

"What the hell was that?" Riley pushed herself off the gravestone.

Elijah squatted, dusting dirt from the edge of an old and rotting coffin. The magic circle symbol and all the others in Owen's rubbings were carved down the center.

Riley's eyes widened in shock at the symbols. "Holy crap."

Elijah dusted the rest of the dirt away from the top, then pried open the wooden coffin lid with the shovel. Its hinges groaned, and wind gusted, blowing dirt into Elijah's face. He wiped his burning eyes with the back of his hand. A fetid-damp aroma bouquet of mildew and rot made Elijah's nose burn. Thick boards blocked an entrance to something underneath.

"There's something down there. I think it's a cellar."

Elijah ran his fingers over the wood slats, pressing down, testing their strength. Hesitating, he hopped inside and thumped the wood. Electricity ran through his arm, and images flashed through his mind.

Quinn giggling, and him kissing her neck while they sat on wood stairs. Time skipped, and she was showing him how to do magic, holding a spellbook in her lap. The following vision was of them making love on a shoreline. The love dissipated, and the image shifted. Quinn's manic screams shook him to his core —she was covered in blood. His blood.

A phantom, chilling breath brushed his ear. A man screaming "North" inside his mind made him wince, sucking him out of the retrocognition. The voice was familiar and traveling from somewhere in the past. Prickling formed in Elijah's chest, and he rubbed the back of his sweaty neck. He rubbed his miraculously almost healed bite mark. It was the same spot he'd been bitten in his past life as Samuel Shaw. He knew that skinwalker Landon hadn't been lying to him; Quinn was Florence, his mistress.

"What's the matter? You saw something, didn't you?" Riley jumped down and handed Elijah the shovel.

"Yeah, this *thing* has been hunting me through lifetimes," Elijah said. "It isn't gonna stop until I kill it, or it gets what it wants. The only thing for sure is I stopped it in every life by dying. The only problem is after my death, the cycle restarts."

Riley's round eyes saddened, and her full lips turned down. Tension-drenched silence swelled in the grave. Her floral perfume intermingled with sweat stuck in Elijah's nose. Riley wrapped her pinky finger around Elijah's and opened her mouth to say something. Her soft soprano voice was drowned out by a menacing howl from the dense woods.

The gentleness in her eyes was replaced by urgency. "You might wanna hurry and find out what the hell is under there. 'Cause I'm pretty sure that bastard is close." Riley lifted herself out of the hole. She cocked and pointed the shotgun, scanning the forest.

Elijah slammed the shovel into the weak wood, breaking it apart. As he ripped away the pieces, a cellar door emerged. He grabbed the handle and shook the door in frustration; it was locked. The salty and damp atmosphere of the southern coast caused rust to grow at an accelerated rate. The nails and hinges were eroded.

"You might wanna back up." He fired his gun at the lock. The bright muzzle flash blinded him for a second, and gun powder stung his face.

He jerked the cellar door open, fighting the dirt and mud rolling down into the faux grave. Elijah grabbed his flashlight and pointed it into the dark cellar; if the answer to save Quinn, Owen, and Shelly was anywhere, it *had* to be hidden here. The only problem was if the torrential rain started again, he would be buried alive.

Overpowering tendrils of energy seeped out of the hole, caressing Elijah's legs and causing his chest to buzz. It felt like the vibrations of music blasting from a massive speaker with no sound. The disruptive sensation surrounded him, touching every part of his body.

"Elijah, you alright? We heard gunfire." Hudson's panicked voice interrupted his thoughts.

"Don't worry. We're good, everything's fine. I found what might be a cellar under Benjamin's coffin. Something that would have been connected to a plantation home."

33

DESPAIR AND TRAUMATIC NOSTALGIA hung in the air, and whirled around Quinn. Her nerves were on edge, and a sickening feeling clung to her subconscious like a parasite to a host. The image of Samuel dangling from the rope wouldn't leave her. There was no telling if she was going to witness the same tragic death happen to Elijah.

Having Elijah ripped away from her so soon after she discovered who he was to her would be cruel. However, their soul group had something on their side now that they didn't have in the 1800s: *time*. Almost two centuries had passed. Mary was weakening, and the spells she'd cast were becoming less effective. Quinn's spell-casting intuition told her the vortex was closing. Mary's window to become immortal was fading.

Leaving Camilla with Parker and Hudson near the dirt road, Kiren and Quinn traversed a dense slope of grassy overgrowth, then a mile later entered into the treacherous wilderness. Kiren clicked on a flashlight and raced to keep up with Quinn.

A reckoning that was catapulted into motion ages ago was on its way. There was nothing any of them could do to stop it from unfolding. Quinn had been confident that Samuel had committed the crimes. But now, she had irrefutable proof of her own that he hadn't.

"The berm from Florence's memory, how much further do you think it is?" Kiren leaped over a fallen tree. She was already covered in sweat.

Quinn raised a quick, shaky hand, pointing North. "It should be right over that hill."

"Your connection to Elijah is strong. It goes back millennia, you know." Kiren pointed the flashlight at Quinn, stopping. "I sensed it when you visited me. The other girl, Riley. She's been keeping you two apart for many lifetimes. But, your story together goes back much farther than her."

Quinn's muscles were fatigued, and every jostle made her feel like they were going to give out. Anger crept through her like slow-growing poison ivy, and she knew the sisters were gaining momentum. Light rain fell, and gusts of wind cooled her. Quinn stopped, leaning against a tree. She closed her eyes and attuned to the power of Mother Gaia. The storm was getting close, and soon it would be another obstacle they all had to overcome.

Faltering vision blurred everything together, making it harder for Quinn to see in the dark. Sharp pains stabbed through her joints. It felt like someone had shoved a dagger through them. Only the replay of Samuel's death and the thought of Elijah's impending demise gave her the strength to stand and keep walking. Kiren was holding the flashlight, sweeping the lush and ominous landscape, and Quinn knew there was something on her psychic radar.

"I have no idea how to tell where the hell Samuel was buried. This area looks vaguely familiar, but this was all land, not marsh."

"What did you see when you suffered the ghost fever? Maybe I can help."

"I've never heard anyone else except for my aunt and Nana call it a ghost fever." Quinn sighed, not wanting to speak about the brutal murder of her soulmate she'd witnessed. "I saw Samuel's death. I watched him hang."

The beam of Kiren's flashlight dropped, and Quinn watched as her face ashened. "That must have been awful."

Swallowing heavily, Quinn crossed her arms, rubbing her shoulders. Her skin stung. Quinn angled herself in the direction of the Shaw family graveyard. "You could see the house from the location where he was hanged. Samuel frequently called Florence his True North and his way home. When they first started courting, they met at the shoreline to make love. There's a tree where he was buried on that same shoreline, and it has the letters TN. That's where it is."

"We don't have long, dove. Death is in the air. Time's running out." Kiren's eyes darkened.

"The tree would be massive by now." Quinn's chest tightened as she contemplated the sight of Elijah's dead body. Tempestuous nostalgia swept through Quinn; something familiar pulled at the dimming light in her soul. Clearing her mind and pushing Helen and the other sisters as far back as she could, Quinn squinted. Confusion ravaged her thoughts.

"I can't concentrate." Quinn stopped, her breathing labored. She coughed. "The sisters are blocking me." Quinn groaned, frustrated with herself. "We're so close I can feel it, but the bitches won't let me access my own memories."

"There's an eyewitness, yes? A spirit who knows exactly where Samuel's buried because he put him there."

"Who?" Quinn wiped the sweat from her forehead.

"Benjamin ..." Kiren paused. "Owen." She wrapped Quinn's arm around her shoulder, helping her walk. "Come, we don't have much time."

The hissing sound of the dead around Kiren and Quinn was barely audible. Quinn grabbed Kiren's hand tightly, and shivers raced through her. It was becoming harder for her to focus and fight off Helen. This time the sisters were stronger and filled with fury. Their rage for being shut out was overpowering, and Quinn knew she was going to pay dearly.

Disembodied whispering flowed through the woods, and Owen's loving and decaying image manifested from a white mist in the darkness. He glanced behind him in the direction of the graveyard and turned back to Quinn, his eyes filled with terror.

Kiren moved in close to him, reaching out a shaky hand, tears welling in her eyes. Low energy vibrated through the atmosphere, and Quinn swore the molecules that created her being were swelling, about to burst.

Kiren kept her eyes on his apparition intently. Quinn could see her squinting in the shadows of her flashlight, and the way she watched him let her know that they were sharing telepathic communications.

"He said there's a tree, four yards that way." Kiren swung her flashlight, pointing in the direction. Owen's spirit shot through the forest, and Kiren ran after him.

Quinn followed her, and after what felt like a lifetime, they stopped. Quinn leaned against a rotting, fallen tree trunk. The wind blew, whipping the scent of saltwater, damp earth, and mildew into her nose.

She watched Owen's apparition fly through a large, towering tree that the world had forgotten, then disappear into the night.

"The letters TN, they're here." Kiren followed the trunk to the ground and found a hidden hole at the roots, then dug with her hands, using the flashlight to help. Quinn followed her, grazing her fingertips over the carved letters. Her heart sped, and a ripple of love flowed through her. Quinn slid down the tree, and her eyes fluttered as she fought to stay awake.

The next thing Quinn saw was Kiren's flashlight in her eyes, waking her from an accidental nap.

"I found a box about three feet under." Kiren set the rotted, wooden box next to Quinn, and she crushed the lid with a nearby rock.

Shoving her hands in, she yanked out a book-shaped item wrapped in torn and ragged, purple silk. Quinn knew right away it was the beautiful silk cloth from Florence's dress. Kiren unwrapped the grimoire and ran her fingers over the surface.

"It's beautiful." Kiren handed it to Quinn.

Familiarity caressed her fingers, and Quinn's mind flooded with images of the spells she'd put into the enormous grimoire two hundred years before. Quinn knew that she'd not only recovered an antiquated spellbook, she'd also recovered a piece of herself that was lost.

34

ELIJAH HELD OUT HIS weapon in anticipation of encountering something that wanted to devour him. He descended the stairs cautiously, testing each one before he placed his full weight. The rocking of the wet wood caused a squeaking under his boots. His intuition told him he was on the brink of a discovery. Elijah paused, lowered his gun, and turned on his flashlight. He knew where he was; it was the cellar he'd visited in his retrocognition. The place Quinn taught him magic two hundred years ago. There was no way for Elijah to tell if they were Samuel's memories or his psychic visions. At this point, it didn't matter; the images were all weaving together in a beautiful supernatural tapestry that created his life.

The heat of the summer night dissipated as he entered the cold, damp enclosure. The smell of algae and rot invaded his nose. Cobwebs coated the cobblestone walls, and the muffled sound of trickling water reverberated through the cellar. There were old shelves with dusty jars filled with herbs and an empty bookshelf. A fireplace was located in the back. Goosebumps formed on his arms, and the high-pitched wails of the dead grew the farther he traveled underground, reaching a crescendo. Etched rune symbols covered the wood beams in the ceiling. Elijah saw a retrocognition of hands furiously etching the runes into the wood. The phantom scent of cedar filled the air, then disappeared.

It was a relative that was close to me.

His vivid memories from the ether of the universe as Samuel fought against the heavy tides of his present mind, struggling to surface. Elijah ran the flashlight along the shelves, hoping the book to save Quinn and Shelly was there. A thick layer of dust surrounded empty voids where the books used to reside, causing his heart to drop. *All* the books had been taken recently. The skinwalkers must have been seeking *the spellbook*. Whoever pilfered the volumes swiped them a while ago. Elijah was disheartened to see that Florence's spellbook was nowhere to be found.

There was a flash of light. Owen's apparition appeared in the corner; it was only the upper half of his body. The breath whooshed from Elijah's lungs as he watched a scene, imprinted in the building around him, repeat itself. Owen frantically grabbed things off the shelves. Elijah eased in closer, observing every detail. He knew Owen was trying to tell him something. There was a stone missing in the wall where Owen stood. The ghostly scene vaporized. Elijah crept closer to the dark hole, shining his flashlight into the abyss. The hairs on his neck stood on end, and Elijah's stomach churned, giving him a warning sign.

It's another room.

Shining, glittering threads of energy gyrated together, radiating from the ground inside the blocked-off room. A vortex swirled like a black hole, flickering, calling to Elijah. Thousands of whispering voices cascaded over each other, fading in and out from another dimension. It was more than a vortex. It was a gate that led to a deathly land he didn't want to enter. A morbid version of Alice's looking glass.

"Ri, you need to see this." Elijah raked his fingers through his thick, damp hair. "Riley?" Elijah said louder, with an undertone of panic. He pointed his flashlight toward the opening. "Riley, are you there?" Elijah heard wild rain slapping the forest floor. The ghostly whispers dwindled, then silenced.

Thudding, rolling, and grunting noises sent shockwaves through Elijah's extrasensory gifts. An urgency prodded him as he made his way out of the cellar.

"Elijah, can you hear me?" Camilla's petrified and strained Hispanic tone came through his earbud.

"Camilla?" Elijah trudged toward the opening and ascended the stairs, pausing in the middle. "You're supposed to be at the church with Quinn."

"Quinn's ... woods, she's ... ing for Samuel's grave."

Static filled Elijah's earpiece, and a *beep-beeping* caught his attention. Elijah paused on the stairs. The battery symbol blinked on the screen; he'd forgotten to shut it off like Hudson had instructed. Something wasn't right; he needed to get to the other batteries.

"What's Quinn's location? I can't hear you."

"Shore ... Samuel's hidden ... could ... life. Kiren ... her ... your sister." Camilla's choppy, panicked voice cut out.

The pack powered down, and the line went dead. "Shit." Elijah smacked the walkie and took the earbud out, letting it dangle from his shoulder.

Heavy breathing came from the outside of the grave as Elijah exited the cellar, removing the walkie receiver and taking the back of it off.

"Ri, could you hand me the batteries from my backpack?"

Elijah holstered his weapon, lifted himself out of the grave, and was greeted by Riley and Jensen. Riley's walkie was on the ground, crushed to bits. Owen's shotgun was on the forest floor, barely visible in the dark, and Riley was bleeding from her right eye. A slim and narrow blister marked her neck and chin, and the scent of burnt flesh was heavy in the air around them. Riley's wild, wavy hair was loose from its ponytail and swirling with the torrent of wind surrounding them. Her hands were in the air, her feral eyes narrowed and, her nose was pointed down. A vicious scowl was etched into her features.

She isn't afraid of Jensen.

An animalistic growl escaped Jensen's lips as they stared at each other in front of the protective circle Riley had created around the graveyard.

Elijah's mind quickly scanned the dark forest, searching for Shelly. He saw her, sitting next to a tree, her silhouette still, her high-pitched weeping muffled by the gag in her mouth. Elijah had no idea what the skinwalker had done to Shelly, or what games it had played on her mind. Guilt spread through him as he considered how tortured Shelly would be by this experience. All because the skinwalker wanted to punish him.

Jensen's pupils dilated to black saucers, her irises a blazing red, thin ring.

Her short, honey-blonde hair was a matted mess, her white-collared business shirt was covered in dirt, and the first two buttons were ripped off. Her skin was ashen, and Jensen bled from her lip. Pure rage and hate drenched every inch of her body as she flicked a glance in Elijah's direction. Jensen steadied her hand as she pointed the barrel of her gun at Riley's head. Her deep, tormented energy saturated the area, and déjà vu froze Elijah. *They'd both been here before.* They were on the land where Samuel lived and where he took his last breaths after being bitten.

Static shot through the bite mark on his arm, and his mouth watered. A sickly-sweet scent drifted from Jensen to Elijah, and he clenched his jaw. The furious waves in the distance crashed against the shore, and he was reminded of Quinn. She was close; he felt her in the air, her soul like a homing device bringing him back from the edge. Elijah would never have guessed the girl he'd known his whole life would turn into the woman that was his soulmate.

"So glad to see you, brother. It's been so long since we've had a good talk. Now remove your weapon, take out the magazine, and throw it into the woods in two different directions." The façade of Jensen melted away, and the familiarity of Samuel's sister exploded through Elijah's memories. He couldn't remember his sister's name; she was a familiar stranger from a century ago.

"Walk away, Elijah." Riley's voice was grim. Blood gushed from her eye wound and down her shirt.

His shoulders tightened. "I'm not leaving you." Elijah removed the magazine and flung the gun into the woods, the magazine toward the shore.

A smile of triumph covered Jensen's face. Both Elijah and Riley stayed still, silent, studying her next move. He had to cautiously discover Jensen's weaknesses, find out her name. Even if he willed the information to come to him, Elijah knew the past memories would only come organically. Jensen was a hundred and eighty years old and had been planning and re-planning Elijah's death through each life. She had tortured and killed him already in many ways. He desperately hoped the memory of each of his different deaths wouldn't surface at once and cripple him.

Elijah eased toward Riley. "Why don't you let her go? We both know it's me you want."

Jensen let out an entertained laugh, curling the corner of her mouth in a wicked half-smile. She knew more about him than he did, and there was a trick up her sleeve.

"It's not all about *you*. You're so blind when it comes to the fairer sex, always have been." Her voice dipped to a conversational tone. Jensen moved toward Elijah, and the tenseness in her stride faded. Riley quickly blocked her with a protective intensity that Elijah had never witnessed before.

"But, since I'm sure you need an act of good faith, check her back." Jensen waved her gun toward Riley. "Go on."

Elijah hated the excited, eager look on Jensen's face. She bit her bottom lip, waiting for the deception to be exposed. Riley's eyes saddened. Elijah wasn't sure what he would find or if he wanted to uncover the truths Jensen was trying to expose.

"I'd rather talk about Shelly."

"I said look; I won't ask again." There was a savageness under the surface of Jensen's soprano tone. She was annoyed at the repetitive conversation. "If you don't, I'll kill Shelly."

Elijah decided to take advantage and moved toward Riley, scanning his eyes over her injuries. She had a scrape on her chin, and the burn on her neck had blistered. Riley removed her raincoat and threw it to the ground. Elijah lifted the back of her soft, sweat covered T-shirt. He saw goosebumps form on the surface of her tanned skin; her back muscles twitched. Riley grunted as she shifted from one foot to the other. A narrow, elongated blister stretched down the center of her back where the silver shotgun had resided in the holster.

Elijah's hand lost feeling as he held up the back of her shirt. Tingles spread across his chest as he processed what he saw.

She couldn't be a skinwalker.

Riley couldn't be the *other* monster that was hunting him.

Riley's the Beta.

Elijah's stomach cramped; his heart lurched into his throat.

"I take it from your silence, you figured out *what* she is? Temperance here has been one of my faithful servants since the beginning. Affairs with the help do tend to drive a woman mad. After Temperance found out about your affair with Florence, she was more than willing to let me change her. She was fine killing you in every life for almost two hundred years. Until she met this *version* of you."

Elijah backed away, easing toward the shotgun, keeping his eyes on Riley. Betrayal crushed his soul. He was in the woods with two monsters that wanted him dead. The blow of finding out what Riley was clouded his supernatural and internal guiding systems. How could she allow Owen to be murdered and Shelly to be kidnapped?

"Change, go on." Jensen pointed the weapon at Riley.

Riley winced and stared at the ground. "Mary..."

"Say my name again, and I'll shoot him." Jensen trained her gun on Elijah's head. "Now change, or he's dead."

Riley turned her face away from him in shame. Kneeling, she hunched her back like a scared cat and groaned in agony. Her bones popped. The sounds of cracking cartilage made Elijah clench his jaw and cover his mouth. Her bones and muscles shifted violently, and she grunted, then screamed in agony. The sickening change in Riley's body slowed, then stopped. Standing, she turned to Elijah with Temperance's face. Her long, blond hair was wild, and her face the same as the woman in the wedding photo with Samuel.

Knowing what Pandora's box she'd opened, Jensen waited in excited anticipation for their relationship to unravel.

"You ... Did you kill Owen?" Elijah didn't even recognize his voice as his own—accusing and disappointed. A gaping hole formed inside him, hollowing out what minuscule love was left.

Temperance stayed quiet. She turned to him, her eyes slowly crawling from the ground to Elijah's face. The truth struck him like a baseball bat to his throat, and he gasped as his legs wobbled.

Tears cascaded down her cheeks, and a deep sob echoed through the forest. "I didn't ... I couldn't ..." Temperance stepped toward Elijah.

"Stay away from me." Elijah backed away, disgusted, wanting to escape into the vortex he knew was underground. "You murdered my brother! What else have you done? Who else have you killed?" Spit flew from Elijah's mouth, his whole body tense, a vicious fever rising within him. The words echoed through space and time, unleashing pent-up fury and betrayal from two centuries.

"The Riley *you* loved, Elijah, doesn't exist. She never did—Temperance killed her before she even met you. Her family has no idea she's dead." Jensen said with a devious grin. "I watched Temperance throw her into the marsh in pieces."

"Elijah, this isn't who I am anymore. I've been doing this for two hundred years, and I don't want to do it anymore. I'm tired of being her slave," Temperance said with conviction. "She's been using me the whole time; to get to this moment right now. I didn't realize until now that—"

"Stop talking!" Elijah's infuriated tone caused Temperance to recoil.

Cold sweat spread across him, and his muscles burned. A surging sting radiated from the bite. His body quivered, fighting the urge to change into the monster he was becoming. Jensen's guard lowered; she kept a tight grip on her pistol, resting it by her side. She was the necromantic puppeteer that had trapped Owen, Temperance, and so many others. She was the stage master that continued to make them suffer through every life. Elijah's hands balled into fists, and his eyes struggled to focus through a red haze.

The graveyard turned into a battlefield, and his defenses were destroyed. He could hear Jensen in the background muttering arrogant bullshit as he steadied himself on a nearby tree. Rain poured from the sky, hammering the muddy ground. Thunder boomed, and lightning flashed, their intervals shortening. The storm was closing in on them.

"He's turning right now." Jensen's muffled voice snapped back into a crystal clear sound.

Jensen jetted to Elijah, whispering in his ear. "That hunger you're fighting only gets stronger. Soon you'll have to feed and change forms to survive. Eventually, that won't be enough. You'll have to kill, eat, and change into *another* human form. It'll become as natural and easy as brushing your teeth."

"You're not going to kill him, not this time. I won't let you keep doing this to him." Temperance was standing tall now, firm in her defiance.

Elijah's throat felt like he'd swallowed razor blades, and he coughed. "I won't be a monster. I'd rather die."

"I believe it." Jensen smiled, taunting him. "Either way, in this life, you're mine to keep—to torture in spirit or as a skinwalker. It's what I've tried to do from the beginning. You have the key, now more than ever, to get Thomas back. This version of you is going to prove to be far more helpful."

Elijah stumbled, trying to escape Jensen; she was too close for comfort. Just then, he saw her head jolt back, and she doubled over in pain. Blood flowed over her fingers as she held her head.

"Elijah, go!" Temperance had hit Jensen over the head with a rock.

Elijah swiped Jensen's gun from her hand. Temperance dropped the stone as Jensen's hand flew back and blasted her face. Temperance flew across the forest, colliding with a headstone. Elijah pointed the gun at Jensen, unable to focus. She swiped it from his hand, bashing him at the base of his skull with the pistol grip.

"You ungrateful bitch." Jensen faced Temperance, and Shelly wailed from somewhere in the woods. "You realize if he gets to your stupid pathetic friends, he'll eat them, right?" Jensen's voice was thick with disdain.

"Elijah can fight it; he can live with it." Temperance's voice was husky and slurred. "Quinn can stop it."

Before Elijah could regain his vision, both Temperance and Jensen morphed into their canine forms. Beautiful red fur along Temperance's spine stood on end. She *was* Beta; she'd been the one that saved him only a couple nights before. Temperance was next to him, guarding him against Jensen. Her back reached Elijah's waist, and her massive paws spread out in a defensive stance. Temperance pointed her snout toward the ground, and her wolf lips curled back in a vicious warning growl. Jensen charged at Temperance, and they somersaulted, violently nipping at each other's necks. The two canines collided with a tree trunk, and the ground vibrated, bark splintering around them.

Sweat trickled down Elijah's back and face. His muscles tensed and spasmed. The primal call, a looming desire in the back of his mind to take a bite of human flesh, now consumed his rational thought. He weighed the decision to run to Shelly. Elijah wanted to save her the way she had saved him so many years ago—but he was starving. The wound on his arm throbbed, sending a twinge through the muscle. Elijah ran to Shelly; her eyes widened with relief. He removed her gag, throwing it to the ground.

"There's something more that she wants." Shelly's right eye was bruised and swollen, and her voice low.

Elijah untied her ankles. "I need you to know something ... I love you, Shelly. No matter what."

Staying focused, Shelly continued. "I think she wants to control your abilities. There's a massive plan she has for you." Elijah recalled what Kiren had said in the reading the day before. That someone wanted to control his abilities.

Elijah helped Shelly stand. "You need to go, now. I can feel the change coming on. All of you need to leave. Hudson and Parker are parked out by the road."

"I'm not leaving you."

Elijah gently put his hands on both sides of her face, making sure she looked him in the eyes. "The desire to taste flesh is overpowering. My strength is growing. You need to go."

Shelly dug her cheek into Elijah's wet shirt. He held her tight.

"I'm so sorry." Keeping her eyes away from his face, Shelly squeezed his hand, then hurried into the consuming darkness.

Temperance flung Jensen across the forest floor. Dirt and branches sprayed into the air as Jensen skipped like a stone over the surface of a lake. A thud vibrated the ground beneath Elijah's feet. A deafening blast echoed through the woods, and Elijah wheeled around. In an instant, Jensen changed back into her human form, and almost as if they were in sync, so did Temperance.

Jensen held her gun on Elijah, the barrel pointed straight at his face, inches from his nose. Adrenaline surged, and he held his breath as she squeezed the trigger. The dead clicking of the firing pin filled Elijah with relief. She was out of ammo.

Charging at Jensen, Temperance's eyes flared with a brimstone-colored glow. Worry and fright painted her expression as she morphed into her wolf form. Jensen flung the useless weapon to the forest floor and lept at Elijah's protector, changing form in mid-air. Jensen caught Temperance by the neck, sinking her fangs deep into her flesh, tossing her. The wolf tumbled violently.

Jensen attacked Temperance in the weak moment, gnawing at her neck, savagely throwing her head from side to side, digging her razor canine fangs deeper into Temperance's exposed, bloody throat tissues. Temperance's wolf form fell at Elijah's feet, blood splattering his pants, intermingling with the mud.

Elijah thought she was dead for a moment until her paws twitched. She rose, trembling, and stood on all fours, resting against a fallen gravestone. Blood gushed from her neck wound down her front legs, saturating the ground and pooling around her paws. Time slowed for Elijah. All the surrounding scents ambushed him, causing a throbbing between his eyes.

Jensen morphed from a wolf back into her human form in mid-stride. Stars spread across Elijah's vision. Temperance changed into her human form, holding her neck, blood gushing between her fingers, as the color drained from her face.

A wound on Jensen's leg oozed blood through her pants, and she grinned maliciously.

"Enough bullshit. Where's Florence's grimoire? We're running out of time." Jensen scanned the forest. "I see you let my hostage go."

Elijah hadn't found Florence's spellbook. He was afraid of what would happen if he told her it wasn't there. Elijah's eyes jumped from Temperance's face to Jensen's as he continued to process Temperance's identity. He had no idea if she'd murdered Owen or if Jensen was manipulating him in a weak moment. He remained silent, watching Temperance's movements, waiting for her reaction.

Conflicting and confusing emotions flooded through him. Rage built inside him at the savageness of Temperance's attack. He wanted to hold her close, protect her, but she'd murdered others to change into a skinwalker. She'd helped murder him in previous lives.

Elijah clenched his jaw, tears wetting his eyes. There was an insatiable need to tear Jensen into pieces, and to experience the warmth of her blood dripping from his chin. Elijah's held his stomach, slightly bending over as he fought off the emerging, starving deviant fighting to escape.

Temperance's face twisted in suffering as she strained to speak—her voice mute. Temperance coughed, and blood sprayed onto her shirt. Her face paled, and her body sunk into the muddy forest floor. It appeared as if the earth was absorbing her—dragging her to the depths of the underworld to pay penance for her spiritual crimes.

Elijah's vision blurred, and his body seized. He leaned against a tree, attempting to regain composure. The skinwalker sickness surged through his veins, taking him over like a neurological poison. Elijah was too far gone. He wanted to run to Temperance but was anchored to the spot where he stood. His eyesight darkened, pulsing in and out. He could sense Temperance's life force fading, and indignation boiled inside of him. He was helpless to stop his transformation. Sounds of cracking bones and the squishing of tissues filled the woods, and the iron scent of blood caused the back of Elijah's throat to itch. He glanced down at his hands, hoping he wasn't shifting.

Jensen's voice was low and condescending. "You know in every life you try to save her. Except, in every other life, she let you die. This was definitely a nice change of pace." Jensen pumped her eyebrows. "It's about time someone did something different. I was starting to get bored."

Elijah's eyesight recovered, and an urgent uncontrollable need to vomit made him clench his jaw. His lips curled back as he swallowed saliva. Jensen gripped Temperance's warm heart in her hand, blood dripping to the forest floor. The empty cavern in Temperance's chest screamed out the finality that Elijah wasn't ready for. Jensen lowered her chin, her demon eyes black with revulsion.

Before he knew what happened, Elijah tumbled with Jensen on the ground, and she tossed him like a ragdoll. Lightning flickered in the distance as thunder shook the ground like an earthquake. Elijah catapulted Jensen through the forest, and her flailing body skipped over a headstone, her back crashing against a large cypress tree. Elijah had only just thought about getting to the silver shotgun, and in that millisecond, he was standing next to it, staring down Jensen with the savage desire to rip her to pieces.

I must be gaining the abilities of a skinwalker.

An unnatural sense of superiority surged through Elijah. Jensen struggled to stand, fumbling. Flashes of lighting pulsed as he stalked toward her, scooping up the shotgun. Aching pain radiated through his hands when he touched the silver weapon. Elijah lost sight of her for a split second, and then Jensen was behind him, gripping the barrel. The second she laid her hand on it, the inscriptions etched into the silver pulsed once with a golden glow, sending Jensen flying a couple feet away. She landed on her back, still close to him, and Elijah spun, shooting at her. Searing pain surged through his hands as the silver bullets tore through Jensen's chest from point-blank range. He could sense that the shotgun was beginning to protect itself from him. The final push for him to become a skinwalker was picking up speed.

Unable to hold it any longer, Elijah threw down the shotgun and ran to Temperance. Kneeling, he let out a short sob. He stroked her head, brushing her blonde, blood-matted locks away from her face. Elijah zeroed in on her features, etching every ounce of pain into the back of his memories along with Samuel. Elijah knew it would haunt him for the rest of his life, but he also knew it didn't matter what Temperance had done. He knew what *Riley* meant to him. She'd been the one to change the course of his life by protecting him. She'd changed and attempted to rectify her wrongs. Blood soaked into Elijah's pants. The iron smell of her life essence made him salivate, and an instant disgust tore through his conscience. Jensen had made him into a monster. The truth of who Jensen was, the pain he'd caused her was eluding him, and he had no idea how long he would be able to fight the repercussions. Elijah knew that no matter what, he would kill himself before he lived with knowing he'd consumed the flesh of someone he'd loved. Then, a surprising realization dawned on him: the ravenous desire for flesh faded when he focused on the positive, how much he cared for the person.

Entities lingered in the shadows of the woods, watching the scene, their tortured spirits flickering. The ghosts were reminders of what Elijah would become if he didn't perform the needed cannibalistic ritual—a lost soul. His sense of hearing intensified, causing a throbbing in the back of his head. Elijah's body quivered as blended chaotic emotions played games with his logic.

Why am I so sad about someone who has done so much evil?

"Don't keep me waiting, brother." Jensen's voice was agitated and mocking.

Elijah stood cautiously, keeping his eyes on Jensen. Her tattered shirt was red with the blood of her already healed wounds. She held the shotgun pain-free, having wrapped her hands in strips of cloth torn from her shirt. Elijah watched as she dismantled the silver shotgun. "Just in case you get any ideas." Jensen winced, grunting as the pain of the silver radiated through her feeble hand protection.

"You didn't have to kill her."

Jensen's tone was nonchalant. "She was in my way. Temperance, or Riley, or whatever *you* prefer to call her, never had the spine to do what was necessary for our survival." Her eyes darkened, and she lowered her chin. "Now, where's the book?"

Spinning away from him for a moment, she picked at a nearby tree. It occurred to Elijah that Jensen knew Quinn was nearby, and she was biding her time. Elijah's eyes frantically searched the woodlands, hoping Hudson, Parker, Shelly, or Camilla weren't going to stumble into their sick and twisted game.

Camilla's comment about Jensen wanting to change him, not kill him from the start rushed over him.

"Your plan the whole time in this life was to change me, not kill me."

"If at first, you fail for one hundred and fifty years, try, try again. I've been looking for a vessel for Thomas for nearly two hundred years. Little did I know what I needed was right in front of me. You have abilities in this life that will be of incredible use." Jensen leaned against the tree and took a coin out of her pocket, flipping it between her fingers. Elijah watched as her chest wound healed itself at an unnatural, accelerated rate. "Keeping you alive long enough to let my dearest possess you and utilize those gifts seemed like an intelligent thing to do."

Jensen paused and turned her nose to the air, sniffing, then stuck the coin back into her pocket. "Your twin flame's here. Her scent's distinct. As a matter of fact, I can hear her stumbling through the woods toward us from that direction." Jensen pointed north. "My sisters should be about ready to kill her too."

"You were waiting for her to get here," Elijah said.

Jensen laughed-scoffed at him. "You idiot. I need *Florence's* grimoire; she was *Florence*. The next best thing *is* her. For her sake, I hope she has it because extracting the memories would be torture—for her, of course, but plenty of fun for me."

Rage flooded through Elijah. He charged at Jensen planting his shoulder in her stomach. She soared through the forest, colliding with a massive rotting stump. Wood shards burst into the air falling around Elijah like confetti. Elijah's neck cracked; white-hot throbbing flared across the base of his skull, and disorientation fractured his vision.

Jensen threw down a thick branch, watching him as he stumbled. It felt like she'd almost broken his spine. She'd moved at such a speedy pace, Elijah never saw the hit coming. His body weakened, and a stabbing pain shot through his stomach. In a second, she was holding a dagger to his throat. The disorientation subsided, and Elijah could feel a trickle of liquid rolling down the back of his neck.

"You might want to keep your anger in check. Or I will slice your throat." Jensen's breath brushed his ear. The closeness of her body caused bile to rise.

Raising his hands in front of him, Elijah nodded in affirmation. Satisfied he'd be obedient, Jensen released him. The skinwalker sickness flooded through Elijah, and he felt his human life slipping away.

Elijah heard the vultures in the background pecking at the dead body of the *real* Jensen, another victim. The *tick-tick* of their beaks hitting bone crescendoed, mixing with the sounds of the deceased. The otherworldly cacophony was unbearable, and he squeezed his eyes shut. The faint smell of lavender, vanilla, and sage drifted on the winds.

Quinn's here.

35

QUINN BURST FROM THE dense, wet forest and stumbled into the circle around the graveyard. Tripping over her heavy feet, she toppled into Elijah's arms, clutching Florence's Book of Shadows to her chest. All five spirits of the sisters appeared at their designated trees after Quinn crossed the threshold. Their ghostly apparitions materialized out of black fog, and they stared at the three of them in the center. Helen stood nearest to Elijah, her dead eyes filled with fury.

Mixed emotions of comfort and fear ravaged him. Holding Quinn in his arms, no matter the circumstances was a relief. Kiren was in the woods; he could sense her. Elijah skimmed the darkness, waiting for his mother to emerge, and when she didn't, he knew instantly that there must be a plan. He could still smell the scent of lavender floating from the darkness.

Kiren made herself smell like Quinn.

Elijah flickered a soft smile at Quinn. Her body was heavy and drenched in rain. She'd used every ounce of energy she had to find him, to help him, to save him. Now it was his turn to try and save her.

"I got here as fast as I could." Quinn's eyes widened at the sight of his shirt covered in blood. "Oh my god. Where's ..."

Elijah opened his mouth to tell Quinn, and Jensen interrupted him. "I tore the little pain in the ass's throat out." She nodded impatiently toward Riley's limp body.

"I'm so sorry." Quinn's exhausted face quivered, tears rolling down her dirty cheeks.

Quinn pressed her face into Elijah's dirty arm. Together, the three of them created a nostalgia that ejected him from his life as Elijah. Memories of his life as Samuel flooded his mind and poured into him from another dimension. Pain from a dark corner of the universe where evil lived, filled him with despair. The two lives mixing caused his ancient consciousness to expand, and memories of a life he'd lived a hundred and eighty years before surfaced.

Temperance and him lying in bed together cuddling, then the sight of her crying when she found out that Samuel had met someone else. He saw Florence sobbing over him and Benjamin holding her as Samuel's limp body was rolled into the ground. A Flicker, then a fragmented memory. Rage, fury, embarrassment. Elijah was fighting with an unknown man. It was a family deal gone bad. The last memory that overtook Elijah was the sight of the man's body dangling from a tree after he was executed.

Jensen stormed over, fury filling her heavy steps. Warm gusts blew her short, blonde hair in whirls. She tore Quinn from Elijah's arms, tossing her to the side while stealing the book from her arms. Quinn stayed on the ground, weak. Elijah charged Jensen, backhanding her. She spun like a hurricane, landing on the spongey ground and mud.

"The spell to save her is in here. If you want it, you'll do what I ask." Jensen wiped her bleeding lip with the back of her hand, smiling like she'd accomplished some hidden agenda.

"I'm leaving. You can have the grimoire, but you're not taking me, and you're not taking Quinn." Elijah turned, making his way to Quinn. "Not again."

Jensen mumbled, chanting with conviction under the raging, cracking live oaks. Wind whipped around Elijah, whistling. A pearlescent energy wave surged through the area, rippling like a stone tossed into the surface of a still lake. Elijah's throat tightened, and his legs cramped. He fell to his knees. Jensen walked to Elijah, clenching Florence's spellbook to her chest, her eyes transfixed on him. Elijah crumbled at her feet, gasping for air, as he rolled onto his back, looking at Jensen. She held a gold coin in her hand, rubbing it with her thumb.

Helen appeared over Quinn, strangling her. Ghostly bodies appeared, hanging from the trees that encircled the graveyard. Energy surged from the trapped spirits and into the ground. Fire flared from the stone circle. Jensen yelled, chanting in another language.

"Why are you doing this?" Elijah yelled over the torrent of the dead.

Jensen ignored Elijah, continuing her crusade.

"Mary Olivia Reynolds." Kiren's raspy, barely audible brogue came from the depths of the night.

Elijah could tell by the way Jensen stiffened that it was her *birth* name. She opened the spellbook, flipping frantically through the pages. The name Mary was a warning for him, a piece of the puzzle to help him survive. The sisters wanted to be released from her grip, which is why they kept appearing, repeating the name of their killer and captor like a twisted mantra. They wanted her grip on their souls to be released.

Kiren continued, "I bind you from doing harm spiritually and physically to my family, friends, and innocents, past, present, and future." Kiren emerged from the shadows, holding a vial out in front of her, grasping it with conviction. Her eyes were deep with concentration, blocking out any fear. "I bind you from spellcasting, necromancy, and any forms of shapeshifting."

An animalistic bellow escaped from Mary's lips, her eyes shifting to the immediate threat. Her body shaking, she dropped the coin, and Elijah swept it up, tucking it into his pocket. He scrambled away from Mary, scraping his legs and arms against the jagged rocks and mud underneath him. Elijah crawled to Quinn as Helen and the other four sisters dissipated. He cradled her weak body in his arms. She coughed, and blood painted her pale, cracked lips. The wounds of her face were coated with dirt, blood rising around the edges of the healing scabs.

"She's your illegitimate sister, and I taught her magic. I'm responsible. This is my fault." Quinn's raspy voice was thick with regret.

"This isn't your fault." Elijah's heart crushed at her pain. He wanted to fix it. "She made her own decisions."

Kiren and Mary were now speaking over each other, their voices getting louder as they commanded their magical powers to demolish their opponent.

"I banish you from showing anything other than the true form you were born into." Kiren's voice was powerful, but he could tell she was getting tired.

The noises of the dead were rising, and the mixed sounds assaulted Elijah's ears. He winced, losing his concentration. Kiren had walked past Quinn and Elijah. She was face to face with Mary now.

Elijah watched as Mary attempted to change into a wolf. Her hideous body morphed into a distorted and disjointed bag of skin and bones, then reverted to a completely different human form. Hysteria pulsed through the air. The healthy plants around Elijah turned black and brittle as Mary leeched the life force out of the forest like a parasite.

Mary's human form was strikingly familiar. Her beautiful eyes and long black hair shocked Elijah. It was the girl who'd brought him Owen's laundry in the dorm, Harper. She'd ultimately warned Elijah about herself. It was wicked.

Quinn guided Elijah's eyes back to her, gently touching his neck. "She has to have a personal belonging of Owen's that she uses to control him and manipulate his soul essence. Take it and use it to free him."

Elijah's mind immediately shifted from Quinn to the coin. Helen disappeared when he grabbed it from the ground. "Like this?"

"The coin, it's connected to all the sisters." Quinn's voice thinned. She reached a trembling hand to his face, running her thumb along his lower lip. "No matter the result of this life, I know we'll find each other again."

Quinn's body flew from Elijah's arms through the flames, landing outside of the circle. A moment later, Kiren was catapulted across the white stones. She crashed to the forest floor, landing next to Quinn. The flames caught Elijah's attention—*fire*. He needed to tear out her heart and burn it to ashes.

Shelly's screaming voice bellowed from the woods. "You will not take another one of my sons, Mary." Shelly stormed from the woods, both hands clenched in fists at her sides. Her ordinarily soft features were hardened with determination. The wind's intensity increased as if in sync with her fury. "I call the elemental gods and goddesses to aid me in my fight. I call on your divine love and judgment." Shelly stuck her palm out toward Mary, commanding and dominating. "I call on all ancestral witches of The Sisters of the Waking world to aid us."

Kiren stood as quickly as she could, grabbing Shelly's other hand. A soft glow burst from the ground when their hands connected, flaring like a powder keg. The two mothers glanced at each other, and a moment of recognition passed between them. Elijah could tell they'd worked together before. They were linked by the love they had for his father and for him.

The herbs Temperance poured in the graveyard weren't in a protective circle. The symbol Temperance created with the salt looked like one of the runes. It was a *binding symbol*.

Kiren's voice lowered to a confident and commanding tone. "I reverse your intentions. I send back all the negativity, hurt, and pain you've caused. I reverse your hexes and spells of evil intent. I block you from hurting another. I cleanse all past lives of pain and wickedness, healing your victims of all ancestral and spiritual trauma." The spirits of the tortured and Samuel's sisters were standing around the circle, staring in at Mary with blind fury. "I bind you from doing harm, practicing necromancy, and shapeshifting."

Thunder shook the ground, and Camilla appeared, throwing bundles of already lit sage into the binding space where Mary and Elijah stood. Camilla hesitated, her face covered in fear. Quinn sluggishly stood, urging her to keep going. Elijah had been wrong—the stone circle was created to keep them out and keep him in. Mary cast it in anticipation of this night. She'd been planning and waiting for this opportunity to control him for centuries.

Mary's eyes were wide, her face drained of color. They'd planned an ambush, and after Temperance's death, Kiren was the perfect backup they needed. Kiren continued as Shelly simultaneously cast her reversal spell. Mary stuttered, flipping back and forth between pages, combating them both at the same time.

Elijah ran to the edge of the circle and tossed the coin to Quinn. He reached the edge of the stones, the fire burning the flesh of his forearm. A phantom wall kept him from going any further. His head whirled, his body shook, and his vision blurred.

Mary had turned her attention to him, muttering words under her breath. The last thing he remembered was Quinn screaming and her terror-filled emaciated face as she desperately reached for him through the flames. His body thrashed as he was dragged across the forest floor by and invisible menace and sucked into the cellar.

36

MARY HELD HER HANDS above her head. Black energy brimmed with red flowed from her palms effortlessly. The runes that were etched into the wood beams of the cellar glowed. A massive fluctuation in the atmosphere whipped around Elijah. It was at that second that the air stopped spilling in from outside. Mary had sealed them in. Elijah could hear the crashing and thundering of the supernatural storm raging above. He assumed they were performing the first step, severing Quinn's cords to the Shaw and Reynolds sisters. His eyes were blurry, and his head throbbed. Mary casted her spells quickly and effectively, directing the spirits around her to block out any harm, protecting her from any further energetic attacks. Elijah clenched his eyes shut, his body, mind, and soul exhausted, his consciousness slipped away.

Heat brushed Elijah's face, and his eyes opened to see flames dancing around a broken piece of wood. A fire, fueled by the bookshelves that had lined the walls, burned in the fireplace. Mary sat next to him, holding the same dagger she'd held to Shelly's neck. The sight of the smoke successfully escaping the fireplace let Elijah know Mary had been better prepared than he'd anticipated.

"They only set me back by an hour."

Elijah sat, leaning against the stone wall. His eyes focused, and the fuzziness faded. Temperance's body lay next to him, her lifeless eyes staring at him as he regained awareness. He was unsure how Mary had gotten both of them in the cellar together, but he was convinced it was a macabre method of torture.

Mary held Temperance's heart in her hands and studied the bloody lump before tossing it into the fire. Elijah's jaw clenched, and an uncontrollable shudder rippled through his body. He turned his head away from the grotesque scene. A sizzling bombarded his ears, and the fluids from her heart spit from the flames, slapping him in the face.

Temperance's carcass rotted before his eyes, the decaying process reaching an unnatural speed, breaking down her body as soon as her heart entered the fire. Her skin turned horrendous patches of black and purple.

Vomit exploded from Elijah's mouth; his throat was on fire. It felt like his stomach had been yanked out through his nose. The nausea settled, and Elijah took in deep breaths, the smell of bile stuck in his nose. Rain pelted the coffin entrance above, and thunder shook the cobblestone walls. Pieces of the mud between each stone flaked out onto the dirty floor.

"Take a bite out of her, or you'll die."

"I'd rather die." Elijah fought back a dry heave, clenching his jaw. Taking a bite out of a decaying body was the last thing he desired to do.

"I'm trying to save your life."

"They're gonna stop you."

"They can't reverse a spell that hasn't been completed. And if they do, I'll kill Shelly and reverse her spells, and everything she's done will be undone since she started casting. I should've killed her when I had the chance."

Mary set Florence's open spellbook next to him, and he ran his fingers over the pages. Static tickled his fingertips. The recollection of the house that used to stand above them two centuries before rolled through Elijah's senses. He could hear the creaking of the wood in the kitchen above them, their servants bustling to make dinner. The scent of food, firewood, and herbs filled the space. Echoes of the distant past reverberated in his ears as if they were currently happening.

"I know you can bring him back. All I want is my husband." Mary sat cross-legged next to him. Her dark hair was wild and matted. "I'm tired of being alone, Samuel." She nudged the grimoire closer. Mary's tone softened, and in a second, he could see the sincerity in her once troubled eyes. Mary had lived across from Owen in the same dorm. She'd watched him, stalked him, then murdered him.

Elijah's supernatural senses were on overdrive, and a vision overtook his mind—of Mary laughing with him on a shoreline, sharing a piece of bread and a bottle of wine. Her energy was different; it was filled with light and hope.

"Mary, you don't have to do this. I know you loved me once."

"I *loved* Thomas. Was the dirty money you got to keep quiet after they murdered him and took his land worth it?"

A vague memory of receiving a massive velvet satchel of coins flickered in Elijah's mind's eye. The gold coin he took from Mary moments before was a part of them. Guilt consumed Elijah. He hadn't taken part in the death of his sister's fiancé, but he was partially responsible. The Shaw men had manipulated the local townsfolk to obtain Thomas's land.

"You could have stopped Father. I took that money, spent all of it after I burnt the house to the ground. He always did love you and Benjamin more. I was an indiscretion. Father's mistake."

"Thomas wasn't supposed to die ... that wasn't our intention. He was only supposed to leave the area." Elijah coughed, covering his mouth.

Goosebumps rose on the nape of Elijah's neck. Ravenous hunger fought its way to the surface, and Temperance's corpse in the corner called to him. Tempting him to take a bite of the flesh and learn what it was like to have power, to live forever.

The past, future, beast, and humanity in him were waging war against each other for the possession of Elijah's soul. Energy from the book seeped into him, soothing the wild wickedness that was taking him by storm. Broken memories raced through Elijah's cloudy mind.

"The vortex, you want me to bring him back into this world. He has no physical body to go ..." Elijah paused. "You want me to give him *my* body. You've never wanted to change *me;* you wanted him to be a skinwalker with you."

"You're smarter than you look. It solves all your problems. You get to save your loved ones, and I get my husband. The only way you could call him from the beyond is with *your* abilities. You and Florence took everything from me. I want you to know what it's like being stuck in a hell that never ends." Mary's voice lowered to a growl. She pointed at him with a shaky hand. "Each life's unresolved pain ... stacking on top of you until it destroys your soul."

"No, I'm not doing it." Elijah shoved the spellbook away. "I have no idea how to cast a spell."

"Don't worry, it's like riding a bike." She shoved the spellbook back.

Pain radiated through his arm, sweat poured from his back, his muscles stiffened all over his body. Elijah doubled over, temporarily crippled by the spasm. Lying in the fetal position, he felt as if he'd swallowed tacks, and they were sliding down his throat, inching their way to his stomach.

Heat from the fire beat against Elijah's back, and he coughed. Blood splattered the dirt floor, and the vortex behind the wall widened, swirling steady and slow.

"Our father's family paid for what they did, and so did my mother's. They all helped him die by perpetuating the lies to save themselves. Not one of them tried to protect me."

Whispering, distorted voices escaped the hole, calling him. Elijah recalled the protection spell Quinn had said earlier and the stone she'd given him that was still around his neck. Elijah pulled out the stone, gripping it.

"I call on the gods and goddesses to protect me from evil seen and unseen." The moment the words left Elijah's mouth, his spell organically flowed. "Protect me and keep me safe by reflecting all harm back onto the sender. I call on the gods and goddesses to protect me physically and energetically." Power surged from the earth through his feet and legs. Quinn's talisman warmed in his hand.

"You're really starting to piss me off." Mary stood, clutching something small in her hand. "But I have always loved a good sibling rivalry."

The dead's whispers grew and pierced Elijah's ears, his head vibrating. A fog appeared in the center of the cellar. Elijah raised himself to a stand, leaning against the wall next to the vortex. Mary held the dagger in her hand, and he glanced at the engraved initials on the handle. *TMD* was Thomas Michael DeLaney.

The dagger belonged to Mary's fiancé.

Mary sliced her hand and set down the dagger on a nearby shelf, grasping Owen's bracelet.

The walls tremored, and Elijah's body tensed. His sight blackened, then faded back into focus. Owen now stood in the center of the cellar where the mist had been forming. Rage clouded his features, and his black eyes fixed on Elijah. Owen's neck was bruised, and scabs from a rope burn formed a line around his neck. Hate emanated from him, causing Elijah's joints to ache. Owen's image flickered, and in a second, Elijah flew across the cellar, crashing against the walled-off room. The stones tumbled around him, and the colorful ribbons of the vortex's edge licked Elijah's fingers.

Owen's entity was on top of Elijah, pinning him down by his neck. Owen drained Elijah's energy from him, and his distorted semi-transparent body leaned inward, squeezing tighter. Owen's nose was inches from Elijah's—his steamy, putrid breath brushed against his cheeks and ears. Owen thrashed Elijah against the wall, and he searched frantically, scanning the space for a weapon, landing on Thomas' ornate dagger.

Mary clenched Owen's bracelet, and blood dripped from her hand. She was in a self-induced trance, connecting with the dead. Her wild raven-colored hair clung to her face, and her fair skin was blotched. The innocent, petite, shy woman he'd met only a few days ago had never existed. Elijah's mind's eye flooded with memories.

Owen and him fishing, Samuel and Benjamin laughing, hugging. Their energies intertwined.

The resentment they felt for each other when Owen died.

The anger and disappointment they felt toward each other as the Shaw brothers.

Benjamin trying to talk Samuel out of the decision to steal the land from Thomas.

Owen sitting with him on the steps of the church at his father's funeral.

Elijah's physical senses faded back in, and he gasped for air. He needed to get Owen's bracelet.

A sinister entity—that Elijah was sure wasn't human—was trying to crawl its way out of the vortex, its black fingers curling around the edge of the gray stones. Elijah was positive it was Thomas' tormented spirit. His violent death had altered his soul, and he was close to a demon. Elijah knew that if he didn't close the vortex, Thomas would escape. Allowing him to possess Elijah or someone else. And that was damn sure something he couldn't let happen. Even if it killed him. Leaving both Thomas and Mary to their own devices with no one to stop them from stealing souls, causing chaos, was a karmic debt he didn't want following him into his next life.

Concentrating, Elijah focused on Riley. *Riley, if you're here, I need your help. I need to be protected.* Nothing. Elijah decided to try again. *Temperance, I need you. Please. Protect me.* Temperance's spirit materialized and stalked from the corner, her eyes intensely focused on Owen. The ground quaked as the two collided, their energies moving and intermingling. Sparks flew like metal scraping the cement from their spiritual battle with each hit.

Elijah choked and gasped. He scrambled, taking advantage of the opening, swiping up Thomas' dagger. Mary lurched, clutching the back of Elijah's shirt, yanking him to the cellar floor. Choking, he fell to the ground, and the dagger flew from his grip, spinning across the dirt floor. Mary nipped at his neck, and her hand grabbed the exact spot where the ghostly handprint had been burned into his flesh. Elijah catapulted her across the cellar, and she collided with the stone wall.

The violent sounds of the two entities fighting in the background shook the cellar, and each boom reverberated like a bomb finding its target in a war. Dirt and clay fell like snow over Elijah and Mary.

Mary stood, stumbled, then lunged at him, gnawing at his neck. Elijah plunged Thomas's knife into her chest. He could feel the jostle of the blade, nicking bone and cartilage. Her warm blood oozed over his hand, dripping to the floor. The bitter-sweet, iron scent of Mary's blood made his mouth water. Her eyes widened in shock, and she jerked away from him, stumbling to the ground. Mary laid on her back, wrapping her hands around the blade.

Elijah staggered to the wall, his blood-covered hands involuntarily shaking as all the muscles in his body seized. He fell to the floor. His mouth watered, and Elijah knew the monster that tried to kill him was the only one that could save him. He crawled to Mary, his joints swelling and his muscles hardening, terrified she'd regenerate if he didn't move fast enough. Intense agony immobilized him; it felt like his flesh was on fire. Elijah removed the dagger from her chest, and it took all the strength he had left to carve out her heart. The tissue was soft in his hands, and the slippery organ warmed his fingers. He cradled the once beating heart in his hand, tears streaming down his face.

The sisters manifested out of a black mist, solidifying. Their black eyes watched him, spectators to his downfall.

I don't want to die. Not now. She's not going to win.

Elijah hesitated, then sunk his teeth into the heart, ripping a bite from the wet tissue. He swallowed quickly, then threw her heart into the fire. The rancid scent of burning flesh and her blood made his throat burn and his ears ache. Energy from the ground swirled around him, and he ripped Owen's bracelet from Mary's corpse, sliding it onto his wrist.

I'm a monster, and I'm no better than Mary.

The breath shot from his lungs, and his chest squeezed, threatening to collapse. Paralyzed, Elijah struggled to roll onto his back. Mary's body rapidly disintegrated, crumbling into bones and dust. Elijah's sight dimmed, and a surge of otherworldly power caused his back to arch and his body to stiffen. The spirits of the sisters and Temperance evaporated into the vortex as it swirled closed. The last image Elijah glimpsed was Owen's spirit kneeling next to him, holding his hand, a beautiful white light surrounding him. As Elijah let go of his fear and anger, he heard Owen's soothing voice, saying, "I love you, brother, always," as he slipped into darkness.

37

FEVERED CANNIBALISTIC NIGHTMARES PLAGUED Elijah while he slept; he'd lost all sense of time, and his mind had disappeared into its own supernatural hellish landscape. Mary stalked him there, hunting him. The wax-like face of Temperance's corpse appeared around every corner, torturing him. The guilt of how he'd failed her those two hundred years ago and how he'd failed her again, weighed heavy on his soul. Elijah knew Temperance and Mary would never be gone. They were a part of him in more ways than he liked. In some way, Mary achieved her goal—she broke him. Healing from one life's trauma was complicated enough, but multiple lives at one time is a whole different notion.

Elijah instinctively knew that past lives were hidden for a reason. If human beings could access the trauma and emotions from multiple lifetimes all at once, there's a possibility they would cease to exist. The massive amount of soul energy would be too much for the fragile human body to endure.

Alternating between sleep and physical torture, Elijah could hear everyone's panicked conversations around him. They hoped he wasn't going to die. The emotional shock of the cellar had scrambled his brain and disabled his ability to communicate. He'd lay in shock for what seemed like years. Elijah's soul and corporeal thoughts were expanding, and it felt like the spiritual upgrade, temporarily separated him from his body allowing him to escape into the consciousness of the universe. When the expansion settled and came to a stop, Elijah's physical senses slowly came back into function.

Kiren sat in a chair next to the bed, reading Florence's grimoire. It was the same place she'd been since they'd come back from Seven Sisters Road. Elijah knew this because every time his body convulsed, or hunger for flesh set in as he made his way through the transition, Kiren was there.

Dust-covered ceiling fans are what Elijah saw when he opened his eyes. The rich, cedar scent of Owen's flannel sheets filled his nose. The softness of the bed wrapped around him. The church was silent. Elijah rolled onto his side and noticed the picture he'd taken from Owen's dorm room of Owen and himself sitting on the bedside table. The memory of Owen sitting next to him as he'd faded into his skinwalker sickness caused a lump to form in his throat. He glanced down to discover the matching leather bracelets on his arm as he repositioned himself on his back. The leather was coated in dried blood—Temperance's and Mary's. Elijah twisted them around his wrist, wishing he could have brought Owen back with him.

The stained-glass windows were lit with the sun, and beautiful colors danced across the floor as the shadow of the palm tree outside rustled in a soft summer breeze. The back door was open, and cool air whirled over him, brushing his cheeks. As if Mother Earth was saying, welcome back.

A crispness in the air told him it was early, and it made him think of the dew that covered Mr. Nolan's farmland on beautiful mornings. Elijah raked a hand through his thick hair and propped himself up on his elbow, joints aching. Glancing down, Elijah noticed the bite on his arm was healed, and the stitches were removed. He touched his cheek, and there was a smooth spot where Allison had punched him.

Kiren glanced up from the spellbook. Leaning forward, she studied him. The light through the stained-glass window backlit her hair, creating a multicolored halo. A soft, comforting smile crossed her lips.

"It's good to see ye again." Kiren scooted the chair closer, grabbing his hand, her loving energy seeping into him. "We thought we lost ye for a moment." Her Irish brogue was tender and soothing as she rubbed her thumb over his sore fingers.

"How many days has it been?" Elijah noted Owen's journal next to him on the bedside table, and he ran his fingers over the soft leather. He picked it up and opened it, flipping through the pages. Elijah stopped at the bloody wedding picture of Temperance and Samuel.

"Three."

The sting of Temperance's death radiated through his soul, and he slapped the journal back down on the nightstand. Shelly emerged through the back door, and Camilla jumped up from the floor in one of the aisles, clapping and squealing.

"He's talking." Camilla jogged to him, then bent down, hugging him quickly. "You're alive. This is so amazing. I'm so glad." A huge smile crossed her face, and she wriggled her whole body as if she was going to explode from happiness.

Shelly sat next to him, wrapping her arms around him, squeezing. "You're alright." Her voice caught in her throat. Shelly took in a deep breath holding back a sob.

Elijah's body ached, and his muscles burned with tenderness, "Easy, I'm a little sore."

"Sorry," Shelly released him, and he plopped back down on the bed. "Guys, he's awake and talking," Shelly yelled out the door, and he heard Parker and Hudson's muffled, excited voices outside.

"Try not to talk so loud." Elijah winced, stretching his stiff neck muscles. his eyes burned, and he licked his chapped lips. "Owen was with me in the cellar. I freed him. I'm not sure if he's moved on or not."

Camilla touched Shelly's shoulder, comforting her.

"I'm sure he'll move on soon," Shelly said, and tears welled in her eyes as she squeezed Camilla's hand.

Elijah glanced next to the bed, and noticed chains that had been newly bolted onto the floor. His shoulders slumped and he noticed a throbbing in his hands. There were ringed scabs around his wrists.

"We had to tie you down. So you didn't hurt yourself," Camilla said quickly.

Except Elijah knew what she wasn't saying, and what was between the lines. They had to restrain him to keep him from biting or killing anyone.

The painful dose of reality made Elijah want to see Quinn, feel her touch. She'd held his hand and read to him; her company had been healing. "Where's Quinn?"

"She's down at the docks, fishing. Connecting with Mother Gaia, healing." Kiren's eyes gleamed. He could tell she was genuinely happy to see him again.

Hudson and Parker flew in the back door, covered in dirt. Hudson's wide grin and caramel eyes lit up when he saw Elijah. "I told you it would be alright." He smacked Parker on the shoulder.

"Guess I owe you forty bucks," Parker said.

Elijah couldn't help but chuckle. It was nice to see them again. Relief waved over him, followed immediately by grief. His confusing emotions about Temperance nipped at his heart. There was something deep inside him that she'd attached to. He knew no matter what in the future when he remembered her, it would be as Riley.

But, how do you mourn the loss of someone that never existed?

Elijah sighed, not really ready to reveal the painful truth to Shelly. "Riley was a skinwalker. She was Samuel's wife, Temperance." Elijah sat and shoved his face into his hands, rubbing his eyes. The pain of her and Owen's deaths grated against his emotions. Tears brimmed his eyes. "She tried to save me." Elijah's heart felt like it was ripped out, the way he'd torn out Mary's. "I'm sorry Shelly. I know you loved her."

The pain of Temperance's death was written all over Shelly's face. She'd already figured it out. Shelly stood next to Elijah's bedside now, her face turning grim. Elijah's throat tightened.

"You shifted while you were out," Shelly said quickly as if the words hurt her to say.

"Into who? Do I still look like ..." Elijah reached for his face.

"Don't worry, you changed back." Shelly stuck out her hand, calming him.

"You shifted into Samuel ... I'm not sure you knew what you were doing," Kiren added.

Elijah's head whirled, and vertigo forced him to lie down. "I don't remember ... that. But if I killed her, then doesn't that mean her spell should fade?"

"It means something went terribly wrong, and there's no telling the way it will play out. There's no telling how much of Mary's spells went undone. But the bigger question is why? How did she get around such a major part of spell work? With the mixture of her magical practices, there's no way to say that this is completely over. The only way we can think of now is to find the original spell she created for you."

Camilla sat next to him and pulled him close and rubbed his back. He nuzzled her shoulder, and his tears dampened her shirt.

"I can't live like this." Elijah sat, wiping his eyes, then heard Camilla hesitate, unsure how to answer him.

"We found justice for Owen, and we still have a month to get the documentary to Turner. In some small way, his story will be told. And lucky enough, yours truly was able to open the secured file. Owen left you and Shelly money in an account. A whole two-hundred grand, we can use it on the church, continuing the research Owen started. It's the best way to remember him. Not to mention it'll help us pay those pesky drug debts."

"I can't believe I got you guys all wrapped up in this. It was the opposite of what I wanted." Elijah sighed, defeated.

"Dude, none of this is your fault. You saved our lives. Mary would have eventually killed us all," Parker said, wiping dirt from his face.

"You're still Elijah to me," Hudson added.

"I found Jensen's body not far from the graveyard. Mary was trying to frame me." Elijah rubbed the back of his neck and swallowed heavily.

"Kiren and I took care of everything. Just don't ask how." Shelly said quickly, shooting Kiren an uneasy glance.

Kiren crossed her ankles, leaning back into her chair. "Your new condition is going to take some time to figure out, so I've arranged for us to stay in Florida." Her voice was tinged with a forced calm; she was sick with worry about her son. "I have a colleague who might know how to help."

"I can't leave. There's no way I can leave my friends."

"Allison is still missing. I had William call and talk to Detective Bohannon, which was not fun by the way. There's no way for us to know what truly happened to him." Shelly said.

"Another reason why we need to leave," Kiren added.

Both of his mothers had made up their minds, and he was too exhausted to argue. "My car?" Elijah raised an eyebrow, hopeful.

"It's in the driveway, and we got the window replaced." Parker smiled.

The despair he'd suffered while in his skinwalker—induced coma dissipated, and for once, Elijah knew what unconditional love was. He was surrounded by family, who, no matter what, would always be there for him. Some weren't his blood family, but they were all his soul family. The only ones missing were Owen and his father. Elijah knew that their deaths would leave a cavern in his heart that would never be filled. No matter who entered his life.

"Wait, just out of curiosity, what was the password for the encrypted file?" Elijah grabbed his T-shirt from the end of the bed, pulling it on.

Camilla giggled, and then winked, "Sandra Nilsson."

Elijah couldn't help but laugh at Owen in that moment. "His girl, good ol' Ms. 2008 Play Boy Bunny."

Elijah watched Quinn as she sat in a red camping chair on the shore, patiently reeling in her line, teasing the fish. He leaned against a tree, staying out of view. Elijah pulled his phone out of his back pocket, hesitating. He wanted to leave it off a little longer, not fully ready to get back to the real world. He hadn't seen the phone since Hudson put it into a plastic bag right before he entered the woods. Elijah clicked on the power button and noticed there was an email from Riley.

Opening the email, Elijah turned away from Quinn, escaping deeper into the forest, using foliage as camouflage. The rawness of Temperance's betrayal and the hurt of her death was complicated, intermingled emotions that would take multiple lifetimes to sort through. He would always remember her as two different people, never knowing which one was genuine. Elijah pulled down the bill of his cap and hesitantly played the video.

Riley's face had a sullen expression, and she adjusted her cell phone, fixing the framing. "If you're watching this, then I didn't survive to stop the email being sent." Elijah could see the church in the background of the video and knew she took it earlier on the same day she was killed. "I know Mary is going to kill me. More so now, since she sent Helen to drown me, branding me with water, marking me as a sacrifice. I wanted to tell you everything from the start. Except, I knew the moment I told you, you would cut me off. That's the way you've always been. First things first, I love you, Elijah. The sting of anger at your betrayal and the intensity of the skinwalker emotions misguided me for a long time. I've loved you through every lifetime, and when I said it in this one, I meant it."

Riley paused, wiping a tear from her eye. "In this life, Mary initially thought you were Samuel, and she wasn't wrong." Riley's voice thinned, tears brimming her eyes. "To change her mind, I convinced her Owen was Samuel." Riley paused, sniffling. "I knew she'd figure out he was Benjamin soon enough. I just wanted to buy extra time to help you survive. To make it more realistic, I cheated." Riley let out a sob. "Causing you the same pain that you caused me so long ago killed me and was the hardest thing I've ever done." Tears streamed down her face, and she wiped them with her forearm. "I never thought she'd kill him. She's never done that before. I loved you and Owen in this life, and I feel privileged to have witnessed the evolution of your lives for the better. Please tell Shelly I loved her. I never wanted this for us."

The screen blackened in the middle of Riley breaking down, and a heart-wrenching cry was cut off at the end. Elijah rubbed the back of his neck, letting out a troubled sigh. He shoved his phone in his back pocket. He had no idea if he would recover from all the damage to his wounded heart, but he knew finding a glass of whiskey would be a good start.

Elijah's eyes drifted to Quinn. Staying out of her view, he admired her beautiful calming energy. Lavender and sage, intermingled with seawater, sailed on the wind, brushing his cheeks, and filling him with a warmth he'd never experienced before. Her curly red hair was tied back in a messy ponytail, and she wore a worn Marlin cap. The cuts on her face were healing. She was still thin but appeared healthier.

The sun was bright, making Elijah wonder where his sunglasses were. The soft lapping of waves on the shoreline soothed him. Elijah smiled and soaked in the simple pleasures of the moment, thankful he was still alive. A warm breeze drifted over him, and he was filled with a sense of relief. He was grateful that *everyone* he'd loved hadn't endured the horrific fate Mary had planned for them. Elijah wished he could undo it all, but that would be impossible. He took off Quinn's necklace, then strode to her.

"Hey."

Beaming at the sound of his voice, Quinn smiled and set down her fishing pole, missing the holder. It rolled onto the ground, and she swiped it up, putting it in its spot. She paused, her sparkling, green eyes watching him.

"Oh ... Hi." Quinn cleared her throat.

Elijah read Quinn's energy and knew she had awakened to their past life connection and what they'd meant to each other on a spiritual level.

"It's Florence, right?" Elijah raised an eyebrow, grinning.

Quinn giggled, jumping up and wrapping her arms around him. Elijah rested his chin on the top of her head. He rubbed her back in slow circles, and she squeezed tighter. "I'm so glad you're alright. How do you feel? You look fantastic for someone who just went through the supernatural ringer. It's amazing." She pulled away, keeping her hand on his forearm.

The light in Elijah's eyes dimmed. "I'd rather not talk about that."

"That's fair." There was no judgment in her expression, and internally, Elijah gave a sigh of relief. A cool breeze waved over them, and the scent of seaweed made his body relax.

The thought that she would find him repulsive weighted on him since he'd regained his awareness. It would have been perfectly natural for her to be disgusted, knowing what he'd done to survive. There was nothing that could change the fact that Elijah had eaten someone's heart.

Quinn grabbed his hand; his chest tingled, and he looked away, turning toward the shore. There was an unspoken understanding under her actions that showed him she would be there to listen when he was ready to talk.

"I have something for you." Elijah held out her necklace, and she took it from his hand, brushing his forearm.

"I hoped it would help," Quinn grabbed his shoulder, squeezing gently.

"It did, for sure. Thank you." Elijah grazed his thumb across her chin.

Quinn sat on the ground, putting the talisman back on, and Elijah sat next to her. He fiddled with grass, plucking a blade. The silence between them was familiar and comfortable. For once, they just existed together. After centuries, Elijah and Quinn had the moment they'd never been able to have. They were enjoying each other's presence without immediate death looming.

A crane flew into sight and landed in the water, moseying around, pecking in the shallows. Binx dashed from the church, barking and chasing the bird. The lab's golden fur shimmered, bathed in the southern sun as he trampled through the water.

Elijah chuckled as Binx raced to him, licking his cheek with broad, slobbery strokes of his monstrous tongue.

"Hell, Binx, stop it." Elijah playfully shoved his wet nose away, and Binx plopped down, resting his head in Elijah's lap, sighing. His wet fur dampened Elijah's leg.

Quinn patted Binx's head, and his ears tucked back. "He's glad you're alright too." She smiled at Binx, then rubbed Elijah's thigh. Her touch held more than desire, it held closure. They'd finally come full circle in their soul journey, and both were traveling someplace new.

Elijah wrapped an arm around her, and Quinn rested her head on his shoulder as they watched the calm inlet.

The storm had passed.

"I have to leave with Kiren," Elijah said softly, every syllable painful to utter. He'd just found her, and now he was going to leave her.

"I know. But I'll see you soon." Quinn raised her head, looking him directly in the eyes. His heart sped up. She smiled with gentle reassurance.

"I don't *want* to leave you." Elijah pressed his lips to Quinn's, and her body melted into his. He rubbed his thumb on her cheek.

Quinn pulled back, staring into his eyes. "After this experience, there's one thing I know for sure."

Elijah leaned in, his lips caressed hers, and the second he backed away to answer, he'd wished he hadn't. His heart hurt less when he was close to her.

"What's that?" Elijah tucked some of Quinn's flyaway hairs behind her ear.

"You're my True North, my way home, and I can never lose you. You're a part of me." Quinn wrapped her hand around the back of his neck and gave him a lingering, passionate kiss.

He could sense how much her beautiful spirit craved his.

"Plus, I mean, how hot is it that I'm a mistress? I think I still have a maid's outfit from Halloween last year."

Quinn winked, and he chuckled. Elijah's cheeks flushed pink as he adjusted the bill of his camo hat. He unwrapped a slim jim and took a nibble.

Being with Quinn soothed his tortured soul; she was the spiritual other half of himself, the Yang to his Yin. Without a doubt, Elijah knew the skinwalker journey he was about to embark on wasn't for her. It was a new chapter in their story that he had to go through alone. Keeping faith that one day the universe would bring him back to the other half of his soul once again, Elijah leaned into Quinn, content.

A silhouette formed in his peripheral vision, and Elijah saw Owen solidify. His aura was ethereal, and his expression loving. His shaggy, blond hair stirred in the summer breeze. Owen smiled at Elijah, and he smiled back.

Love you, brother.

Owen gave a half-smile and winked, acknowledging he'd received Elijah's telepathic communication. His spirit glittered, shimmering like an angel, then dematerialized into a fog, drifting off into the marshland of the coast.

For once, watching Owen disappear didn't hurt. Owen was happy, safe, and had moved on to the next dimension. In the next life, if Elijah was lucky enough, Owen would be his brother again. And next time, come hell or high water, Elijah would get things right.

Acknowledgments

I have been inspired by many sources for this book. The original folklore of Seven Sisters Road takes place in Otoe County, Nebraska, and was the one thing that started my creative juices flowing and the development of this story. There are many theories of what happened on the land, but there is no historical documentation showing whether seven sisters were murdered.

My second inspiration was that of the Navajo skinwalker beliefs. In no way does this story depict the belief systems of the Navajo tribe or their spiritual practices. I used the skinwalker folklore because it inspired me on a deeper spiritual level. I found myself pondering who we are as humans, which led to the realization that we are all made up of light and dark energy, but it is our decisions through life that define who we are as individuals and whether or not we choose to live in the dark or the light.

I would like to thank my writer's groups. Among those dedicated individuals, Jeff Young, Kelly Loomis, and Sophia Alexander who helped me make my work sparkle and shine through the pandemic, late-night Zoom meetings and my desire to set the manuscript on fire. They have been encouraging and supportive, and I could not have done it without them.

Lastly, a world of thanks to Dawn Cordray, who has been a critique partner, Beta-reader, sounding board, encourager, writing accountability manager, and, more importantly, a kindred creative soul and friend.

Track List

I ALWAYS LOVE to build playlists for my characters and the overall theme of the story. Music has been and always will be a massive inspiration to me. There is nothing like a song that speaks to me and allows me to watch the scenes play out in my mind, bringing my characters to life. I thought you might enjoy some of the music I used to pen this novel. Please remember to support the artists by buying their tracks and following them on social media if you love the music too.

"Hurts too Good"	Ruelle
"Will it Ever Be the Same"	Young Summer
"Got You Where I Want You"	The Flys
"Your Hands"	GRAE
"Shadow's Fall"	Regina Price
"Is it Really Me You're Missing"	Nina Nesbitt
"Way Down We Go"	Kaleo
"Sound of War"	Tomee Profitt (feat. Flurie)
"Coming up For Air"	Signals In Smoke
"Still Here"	Digital Daggers
"Kids (Aint All Right)"	Grace Mitchell
"Simple Man"	Lynyrd Skynyrd
"Raise Hell"	Dororthy
"Animal"	Spring King
"Bones"	MS MR
"Go Fast"	Endway
"Even If It Hurts"	Sam Tinnesz
"Highway to Hell"	AC/DC
"Best Of You"	Foo Fighters